USA TODAY & WSJ BESTSELLING AUTHOR
SIOBHAN DAVIS

Copyright © Siobhan Davis 2022. Siobhan Davis asserts the moral right to be identified as the author of this work. All rights reserved under International and Pan-American Copyright Conventions.

This is a work of fiction. Names, characters, places, incidents and dialogues are products of the author's imagination or are used fictitiously. Any resemblance to actual people, living or dead, or events is entirely coincidental.

This book is sold subject to the condition that it shall not, by way of trade or otherwise be lent, resold, hired out, or otherwise circulated without the prior written consent of the author. No part of this publication may be reproduced, transmitted, decompiled, or stored in or introduced into any information storage and retrieval system, in any form or by any means, whether electronic or mechanical, including photocopying, without the express written permission of the author.

Printed by Amazon

Paperback edition © February 2022

This edition © July 2023

ISBN-13: 978-1-959285-32-8

Editor: Kelly Hartigan (XterraWeb) editing.xterraweb.com

Proofread by: Bre Landers, Lauren Lesczynski, Brenda Parsons, Elizabeth Clinton, Aundi Marie, Megan Smith, and Amanda Marie (Draft House Editorial Services)

Cover design by Robin Harper of Wicked by Design

Cover image © Depositphotos.com

Interior imagery © Depositphotos.com

Formatted by Ciara Turley using Vellum

A new emotional and angst-filled stand-alone taboo romance from *USA Today* & *Wall Street Journal* bestselling author Siobhan Davis.

He's my eighteen-year-old son's best friend, and I'm old enough to know better.

My marriage is falling apart, and Vander's home life is tragic.

Yet, his broken parts speak to mine, and amid all the chaos, a true connection is formed.

The only peace I find is in those stolen moments when we share our darkest secrets and our deepest desires.

This thing between us has disaster written all over it. But I'm powerless to resist the magnetic pull that draws us closer and closer.

Until lines are crossed, boundaries are broken, and everything I thought I knew about myself is undone.

Note from the Author

This reverse age-gap romance contains mature scenes, some dark themes, and situations that may push your boundaries. Check out the trigger warning page on my website at www.siobhandavis.com. Please note this trigger list contains spoilers.

For Kelly and Louis.

"In dreams and in love there are no impossibilities."

János Arany

"Love does not label."

Marcus Aurelius

Chapter One

Kendall

"You're up," Shirley says in that "don't fuck with me" tone she likes to use whenever she's in charge of something. Wine dribbles out of my mouth and down my chin as she forcefully yanks my chair back, the wooden legs screeching against the tile floor in protest. Shirley is so anal about our annual psychic night, ensuring everyone attends their session at the exact appointed time. Instead of running a furniture business with her husband, she should be training recruits in the military or something. She'd have them all quaking in their boots.

Setting my wineglass on the table, I stand, smoothing a hand down the front of my dress. "I'm not sure I'm in the mood for this tonight," I admit, glancing anxiously at Mirabelle sobbing loudly in the corner of Shirley's Shaker-style kitchen. Something the psychic said really spooked her, and I don't know if I'm courageous enough to hear my truths tonight.

"You know you can't pass it up," Viola says, eyeing me with concern. We've been best friends since middle school, and she knows why I'm having second thoughts. Which is most unlike me, because I started our annual tradition.

I'm fascinated with things we can't explain or control. I was that kid who bypassed rides at carnivals and headed straight for the fortune-teller's tent, full of curiosity and excitement. When Curtis and I first moved to this street—when West and Stella were toddlers and Ridge was just a twinkle in my eye—I decided to host a psychic night at our house to break the ice and get to know my new neighbors. It quickly became an annual get-together for us girls, and we alternate houses every year.

We used to hire different psychics until we stumbled upon Dee three years ago and we knew we hit the jackpot. There are a lot of frauds in the game, but I firmly believe there are people out there with genuine ability. People who have a gift for looking into the past and the future and who see things most of us mortals don't—like Dee.

I'm enthralled by the thought someone can guide us through life's murky waters, shining a light on things that could be construed as preordained. But I believe we still have free will. We still have choices, and we choose the path we travel.

Which is why I'm not going to chicken out.

I smile at my best friend. "You're right." I take a large mouthful of my wine for bravery. "Time to pull up my big-girl panties."

Viola squeezes my hand while Shirley taps her foot impatiently on the floor. Stepping away from the table, I follow Shirley out of the kitchen and ignore the nerves pricking at my skin. "I thought you liked Dee," she says, as we walk down the hallway to the small study on the left just inside the front door.

"I do. She's given me good advice these past few years." I'm just terrified of what she might confirm tonight.

Shirley stops, placing her hand on my arm. "Is everything okay?" Her brows knit together as she stares at me, and I'm surprised. We don't have this kind of relationship. She's my closest neighbor and someone I know I can rely on if I need a cup of sugar or someone to watch Ridge for an hour if there's a work emergency and Stella isn't around to take care of her little brother. We do family dinners a couple of times a year, but largely we stay out of each other's hair, and I like that. Close, but not too close. We don't confide things in one another, and I'm not about to start. I like the friendship we have as it is. If I need to vent, I have Viola and June—my bestie from Bentley Law, where we both work.

"Everything is fine," I lie, offering her a more robust smile. "I'm just tired. I've been pulling long shifts at work for weeks now, and I'm exhausted." That's no lie. Things are crazy busy at the office. Late nights and weekend work has become far too much of a regular occurrence lately. I'm close to blowing a gasket. Family time is precious to me, and my kids are growing up way too fast. I don't want to miss time with them, and I'm getting fed up having to work overtime. I plan on speaking to my boss about it this week.

"I know we're not as close as you are with Viola, but I'm here for you too. I just want you to know that." Her features soften as she looks at me, and I wonder if she knows something. I didn't confide in her three years ago, but it's not inconceivable to imagine she heard something through the grapevine. If she heard rumors, she never addressed them with me. That's one thing you can count on with Shirley. She's discreet.

"Thanks, Shirley. I appreciate that. You're a great neighbor and friend."

"I can say the same for you." She drops her hand from my arm, jerking her head forward. "Come on. We're getting behind on the schedule."

Pursing my lips and trapping a smile, I follow her into the study where Dee awaits.

I sit down in the chair in front of the desk as Shirley exits the room, softly closing the door behind her.

The older woman behind the desk smiles warmly at me. "Kendall. It's great to see you again. How have you been?"

I shrug. "So-so."

Her piercing green eyes drill into mine. "Are you still working at the law firm?" She clasps her hands on the desk while maintaining eye contact with me.

"Yes. Curtis got a big promotion at work nine months ago, and I put in a request to move to part-time working, but it was denied. It's very busy at the moment. We won a few new high-profile accounts, and the timing isn't right. I'm the only office manager, and there isn't anyone else available to pick up the slack. I am hoping to reapply after Christmas, when things should be a little quieter."

Her gaze continues probing mine, but it's not uncomfortable. I felt a connection with Dee the instant I met her, and we just clicked. I feel relaxed in her presence, even if I'm anxious over what she might say. Her insights have been spot-on in the past, and I know she's the real deal. I have considered organizing a few private readings during the year, but I just haven't found the time to put that in motion.

"And the children? Are they well?"

I nod, and a genuine smile ghosts over my mouth. My kids are my everything. They keep me going on days when it feels like I can't function. "They are all doing great. West is a senior this year. Stella is a junior, and Ridge has one more year before he starts middle school. They are growing up so fast. I wish I could slow down time."

"Wouldn't that be wonderful?" Her warm smile comforts me like luscious hot chocolate on a wintry night, and I sink into the leather chair, unwinding a little.

She cocks her head to the side, studying me. "I can tell

Always Meant to Be

something is playing on your mind. What can I do for you, Kendall? What would you like to know?"

Drawing a brave breath, I grip the edge of the chair as I exhale slowly. "I think it's happening again," I admit, swallowing over the massive lump clogging my throat. "I think Curtis is cheating on me." I unstick my tongue from the roof of my suddenly dry mouth. "Is he?"

Her brow puckers, and her tongue darts out, wetting her lips as she stares contemplatively at me. Anxiety blooms in my chest as the seconds tick by. "I'm not seeing anything in relation to your husband, and I sense you already know the answer to your question."

"I have suspicions but no proof. He's smarter this time."

"You need to speak to him."

Air whooshes out of my mouth. "I know." Like I know I've been delaying the inevitable conversation. But I won't go through this again. I can't. I won't be played like a fool or treated like less than I deserve.

"Ask me what you really want to know." She pins me with that all-seeing look of hers.

Her intensity brings *his* image to the forefront of my mind, and my heart picks up speed behind my rib cage. My chest visibly heaves, and my palms grow sweaty. "You see him?" I whisper, afraid to say it out loud. I can't even force myself to think about it, let alone articulate the thought.

"I do. I saw him the first time we met."

I suck in a shocked gasp at her admission. Vander had only moved to the area with his parents a few months before our first session, and I resolutely refused to think about him as anything but my eldest son's new best friend. He was fifteen then. *Fifteen.* And...I force those thoughts from my mind. It was around the time Curtis had his affair and my mind was a mess. That's the only way I can explain my weird reaction to someone who was only a kid at the time. I haven't thought of him like that in the intervening period. Not until more recently when the connection seems to be growing stronger.

And Vander is no longer a kid.

He's eighteen. Six foot three inches of pure masculinity wrapped in the most tempting package. His quiet confidence, sharp wit, brooding manner, and keen intelligence is as appealing as his appearance and—

I stop that train of thought. No good will come from it. He's West's best friend. He's eighteen and a senior in high school. I should not be having wicked thoughts about him. It's only because my marriage is falling apart and he pays me more attention than my husband does.

It's just a stupid infatuation.

Nothing will come of it.

Because I won't let it.

"Beating yourself up over it won't make any difference," Dee says, leaning back a little in her chair. "In this life, we don't always get to choose."

"What does that mean?"

"I think you know what it means."

"It's wrong," I whisper, and my cheeks flush with the recognition she sees the immoral thoughts I've been having.

"Why?" She sits back fully in her chair, and her eyes soften as they latch on mine.

I clear my throat, deciding to own up to my feelings. It's not like Dee is going to tell anyone. "Take your pick. I'm too old. He's too young. I'm married. His home life is a nightmare. He's West's best friend." I tweak my lips with my fingers as I stare out the window into the dark night. "I'm delusional and imagining things that aren't there."

"Like what?"

Always Meant to Be

I turn my head, refocusing on Dee. "Like the way he looks at me," I whisper.

"How does he look at you?"

"Like he has a hotline to my soul and my innermost thoughts and feelings. Like he *sees* me."

"Perhaps he does."

I shake my head. "He's not supposed to."

She arches a brow, leaning her elbows on the table. "Isn't he?"

I frown, wondering what she is getting at. "It almost sounds like you want me to act on my feelings."

"I don't tell you what to do or steer you onto any path, Kendall. You know that. I can only tell you what I see."

"And what is that?"

Her eyes probe mine intensely. "I'm not sure you're ready to hear this yet, but I'm going to tell you anyway. I think you should keep an open mind."

"I'm more open-minded than most, but even I'm struggling with this."

"Maybe you need to stop fighting it and delve deeper to uncover the hidden truth."

"What hidden truth?"

"Do you believe in soul mates?"

I nod without hesitation. "Absolutely. But I also believe most people won't find theirs in a single lifetime."

A triumphant smile coasts over her mouth. "I wholeheartedly agree. When you think about the billions of people on the planet, it seems like an insurmountable challenge, right?"

"We discussed this very topic at my philosophy class last month. Some of my classmates believe in soul mates. Some don't. Some believe you can have more than one."

"What do you believe?"

"I believe there is another person out there who shares half my soul, but the chances of ever meeting him is beyond slim, and I have made my peace with that. I thought I'd found someone I connected with. Someone I could build a life with, and be happy, but I don't believe in that anymore." I'm getting dangerously close to voicing the truth hidden in the deepest part of my heart.

"What if I said you have already met him?" she says, and I almost fall off my chair. "Already loved him, in successive lifetimes, because it's a connection so profound, a love so complete, it cannot die."

"What?" I blurt, staring wide-eyed at her. Surely, she doesn't mean…

"In every lifetime, you find one another because the bond is so strong nothing can keep you apart. Not oceans or mountains or timing or other people." Her eyes drill into mine. "Not age."

My mouth hangs open, and I'm sure the shock I'm feeling is written all over my face.

"Nothing else matters but the connection you share." Reaching across the table, she takes my hands in hers. "Search your heart, Kendall. The truth you seek is there. In every lifetime, you battle obstacles and fight through considerable pain and turmoil to find one another again. But find him you have."

"This isn't real." I'm drowning in uncertainty and a whole host of emotions I have no way of dealing with. "You can't mean what I think you mean."

"Vander is the other half of your soul, Kendall. It's up to you what you do with that knowledge."

Chapter Two

Vander

"Where's Hazel gone?" I ask when my buddy West drops down on the couch alongside me. "God's Plan" by Drake pumps out of portable speakers, bouncing off the stone walls of the carriage house that is more my home than the lavish mansion at the front of my parent's property.

"I dropped her off at home. She has a curfew." Snatching the joint from my fingers, he brings it to his lips. I'm not surprised he's returned without his girlfriend or that he's in the mood to party. He's still reeling over what he learned last weekend. Truth is, I'm pissed too. Though I have a less legitimate right to be.

Behind us, a small crowd of our friends is talking, dancing, and drinking. Friday night sessions are a regular occurrence because I'm the only one of my friends with a private space where we can party without parental interference. My mom is most likely in a drug-and-drink-fueled haze of her own making, passed out in the master suite at the house. Dad is traveling this weekend, which means he's wining and dining clients and screwing whatever sidepiece is his latest fuck buddy. They rotate as fast as the line at Chick-fil-A, and there seems to be a never-ending supply of gold-diggers and whores willing to take a ride on his dick. He fucking disgusts me, but I hate him for much more than his cheating.

"That's what happens when you date high-schoolers," I tell my best bud before finishing my beer and setting the empty bottle on the floor by my feet.

"I love her," West replies without hesitation.

He was a total player until he fell for his girlfriend, and now he's a changed man. It's been over eighteen months, and those two are still crazy in love. I'm happy for my buddy, but it's not for me.

"Don't knock it till you've tried it," he adds.

I shake my head, watching him take a long pull on the spliff before I snatch it back. "You know me. I like my women older and to keep it simple." Dazzling blue eyes and long blonde hair fill my mind's eye as I take two hits of the joint. Briefly, I close my eyes, savoring the mental picture, before I remember what an asshole I am for thinking about Kendall while West is sitting beside me.

"Aren't you sick of all the one-night stands?"

I open my eyes and pass the joint back to him. "Casual sex is uncomplicated, and that's all I have time for." Dragging anyone into my fucked-up life wouldn't be fair, and there's only so much a guy can handle. It's one of the reasons I don't fuck girls from school, preferring to find my fuck buddies at UCCS. High school girls equal drama, and I've got enough of that in my life. College seniors are more mature and less work. The University of Colorado campus in Colorado Springs is prime hunting ground, and I usually hit up a couple of college bars on Saturday nights with a few of my older buddies from the boxing club. However, it's been months since I hooked up with

Always Meant to Be

anyone, because I'm too fixated on the one woman I want and can't have to even attempt to fuck anyone else.

We moved to this town a little over three years ago when that prick I call Dad changed jobs. If you ask him, he'll tell you it was a career move when really it was to avoid a big scandal. I wasn't happy about the move, at the time, but I actually like it here. I have good friends, found a sport that lets me channel all my pent-up frustration, and commandeered the carriage house on our grounds as my own personal sanctuary-slash-studio.

And I met *her*.

Blood rushes to my dick, and I subtly adjust the semi in my pants. It's not cool to spring a boner about his mom when I'm hanging out with West, but lately I can't get Kendall Hawthorne off my mind. It was easier to push my feelings aside when I was younger and could do nothing about them. But now I'm eighteen, old enough to act on them, and it's like my brain and my body have decided to run free, indulging all my pent-up fantasies, and it's all I can think about. Nothing helps to distract me, and I have zero interest in other girls. Staying away from West's house has made no difference, and even pounding my fists into the punching bag until they bleed only works temporarily.

"You know most of Hazel's friends are in love with you," he says, handing the joint to Shepherd as our other friend Bowie emerges from the bedroom with a smirk on his face. "Pick one and we can double date for a while."

Milana slinks out past Bowie, making a beeline for the door with her head down, her long pink locks curtaining her pretty face. West bursts out laughing as Bowie flops down on the couch across from us. "You dirty dawg." West wears a shit-eating grin, but I see the pain behind it. Cheating is a sore point. "Abel is gonna kick your ass when he finds out you're fucking his girl behind his back."

"What happened to the bro code?" Shepherd asks, looking disgusted, but I can tell it's a front to hide his pain. I don't know how long Shep has been in love with Bowie because I only noticed recently. I'm not sure any of our other friends have worked it out, and it's obvious as fuck Bowie has no clue. From what I've seen, he's strictly hetero, but who knows? Maybe he's into dudes too. Shep is proudly bi, and he's had flings with guys and girls, so it's no secret where he stands. I feel for the dude. I know what it's like to want someone who will most likely never want you back.

"My brother is a dick." Bowie accepts the spliff from Shep, taking a couple of long, lazy tokes.

"I'd kick Ridge's ass if he ever hit on my girl," West says, grabbing a couple of beers from the ice bucket on the coffee table situated between both couches.

On this level, there is a decent-sized living area with a kitchenette occupying most of the space. The bedroom and small bathroom with a toilet and shower is to the right. Upstairs houses my art studio, which I keep locked any time I have company. I normally sleep at the main house, preferring not to leave Mom alone at night, but on weekends or times when I paint late into the night, I crash here. It's wired for electricity, so I have Wi-Fi, a TV, small refrigerator, a microwave, and a freestanding stove, and I bought a few plug-in heaters. The carriage house has everything I need to lock myself away from my warring parents when shit hits the fan, as it often does.

West hands me a beer while popping the top on his own.

"Good thing Ridge is only nine and you don't need to worry about that," Shep says. "Unlike Abel." He fixes Bowie with a knowing look. "I don't care how big of a dick your brother is. You shouldn't be fucking his girlfriend."

"Shep is right," West agrees, drinking a mouthful of beer. "No good can come from it. You need to keep it in your pants."

Always Meant to Be

It's good advice. Advice I should heed. Because obsessing about West's mom is a shit show in the making. My buddy would be pissed if he knew the fantasies I've had about his mom, but I can't find it in myself to feel guilty for wanting her. I only feel guilty for thinking those thoughts when my buddy is next to me, because if he knew the truth, it'd make him uncomfortable. But I refuse to feel shame or remorse for feeling the way I do about Kendall. I don't even regret what happened at my birthday party, except maybe I was wrong to back down, because it's not making any difference in how I feel, and it's becoming damn hard not to do something about it. Especially after hearing what that asshole husband of hers has done. I want to beat the crap out of him and then take care of his wife the way she deserves to be cared for.

If Kendall was mine, I would worship the ground she walked on. Spend hours showing her what a queen she is with my mouth, my fingers, my...

Shit. I drag a hand through my hair. I can't think those things here. Short of a lobotomy, I don't know how to evict thoughts of Kendall from my mind. And I'm pretty sure I don't really want to.

"Mom." I hover over my parents' bed, staring anxiously at my mother as she sleeps. Little puffs of air slip through her collagen-enhanced lips as she softly snores. Her reddish-brown hair fans around her face on the pillow, and although she's forty-seven, there isn't a gray hair in sight. Not that Dad would permit it. I wouldn't be surprised if he left instructions at the hair salon like he does at the cosmetic surgeon's office. Dad has little interest in Mom, but he won't let her disgrace him in public, so she is forced to do his bidding when he comes calling.

The rest of the time is spent in a numbed-out haze.

Rubbing at the tight pain across my chest, I gently shake her shoulders. "Mom. Wake up. You need to eat."

She stirs, moaning as she curls her knees up to her chest under the covers. "Go away," she mumbles, swatting me with a floppy arm. "I have a migraine."

I exhale heavily, silently praying for strength that is in diminishing supply. "Sit up," I say in a more forthright tone. "Eat something, and then I'll get your migraine meds." My eyes sweep over the pill bottles on her bedside table, most of the contents gone. An empty vodka bottle lies across the carpeted floor. Vodka is her poison of choice because it's odorless and it can't be smelled on your breath. She told me that one time, when she was explaining how she manages to function in public when attending one of Dad's events. It takes a lot for her to get drunk these days, so downing a half bottle of vodka before she leaves the house slices the edge off her nerves while enabling her to play the part of rich attorney's wife to perfection.

"Leave me alone." She swats at me again, and I rub a tense spot between my brows, struggling to hold on to my patience.

I don't ever want to lose my temper or lash out at her. She deals with enough of that from my dad, but she makes it so hard to be kind and loving and patient. "Diana." My tone is firm and bordering on aggressive as I say what I need to say. "Sit the fuck up and eat or I'm calling Dad." I never would, and she knows it, yet we play our usual game.

Her eyes pop open, and her mouth curls into a frown. "Don't call me that. I'm Mom to you."

I wish she was. But the only parental figure around here is me. Which is fucking laughable. I only turned eighteen during the summer, but sometimes I feel ancient.

Always Meant to Be

Like I have lived a thousand lifetimes in those eighteen years and I'm world-weary.

"You need to eat, Mom." I help her to sit up against the headboard, hating how frail she feels under my large palms. "You're too thin. You need to take better care of yourself." I know I'm preaching to a void, but I won't ever stop trying.

"You're a good boy, Vander," she says, in a moment of rare acknowledgment. Her fingers sweep the hair tumbling across my brow, pushing it out of my eyes. "A good son." Her tired green eyes lock on to my face. "You're the only one who cares." Sadness is a dark shroud covering her face, and I wish I could contest her statement, but I won't lie to her. Her parents are dead, she is an only child, and she has no true friendships. Only acquaintances. Most are the wives of men Dad does business with or wives of his golf buddies at the nearby club and resort, and they only tolerate her at best. Her only friend—an old roommate from college—lives in Europe with her husband, and she hasn't seen her in years.

"I love you." Gently, I give her a hug, squeezing my eyes shut when her fragile limbs cling to me in desperation.

"I love you too." When she pulls back, tears are rolling down her face. "I'm sorry I wasn't a better mother. I'm sorry I'm so weak."

I have heard all of this before. Along with futile promises to change. She has tried. Countless times. But it's never enough. *I am never enough.* And I have had to come to terms with our one-sided relationship because continuing to harbor hope was killing me.

I sit on the side of the bed, spoon-feeding my grown-ass mother the smoked-salmon scrambled eggs I made her because her hands are shaking so bad she can't hold the silverware. As I make my mother eat, I wonder what the fuck I did to deserve this shitty life.

After she has finished, I hand her the migraine meds and a glass of water, staying beside her until she falls back asleep. My heart feels like a lump of stone in my chest as I watch her sleep, imagining how and when this will end. Because it can't continue like this. Slowly, she is killing herself, and I'm forced to be a bystander. I wish I knew how to help her, but none of my interventions ever work. And they never will. Not as long as it suits my father to keep my mother in chains.

I scrub my hands over my face, and my limbs feel weary with exhaustion as my cell vibrates in my pocket. It's a text from West, inviting me to Sunday dinner. It's a long-standing invitation. One Kendall issued when she realized the kind of homelife I'm forced to endure. I haven't attended in months because I'm trying to stay away from her—the woman who is the holder of my heart and my dreams.

But I'm vulnerable today. A bit hungover from last night and heartsore because Mom is a freaking mess. Seeing Kendall's face will make everything seem better. So, I message West back, telling him I'll be over later.

My mind churns as I exit Mom's bedroom and quietly close the door, my thoughts instantly turning to the woman I have forbidden feelings for. I used to think the way I felt about Kendall was because she's the perfect example of how a mother should be. Like she was the embodiment of everything I should have and was denied. That I was compensating for the lack of motherly affection in my life by channeling those sentiments in her direction.

But now I'm older, I know I was wrong.

That's not it at all.

The feelings I have for her are not motherly in any way, shape, or form.

And I'm not compensating for the lack of a mother figure in my life.

Always Meant to Be

It's just *her*.

Everything about her enchants me. It's not only her gorgeous face and tempting body. It's the very essence of who she is as a person. Something in her speaks to the very core of me, in a way I can't properly explain. No other woman has ever attracted me on this level, and I'm beginning to think no other woman will.

Kendall is one of a kind. From her carefree sense of humor to her obvious intelligence. Her compassionate and caring nature that sees her sacrifice and do so much for her loved ones and the community. A shared passion for understanding the intangible and the inexplicable, and her dogged determination to live the fullest life. She inspires me and gives me hope, and I can't help but be drawn to her.

Society would say it's wrong to feel like this.

That I'm too young—for her and to know my own mind.

But I *do* know my own mind.

I know what I'm feeling.

What I have felt from the moment she first entered my orbit.

I couldn't explain it then.

But I can now.

I'm in love with Kendall Hawthorne.

I love my best friend's very married mother.

I just don't know what the hell to do about it.

Chapter Three

Kendall

The doorbell chimes, and butterflies swoop into my belly. I hadn't expected Vander to accept West's invitation. He seems determined not to join us for Sunday dinner anymore, and while it disappoints me, I know it's for the best. I'm not sure what's changed today, but I know why my stomach is lurching like a herd of wild elephants is stomping all over it.

"I'll get it." West yells from the living room, at the same time Stella puts the chef's knife down and moves away from the kitchen counter.

"Stay put, missy." I pitch her a knowing look. "Let your brother greet his friend." Stella will try everything and anything to get out of helping around the house. While I have tried to pass my love of cooking and baking to my only daughter, I threw in the towel a long time ago.

Stella is the quintessential tomboy, more at home playing sports and climbing trees than slaving over a hot stove, and I wouldn't have her any other way. She is true to herself, and she owns it, making me incredibly proud. Yet, I worry about her more than the boys because she is stubbornly brave and reckless and prone to acting without thinking.

Living with her is interesting too. If chaos descends, you can bet Stella is at the center and relishing it. She likes pushing buttons and testing boundaries, and we have been at our wits' end with her on several occasions over the past few years, but she seems to have moved past that destructive rebellious phase. Her bedroom is like a bomb site and way messier than the boys' rooms. Something neat-freak West always teases her about. I don't bother calling her out on it anymore. I just close the door and ignore the chaos. She's almost seventeen. Old enough to tidy her own shit.

Since Curtis's big promotion and accompanying salary increase, I hired a lady to come in to clean and do laundry once a week. I work full-time and run the household and the kids almost single-handedly now, so I refuse to feel guilty for hiring some help. Ruthie is a godsend, and there is nothing like coming home on a Friday, after a long working week, to a sparkling house and an empty laundry basket.

"Why don't the boys have to help?" Stella whines, dumping the cooked carrots in the strainer.

"The boys will clean up after dinner. You know the drill." Whoever cooks and preps doesn't have to clean up and vice versa. The kids know the rules. I'm all for equality in this house, and I have tried to instill the right values in my children. The rest is up to them.

"Where's Dad?" Ridge asks, ambling into the kitchen from outside, traipsing muck all over my pristine kitchen floor.

I glance at the clock on the wall over the window with a frown. "He should be on his way home now. I'll text him." I pluck my cell off the window ledge and tap out a quick message to my husband while I tell my youngest son to go wash up for dinner. Hushed conversation filters in from the hallway, and butterflies race from my stomach to my chest. I wet my lips and fight a fresh wave of anxiety as footsteps approach. "Put the vegetables into bowls and cover them," I instruct my daughter, hoping she doesn't hear the slight tremble in my voice. "We'll keep everything warm in the oven until Daddy gets here," I add as my phone pings with a message from Curtis confirming he's just leaving the golf club.

I'm cleaning mud off the floor when West and Vander step into the kitchen. My palms are clammy around the handle of the mop, and blood rushes to my head, making me a little woozy. It feels as though all the oxygen has been sucked from the room, and every hair on my body lifts in potent awareness. I'm not sure I have ever felt someone's presence in every molecule of my being like this before. It's like the second Vander enters my space I'm acutely aware of it. As if I'm uniquely attuned to his aura and can recognize it as soon as he's near.

It's disconcerting, putting me even more on edge. I've been a bit of a basket case since Friday night when Dee sent me into a complete tailspin.

"Mom." West's deep voice reminds me I need to get my shit together. "Vander's here."

Plastering a smile on my face, I lift my head and stare at my son's best friend. It's the first time we have seen one another in months, and it takes every ounce of willpower not to gasp when my eyes lock on his.

I didn't think it was possible, but he's even more magnetic. An invisible charge ignites the space between us, and I feel an almost insurmountable urge to run to him. Every part of me strains toward him, as if I'm being drawn by some magical force. It only adds to the confusion I feel.

Vander incites attention whenever he steps into a room. It's not only because he's utterly gorgeous—tall and broad with ripped abs and bulging biceps that can't be ignored. The growing number of tattoos covering his skin showcases his artwork to perfection. I know, for a fact, he has designed and drawn every piece of ink that adorns his tempting body. His tight black shirt is rolled up to the elbows, displaying new ink on his lower arms, and I see more creeping up his neck from the collar of his shirt. He has his nose and eyebrow rings in today too, and his piercing green eyes are smoldering as he stares at me.

No, it's more than how striking he is to look at. He has this way of carrying himself that commands attention, whether he wants it or not. He oozes masculinity in a way I've never noticed in any man before. He's only eighteen, but he's definitely not a kid. Vander has always seemed older, in looks and disposition. His dysfunctional upbringing has forced him to mature at a young age, and that's one of the things that sets him apart from his peers.

"You feeling okay, Mom?" Stella asks, narrowing her eyes at me. "You're acting weird."

Heat creeps up my neck at my daughter's words, confirming I'm being obvious in the extreme. "Apologies. I was daydreaming," I lie, setting the mop against the wall and plastering another smile on my face. I walk toward Vander with a pounding heart. "It's good to see you, Vander. We've missed you."

"I have been busy," he says, thrusting a bunch of roses at me. The deep, rich tone of his voice does strange twisty things to my insides, and it's a struggle to remain composed. "Thanks for inviting me," he adds, stabbing me with intense eyes that seem to see all the way through to my soul.

"You know you're always welcome in our home." I take the flowers, and a genuine smile materializes on my face. "Thank you. You know you don't need to bring anything, but I appre-

Always Meant to Be

ciate it." Especially when it's been years since my husband has done anything as considerate.

In the aftermath of his affair, Curtis bent over backward to make things up to me. Showering me with affection and gifts, but it all felt fake and forced, and I couldn't bring myself to appreciate it. By the time I had thawed, Curtis had reverted to form, and the affection and gifts were a thing of the past.

Vander always brings flowers or chocolates when he comes to Sunday dinner, and I know it's because he's grateful to be included and appreciative of a home-cooked meal. His sincerity is never in doubt. I don't know where he collected his manners because it's not like he's had any role model to look up to. I think he is just inherently good.

"You're such a suck-up." West thumps Vander in the arm while grinning.

"You're lucky you have a mom who cooks Sunday dinner. Maybe you should be more appreciative." His eyes pin West in place, and the meaning is clear.

The smile slips off my son's mouth. "I didn't mean anything by it." West turns to me with a somber expression. "You know I appreciate you, Mom, right? I couldn't have asked for a better mother, and I love you. You're the best."

My heart swells at his heartfelt words. I stretch up and kiss his cheek. "I know, honey, and I love you too." My boys are very affectionate with me, but West did go through a phase, from thirteen to sixteen, when it apparently wasn't cool to hug your mom or tell her you loved her. He's really grown up in recent months, and I think his girlfriend, Hazel, is a good influence on him too. I have noticed he is freer with the affection, and I love it. There is just something about the bond between mother and son that is vastly different from the bond I share with my daughter, but I cherish the relationship I have with Stella too.

Opening the overhead cupboard, I stretch up to grab my favorite glass vase when warmth hits me from behind.

"Let me get that," Vander says, reaching over me. While he is careful not to press up against me, he is so close I can feel his body heat, and my knees almost buckle. I hold my breath, grabbing the counter to steady myself as my heart skips a beat and all manner of physiological tells happen inside me.

"You want me to fill it?" he asks in that low, deep tone of his, and it's a miracle I don't melt into a puddle of goo at his feet.

"I've got it." Getting a grip, I take the vase and smile up at him. "Thank you."

Moving to the sink, I conduct a stern inner talk with myself as I fill the vase with water. I'm acting like a lovesick teen with a huge crush, and I need to get over it.

"Has something happened I should know about?" West asks as I twist the faucet off and turn around to grab the bouquet of roses.

Vander shrugs, but the casual movement is out of sync with the taut pull of his shoulders. "New day. Same ole shit." He rubs the back of his neck, and my heart aches for him as I fill the vase with flowers. I don't think Vander has ever had the opportunity to be a normal child because his parents are too fucked up and selfish to think about all the ways they are hurting their son. It makes me murderous every time I think about the shit he has had to endure.

"Are your parents at home?" I softly inquire, setting the vase down on the island unit and smiling at the glorious blooms. Pink is my favorite color, and I wonder if Vander has somehow deduced that. If it's why he only ever gets me pink flowers.

"Mom's sleeping. Dad's away."

Always Meant to Be

I nod. "That's right. I forgot Greg was with Leland at the Einhorns this weekend."

Ernest Einhorn is one of our new prestigious clients. He spearheads a multibillion-dollar satellite communications company that is headquartered in Denver. He owns a massive estate in Boulder, and he invited Leland—the owner of Bentley Law—to spend the weekend. Leland has three senior partners in the firm, but he worships Gregory Henley like you wouldn't believe. So, it was no surprise he chose him to accompany him this weekend. Greg is most definitely Leland's favorite child, much to the consternation of the other two partners, who resent him as much as they admire him.

No matter how much I hate Vander's father—and I loathe him with the intensity of a thousand suns—I've got to admit Greg has brought in a ton of new business since joining the company three years ago.

A muscle clenches in Vander's jaw, but he clamps his lips shut. I know he confides in West—and he has confided in me too in the past—but he is never outrightly critical of his parents, which says a lot about his integrity. I'm not sure I'd be as gracious, given the circumstances.

"I'll save a plate for Diana," I tell him, wanting to switch the subject. "You know I always make far too much food." My mantra is it's better to have too much than not enough. That, and I rarely use any measuring utensils.

"Thanks, Kendall." His eyes sear into mine, conveying so much with one look, and I struggle to breathe.

Vander has this way of looking at me that is super intense, and it's easy to forget anyone else is in the room. We have always had this powerful connection, although I have worked hard to deny it over the years. Things came to a head at his eighteenth birthday party, during the summer, and I've been freefalling ever since. Now, with Dee's revelations, I'm spiraling again. It's quickly reaching a point where I'm incapable of denying anything when it comes to him, and that is worrisome on a whole other level.

When did my life become so complicated, and what am I going to do about Vander and Curtis? I wish I had answers, but I'm clueless and struggling to keep my head above water.

And, right now is not the time to be thinking these things.

Chapter Four

Kendall

Forcing myself to look away, I suck in a deep breath, praying I have the strength to get through this dinner intact.

"You're acting weird too." Stella peers up at Vander with knitted brows. "It must be something in the air. I hope it's not contagious. I have a date for the movies tonight, and if he starts acting weird, I might have to bail and come hang out with you." She waggles her brows and licks her lips.

"Quit with the flirting, beanpole." West nudges his sister in the side. "You know I hate you doing that with my friends."

Stella rolls her eyes. "You're no fun since you started dating Hazel. It's like she has sucked all the life out of you."

West's face darkens, and I swing into action, moving in between my two hotheaded teens. There are only thirteen months between them, and though they are very close, they fight like cats and dogs a lot of the time. Refereeing is a common requirement to keep the peace. I place a warning hand on West's chest while I fix my daughter with a chastising expression. "Stella. That's not a nice thing to say to your brother, and you should apologize. I thought you liked Hazel?"

"I do," she admits, looking a little sheepish. "But it doesn't change the fact West is so boring now." She shrugs, fighting a grin. "Sorry, not sorry," she mumbles.

"You wouldn't have said that if you saw him Friday night." Vander leans back against the counter and winks at his friend. "Boring is not a word I would ever use to describe your brother."

I hold up a hand. "I think the less I know, the better." I like being involved in my kids' lives, and I like that they talk to me about stuff going on, but there's a limit to what I want to, or need to, know.

"Chill, Mom." West slides his arm around my shoulders, smacking a kiss to my temple. "I just smoked some weed, drank a few beers, and got a little rowdy with my friends, but it's nothing to be ashamed of." His lips twitch as he stabs his sister with a look that is part mischievous and part murderous. "It's not as if I went skinny-dipping with a bunch of football players, flashed everyone the goods, and kissed at least two of them."

That most definitely was on the list of things I didn't need to know.

I look at Stella. "Do we need to have a conversation again?"

She rolls her eyes while jabbing her finger in West's direction. "You have a big mouth, and I'll get you back." Her blue eyes flit to mine as she plants her hands on her hips and tosses her long dark hair over one shoulder. "It's nothing to worry about, Mom. I'm pretty sure you and Dad were doing way worse at my age."

Fuck, we probably were. I met Curtis when I was fourteen—I was a freshman and he was a sophomore—and we were joined at the hip from that moment on. I wish I could refute her claims, but I won't lie to my kids.

Always Meant to Be

Out of all our children, Stella is the one who is most like a mix of me and her father. She's tall, like her dad and her older brother. Dark like Curtis too, but she has my blue eyes and my stubborn streak. I remember being determined and reckless at her age too, which is why it's so hard for me to chastise her for doing things I did.

And I can't say I want more for her from life without sounding like a hypocrite or like I regret the choices I have made. That would be akin to admitting I'm unhappy with how my life has panned out when I would never say that. Not even when I am miserable at the thought my marriage is unsalvageable and divorce most likely awaits me in the future.

My kids are my world. Period. Although I had to sacrifice my dreams when I got pregnant at seventeen, I still wouldn't change a thing. West, Stella, and Ridge are the absolute best things to have happened to me, and nothing will ever change that. However, that doesn't mean I want my daughter to follow the same path. I want her to be carefree for as long as possible.

Life is long. There is plenty of time for responsibilities.

"Your brother is only looking out for you, and I'd rather you not make me a grandma at thirty-five."

"Oh my God. You'd swear I was fucking the whole football team!" Stella throws her hands in the air.

"What the what?" Curtis barks, stepping into the kitchen at the worst possible moment.

Out of the corner of my eye, I notice Vander stiffening and straightening up. He folds his arms over his chest, and his jaw pulls tight as he stares at my husband with a dark look. Prickles of apprehension dance over my skin, and I rub at the pressure sitting on my chest. I only relax when Vander looks away from Curtis and lowers his eyes to the floor.

Curtis fixes our daughter with a ferocious look, and I need to deflect this and fast. My husband takes the cake when it comes to overprotective fathers. Not that I fault him for it. Stella has always been the apple of his eye, and he's been completely and utterly in love with her from the second she took her first breath. Last year, when her boyfriend of a year dumped her shortly after taking her virginity—something I only know because I overheard Stella confessing to her best friend—I thought I would need a restraining order to keep West and Curtis from beating his ass.

My husband's brown eyes land on mine. "What's going on? Please tell me I didn't just hear what I heard."

"It's nothing. You know how Stella likes to shock. She didn't mean it literally." I hope. I know, from personal experience, how easy it is to get a rep in high school and how nasty teenage girls can be. I don't want that for Stella.

"Stay away from football players!" Curtis warns Stella. "They're bad news."

"Hey," West pipes up. "Not all players are bad news." He points at himself. "I'm a good guy." His eyes narrow to slits as he eyeballs his father. "Unlike some I could mention," he murmurs, drilling his dad with a sharp look.

What the hell is that about?

"Tell that to the string of broken hearts you left behind until Hazel tamed you," Stella retorts as Ridge strolls into the kitchen, humming under his breath. He goes still, his observant gaze moving to his siblings, sensing trouble brewing.

Tossing West's cryptic comment aside to dwell on later, I say, "Okay, enough. Let's eat." I want to end this standoff before World War Three erupts. "Stella, give the boys a dish each to carry while I carve the meat."

Surprisingly, Stella obeys without protest while I transfer the roast lamb to the wooden board and remove the electric carving knife. When the kids have left the kitchen, Curtis comes up alongside me, giving me a cursory once-over.

Always Meant to Be

I'm instantly on guard. "What?" I ask while simultaneously plugging the knife in.

"Is that a new dress?" He leans against the counter, eyeing me with what looks like interest. It's hard for me to tell because my husband hasn't shown any interest in me in months. If I'm being honest, it's actually been way longer than that.

"Yes. Why'd you ask?"

He shrugs before unfurling to his full height. My husband is hot and as handsome as when I met him. He takes good care of himself, working out early every morning at the company gym, and he also jogs, cycles, and takes regular hikes with the kids. His dark hair is kept short, and the scruff on his face is always neatly trimmed. His chocolate-colored eyes contain the same swirling depths, but the attraction isn't the same. When I look at Curtis now, I see a handsome man who garners attention wherever we go. But the all-consuming need to be near him, the unquenchable need to touch him—that I felt for a long, long time—is absent now, and I don't think it will ever return. Whatever spark we had has died, and it hurts to admit it to myself.

But it's the truth, and I can't force myself to feel things I don't.

Darting in, he kisses my cheek. "You look pretty. Is telling my wife that a crime or something?"

I clutch the carving knife tighter in my hand, hating how I'm instantly suspicious of his motives. "Honestly? It's been so long since you've even noticed me, Curtis, that any kind of compliment stands out."

"That's not fair, and you know it."

Anger swims in my veins, and I glare at him. "Don't do that. Don't insult my intelligence."

"You act like this is all my fault." Crossing his arms over his chest, he seethes as he glares at me. "I fucking apologized, but you're never going to forgive me, are you? You said you have put it behind you, but you won't ever stop punishing me for it, and I'm tired of the bullshit, Kendall. I made a mistake, and I have tried to make it up to you, but nothing is ever good enough." He spins around, sneering when his gaze lands on the vase of flowers. "You don't need me to pay you attention when you have Vander fawning all over you with his little schoolboy crush."

Blood drains from my face, and nerves fire at me from all angles. Curtis snorts in a derisory manner. "Not that I blame the kid for his mommy issues. If I had that drunken slut for a mother, I'd be drooling over my best friend's mom too." With those awesome parting words, my husband leaves the kitchen while I try to ignore the hurtful insinuation and slice the lamb with trembling hands.

"That was delicious," Vander proclaims, placing his silverware down on his empty plate. "Thank you." He lifts his head to look at me, and I silently beg him to keep his game face on. I'm sitting at one end of our table while Curtis sits at the other end, and it's feels symbolic. The kids sit on either side between us. The atmosphere has been strained, and I'm sure everyone has noticed, even if Stella and West have kept the conversation going during the meal. It's hard to miss the angry slash of Curtis's jaw or the hostile glares he sends in my direction.

I wonder if this is all an attempt to deflect the truth. To begin setting up the blame before everything is revealed. I am even more convinced than ever that he's having another affair.

"You're welcome." I smile softly at Vander as I push my barely eaten plate away.

His brow creases as his gaze lowers to my food. "Weren't you hungry?"

"I don't have much of an appetite today."

His frown deepens, and fully-fledged anxiety returns when I spot my husband glowering at Vander. I almost laugh at the irony. I'm not the one committing adultery—unless you count the thoughts in my head—yet Curtis is treating Vander like he's affronted him, when I'm the only one who has the right to feel aggrieved.

"Dad." Ridge finishes his dinner and climbs out of his chair. "Can we go out on our bikes now?"

Curtis's gruff demeanor softens as our youngest stands beside him. "Sure thing, bud." He tousles Ridge's white-blond hair and kisses his brow. "Help with the cleanup while I change out of my golf clothes. We'll head out then." Curtis stands, throwing his napkin down on his chair before exiting the room, without so much as a thanks or a look in my direction.

Asshole.

He's not the only one who works hard all week. Yet his weekends are for leisure. Drinks with the boys on Friday nights. Golf with his cronies at the club. Hikes and camping trips with the kids. I don't begrudge him spending time with the kids, and he's a far better father than husband, but it wouldn't kill him to cook dinner sometime or to run me a bath or offer to come with me when I volunteer at the retirement home on Saturday afternoons.

He makes no effort with me anymore, and I'm sick of him using his affair and my understandable reaction as an excuse. I have stopped trying to organize date nights because there was always some excuse as to why he couldn't attend. Now, the only times we socialize are when one of our friends hosts a dinner or there's an event with work or at the golf club.

"What's going on with you and Dad?" Stella asks, yanking me from my head.

I look around the dining room, noticing the boys have left and most all of the table is cleared.

"What do you mean?" I blurt, caught completely off guard.

"We're not stupid, Mom. I saw the looks he was giving you, and you got a couple of sly digs in."

I have tried not to let stuff show in front of the kids, but it's reaching a point where neither of us are able to keep it trapped inside. We need to have this out, once and for all, and make some tough decisions. I don't want our actions to mess up the kids or hurt them anymore than they will be. I don't want to upset Stella now, but I'm not going to sugarcoat it either. I won't disrespect my daughter by lying to her or pretending her observations are wrong. "There is some stuff your dad and I need to discuss. I'm sorry if you picked up on the tension at the dinner table. That wasn't my intention."

"Is he cheating again?" West asks, from behind, and I spin around. His eyes burn with anger as he clenches his fists at his sides.

"What?" Shock whips through me as the horrific truth registers—*they know*.

"We know about that slut who used to work for him," Stella softly says, coming around the table. She slides her arms around me.

"How?" I ask.

"You know that dinner I went to at Hazel's aunt's house last week?" West says, and I nod. "She was there. The whore that used to be dad's secretary. She's going out with one of Hazel's cousins now, but she enjoyed telling me how she used to work for my dad, and well...she said enough for me to know what happened."

Always Meant to Be

"Tell me exactly what she said." I hold my head up, bracing for it. "I can handle it."

Pain spreads across West's face, and that cuts me to the bone. I never want my children to suffer for the sins of their father. I thought taking him back was the right thing to do. To protect them from the truth. But lately, all I've been doing is second-guessing myself.

"Tell her." Stella eyeballs her brother.

A muscle pops in West's jaw, and the skin on his knuckles blanches white he's clenching his fists so hard. "She said I looked like him, and then she pressed herself up against me and said she wondered if I looked like him everywhere while—" His lips purse, and his jaw locks tight as he deliberately stops speaking.

"While she grabbed his dick through his jeans and tried to feel him up," Stella hisses, her eyes spitting fire. "I want to cut the bitch."

"Get in line." I lean in and hug my daughter. "I love you." I dot kisses into her dark hair.

"Love you too, Mom." She squeezes her arms around me, and then West is there, hugging us both too.

Tears prick my eyes as I palm each of their faces while enveloped in their comforting embrace. "I love you both so much, and I'm sorry you had to find out like that."

"Why didn't you tell us?" West croaks, his eyes looking suspiciously glassy. "I knew something was up that time because Dad was gone for ages, and he's never been away on business for so long."

I kicked Curtis out when I discovered he'd been having an affair with his then twenty-three-year-old secretary, only letting him back after five weeks for the kids' sakes. "I'm sorry I didn't tell you the truth, but I wanted to protect you both. You were already at a sensitive age and going through so much. I didn't want you to worry." Swallowing my pride and my hurt, I say what needs to be said. "I don't want either of you to hate your father for this. What happened is between us as husband and wife. He is still your father. What he did doesn't change that."

"Fuck that shit." West removes his arms from around me and his sister. "He disrespected you, and I'm not cool with that."

"How could he do that to you?" Stella is tough as nails, but she's on the verge of tears.

"He's a fucking idiot." West cracks his knuckles. "I mean, look at you." He waves his hands in my direction. "You're fucking beautiful. All my friends have a hard-on for you, and they can't believe you're my mom 'cause you look so young. You're always top of the MILF lists."

I don't know if I should be flattered or grossed-out.

"It's way more than you being gorgeous," Stella adds. "You're smart and funny and just so freaking nice. You look after those smelly old perverts in the nursing home with a smile on your face. You're the first to offer to help when any of our neighbors or friends are in trouble. You attend those boring meetings at the schools, and you always bake cupcakes and treats for bake sales when other parents just pretend the store-bought crap they supply is homemade. You don't even get mad when I pull stupid shit, taking the time to explain to me why I should be more considerate of my actions. Hell, even your weird philosophy obsession is endearing." She chokes over a sob. "It's like Vander said. We're lucky. Dad is lucky. What kind of a dumbass doesn't see that?"

I grab my eldest kids into a big hug, clinging to them and fighting tears. "God, I love you." I hold them tighter. "I can't answer for your father. We need a family meeting to talk about this. Just the four of us. Ridge is too young."

"I don't want to talk to the asshole," West says, ripping out of my arms. "There's nothing he can say that'll make this right."

"Honey." I take his hands, squeezing them. "Don't do this for him. Do it for me."

"Why, Mom?"

"Because this family means everything to me, and if I can forgive your father, then I'd like for you to try. I don't want this to tear us apart. Maybe now you both know we can get it all out on the table and try to move past it." I don't know if that's possible, but we've got to try.

First, I need to have a separate conversation with my husband, and it can no longer wait.

Chapter Five

Vander

I turn the faucet on too fast, uncaring when water splashes over my shirt as I angrily rinse plates before loading them in the dishwasher while West and Stella talk to their mom. I heard most of the conversation, skulking behind the door to the dining room, listening to Kendall make excuses for that pathetic piece of shit she's married to. When I'd heard enough, I returned to the kitchen before I did something reckless—like bound up the stairs and ram my fists into Curtis's smug face.

I have never warmed to that man, instantly seeing through him. He loves the sound of his own voice and thinks the world revolves around him. I have seen the way he flirts with other women at events, and he is almost as bad as my father. He doesn't hit his wife or his children, but that's the only difference between him and Gregory Henley. In every other regard, they are two peas in a pod. I used to be surprised they didn't get along until I realized it's because they're too alike and too competitive. Now that Dad is handling the account for the defense contractor Curtis works for and West's dad is moving up the ranks, they are forced to spend more time together, on and off the golf course, and I bet the jabs are flying.

Loading the last plate into the dishwasher, I remove a tablet from the box under the sink and turn it on. Then I fill the sink with warm soapy water and get to scrubbing the pots. I need to keep my hands occupied so I don't run upstairs and beat the shit out of that cheating prick.

My hatred for Curtis Hawthorne was instant and instinctive, for the reasons already mentioned. But it was more than that. The overriding thought in my head the first time I met him was *"You have something belonging to me."* It's as if some little voice was in my ear, chanting it over and over until it permanently lodged in my brain. It didn't take much to convince me when I met *her*.

If my reaction to Curtis was strong, my reaction to Kendall is something I have never been able to adequately describe. It was more than a fleeting reaction, a crush, or insta-lust. It was like something clicked inside me. The darkness that lurked within me instantly retreated, blinded by the light and goodness exuding from her like liquid sunshine. It was as if all the jagged pieces of my heart finally slotted perfectly into place and the cracks began to knit together.

The second I laid eyes on her, an intense sense of relief washed over me, unlike anything I have ever felt before. But it went beyond that too. The emptiness that always existed inside me vanished, and I felt whole, complete, reborn, replenished. Like I do every time I'm in her company.

I'm still not articulating it correctly, but I don't need words. Not when I have this connection to her. This bond that feels like it can never be broken, even if Kendall is still in denial.

I don't care what anyone says.

I know what is true, and Kendall is *mine*.

"You didn't have to do all that by yourself," she says,

entering the kitchen, immediately soothing the ragged edges of my frustration and rage.

"I needed to occupy my hands; otherwise, I would have found a better way to expend this restless energy," I truthfully admit, placing the last washed pot on the drainer and pulling out the plug in the sink. I turn around to face her as I swipe the towel from the counter and dry my hands. I drill her with a pointed look so she understands exactly what I'm saying.

Her stunning blue eyes examine my face as she steps back, creating some distance between us. I have no clue where West and Stella are, but I hope they remain gone because I need to get a few things off my chest, and I'm done pussyfooting around our feelings.

I walked away three months ago, and it fucking killed me.

I'm not doing that again.

I am going to fight for her, and I'm not giving up until she's all mine.

"West told you," she whispers, as her cheeks stain red.

"Yes," I say through gritted teeth. "But I've always known what kind of man your husband is." I step closer to her, casting a quick glance toward the kitchen door to ensure no one is around. My heart races as I stare into her beautiful face. "Don't do that. Don't look ashamed. You haven't done anything wrong. This is all on him, and he doesn't deserve you." Lifting my hand, I brush my fingers down her cheek, enjoying the feel of her silky-soft skin under my touch. "He has never been worthy of you."

"What...what are you doing?" she whispers, tilting her chin up and peering into my eyes.

"You know what I want. I think I made that perfectly clear the night of my birthday." My mind wanders to my eighteenth birthday party, and I recall the events of that night, like I've done so many times since.

I'm drunk, which would be an issue if we'd held my birthday party at the golf club like Dad wanted. But, for once, Mom stood her ground, and to both our surprise, Dad relented, permitting her to host the party at our house. I'm under no illusions. My parents aren't throwing this party for me because, honestly, I couldn't care less about celebrating my birthday. I'd have been happy hanging out with my friends at the carriage house. No, this isn't about me. This is about keeping up appearances. *Why else are all my parents' friends and Dad's golf buddies and coworkers here?* This is just for show. It's not like my parents actually give a shit about me as a person. To mom, I'm her caregiver. To dad, a possession to manipulate into doing his will.

Dumping the last of the whiskey into my glass, I knock it back, enjoying the burn as it glides down my throat. Gayle Turner slides onto the stool at the bar beside me, but I ignore her, like I've been doing all night. I don't fuck around with the girls from my school, and everyone knows it, so she's wasting her time.

Mom hired caterers to handle the party food, and they set up a fully stocked bar with staff to manage it. I don't know how big of a bribe Dad paid to get them to turn a blind eye to all the underage drinking, but none of my friends have been asked for ID. As I sweep my gaze over the room, I see I'm not the only one who is drunk.

West has slipped out to one of the bedrooms with Hazel, so this is the first real opportunity I've had to watch Kendall. Even when I'm drunk, I know better than to watch his mom in his presence. West is the best friend I've ever had. We are as close as brothers, so I know he'd be shocked if he knew the intensity of my feelings for his mom. Lately, my dirty thoughts and wicked fantasies have gone into overdrive, and I don't know how much longer I can hold back and not do something or say something.

I'm eighteen now. Legally an adult. So, technically there is no legal reason why we can't be together. I find it laughable that I'm allowed to vote, have sex, and get married but not drink. *What kind of moron devised that law?*

"Want to get out of here?" Gayle asks, wrapping her bony hand around my lower arm and shoving her face into mine. Her dress is cut so low at the front I can practically see her nipples. It's not, in any way, appealing to me.

I yank my arm from her grip and stand. "Not if you were the last woman on the planet," I cruelly say, hoping that might drive the point home. All night, I have been politely declining her advances, but I'm done playing nice.

"You're such an asshole."

"Because I'm not interested in you?" I lean down with a dark glare. "News flash, honey. It's my birthday. My house. My body. What I do on it, in it, and with it is my business. Leave me alone or get the fuck out." It's rude as fuck, but I'm past the point of caring. Without waiting for a reply, I stalk off in search of my prey.

I find her a few minutes later, talking to her neighbor Shirley and a petite redhead with big boobs. I've met her before. She works at Bentley Law too. June something or other. She's in charge of marketing, and I know she's Kendall's best friend at the office.

I watch Kendall from a distance for a few beats, just drinking her in. She always looks hot, but goddamn, she looks straight fire tonight. Her long blonde hair hangs in soft waves over her shoulders, and she's wearing more makeup than usual. Her lips are a vibrant red, and I want to suck, bite, and lick the lipstick off until her mouth is swollen and bruised from my kisses. A tight, strapless, little black dress hugs her gorgeous curves, stopping just above her knee. Her shapely slim legs are encased in a pair of black and gold high heels, and visions of having them wrapped around my shoulders as I fuck her instantly surge to the forefront of my mind. In my head, I have fucked her in all manner of ways and locations. Blood rushes south, thickening my cock behind my jeans, and my fingers twitch at my side, itching with the craving to touch her.

No other woman has ever stood a chance with me. From the moment I met Kendall, she is all I see and everything I want.

I am done fucking waiting.

Her eyes lift, and her head turns in my direction, as if I called her name. We stare intensely at one another, like we have so many times before, and I know she feels it too. Sparks explode in the gap between us, like the fireworks streaking across the sky outside. The crowd gasps, oohing and aahing as people make their way out onto the balcony.

Shirley walks off, and June moves to follow her, grasping Kendall's hand and breaking the spell enchanting both of us. I move on autopilot, sobering up as I walk toward her with purpose.

I don't really know what I'm doing, but I'm doing it anyway.

"Don't go," I whisper, circling my fingers around her slender wrist. I press my mouth to her ear. "I need to speak to you. We can do this in private or here. I really don't fucking care. I would happily shout my truths for the entire world to hear, but I don't think you'd like that."

Her eyes pop wide, and her mouth forms an O as June stops, turning to look at us with curious eyes.

"I'll follow you," Kendall says, rapidly composing herself.

She flashes her friend a convincing smile. "West needs me. I'll be back as soon as I can."

I chuckle under my breath as I take her hand and lead her toward the door to the hallway.

She rips her hand from mine, pinning me with a warning look, and I chuckle again. "Vander," she whispers in a breathy tone that turns my dick to steel. "You're drunk."

"Guilty as charged." I grin as I steer her into the hallway. A few people are out here, but I ignore them, walking past closed doors until the hallway clears and we are out of sight. Grabbing Kendall's hand, I pull her into the library, closing and locking the door behind us.

She slams up against the door, flattening her palms on the wood and staring at me with panicked eyes. "What are you doing?" she asks in a sexy tone that does weird things to my insides. I know she isn't aware of how seductive she sounds when she lowers her voice, but it never ceases to turn me the fuck on.

"What I should have done a long time ago," I purr, caging her in with my arms and leaning down to press my face into her neck. I inhale her intoxicating scent. At the first smell, it's a delicate, light, floral scent until darker notes of spice tickle my nostrils, and I growl against her smooth skin. It's the perfect perfume for her. Scintillating goodness mixed with an undercurrent of naughty deliciousness. Just like the woman wearing it. "God, you smell divine. Like sunshine and temptation." My tongue darts out, and I lick a slow path up the column of her elegant neck. "You're perfect."

"Vander. No." She tries to sound commanding but can't pull it off.

My tongue laps at the pulse point throbbing in her neck. "Don't lie to me, Kendall. I know you want me the way I want you. Your body betrays you every time."

Her small hands land on my chest, and she pushes, trying to dislodge me. "Stop it," she hisses. "We can't do this."

"Why?!" Reluctantly, I raise my head and step back. Her hands fall off my chest, and I instantly miss her touch. I won't ever do anything to make her uncomfortable. No matter how badly I want her and that I can see all she is hiding from herself.

"*Why?*" Her face mirrors the disbelief in her tone. "You know why! I'm married. You're my son's best friend, and I'm far too old for you."

I notice she doesn't deny our connection or refute my feelings or hers. I can work with that. "You can't deny you're attracted to me. That you have feelings for me. I know I'm not alone in feeling this." I take her hand and place it over my chest, where my heart is pounding like crazy because we both love being this close to her. *Imagine what it would be like to be able to touch her at will?* The closest feeling to euphoria settles deep in my chest, my body thrumming with the righteousness of the emotion and her. "I see you, Kendall. I see what you try to hide from yourself. But you can't hide it from me. I know." I pierce her with the full intensity of everything I feel for her.

"It's wrong," she whispers, forcing herself to look away.

"Nothing is ever wrong, just more or less correct."

Her head picks up, and she whips her eyes to mine, shock splaying across her face. "Did you just quote Marcus Aurelius?"

I grin, nodding. "Thank you for the book. I have highlighted it to shit already." My actual birthday was on Monday, and Kendall gave me the book as a gift when I came over to hang out with West that night. She had also baked me a cake, and if I wasn't already in love with her, that would have sealed the deal.

Her features soften, her eyes blaze brightly, and her mouth

curves into a smile, and I'm transfixed. She is the most beautiful woman in the whole world. When she looks at me, nothing else matters.

Only her.

Fuck it. It's all or nothing now. I hold her hand over my heart as I lower my face to hers, leaving only a tiny gap between our mouths. Her chest visibly heaves, and a rosy hue creeps up her neck and onto her cheeks. I swear she has stopped breathing. "My heart beats only for you." I squeeze her hand. "Do you feel that? You sustain it. You make it grow. You fill it so fully that none of the other shit in my life matters. The only thing that does is you." I rest my brow against hers, peering deep into her eyes as I admit the ultimate truth. "I love you, and there is absolutely nothing wrong about that."

Chapter Six

Kendall

Vander is staring at me, but his mind is gone, and I suspect he's reliving the night of his eighteenth birthday party, like I just was.

"*I love you, and there is absolutely nothing wrong about that.*" His words are etched in my brain, and I think of them, and him, often. The memory provides both comfort and pain. Comfort because, when I'm at my lowest, I think of the way Vander looked at me when he admitted his feelings, and I have never felt more loved or cherished than in that moment. Pain because it can't happen, no matter how we feel.

I might be unhappy in my relationship, but I'm still married, I'm no cheater, and I won't disregard my wedding vows because I won't be responsible for tearing our family apart. No one would understand, even if I did. Least of all, West, and my kids come first. That's why I fled Vander's house after he uttered those words, without replying for fear of saying or doing the wrong thing.

Because I was tempted.

So fucking tempted.

But my life is already complicated, and I won't add to it.

"Vander." Removing his hand from my face, I sidestep him, glancing over my shoulder at the door, grateful no one witnessed what just transpired between us. "You can't get involved."

"The hell I can't," he says, snapping out of his head.

He runs a hand through his hair, messing up the styling, sending waves of dark locks tumbling across his brow, and oh, how I long to touch him. I wish I knew what it feels like to thread my fingers through his hair, press my lips to every inch of his body, and let him move inside me. I subtly squeeze my thighs together as liquid lust rushes to my neglected core, reminding me I'm still a sexual being. I should be ashamed for having such thoughts, but lately, I am finding less and less reason to feel guilty for the naughty fantasies I've had about Vander Henley.

It should feel wrong. He's only eighteen, and he's my son's best friend. So why does it always feel so right?

"Does he know?" he asks, effectively yanking me from the forbidden thoughts swirling in my head.

"Know what?" My brow scrunches in confusion.

"How we feel about one another."

"I never told you how I feel," I stupidly blurt because now definitely isn't the time for this conversation.

A cocky grin spreads across his kissable mouth. "You don't need to say it for me to know. I'm not the only one who steals sneaky looks or enjoys spending time together, and you forget I see you, Kendall." He moves in, closing the gap I just created, taking my hands in his. "I know who you are, and I see the things even you don't see or refuse to acknowledge." Warmth seeps into my hands and up my arms as his callused palms cover mine. He frees one hand, lifting it to my scalp as his fingers tangle in my hair. Angling my head back, he stares at my mouth like he wants to devour it, and I'm seconds from throwing all caution to the wind and telling him to do it.

When he looks at me like this, touches me like this, all logical thought and previous convictions fly out the window.

"Our souls are carved from the same entity. You are the other piece of me. I was meant to find you, Kendall. We were always meant to be."

I can't contain my shocked gasp as he edges eerily close to confirming Dee's assertion. I don't know what is going on here, only it feels like I'm losing control. That I can't stop whatever force is at play, no matter how hard I try.

Leaning in, he presses his mouth to my ear. His warm breath ghosts over my skin, eliciting a rake of delicious shivers. My core pulses with need, and internally, my soul screams at me to take what is mine. "It's always just the beginning," he whispers into my ear, quoting Marcus Aurelius again, and a powerful shudder works its way through me.

How am I expected to resist him when he quotes philosophy at me?

But resist him I must.

It doesn't matter what he says or what Dee believes; Vander is eighteen. He's got his whole life ahead of him, and starting something would not end well.

I'm aware I'm especially vulnerable now, but I've got to stay strong. "Why are you doing this now? I thought you understood. That's why you stayed away." He eases back, still holding my hands. I should pull away, but I don't. I feel an inner peace whenever I'm touching him, and I cling to it like a lifeline.

"I purposely stayed away because you weren't ready to admit the truth, but I'm done waiting, Kendall." He drops my hands, clasping my face in his large, warm palms. "I'm going to fight for you now because you belong with me. That asshole has never appreciated you, and you're not happy. West and Stella see it, and I see it. I was wrong to walk away, but I won't be making that mistake again." Steely determination washes over his face. "Leave him. Be with me. Let me love you the way you deserve to be loved."

My jaw trails the floor as I stare at him, speechless and completely floored. This is nuts. He's still in high school, and he has plans to go to college. Even if we could get over the other obstacles, I won't be the reason he changes his plans and alters his future.

Vander chuckles, and his eyes radiate love and adoration. God, it would be so easy to get lost in those mesmerizing emerald depths. To imagine a world where there are no barriers separating us and no one would care if we were together, a world where we could be happy. I can see it. Easily. That thought alone should shock me, but I have always been able to look beyond the exterior and see the truth of the man standing before me. Sometimes I have to remind myself of his age because, when we spend time together, I often forget.

But that vision is just a dream. The reality is, there are too many obstacles in our path, and I have a family. A family I can't just give up. If I can patch things up with Curtis, and we find a way to make things work and keep our family intact, that's what I must do. Even if it means sacrificing my happiness and the potential love of a lifetime with the guy standing before me, opening his heart, and shielding nothing.

"I can't leave Curtis," I finally say, removing his hands from my face and stepping around the other side of the island unit, creating a physical barrier between us. "He's my husband. The father of my children."

"He's a cheating douchebag, and you're not happy."

"My happiness doesn't come into it." My hands tremble as

Always Meant to Be

I remove the Saran Wrap from the drawer and cover a plate of food for Diana.

"Bullshit." He slams his clenched fist on the marble countertop. "You can be a loving mother and be happy too. Those things aren't mutually exclusive."

"You don't understand. It's—"

"I fucking understand more than most," he seethes, and a muscle pops in his jaw. "If my mom had left my dad when I was a kid and he first started beating her, she would've had a chance at being happy, and I sure as shit would be a lot less scarred. Don't fool yourself into thinking you're doing the right thing for your kids by staying with him."

It's scary and sad how much Vander understands.

"That's why you took him back after he cheated, isn't it?" he prods.

I glance at the door again, knowing Curtis and Ridge won't be back for ages, but I'm not sure where West and Stella have gone. They could reappear at any second, and I can't have this conversation here. "This isn't the time or place for this conversation."

He grinds his teeth, and I hate to see so much anger and pain on his face. "Answer me one thing, Kendall, and I'll go."

I wrap my arms around myself, instinctually knowing I need it.

"Do you love him?"

"I'm not answering that. It's none of your business."

He grins. "You just did." He stalks around the island unit, and I scramble back until my spine hits the wall. He towers over me, consuming me completely without even touching me. "Do you love *me*?"

My heart thrashes against my chest cavity, and my mouth turns dry. "What?" I croak, grasping for time.

"You heard me." His eyes bore into mine. "I love you, and I want to hear you say it too."

At times when I forget Vander is a teenager, his youthful arrogance rears its head to remind me. "That is very presumptuous of you."

His grin is borderline scary. "Stop deflecting, Kendall baby." He grips my chin tight, angling my head up. "Answer the question. Do you love me?"

"No," I snap.

His nostrils flare as he leans in close to my face. "Liar." He brushes his lips across my mouth.

It's only fleeting. Not a proper kiss. But, my God, I feel it everywhere, and my knees almost buckle underneath me. My heart is careening around my chest, about to force its way out of my body and grow wings.

"Let's try that again. I want the truth this time."

"I don't know," I whisper, and that *is* the truth. I know I have strong feelings for him. Feelings I have no business having, but I haven't labeled them. I don't know if it's because I can't decipher what I feel, my situation with Curtis is messing with my head, or I'm just too chickenshit to admit it.

His fingers loosen their grip on my chin as he stares into my eyes. "I won't push you, but I'm not backing down this time." He lets go of me and steps back, taking all the warmth with him. "You know where I am if you need me. I'll be waiting." He takes the plate for his mom. "Thanks again for dinner," he says, walking off without another look at me.

I watch him leave the kitchen with scattered thoughts and a racing heart, both relieved and disappointed.

Always Meant to Be

"We need to talk," I tell Curtis later that night when Ridge is in bed. My husband went out for a few hours after he returned from his bike ride with our son, and I have no clue where he went. When he came home, he went straight to his home office, and he's been holed up here ever since. I want to sit down with Stella and West, which is why they are waiting in the living room for us. But first I need to know if it's happening again. I fold my arms and level my husband with a solemn look. "Are you having another affair?"

He sits back in his chair, arching a brow as he stares at me with indifference. "I wondered how long it'd take you to start accusing me again."

"Just answer the goddamn question, Curtis." Acid churns in my gut, and pain pounds in my skull.

"Don't take that tone with me. I have done everything you asked of me over the past three years, and nothing is ever good enough for Little Miss Perfect." He leans forward in his chair and glares at me. "This is so typical of you."

"You're deflecting." I rub at the tight pain spreading across my chest. "I guess I have my answer."

"No," he barks. "I'm not having another affair."

"Look me in the eye and tell me," I demand.

He stares straight into my eyes as he says, "I'm not having an affair."

I'm not sure I believe him, but I have no proof this time. I guess I'll just have to accept him at his word. For now. My shoulders slump in relief, and I uncross my arms, letting them hang by my sides. "The kids know about Lydia."

"What?" He scrubs a hand along his jawline, glaring at me. "You fucking agreed to keep it a secret!" he snaps.

"I didn't tell them!" I shout. "That stupid conniving slut did!"

"Mom's right," West says, storming into the room. He

wraps his arm around my shoulders, and I could cry. I let my son comfort me as he glares at his father. "Mom hasn't said one word to me or Stella. I know because Lydia's dating one of Hazel's cousins."

"Or she was," Stella murmurs, entering the room and closing the door. I guess we're doing this in here. "Hazel told her cousin that his girlfriend hit on West, and he dumped the cunt." A gleeful expression spreads over her pretty face, and I'm enjoying this too much to call her out on her appalling language. "Good riddance."

A look of thunder ghosts over Curtis's face as West steers me to the leather couch in the corner. "Is that the truth, son?" he asks, getting up and walking toward us. West situates me in between him and his sister, keeping his arm around me as Stella moves closer, and I have never loved my kids more than in this moment. Their support gives me the courage to lift my head up high and remember I am not the one at fault here.

Curtis drops into the high-backed leather chair, leaning forward on his elbows, unable to hide the hurt look from his face. Wow. He really is a piece of work. West sneers at his dad while he tightens his arm around me. "Your whore wanted to test-drive the hotter, younger version, but I kicked her skanky low-life ass to the curb. Like you should have done, you pathetic piece of crap!"

Chapter Seven

Kendall

West jumps to his feet and stalks to his dad, caging him in as his hands land on either side of the chair, and he leans down, putting his face up in Curtis's. "How could you do this to Mom?" he hisses, a muscle clenching in his jaw. Stella nods at her brother, encouraging him to go on, while she slides her hand into mine. I cling to my daughter, too choked up to speak. Maybe it's not right to let my kids act like this, but they have an entitlement to their feelings, and I won't stop them from venting if it's what they need to do. "How could you disrespect her like this?"

Curtis has the decency to look ashamed, but I have no clue if it's genuine or not. While he showed remorse in the initial aftermath, I haven't seen much of it these past couple of years. I'm beginning to realize the man I have been married to for seventeen years is no longer the same man, and I don't know him. Not like I thought I did.

"Marriages are hard, son, and relationships are complicated. This is something between your mother and I. It shouldn't concern you or your sister."

"That's freaking bullshit," Stella says, sitting up straighter. "We both knew something was going on. You left, Dad. Mom didn't have to tell us she kicked you out for us to know it wasn't normal."

"And then you came back, and she flinched every time you went near her," West says, easing away from his father. Reaching out, I take his hand, pulling him back down beside me.

Curtis looks uneasy as he watches the three of us. He can see which side our children are on. The thought warms my heart, but at the same time, I need to intervene. I don't want their relationship with him damaged because of something he did to me. He is still their father. If we can't fix this and we split up, they need to have a relationship with him, and I owe it to my kids to do what I can to enable that. "It was hard for me, at first," I admit, my gaze bouncing between my kids. "The trust was broken, and I was very hurt. But we went to couples counseling and worked hard to move past it."

I smother my bitter laugh, convincing myself I'm lying with good intentions. Curtis attended two sessions and then refused to come again. I attended the other four alone. Maybe I should have given him an ultimatum or divorced him when he refused to put any real effort into making amends, but I was so messed up and desperately trying to keep my family together, so I let it slide.

West and Stella exchange a look.

"Say what you need to say," I tell them. "Get everything out on the table now, and hopefully we can move past this."

"You're not happy," Stella says. "Either of you. We're not blind."

"I *am* happy," Curtis protests, gripping the armrests tight. "I love my family, and I'm in a good place in my career. If you have picked up on anything, it's the stress of my new job. I have a lot of additional responsibilities, and I'm feeling the pressure."

That's not exactly a lie, but it's not the full truth either.

"Don't talk shit, Dad." West sends daggers at Curtis. "We're not little kids. You can't pull the wool over our eyes anymore." The anger glides off his face, replaced with the saddest expression. His eyes turn glassy. "I don't see any love," he whispers, pressing a fierce kiss to the top of my head. "It was so obvious on vacation. I hated the way you spoke to Mom. I hate the way you treat her. It's not right."

"She's our mother." Stella's voice ripples with emotion. "Your wife, and she doesn't deserve this. She always puts us first, and it's not fair."

Shame zips through me, and I lower my eyes to my lap. It's embarrassing I have let it get this far. That my kids have seen the painful truth while I have kept going about my life pretending like my marriage isn't hanging by a thread.

"You're right," Curtis quietly says. "I'm so sorry."

"Are you getting a divorce?" Stella inquires.

"Absolutely not." I lift my head in time to see Curtis vehemently shaking his head. He slides to the floor and kneels before us, taking our daughter's free hand in his and bringing it to his lips. He kisses the back of her hand. "I'm sorry I failed our family." Letting her hand go, he moves over in front of me. "I'm sorry I failed you." Tears pool in his eyes, and I want to believe him, but I'm finding it difficult. "I know I haven't been trying hard enough lately, but I love you, Kendall. I love this life we have built, and I will do better. I promise. I don't want a divorce. I want to fix things."

I'm kind of numb as I listen to him saying all the right things. I glance at my son and daughter, and both stare at me with hopeful anticipation, and I know I need to do this. "I love you too." The words feel hollow to my ears, and my heart doesn't react at all when he leans in and kisses me. I can't remember the last time he kissed me, and I feel overwhelming sadness as his lips brush against mine. The stark contrast to how I felt earlier when Vander did the same thing is telling.

Then, I felt tingles everywhere, and I had to fight a vicious internal battle not to grab his head and kiss the living daylights out of him.

Now, I have to hide a shudder and quell the urge to shove my husband away.

I force the brightest smile on my face as I turn to my children. "We don't want you to worry. Your dad and I promise to work on our relationship. What's most important is how much we love you both and your younger brother."

"You guys are everything to us," Curtis says, and it's the only thing we agree on anymore. "I am sorry I let you down. I'm ashamed of my actions, but you need to put it aside and let me and Mom work through it."

West darts in, kissing my cheek before standing. "I can't promise that, Dad. I won't let you hurt Mom again. Treat her right, and there's nothing to worry about."

Curtis clamps a hand down on West's shoulder. "I can do that, son." He yanks him into a hug. "I'm proud of the man you're becoming and excited for your future." He stands back, smiling a proud smile. "You just focus on school and football, and let us take care of the rest."

"Are you sure you're okay, Mom?" Stella asks, inspecting my face carefully.

"I'm fine, sweetheart. Daddy's correct. Just focus on school, and enjoy being a junior. Responsibilities come around quicker than you'd think. Enjoy being carefree, and live your best life." I hug her tight. "Try to put this out of your mind, and let us be the adults." I brush dark locks out of her eyes. "Okay?"

They nod. We are silent as our kids exit the room, seeming

happier than they were when they came in. West glances back at us, offering me a soft smile. I can tell he's still concerned. No doubt Stella is too, and I vow to do better. They shouldn't be worrying about this.

"Drink?" Curtis asks, closing the door and striding toward his liquor cabinet.

"No thanks." I settle my hands on my lap, watching as he fixes himself a whiskey. He walks back over, reclaiming the chair rather than sitting beside me. "Did you mean it?" I ask, staring him in the eyes.

"Which part?" He waggles his brows as he swirls the amber-colored liquid in his glass.

"All of it."

He stares at me as he drinks a healthy mouthful of his drink. Nerves jangle inside me as I watch him sizing me up with cunning eyes. Right now, Curtis Hawthorne is a complete stranger to me. As if I haven't known him for over twenty years. There was a time I could tell what he was thinking just by glancing at him. Now, I have no clue, only that the cold, sneering, superior glaze of his eyes warns of impending cruelty.

"I meant it when I said West needs to focus on school and football. We can't mess up this opportunity for him. He could go all the way to the NFL. He could have the chance I missed out on when I broke my arm. Nothing can distract him from that."

I have always known Curtis is living vicariously through our son. If I didn't know West lived and breathed football, I would have stopped Curtis from pushing him so hard, but the truth is, it's what West wants. "I agree. It's the same for Stella. Junior year is still an important year. We need to try harder. I had no idea they had noticed so much."

"They're smart kids." He drains his drink before lifting his eyes to mine. I see zero warmth or compassion there. "So, we need to put on the show of a lifetime. At least until Stella graduates high school, and then we can divorce."

Although I have been thinking of divorce a lot recently, his words are still a blow. I'm not sure what expression he sees on my face, but he laughs, and it's a mean, spiteful sound. "God, you're so fucking gullible." He snaps his fingers in my face. "Wake up and smell the coffee, Kendall." He crosses an ankle over his knee. "I told them what they needed to hear. Of course, I don't love you. I haven't for a long time. Why do you think I was fucking Lydia?"

"Because you're a disloyal asshole." I'm happy my voice doesn't shake even though I'm trembling inside.

"No one could live up to your expectations, Kendall. You just have to be the perfect wife. The perfect neighbor. The perfect employee. It's fucking exhausting, and you left no time for me. If you want to blame someone for my affairs, blame yourself. You dropped me like a hot potato the instant the kids arrived. And when my football dream ended, you weren't there for me. All you cared about was I got a good job to support us."

"That's not fair! You know I was devastated for you, and what about my dreams?" I thump a hand over my chest. "You know I wanted to study philosophy in college and pursue a career in social research. Things haven't exactly gone the way I planned either, but we have a good life. Amazing kids. Why couldn't it be enough for you?"

"That's your problem, Kendall. You lack ambition in all aspects of your life. You might be content with vanilla sex once a week, but I need more excitement. I want a woman who knows how to please a man in bed. Someone adventurous who prioritizes her man. That's not you."

His words cut through skin and bone, pulverizing my heart, like intended. I want to tell him I was bored with our sex life too—not that we've been having any for months. I was more

Always Meant to Be

than willing to try different things, and he fucking knows it. I should defend myself, but I can't speak past the painful lump clogging my throat. It's clear he has harbored resentment for a lot longer than I realized.

"And let's be honest," he continues, moving to the liquor cabinet to refill his drink. "It's not like we got to choose. You got yourself pregnant and sealed our fates."

Anger flares in my gut, and I swallow past the lump. "Last I checked, there were two of us involved, and I did choose. I chose you."

"Well, I didn't choose you." He returns to his seat, flashing me a dark grin. "I did the right thing for my family, and that's what we're going to do now."

"Fuck you." I clench my hands into fists.

"No thanks. I'd rather screw a corpse."

Hurt scuttles through me, and I fail to disguise it from my face.

He leans forward, gripping my face tight. "You need to work on your poker face, wife. This won't do." He lets me go with a disgusted grunt. "The kids need to be convinced, and you're going to play your part."

"Like hell I will. I'll be filing for divorce the second I step foot in the office tomorrow morning."

"No, you fucking won't." He gulps back his drink. "I don't even have to threaten you to make you toe the line because you'll do it for the kids."

"Divorcing you is what's best for the kids."

He drains the dregs of his drink and stands. "Not right now it isn't, and we both know it." He shoves his hands in the pockets of his pants and his features soften a smidgeon as he looks at me. "You're a great mother, Kendall. I would never, could never, take that from you. I know you'll do this because divorcing now will upset West and Stella and derail their futures. You love them selflessly. I know you'll do it for them."

I hate that he's right.

"We just have to play the loving couple in public until Stella graduates," he reconfirms. He obviously doesn't give a shit about upsetting Ridge. "Then we'll divorce. You can have the house, and I'll give you a generous cash settlement."

"Did you ever love me?" I foolishly ask.

He shrugs. "At the start I did, for a while. But everyone knows first love never lasts. I was actually planning to break up with you before I left for college, but you got pregnant, and I couldn't pull the plug then." Pain, like I have never felt before, rips my insides to shreds as I contemplate how everything has been a lie, and I gobbled it up like a naive fool. "Then I was going to leave you ten years ago, but you got pregnant with Ridge."

I remember the arguments we had when I revealed I was pregnant again. Ridge was a surprise baby, and while he hadn't been planned, I was thrilled. Curtis went crazy when I told him, even demanded I have an abortion. I told him no, and he left for a couple days, eventually returning, but it was no picnic. We had a rocky time until Ridge was born and Curtis's paternal instincts kicked in, like I hoped they would.

I raise a shaky hand to my mouth, fighting to keep my tears at bay. I can't believe he was acting this entire time and I didn't see it. I feel like such a gullible idiot. I invested so much in my marriage, yet it was doomed from the start because my husband didn't love me. Pain eviscerates my heart, and the urge to curl into a ball and sob is riding me hard. But I won't give this lying, cheating bastard any more of my tears, so I force them back inside and work hard to conceal the emotion from my face.

"I was planning on leaving you around the time I started my relationship with Lydia. Ridge was six, and West and Stella were teens. I figured they were all at ages where it wouldn't upset them too much, but that stupid slut planted evidence on me knowing you'd find it and discover our affair. Stupid bitch thought I'd leave you for her. As if." He laughs, and it sends nasty shivers down my spine. "She was just a pretty hole to fuck my boredom away. When you kicked me out and threatened to divorce me, it killed me being away from the kids. It made me realize I couldn't go through with it until West and Stella had at least grown up."

"Every promise you made at that time was a lie," I say.

"Not every one," he replies, staring down at me with no remorse. "I love my kids. I would die for them, and I returned because of them. But I haven't loved you in a long time, Kendall. Any woman with half a brain would have figured it out a long time ago."

It's not enough to rip my heart from my chest and destroy every memory I've had from the time I was fourteen; now he has to insult my intelligence too.

"Affairs," I say, staring at him with mounting horror as I recall something he said a few minutes ago. "You said affairs earlier. Not affair."

An evil grin materializes on his face. "I've been cheating on you for years. The first time was during freshman week at college, and I've taken plenty of lovers since. It's the only way I could tolerate playing happy family with you."

That means he cheated on me before we were even married and every time I was pregnant with his child. Yet he continued to have sex with me while screwing other women, putting my health at risk. Nausea churns in my gut and travels up my throat as the true extent of his deception becomes clear. "You unimaginable bastard." I climb to my feet as blood rushes to my head. "I hate you."

He shrugs, letting my words float aimlessly over his head.

"Your feelings are inconsequential to me. Just play the role of dutiful wife and mother, and in less than two years, we'll be free of one another."

Except we won't ever be truly free of each other. We will be tied to one another for life through our kids. The thought depresses and devastates me. I clutch the arm of the couch as I sway, my legs threatening to go out from under me.

"I'm going out." He grabs his jacket off the hook on the back of the door. "Don't wait up. I'll be fucking my girlfriend for hours because she understands how to please her man." Clearly, he lied earlier when he denied he was having an affair, but he obviously feels there's no need to hide it now West and Stella know part of the truth. Curtis casts a derogatory look over me, and I wonder what I ever saw in him. "You're a mess. Use the time to pull yourself the fuck together." He points his finger at me. "You don't want to see what I'll do if you don't make this convincing for the kids."

I fall back on the couch as he exits the room, waiting until I hear the front door shutting, before I fall apart.

Chapter Eight

Vander

I'm returning home from the boxing club, just after ten, when I see Kendall walking in the direction of my house. She's not in her usual walking gear. She's wearing the same dress she wore to dinner earlier with no coat or clothing covering her bare lower arms. I know it's milder than usual for early November, but it's still fucking cold at night, and she'll get sick walking around like that.

Speeding up, I drive past her and pull over to the curb up ahead. Killing the engine, I hop out and run toward her. Panic jumps up and slaps me when she passes under the streetlight and I see her tear-streaked face. "What's wrong?" I blurt when I reach her. "What's happened?"

Tears roll silently down her face as she tips her chin up. Haunted eyes stare at me, and bile swims up my throat. I worked hard to release my frustration in the gym, and I was feeling more relaxed by the time Jimmy kicked me out of the place at closing time. But now a fresh layer of stress settles on my shoulders as concern washes over me. If that bastard has hurt her, all bets are off. I will fucking squeeze the life from his pathetic body and not feel a single regret if he is the cause of this. "Did he hurt you?" My eyes quickly skim over her body, checking for signs of injuries.

"Not physically," she croaks, almost choking on a sob. She shudders before wrapping her arms around her body. Her teeth chatter, and her lower lip wobbles as she sniffles. Carefully, I touch her arm and she's ice cold.

"Fuck, Kendall. You're freezing." I rub my hands up and down her arms before pulling her into my side and circling my arms around her, hoping she siphons some of my body heat. I'm conscious I stink to the high heavens and a fine sheen of sweat coats my skin. But I couldn't give two shits about that now. Getting her warm, and taking care of her, is all that matters right now. "You're coming with me."

I definitely know something is wrong when she mounts no protest, letting me lead her to my truck and helping her into the passenger seat, without uttering a word. I run around to the driver's side and climb behind the wheel. Turning the engine on, I switch off the stereo and crank the heat to the max. Kendall has her arms wrapped around her middle again, and she's staring numbly out the window. Reaching over, I grab the seat belt and buckle her in, doing my best not to touch her because she's clearly upset, and I don't want to do anything to make it worse.

I drive down the street, past the entrance to my parent's house, and take a sharp left, turning down the rear lane I use when I'm at the carriage house. Tall oak trees and pine trees border the lane on the right side, towering over the side of our property, affording us complete privacy. The woodland is actually the western side of Palmer Park, which is a large park set over seven hundred and thirty acres with forested areas, an abundance of walking, hiking, and running trails, picnic pavilions, playgrounds, and various athletic fields, as well as a dog park. The stunning views over Pikes Peak from the top are legendary around these parts, and I sometimes go there when I need to be alone or I need space to think.

The truck bounces over bumpy terrain, jostling us a little as I head toward the rear entrance to my house. I slow down as we approach the high wooden gates, pressing the button on my key fob to unlock them. Kendall continues to stare into space as I maneuver my Chevy through the gates and park it on the side of the carriage house. The gates close automatically behind us as I kill the engine and consider my next move. We are far enough away from the main house not to worry about my parents, especially since they rarely come out here, but I won't take chances with Kendall. So, I hop out and do a quick check of the grounds and the carriage house, ensuring there are no surprises lying in wait.

Once I'm assured the coast is clear, I help Kendall down from the truck and escort her inside before locking the door and throwing my keys, wallet, and phone down on the kitchen counter. For the first time ever, I'm sorry I haven't done more with this place. I wish I had a fireplace and a proper bathroom so I could light a fire and run her a bath. "Come sit," I say, steering her over to one of the couches. Gently, I push her down before turning to switch both heaters on to the max. "Stay put." I run to the bedroom, remove one of my hoodies from the freestanding rail by the wall, and grab the heater from that room before returning to Kendall.

I plug in the third heater, hoping the space warms up quick. "Put this on." I thrust the hoodie at her, hating the forlorn expression on her face as she clutches it to her chest. At least she has stopped crying. Bending down, I peer into her eyes while brushing the dampness off her cheeks. "You need to get warm, sweetheart. Put this on, and I'll make you coffee." I walk toward the tiny kitchenette.

"I need something stronger," she rasps in a throaty voice that is testament to the tears she's shed. "I know you have alcohol here." Kendall knows we drink, and she sometimes buys beer for us. She told West she'd rather we didn't drink cheap shit that'll strip the lining from our stomachs, but she doesn't outrightly condone us getting drunk either. My parents couldn't give two shits. Honestly, it would be hypocritical of Mom if she did. Our house is an alcoholic's paradise. Dad has an extensive liquor cabinet he keeps fully stocked. God forbid Mom has a chance at getting sober. I feel zero remorse when I regularly raid Dad's stash. He knows I take it, and he couldn't care less.

"I don't have any Sancerre, but I can go up to the house to get some for you, if you like?"

She stares at me, her eyes blinking excessively. "How'd you know that's my favorite wine?"

My lips curve at the corners. "I observe everything to do with you."

"Like that's not creepy," she says, fighting a barely there smile.

"I want to know everything there is to know about you. Shoot me if that's a crime."

Her eyes well up, and I curse under my breath. I make a move toward her, but she holds up a hand. "It's fine." She angrily swipes at the tears leaking from her eyes. "I can't control my tear ducts tonight, and you're too sweet." She offers me a watery smile. "What booze do you have here?"

She slides her arms into the hoodie and zips it up. It swamps her, and she looks so tiny and fragile, and I just want to bundle her up and make everything better. I fucking love seeing her in my clothes, and the usual possessive streak I feel in her presence charges to the fore. I want to lock her away with me and never let her go.

"Vander?"

I snap out of it, rubbing a hand across the back of my neck. I can't believe she's at my place. Or that it looked like she was coming to me, seeking my help. She has no clue how much this means to me or how much hope it gives me. I hate she's upset, but I can't be sorry she's here. "I've got Bud or tequila." I haven't had a chance to restock my supplies since West drank me dry on Friday, and I made a further dent in it last night.

"Tequila works," she says, surprising me. I've never known her to be a big drinker.

"How about I make you some coffee for now, and after I shower, we can share the tequila?" I don't want to leave her alone, but I stink, and I need to change out of my workout clothes.

Her eyes trail my body, from head to toe, and heat spears my flesh in every place her gaze lands. "Okay," she whispers, pulling her eyes back to mine. "You were at the boxing club? I thought Sundays were your day off?"

I love how she remembers my training schedule. "They are, but I needed to let off some steam, so I went a few rounds in the ring with Crusher." I switch the Keurig on before removing a mug from the cupboard.

"You still hang out with him?"

"We mostly train together and sometimes hang out at one of the bars around UCCS. He's a senior there now," I explain, as I pour coffee into the mug and add some creamer. I know she doesn't take sugar. Inspecting the contents of my refrigerator, I silently berate myself for not picking up some groceries on the way home.

I walk toward her with the coffee. "Do you want something to eat? The pickings are slim. I have some chopped fruit, a couple protein bars, or some chips left over from Friday, but they might be stale."

A genuine smile appears on her mouth as she takes the coffee from me. Our fingers brush in the exchange, sending fiery tingles shooting up my arm, but that's nothing new. "Wow, you're really spoiling me."

I'm not sure what expression she sees on my face, but it's enough to have her reach out and squeeze my hand.

"Hey. I was teasing. I don't want anything to eat. I think my stomach would revolt if I tried to force food down." And just like that, the smile drops off her face, and the sad, devastated expression is back.

I want to know what he did to her, but I need to shower and change so I can give her my undivided attention. Crouching in front of her, I tuck a stray piece of blonde hair behind her ear. "I'm gonna grab a shower real quick. Drink your coffee and make yourself at home."

She visibly gulps, but she's got that faraway look in her eyes again.

I stop at the doorway to my bedroom. "Kendall?"

She looks over her shoulder at me.

"Don't leave. I'll be right back."

I maintain eye contact with her until she nods, but I'm not entirely convinced she won't be gone when I come out.

Chapter Nine

Vander

I take the quickest shower in the history of showers, and my body is barely dry when I pull on a pair of gray sweats and a long-sleeved white tee. I slip my feet into a pair of Nike slides. After dragging the towel through my hair, I run my fingers through it and spray on some cologne before exiting the bedroom.

My shoulders collapse in relief when I find Kendall still here. The room is noticeably warmer, thank fuck, and she has ditched her ballet flats, curling her legs up under her, still swaddled underneath my hoodie. Her shoes aren't the only thing she's ditched. The half-drank coffee is cold in the mug on the coffee table, and she's found the tequila. Along with the portfolio for my college submissions. It's resting on the table, and she's slowly flipping through it as she drinks straight from the tequila bottle. A look of fierce concentration glides over her beautiful face as she studies it carefully while sipping tequila like it's lemonade.

There is something so painfully beautiful about this visual that I stop and stare, even though I should probably be freaking out she's going through my drawings because I know what she'll discover.

But fuck it. I've already laid my cards on the table. She knows how I feel about her. I'm going to own it.

I watch her expression transform as different emotions surface while she flicks through my artwork, and my heart swells behind my chest. She's so entranced she hasn't even noticed I have returned to the room.

Watching her wearing my clothes and looking cozy on the couch as she drinks tequila from the bottle without flinching, while leafing through the physical manifestations of my soul, is profoundly beautiful, and I wish I could freeze frame this moment and capture it for eternity.

If she wasn't so vulnerable tonight, I'd suggest she pose for me. But I can't be selfish. Not when she's upset. Taking another few seconds to watch her, I commit the visual to memory so I can draw it after she's gone. Reluctantly, I clear my throat, announcing my presence. "Hey. I see you found my portfolio."

"I did." She glances at me briefly before returning her attention to my artwork. "I hope you don't mind me looking, but you know I've always loved your drawings. You've gotten even better." Her fingers glide over my interpretation of the view from the bridge at Helen Hunt Falls. She doesn't even look up as I sit down beside her. "You are incredibly talented, Vander. This is impressive work," she adds, flipping the page.

I wait with bated breath for her reaction.

She stares at one of the many portraits I have drawn of her, her finger tracing over the lines of her stunning face. "When did you do this?" she softly asks, turning her head to look at me.

"It was the start of the summer. I was hanging with West in his room, and you were sitting on the loveseat in the backyard, rocking back and forth as you stared into space." Angling my body, I twist around so I'm facing her. Our knees brush in the

Always Meant to Be

process, and that's all it takes to warm every part of me. I long to pick her up, deposit her in my lap, and just hold her close.

Her touch stirs so many sensations in me. Some soothing. Some arousing. Some confusing. But I always *feel*. Kendall makes me feel things that shouldn't be familiar, yet they are. Every fleeting touch is like a memory seared into my skin, and it takes monumental willpower not to react to it in a visceral way.

Unable to resist touching her, I tuck another piece of her hair behind her ear, my fingers lingering against her cheek. "You looked so incredibly sad, and I couldn't tear my eyes away from you. I watched you through the window, for as long as I could get away with it. That night, I couldn't sleep because your pain tormented me. I felt your anguish as if it was my own, so I got up, grabbed my pad, and started drawing."

Her eyes widen before she lowers them to the picture again. "You drew this from memory?"

I drew most all the pictures and paintings of her from memory because I couldn't risk taking a photo. Moving my hand from her face, I press my fingers to my head. "You're imprinted in here the same way you're imprinted in my heart." I place my hand over my chest, right where my heart thuds steadily. "You're all I see, Kendall. Even when I close my eyes."

A strangled sound emits from her throat, and her eyes well up again.

"Please don't cry, baby." I brush her tears away before pressing a kiss to the top of her head. I squeeze my eyes shut for a second, wishing I could absorb her pain and remove it. "It's killing me to see you like this."

"I don't know how to process everything I'm feeling," she admits, remembering the tequila and swallowing a mouthful. She hands it to me. "I know you want to know what's happened, but I can't talk about it. I can't say the words." More tears stream down her face as I take a healthy glug of the earthy, semisweet liquid. "It's hurts too much."

"I'll kill him," I hiss, unable to contain the anger I feel toward her husband. "I will fucking bury him for hurting you."

She shakes her head, sending waves of golden-blonde hair cascading over her shoulders. "He's not worth it." She swipes the bottle from my hands, taking another drink. "I don't want to think about it or talk about it. I just want to spend time with you." Tentatively, she reaches out, threading her fingers through my damp hair. "You have beautiful hair, Vander." She sets the tequila down on the coffee table and turns to me. Her fingers trail down my face, and I can't move, can't breathe. I'm afraid to move a muscle and break this spell. "A beautiful face too." Softly, she explores my face, her fingers sweeping over my eyes, my nose, and my cheeks. She drags her lower lip between her teeth as her fingers run through the bristle on my chin and cheeks. Things get interesting in my pants when her fingers keep moving, trailing down my neck, along my collarbone, and onto my chest. My dick is hard as a rock, and she's barely touching me—her touch is addictive, and I can't get enough. Her hand comes to a stop over my heart. "But this is the most beautiful part of you. You have the biggest heart, Vander. I think you're amazing."

"I think you're amazing too." I lean in, unable to hold myself back any longer. "And beautiful doesn't come close to describing how utterly stunning you are." I clasp her face in my hands, pleased her skin is warm to the touch, and lower my eyes to her luscious lips.

I need to kiss her, hold her, love her.

I can't restrain myself any longer.

My heart is going crazy as I line our mouths up, keeping my gaze fixed on her. She grips my shoulders, and her touch seeps soul-deep. Adrenaline courses through my veins as I move to close the gap between our lips, ready to properly kiss her for the first time, when she pushes on my shoulders and twists her head so my lips brush against her cheekbone instead.

"We can't, Vander." Her eyes flood with compassion as she drops her hands to her lap.

My hands lower to my sides. "Why not?" I grind my teeth to the molars. "Your husband isn't loyal, so what difference does it make?"

"Two wrongs don't make a right."

"Why can't you just take something for yourself? I want you, and you want me. How can that be wrong?"

"You deserve more than I can offer, and you're too young to be dragged into my mess."

"That's not your decision to make, and my age is irrelevant. Love doesn't discriminate. I couldn't give a flying fuck about our ages. All that matters is how we feel."

"It's not that simple, and I can't be selfish. You have enough on your plate already."

"Again, that's not your call to make, and there isn't a single fucking selfish bone in your body. My life is already a shit show. I've confided enough in you over the years for you to understand that." She doesn't know the half of it, and right now, I'm glad I sheltered her from the worst of it. She is still hiding from her feelings, and I'm beginning to think I will never be able to get through to her. "You're the only bright spark in my existence. The only person who makes it easy to forget the chaos." I wind my fingers through her hair and force her gaze to mine. "Why can't love be enough? Fuck everything else."

She shakes her head, removing my hands from her hair. "Starting something could hurt a lot of people, including us, and the truth is, I'm too confused right now, Vander." Strain is etched upon her gorgeous face, radiating from her azure eyes as she pleads with me for understanding I'm not sure I can give her. "I can't make sense of anything I'm feeling, and I can't give you what you want."

"Can you at least admit you feel something for me?"

She worries her lower lip between her teeth again, and I beseech her with my eyes. I need her to give me something. I need some hope to cling to because the next few months won't be easy. Dad could figure out what I'm up to and ruin all of my carefully laid plans.

I have few good things in my life.

If I have to give up my dream of being with Kendall, I don't know how I'll cope.

I need her. Like I know she needs me. No one will ever convince me there is anything wrong with that.

Her features soften as she touches my cheek. "I do have feelings for you, Vander." Her lips part, and her tongue peeks out. "Feelings I shouldn't have but I'm struggling to fight."

My heart swells and butterflies swoop into my belly. "Don't think, baby." I rest my brow against hers as my hands land carefully on her slim waist. "Just feel. Be selfish for once, and take something for you."

Her arms go around me as she pulls me into a hug. I hold her tight, inhaling her spicy floral scent and marveling at how incredible it feels to finally have her in my arms. She buries her nose in my hair, and I have a sense she's doing the same as me. Absorbing it all. Committing it to memory. Swallowing it like the most tempting nectar. "I care about you too much to be selfish," she whispers in my ear, still clinging to me. "I care about you enough to not ruin your future." Easing back, she stares at me with fresh tears in her eyes. "I'm a basket case right now, and I won't drag anyone else down with me."

Shucking out of my hold, she stands, taking the portfolio from the table and closing it. She hands it to me. "You have a goal, and I know everything hinges on you getting accepted into the art program at Yale. Your father can't force you to follow in his footsteps, but he can try to stop you pursuing your dream." She kneels in front of me, taking my hands in hers. "You are so talented, and I want this for you. That's why I can't distract you. You need to focus on your future."

I set the portfolio back on the table. "You could never be a distraction." I squeeze her hands, loving how small and soft they feel against my larger palms and rougher skin. "You are one of the few people who support my dreams. I need you, Kendall," I add in a whisper. "Having you by my side would help me to maintain focus. Right now, I'm going crazy thinking about you all the time." I brush my thumb along her lower lip, as my mouth curves into a smirk. "Really, when you think about it, you can't not be with me." I waggle my brows. "You're a much bigger distraction when I can't have you."

She laughs, unable to contain her grin. "Nice try, but I'm not buying it." Her grin softens to a smile as she removes her hand from mine and climbs to her feet. "I live with two teenagers. You can't manipulate this woman."

I stand, looming over her. "That's not what I'm doing. There's a difference between enticing and manipulation. I would never manipulate you. It's not my style." I place my hands on her hips and move closer. "Just give us a chance. No labels. No commitments. We do this and see where it takes us."

She steps back, shaking her head. "No, Vander. I know what it's like to lose your dream. I won't stand in the way of yours. You need to put me out of your mind and focus on getting into the art program at Yale." She slips on her shoes. "I shouldn't have come here. It's not fair to dump all of this in your lap."

I fold my arms over my chest as irritation prickles at my skin. She won't even fucking consider it, and I still know shit.

"You haven't dumped anything in my lap. You haven't told me a damn thing."

"It's better you don't know." She moves to unzip my hoodie, but I stop her.

As quick as it flared, my anger fades. I don't want her to leave. "Don't go. Please stay." I shouldn't have gotten all heavy with her. It was selfish of me to go there, and I wish I could rewind and steer the conversation on a different path.

"I want to. I truly do. But it's best I leave. I don't trust myself right now, and I'm not going to mess up our lives by doing something we would both end up regretting."

Speak for yourself. There is nothing I could do with her that I would ever regret. But I know when to shut my mouth. Nothing else I say will sway her, and there's no use trying.

She yanks the zipper down, preparing to remove my hoodie, but I shake my head. "Keep it. It's freezing out." I swipe my keys from the counter. "And it's late. I'll drive you home."

"It's only a five-minute walk, and I'm a grown woman."

I slant her with a firm look. "It's still not safe. If you think I'd let you walk off by yourself, you clearly don't know me very well." I take a step closer. "I'm driving you home. End of discussion."

Her eyes penetrate mine, and I see the moment she concedes. "Okay." Looking down, she curls her fingers briefly against mine. "Thank you for tonight. I know I shouldn't have come here, but I'm not sorry I did."

Chapter Ten

Vander

"Let's go to the diner," West says the following day at school as the bell chimes for lunch break. "I really need to talk to you."

"I'm down." I sling my bag over my shoulder and fall into step beside my buddy as we exit the classroom and make our way through the crowded hallway. He's tapping away on his cell, most likely texting Hazel.

"Hey, Van." Gayle Turner lounges against her locker, wiggling her fingers and smiling at me.

I jerk my head in her direction, in a brief acknowledgment, and pick up my pace. West chuckles as he pockets his cell. "That girl is persistent."

"She's a pain in the ass. I've told her countless times I'm not interested, in countless ways, and nothing gets through to her." I have tried letting her down nicely, and I have deliberately been a prick. Nothing seems to faze her. She's got balls, I'll give her that.

"Maybe you should just fuck her. Give her something to brag about, and it might do the trick."

"I'd rather stick rusty nails in my balls."

West chuckles again as we push through the double doors, out to the student parking lot. "You need a girlfriend. She'd back down then."

"You think?" I arch a brow. "Girls like Gayle love a challenge. If I had a girlfriend, she'd probably make it her mission to break us up. Try to get me to cheat or create the illusion I was." We reach my truck first, and I unlock the doors, throwing my bag in the back before climbing behind the wheel.

West slides into the passenger seat, turns the stereo on, and cranks the volume to an ear-shattering level. Beats rumble the windows as I pull my truck away from school, heading downtown.

The diner is quiet today, even for a Monday. After we've placed our orders, we settle back into the booth, across from one another. I wait impatiently for my buddy to start talking. I'm dying to know what happened after I left his house yesterday.

"My dad admitted the affair," he eventually says, staring out the window with a troubled look in his eyes.

"He didn't have much of a choice," I retort, working hard to keep the anger from my tone.

He turns to face me. "He apologized to Mom and us, said his family was his priority, and he was stressed 'cause of his new job."

A likely fucking story. I don't believe a word out of that asshole's mouth, but I can't share those thoughts with West. I've got to put my feelings for Kendall aside and be here for my best friend. "What'd your mom say?" I ask, lifting my bottle of water to my lips and feigning nonchalance.

Always Meant to Be

"She said it's between her and Dad and they would try harder to fix things. That I should focus on school and football."

"I can't believe she took him back after he cheated. She should've kicked his disloyal ass to the curb."

Pain glimmers in his eyes, and his Adam's apple bobs in his throat. "There's a big part of me that agrees with you, but another part of me is so fucking relieved she didn't." He rubs at his temples. "That makes me a selfish prick, right?"

"It's your family, and you're scared. I get it."

He exhales heavily. "I'm still so fucking pissed at him for doing that to my mom."

Understatement of the century, bud. I could easily murder Curtis Hawthorne and not lose any sleep over it. I dig my nails into my thigh under the table in an attempt to quell the red rage sweeping through my veins. Every time I think about how he has disrespected Kendall, I want to rip his head from his shoulders and slice his cock off.

Tears prick his eyes, but he quickly averts his gaze. A few tense beats pass before he lifts his head, eyeballing me. "He said all the right things, and Mom reassured us too. I left the room thinking everything would be okay, but after this morning —" Air whooshes out of his mouth as he shakes his head. "I don't know, man. I really don't know."

My hackles are instantly raised and I lean forward, pressing my elbows to the table. "What happened this morning?"

He cringes, opening his mouth to speak just as the waitress appears. We don't talk as she sets our food down in front of us. West twirls the pasta around his fork, and I try to remain patient as I wait for him to elaborate. "They were all lovey-dovey at the breakfast table," he says, just as I've swallowed a mouthful of pasta. I almost choke on it, reaching for my water and knocking it back.

"It looked so forced," he admits when I have stopped spluttering. "I could tell Mom wasn't comfortable." He sets his fork down and cradles his head in his hands. His shoulders shake, and I feel for my buddy. I say nothing, quietly eating as I wait for him to compose himself. His eyes are glassy when he finally makes eye contact with me again. "What if she's only doing this for us? What if that's the only reason she took him back three years ago? What if he's still cheating and that's why she's miserable?" He lifts his fork, twirling more pasta around it.

I wonder if that's why Kendall was upset last night. Everything West has said about their conversation hasn't raised any red flags, so he could be onto something. Not that I can voice those thoughts. Unless I have proof, I can't encourage the theory. It wouldn't be fair to him. It's on the tip of my tongue to suggest we follow Curtis to find out once and for all. But I can't do that to West. If his dad is cheating again, catching him in the act would devastate him. If Kendall is going to all this trouble to keep her kids shielded from the truth, I can't suggest the spy route.

But there is nothing stopping me from watching the asshole.

I mull it over, thoughts flitting through my head while I carefully consider my reply, trying to be West's buddy, because he needs me. "If she did, that was her call to make, and she did it because she loves you."

"I don't want her to be miserable, but I don't want them to divorce either. Fuck." He pushes his plate away, grabbing fistfuls of his hair.

I have prayed my parents would divorce for years, and here is poor West praying his parents don't while I'm silently hoping they do. I'm a shitty fucking friend, and I need to do better. "Look, man, there isn't anything you can do, and worrying about something that might not come true is a waste of time. I know you're worried. I hate that for you, but you should do what your parents said. Just focus on your grades and winning the state championship. Playing for the Oklahoma Sooners is a shoo-in then. Let them worry about their marriage."

"I definitely think it's a good idea to apply to a number of art schools so you have options. But if your heart is set on Yale, you really should talk to your parents, especially now you have sent in your early application. They are alumni, and I'm sure they can help," Mrs. Wills says from across the desk.

It's my last period of the day, and I usually enjoy sessions with my guidance counselor, but today she's decided to bust my balls for some reason, and I'm not in the mood for it. I've been feeling shitty since lunchtime.

"Lots of students think their parents won't be supportive and they are pleasantly surprised."

My knee bounces up and down as agitation sweeps over me. "My father has been ramming Yale Law down my throat from the time I was in diapers. He has plans to buy the current law firm he works at when the owner retires in a few years. He thinks we're going to run it together as father and son, and there is nothing I can say, nothing I *have* said, that will change his mind," I say, through gritted teeth.

"But surely, he wants his only son to be happy?" she asks, twirling the strand of pearls around her neck. I don't know what age Mrs. Wills is, but she always dresses like a grandma in cardigans, high-necked blouses, and austere skirts that hit her calves. She looks way older than Kendall, but Kendall looks super young for her age, so it's hard to gauge. Anyway, she's old enough to have been around the block. She can't be this naive.

I slam my hand down on my knee to stop the bouncing motion. "Dad doesn't care about my happiness. He cares about me carrying on his legacy. My parents struggled to conceive, and I'm their only son, so it's all on me."

She scribbles something down on her notepad, and I glance at the clock over her head, willing time to speed up.

"Has he seen your art?" she asks, trying a different approach.

"Not since I was a young teen."

"Well, there you go!" She smiles, clasping her hands on top of the desk. "You need to show him your portfolio. I bet he'll be blown away by your talent and realize your future lies on a different trajectory."

A muscle pops in my jaw and I grind my teeth so hard it's a miracle I don't chip a tooth.

"If you're worried, I could talk to them on your behalf," she adds. "I'm more than happy to set up a meeting."

Over my dead fucking body is she going anywhere near my parents. I'm all out of patience, and she needs a reality check. I lean forward and stab her with a sharp look. "When I was thirteen, my father gathered up all my sketch pads, canvases, easels, paints, and art books, and built a bonfire with them in our backyard. He told me I was on the way to becoming a man now and art was for kids and pussies. He forced me to pour the gasoline and light the match. Then he made me watch my dreams go up in flames."

Swiping my bag off the ground, I stand, preparing to leave, even though there are still twelve minutes on the clock. She can write me up. I have zero fucks to give. "Gregory Henley doesn't give a fuck about my talent. He only cares about himself." I sling my bag over one shoulder and glare at her. "Getting accepted into Yale to study art is my lifetime dream. I think I'll probably get a place, but getting to go is another matter entirely. My father won't pay for it, and with his contacts, he'll stop me from getting any kind of scholarship. I don't even care about the money. I'll take out student loans when the inheritance my grandparents left me runs out. My biggest fear is he'll get the offer rescinded, and that is why he can't find out what I'm planning."

The chair screeches as I push it back, stomping toward the door. I turn around as my fingers curl around the door handle. "I know you mean well, and I appreciate all you have done to help me, but you need to drop this. Your responsibility is to assist me. To help me to achieve my academic goals. My father can't know, which means my mother can't know either. Please don't reach out to them. Trust me when I say it wouldn't end well for either of us. He is not the kind of man you want to cross." I let those words linger in the tense air for a few beats before I open the door. I cast one final glance at her. "They need to remain in the dark."

Chapter Eleven

Kendall

"We're staging an intervention," June says, appearing in the doorway of my office with a determined look on her pretty face.

"Who is?" I inquire, setting my pen down on my pad.

"Your two besties," Viola replies, popping her head over June's shoulder.

"What are you doing here?"

June rolls her eyes. "Staging an intervention. Duh." She walks over and flippantly turns my computer off.

I purse my lips, my gaze bouncing between my two closest friends. "I still have work to do."

"No, you don't. It's after five on a Friday night. Your working week is over, chica." Viola grabs my coat from the coat hanger and stomps toward me. "You have worked late every night this week and given both of us every excuse under the sun to avoid talking. It ends now." She thrusts my dusky-pink woolen coat at me.

"We're your best friends." June props her butt on the edge of my desk.

"We know you inside and out, and we know something is wrong," Viola adds, planting her hands on her shapely hips.

"We want to help," June supplies.

"We need to know," Viola says.

I hold up my hands. "All right. Enough with the tag team." Leaning back in my chair, I sigh heavily. "I was always planning on confiding in you," I truthfully admit, looking both my friends in the eyes. "I just needed some time to process first, and I was hoping to tell you when I could finally control my tear ducts." Moisture stings my eyes, but I rub them, shoving the tears back down inside. I have cried enough tears this week because of that prick. Anger comes and goes, but the overriding feelings are hurt, sadness, disappointment, embarrassment, and regret.

Viola glances over her shoulder, checking no one is outside, before swinging her gaze to me. "He's cheating again, isn't he?" she softly asks. I shared my suspicions with my friend a couple of weeks ago, so I'm not surprised she's made the correct assumption.

I nod, gulping over the lump in my throat.

"That fucking asshole!" June hisses, reaching over to take my hand. She squeezes it. "He has never been good enough for you, and you deserve so much better."

"You do," Viola agrees, nodding. Coming around my desk, she pulls me to my feet and hugs me. A sob rips from my throat as I cling to my childhood bestie. Viola squeezes me harder before easing back. "You can tell us everything, and we'll help you to figure this out. We're getting takeout at my house, and I already stocked up on wine and vodka."

"I can't," I say, tidying the papers on my desk. "I've got to get home to Ridge. West has a date with Hazel, and Stella is going out with her friends." I don't mention the prick I'm

Always Meant to Be

married to won't be home because he'll be out fucking his girlfriend.

"Ruthie has agreed to watch Ridge and the twins," Viola says. "I talked to her earlier, and she said she didn't have any plans for tonight. She's cool to stay home with Ridge and my two hellions."

"You're sure?" I inquire, as I put my coat on, because I don't usually ask my cleaning lady to babysit, but she has helped me out with emergencies in the past.

"Positive. I think she was happy to be asked, and you know she's trustworthy. The kids will be fine with her." She circles her arm around my shoulders. "It's covered. You're ours for the night. Let's go."

"Okay. Tell us everything," June says ninety minutes later, handing me a large wineglass, in the comfort of Viola's cozy living room. Viola got the house in the divorce five years ago, and her ex-husband lives four miles away with his new partner, Brian. They share joint custody of their thirteen-year-old son and daughter, and if there was a poster child for the perfect divorce and co-parenting model, it would be Viola Johnson. Not that it was smooth sailing initially, but they did what was best for the kids and manage to keep things amicable by putting their best interests first.

June drops down beside me on the couch while Viola is curled up in her leather recliner in front of a roaring fire. The room is toasty warm unlike the chill emanating from my soul. "It's all been a lie," I admit before gulping back a large mouthful of white wine. "Every fucking moment of my marriage has been fraudulent," I say, staring at Viola. She was there for the entire thing, and I need to know if she was as taken in as I was.

"What exactly does that mean?" Her brow creases as she sips her wine.

"It means he's been cheating on me since I was seventeen." I proceed to tell June and Viola everything, and they listen attentively, drinking their wine, their faces growing redder, their expressions angrier, the more I talk, but they don't interrupt. They let me get it out, and it spews from my mouth like projectile vomit. I didn't realize how badly I needed to confide in my friends until now.

"Oh my God, Kendall." Viola rubs a hand over her mouth and sighs. "I cannot believe he's done that or what he expects of you now."

"Did you ever notice?"

She shakes her head. "Never. He always seemed so in love with you."

"He's a motherfucking psychopath," June seethes. "How dare he treat you like that!" Of the two, June is the more free-spirited, hotheaded one, so I'm not surprised she's reacting in anger.

"That's not even the worst of it. He was having phone sex with her the other night," I admit, digging my nails into the palms of my hand. I'm still shocked, enraged, and devastated anytime I think about it. "He knew I was in the en suite bathroom, and he still jerked off while talking dirty to her over the phone."

June hops up, steam practically billowing from her ears. "That motherfucking bastard, asshole, jerk, douche, shithead, pissant, dickwad, prick, son of a bitch, ass maggot, Tiger Woods wannabe, lying, cheating piece of goddamn shit!" she roars, letting loose a string of colorful insults, which impresses me. She stops only to draw a deep breath. "I want to kill him with

Always Meant to Be

my bare hands. I want to beat the ever-loving shit out of that good-for-nothing cheating scumbag." Her face looks murderous as she continues. "No, that's not torturous enough. I want to chop him up into tiny pieces and feed them to the slut he's currently fucking. Then I'll set her on fire and cackle my head off while I curse them both and wish them a long and painful afterlife in hell."

"Creative. I like it." I have had a lot of similar thoughts, but she's more imaginative than me. Must be the marketing part of her brain.

She's not done though. "I hope his tiny disease-ridden dick falls off and he gets scabies and has itchy pubes." She stomps across the floor, clenching her fists and snarling. "Oh, oh, I know!" Her eyes light up, and her gaze dances between me and Viola. "You need payback, Ken, and we need to start a list." She jabs her finger in Viola's direction. "We can have some real fun with this." Her eyes glow with mischief. "I read this post on social media one time about a woman who suspected her husband was cheating after she found a half-empty box of condoms in his car."

She gleefully rubs her hands. "She poked holes in the wrapper of each condom and soaked each one in habanero pepper juice before putting them back in the box. The next day, her husband left saying he was running an errand or something. Then a few hours later—wait for it—she got a call from her best friend saying she'd just had sex with her new man and now she was on fire down below. Can you believe it?"

Her eyes pop wide and she shakes her head. "Imagine calling your lover's wife asking for advice?" Her eyes narrow. "I'd have cut the bitch. Anyway, then her hubby came home and ran straight to ice his dick, creating some elaborate story to try to excuse it, but she knew the truth." She sinks onto the couch and grabs my hands, her face alight with excitement.

"That's what you should do! Give his current slut a nasty itch she'll feel for days."

A giggle bubbles up my throat as I stare at her hopeful face, and I set it free. Perhaps that *is* what I need to do. Make Curtis's life hell while outwardly he has to keep pretending with me. We're all laughing; it's a great tension reliever, and it feels great.

Until it doesn't.

My laughter quickly transforms to sobs as I fall apart in front of my friends.

Viola joins us on the couch, and I cling to my friends as I sob onto their shoulders. A tsunami of emotions lays siege to my insides, and I give in to them as it all comes crashing down. My chest is wracked with pain as I unleash everything, emitting deep body-encompassing sobs, my insides twisted in agony, as I purge the emotion stripping me raw. They hold me, without speaking, letting me expunge it, as I cry my heart out.

The doorbell rings, and Viola kisses the top of my head before leaving to retrieve our takeout. That forces me to pull myself together. I ease out of June's embrace, sniffling and swiping at the tears making a mess of my face. My body aches as stress infiltrates every nook and cranny of my being. June hands me a couple of tissues, and I blow my nose and dry my eyes as Viola reappears with the delivery bag. I'm emotionally and physically drained, and I don't know how much more of this I can tolerate before I lose my mind.

"At least I don't have to worry about either of you fucking Curtis," I rasp, my throat scratchy and sore. I offer them a shaky smile. "I know you would never do that. Imagine being betrayed by your husband *and* your best friend. That would really suck."

"Your situation is no less of a betrayal." Viola dusts another kiss on my head before dropping the bag on the coffee table. "I

Always Meant to Be

think we'll eat in here. Can you get plates and silverware from the kitchen?" she asks June.

"Of course." June gives me another quick hug. "You're going to be okay," she says before traipsing into the kitchen.

"She's right." Viola slides her arm around me. "I know it probably doesn't feel like that now, because it's all such a shock, but you will be."

I sniffle, biting down on my lower lip.

"I know you're enraged, but—"

"That's the thing," I say, cutting her off. "I am, but it comes and goes. I just feel this overwhelming sadness for everything that's been lost. Along with the hurt and the humiliation, I'm concerned about the kids. About what this will do to them when they eventually find out."

"I understand completely," Viola says, as June comes back into the room. "Of course, they are a huge consideration but you need to work out what's best for you too. You can't mother them until you take care of yourself."

"I know what you say is technically correct, but I don't have that luxury. I won't fail my kids as a mom. They are my first priority. Protecting them is my primary goal. I'll hurt myself if it means keeping them sheltered for as long as I can."

Viola looks like she wants to disagree, but she clamps her lips shut.

"I feel like I failed as a wife, but I won't fail as a mom." Being a mom is the only reason I could get out of bed every day this week. I can't neglect my kids or my responsibilities, and keeping busy with my normal life is as vital as oxygen to me right now.

"Failure isn't in your DNA," Viola says. "The only one who failed is that liar you married."

"I wouldn't expect anything less of you, Kendall, because you're a freaking amazing mom," June says, setting the plates and silverware down and opening the bag. "But speaking as someone whose parents divorced when I was ten, I tend to agree with Viola. You need to consider what's best for you too," she adds. "I was super upset when my parents first told me, and I was quiet and withdrawn a lot, but over time, I realized it was the best thing for everyone."

She places cartons on the table, opening them up and shoving some spoons in. "They were always fighting, and things were pretty tense. After they split, Dad made more of an effort with me, and I actually enjoyed spending time separately with them. Both ended up meeting new partners, and they're much happier now." June places three cushions on the floor, and we sit cross-legged around the coffee table. "I know your situation isn't the same, and I'm not trying to tell you what to do, just that sometimes the right thing for kids *is* divorce."

"Except Curtis won't make that easy for her until it suits him." Viola's eyes narrow to pinpricks as she stabs a prawn and pops it in her mouth.

"He can't stop it if it's what Kendall wants," June says. "Colorado is a no-fault divorce state, and adultery doesn't come into it. Ken can file for divorce claiming the marriage is irretrievably broken. Curtis can try to contest it, but it's rarely successful. Same if he tries to go for full custody. There isn't a court in the land who would deny Kendall her maternal rights."

I spoon some chicken fried rice and noodles on my plate, but I still don't have much of an appetite. "I know I could file for divorce and get joint custody. He probably wouldn't even fight it that much if it meant he could be with his whore. But he has a point in relation to the kids. I hate Curtis, and he's been a lousy husband, but he's a decent father, and he is putting their needs first. I have to do the same."

"Think about this practically," Viola says. "How the hell can you make that work knowing what you do now?"

"That's the million-dollar question. This week has been hell," I admit, in between drinking my wine. "I don't think I can endure two years of pretending. I can barely look at him without wanting to stab him in the eye. I just want him gone." I slowly chew a forkful of food.

"Please tell me you're not still sleeping in the same bed," Viola says.

I rub at the tightness in my chest. "We retire to bed together at night, to keep up appearances, but as soon as the kids are asleep, I move to the guest bedroom and get up before any of them wake."

"That cheating scumbag should be the one sleeping in the guest bed. Not you." June gnashes her teeth as she dumps more food on her plate.

"This doesn't bother him in the slightest. He's going around the house whistling and singing in the shower, like he doesn't have a care in the world." I gulp back more wine. "How can he be this callous? This cold? It's like he has no emotion at all. He must see how much this is hurting me, but he just doesn't care. That hurts as much as the betrayal. He has zero remorse, and he doesn't give a fuck what this does to me. All he cares about is screwing his whores and protecting his reputation with the kids."

"Maybe you should tell them. They're well-adjusted kids," Viola says. "They might handle it better than you think." She nudges my fork, encouraging me to eat with her eyes.

I force another mouthful down. "I can't take that risk. I won't derail their future because their father couldn't keep his dick in his pants."

"I don't think you should make any firm decisions yet," Viola says. "Though our situations are vastly different, I remember how much my emotions seesawed during that time. You need to get a handle on things to fully understand how you feel, and only then can you decide what to do. But you do need to make a plan and start preparing for the future. You're smart. Smart enough to outwit that slimeball. Maybe you should talk to a therapist."

"And a divorce attorney," June says. "I'm sure Leland would represent you if you asked him."

"I can't involve anyone at work. I'd prefer to keep what's going on at home separate from my professional career, and I wouldn't trust Greg not to say something to Curtis. While they're not friends, they are golf buddies. I can imagine Greg patting Curtis on the back if he found out. Knowing him, he'd go out of his way to ensure Curtis screwed me over."

"From one cheating asshole to another," Viola says, disgust clear in her tone.

"Valid point." June agrees. "I can get a few names in other firms. Discreetly, of course." She arches a brow, and I nod.

"I have given it some consideration this week. It can't hurt to talk to someone. To explore all options."

"I can give you the number of the woman I spoke to during my divorce. She was helpful."

"Thanks, Vi."

"You should start documenting everything and recording your interactions with him," June suggests. "Build an arsenal of ammunition. You never know when you might need it."

"That's good advice, but right now, I'm doing all I can to avoid him outside of putting on a front with the kids."

"Whatever you decide, just know we're here for you." June reaches across to squeeze my hand.

"We will support you every step of the way," Viola agrees.

A devilish glint appears in June's eyes. "Hell, I'm even down for murder. We can chop him up together. Whatever it is you need, it's yours."

Chapter Twelve

Vander

"Who pissed in your cornflakes?" Crusher asks, holding the pads while I throw vicious jabs in rapid-fire succession. "You have been in a shitty mood all week."

"I've got a lot on my mind," I grunt, keeping my fists raised and pummeling the pads.

"Anything I can help with?" my buddy asks, and it's timely.

"Actually, there is one thing. Want to head to TJ's later?"

"Sure thing." He slaps me with the pad. "You're open. Fists up."

I go another few rounds with Crusher before calling time on my pad work and heading to the other side of the boxing club, where the equipment and mats are located, to begin my strength training. It's late Friday night, and most of the guys have finished their sessions and left already, so the place is virtually deserted.

I complete a few sets of push-ups, pull-ups, squats, and dips before doing three rounds with the sway bag, and then I call it a night. I want to talk to Jimmy before he closes up.

Mopping my brow with a towel, I drape it around my neck and head toward the small office Jimmy uses to handle business. I chug half a bottle of water down my parched throat before stepping up to the door. It's ajar, so I poke my head in. "You got time to talk?"

He looks up from the papers spread all over his desk with an instant smile. "For you, kid, always. Come in and shut the door." He sets his pen down and claws a hand through his thick gunmetal-gray hair.

I sit on the worn brown leather couch pushed up against the side wall and swallow. I need to talk to someone before I drive myself crazy, and Jimmy is the only man for the job. I can't talk to West or any of my buddies, for obvious reasons. Jimmy has looked out for me since I joined the club a few months after moving to Colorado Springs, and he's always been like a father figure to me. He takes an active interest where my old man doesn't give a shit. Dad doesn't object to me coming here—boxing is a manly sport, so he approves even if he can no longer beat me because I beat back harder—but he doesn't champion it either.

"What's up, son?" Jimmy removes his black-framed glasses and pinches the bridge of his nose. Placing the glasses on the desk, he rests his hands in front of him and gives me his undivided attention. "You look troubled, and I've noticed you've been putting in extra time all week. What's on your mind?"

I clear my throat and sit forward, leaning my elbows on my knees. "I need some advice."

"Then you've come to the right place." Jimmy retrieves a bottle of whiskey and a glass from his desk drawer. "I assume you don't want one," he says, arching a brow as he pours a generous measure.

I shake my head. "I'm driving tonight." Sometimes I jog to and from the gym, if I have missed my daily five-a.m. run. I'm conscious of my family background, and while I like a drink as much as the next guy, I don't usually overdo it. I'm constantly watching in case it becomes a crutch. When I first moved to town, I was abusing alcohol and drugs. Using them to numb my pain until I found West and boxing. They set me on the straight and narrow. Kendall helped too. She suggested I needed a physical outlet to vent my frustration and stress. She even found this place for me.

"Spit it out, son." Jimmy leans back in his chair, lifting the glass to his weathered lips.

"There's this girl, well, woman and..."

A wry chuckle rips from his lips. "I thought it might be girl trouble, but it's not like you to seek advice with the ladies. From what I've heard, you do just fine."

I roll my eyes. "I swear the guys are worse gossips than high-school girls."

"True that." His warm brown eyes crinkle at the corners as he chuckles again. "Go on."

"It's complicated." I scrub a hand down my face. "I don't have anyone to talk to, and I know I can tell you and you won't judge me or betray my confidence."

He nods, leaning forward a little. "Color me intrigued."

"I love her," I blurt. "I have for a long time, but I only let myself admit it recently because—" I pause to take a drink of water, my mouth suddenly feeling dry.

"Because?" Jimmy coaxes when I drain the water and toss the empty bottle in the trash.

"Because it was inappropriate, and nothing would have happened."

"Inappropriate how? Who is this woman?"

"It's Kendall Hawthorne," I admit, my heart galloping. A tiny hint of shock splays across his face. "She's West's mom." He is aware who West Hawthorne is. Most everyone in town knows our QB because he's a star on the field and clearly going places.

He steeples his fingers against the thin layer of silvery scruff on his chin. "I know who she is. You never forget a woman like that." He chuckles again. "I still remember the day she showed up here. Pretty as a picture but clearly out of her depth. The guys were tripping over themselves to offer her assistance."

"I'll bet." I rub a hand along the back of my neck. "I tried to just see her as West's mom. To tell myself it was only a stupid crush or hormones or the fact she was nice and tried to help me." I shrug, attempting to loosen the tense muscles in my shoulders. This is harder to admit than I thought.

"But it's not."

"It's not." I lick my lips, preparing to admit something I'm scared to even admit to myself. "This is going to make me sound like a pussy, but it feels like fate brought me here to find her. The instant I met her, I felt the most intense connection, and it hasn't gone away. It's only gotten worse, and—" I stop talking, knotting my hands together and looking at the floor as I prepare to say the words. "I see her in my dreams. See *us*, but it's like we were from a different time."

"What do you mean?" he asks, and I look up. I don't see any derision or humor on his face, and that spurs me on. "It's the same dream I've been having for years. We're in a river. It's nighttime, and the moon casts shadows over the pyramids in the background. Palm trees line both sides of the river, and rudimentary mud-brick homes are scattered in the near distance. We're alone. We have our arms around one another, and we're kissing." My heart careens around my chest as I visualize the image in my mind's eye. I have seen it so much in my dreams I can instantly recall it. "I'm older, and she's younger. We look different, but it's still her. When I look into her eyes, I see through to her soul, and I know it's Kendall. Even though it's only a dream, I *feel* her in my arms. I feel her heart beating against mine and her pulse thrumming against my fingertips. I feel the featherlight touch of her hand as she runs it up and down my chest and the warmth of her breath against my ear as she whispers how much she loves me."

I glance up at the old man. He's watching me with keen intensity. Jimmy nods, urging me to continue.

I drag my lip between my teeth as pain lances through my chest. This part always hurts. "After we're together, I help her to dry off at the river's edge, and then I hold her hand and lead her away. I guess I'm taking her home, but we stay in the shadows, running under the trees and crouching along low walls. Until a group of men surround us. They're dark-skinned, wearing loincloths and carrying spears and shields. They take her from me. I'm fighting. Kendall is screaming and then—" My eyes lock on his. "Then everything turns black."

"Well, shit."

I blow air out of my mouth. "That's one way of describing it."

His lips curve at the corners. "You sure you're not high, son? You take one too many hits to the head?" I narrow my eyes at him, and he chuckles. "I'm just yanking your chain." He swigs another mouthful of whiskey. "That's very intriguing."

"You don't think I'm crazy?"

"No crazier than most men."

"Well, that's reassuring. Thanks," I mumble.

He chuckles again. "The brain is a fascinating organ. I've studied it a little, what with the risks involved in this business. Read all manner of unexplainable things. I don't think we'll ever unravel the mystery of how it works."

"You think I have some issue with my brain?"

He shakes his head. "No. Not at all. I'm just saying the brain is capable of a lot, and there is much we don't understand about it. Who knows what our dreams are or why some people dream and others never do? Why some vividly remember their dreams and others forget them the instant they wake? Are they past recollections of a different life? Glimpses into the future? Is it a worry or concern manifesting in strange ways like a puzzle we're unable to figure out? Or is it our brain trying to tell us something or guide us along a certain path?" He shrugs. "We don't know. We never will. At least not in our lifetime."

"Kendall would love you. She's big into philosophy."

"She the reason you carry that dog-eared paperback with you everywhere?"

I nod. "She gave me a copy of *Meditations* for my eighteenth birthday. It's one of the best books I've ever read."

"Tried reading it once," he says. "There's definitely some wisdom amid all the nonsensical ramblings."

"That book speaks to my soul," I truthfully reply, pointing to my inner arm. "Got a couple of quotes inked on my skin."

He strains forward over the desk. "What's it say? These old eyes can't read it from here."

"Divine tolerance and divine fury," I confirm. "I'm equally split between the two." I stand, carefully removing my sleeveless training top and showing him my back. "Got this done on Tuesday; that's why it's still a little red and swollen."

He doesn't need to put his glasses on to read the large lettering that is inked in a curved arc from left to right across the back of my shoulder blades.

You become what you love

He frowns at me. "That's a big-ass tattoo. You shouldn't have been training this week."

"I barely felt the pain," I admit, putting my top back on.

Always Meant to Be

"I've been so frustrated and worried about Kendall I can scarcely feel anything else."

"Before you tell me the rest, tell me what you believe the dream is."

"When I first started having it, I thought it was my subconscious turning my crush into reality, but the dream is so vivid, and it's always the same. No detail is ever different. I think it's a message." I eyeball him. "I think our souls have lived before. I think we've been together in another lifetime and I'm meant to be with her in this one."

"That's pretty heavy."

"I know." Silence descends for a few beats. "You haven't said anything about her age or the fact she's my best friend's mom."

He shrugs. "Love is love. I'm old. I've seen what this life has to offer. Experienced plenty. I lost my Dolly far too young. Not a day goes by where I don't miss her. The day my wife died, a part of me died too. If it wasn't for this place and you hooligans keeping me sane, I think I might've lost the will to live a long time ago. If it's meant to be, it will be. True love will always trump obstacles in its path."

I wish Jimmy was my dad. He always knows the right thing to say, and he always really listens. Emotion clogs my throat, and it's hard to speak. "I don't know if I ever thanked you. You and this club saved me from myself."

"No, my boy. You saved yourself."

"I knew I was right to come to you. I already feel better, but I still don't know what to do."

"Fill me in on the rest," he says, and I do, explaining, in summary, everything that happened from the time I moved here. How she has always looked out for me, welcomed me into her home, supported me when things were particularly shit at home, listened to me, and encouraged my dreams. I finish with a summary of what went down at my birthday party and last Sunday.

"Well, shit. That's not good."

"Nope." I toy with the hem on my top. "Her husband is a cheating bastard, and I wish she'd leave him."

"She might yet. Give her time to process it."

"I'm running out of time. I'll be leaving next summer for Connecticut, and I won't be coming back."

"You have the rest of your life, and Kendall is still young too. Perhaps the timing isn't right yet."

"How do I do this? I can't spend the next seven or eight months tiptoeing around her knowing what I know and how I feel. She has feelings for me too. She admitted as much." I swallow thickly. "I laid my heart on the line, and she rejected me, and now I don't know what to do or where I go from here. Forgetting her is not a possibility. She's the star of my fucking dreams, and she's embedded in here so deep," I add, tapping my head, "I can't get her out. It feels like I'm going insane."

"She didn't reject you so much as she's unwilling to allow the idea of you to be. She admitted she has feelings for you. No matter how inappropriate she might believe them to be, she's not denying they exist. That's what's important."

"I don't know what else to do. She knows I love her, but it doesn't seem like enough."

"You made a rookie mistake, son."

I tip my chin up. "In what way?"

"You came in too hard and too fast."

"I always want to be honest with her. How is telling her I love her wrong?"

"I get it, kid. You got excited. She was at your place, wearing your clothes, sharing your space, and encouraging your ambition. You could see your dreams coming true, and you went full throttle. It's one of the things I admire most about

Always Meant to Be

you. You see what you want, and you go for it. I imagine that is part of your appeal for her, but put yourself in her shoes. There is so much at stake. Too much to risk starting something with you, no matter how she feels."

"What should I do?"

"Well, you shouldn't interfere in her marriage. Kendall needs to make that call free of any influence from you. Otherwise, that could end up hurting you both down the line."

That is easier said than done, but I get the point he's making.

"The only thing you can do is be there for her, in whatever capacity she needs. You have had a friendship of sorts through her son. Extend a new hand of friendship. Let her know you understand nothing else can happen now but you are there for her as a friend. I'm betting she needs as many of those as she can get right now."

Chapter Thirteen

Vander

"Fucking asshole." I toss my bag onto the back seat of my truck and slam the door, grinding my jaw and clenching my fists.

"Problem?" Crusher throws his bag in beside mine.

"I can't head out to TJ's after all. My fucking father has summoned me home." I run a hand through my damp hair as a frustrated sigh heaves from my lips.

"Give him the middle finger. That's what I do when my old man's being a demanding prick."

Most of my friends know my dad is a giant asshole, but very few know the true extent of my fucked-up home life. I would love to give Greg Henley the middle finger, but I won't be the one who pays the price if I refuse to play ball.

When Dad realized he could no longer beat me into submission, he switched to using Mom as bait. Now we play this sick game, and it's the very reason why I can't throw caution to the wind and head out as planned. If I don't make an appearance, he'll take it out on my mother.

"That wouldn't work with my dad," I say, opening the

driver's door. "Hop in and I'll drop you off. I'll explain the favor I'm looking for on the way."

I pull my truck in front of the house twenty minutes later and kill the engine. I take a minute to prepare myself before I hop out. I always have to psych myself up for a conversation with the psychopath.

I open the front door and step into the circular lobby of my parent's plush home. All the blood leaches from my face when a shrill scream greets me. Slamming the door shut, I dump my bag on the floor and run past the curved stairwell, heading in the direction of my mom's screams. From the proximity, I can tell my parents are in the study.

The door crashes against the wall as I burst into the room with a shout. "Let her fucking go!" I roar, racing across the room like a bull charging at a red flag. Mom is on her knees in front of my father. His hand is wrapped around her hair, and her head is arched back at an awkward angle. Blood trickles out of her nose and over her lips. The corner of her shirt is ripped, and dad's tie is askew, his face red with anger or exertion or both. "I said let her go." I push his shoulders, throwing all my strength into the move, and he stumbles back, releasing her with the movement. I shove him into the cabinet, and the glass rattles as his spine makes contact. "You fucking prick!"

Mom whimpers behind me while Dad sneers. "Get your damn hands off me or you know what'll happen next."

Fueled by a ton of pent-up frustration and beyond enraged at this situation, Kendall's predicament, and the futility of my feelings for her, I punch him in the face.

"No, Van!" Mom screams. "You'll only make it worse."

Always Meant to Be

Feeble fingers curl into the back of my sweaty top as she attempts to pull me back.

Dad's pupils narrow and darken as he dabs at the blood now pumping from his nose. "You clearly want me to beat your mother bloody," he says, ramming his fist into my stomach.

It hurts, because he has plenty of experience throwing punches, but not as much as he likes to think. My abs are a solid wall of muscle, and it'll take more than that to inflict real damage.

I punch him in the face again, and blood flies from his nose, spraying my shirt.

His fist swings out, and I could duck down, but I want to feel pain. I didn't get here fast enough, and he took it out on Mom. I can take one for the team. His fist glides against my cheekbone, but I barely feel it. I punch him again, enjoying the fact he'll have to show up at the office on Monday with a swollen nose and a black eye.

"Vander, please. Stop."

Mom's pleading sobs and the potential retaliation are the only things that get through to me. Pinning my father with a warning look, I step back, shielding my mother with my body. "If you touch her again, I will call the cops," I say with lethal calm. "I am done letting you use Mom to keep me in line."

"Be my guest." He removes an embossed handkerchief from the inside pocket of his suit jacket and wipes his bloody nose. "I know all the cops in this town, and my reach extends far. I'll have the charge dismissed before the ink is even dry on the report. Same goes for any threats involving the media. I'd slap them with an injunction and sue their asses before they could post or print a word. You don't hold any power in this situation, son. I can do whatever I want. Besides, your mother will never tattle on me. Will you, Diana?"

My arms hold Mom in place when I feel her moving

behind me. The second she leaves the protection of my body, he'll go for her.

"I asked you a question," Dad hisses, glaring over my shoulder at his broken wife.

"No," Mom croaks over a sob.

"Why are you here?" I widen my legs and shoot daggers at him.

"This is my house! I live here."

"Barely," I retaliate. He has a penthouse apartment in Denver, close to Bentley Law, and he tends to stay there most weeknights. On weekends, he only returns home if he's playing golf or there's an event locally my parents must attend. He's been absent a lot lately, which has been a blessing. "Not that I'm complaining. Mom and I do fine without you."

"You're really testing my patience, boy." Brushing past me, he stalks toward the liquor cabinet. "Sit down," he snaps over his shoulder. "I need to talk to you."

"Why don't you go and run a bath, Mom?" I suggest. "I'll come up when I'm done with Dad and see to your nose."

"Sit the fuck down, Diana." Dad stalks toward us, nostrils flaring and eyes as black as the night sky. He slams an unopened bottle of vodka down on his desk, snarling at Mom. "That should keep you happy while I talk to *our son*."

Mom slides out from behind me before I can stop her. Dad swings around and throws a punch. His fist lands on the side of her jaw, and she collapses like a sack of potatoes.

I go for him again, and he pulls a gun on me, pressing the muzzle into my stomach. "Enough!" he grits out. "You seem to have forgotten who calls the shots around here. Sit your ass down and shut up until I ask you to speak. If you want to protect your mother, you know what to do."

I grind my teeth to the molars, and a muscle ticks in my jaw as we face off. Mom is crying as she climbs to her feet, swiping

Always Meant to Be

the bottle of vodka and unscrewing the cap. Disgust is etched upon dad's face as she drinks straight from the bottle. He created the monster, but now he can barely tolerate looking at her.

"Sit." Moving the gun to my side, he pushes me toward one of the chairs in front of his desk. Accepting defeat, I sit down without uttering another word. I often wonder why I bother fighting Mom's battles when she makes zero effort to defend herself. She's a slave to booze, and it's like nothing else matters but getting that next fix. Not her husband's swinging fists. Not her son's sanity or safety.

Mom yelps as Dad grabs her by the hair, throwing her into the chair beside me. She doesn't drop the vodka though, clutching it protectively to her chest, like it's a baby. Frustration washes over me. I feel a whole host of emotions whenever I contemplate the life my mom leads. Anger is a recurring sentiment, along with exasperation and a sense of helplessness, but overwhelming sadness is the most regular feeling. She's a shell of a person, existing from one bottle to the next. I don't know that she has many moments of lucidity. Most all she has known these past twenty years is pain and self-loathing.

Sometimes, I wonder if she would be better off dead. Occasionally, I think she'd be doing me a big favor popping too many pills and washing it down with Mr. Grey Goose. This noose around both our necks would die with her body, and maybe that would be for the best because this is no way to live.

And the truth is, it already feels like I've lost my mom. I lost her a long, long time ago.

Remorse courses through me as those thoughts land in my head, like always. I'm a shitty son for wishing her dead, but sometimes it's hard to be understanding and show compassion. I know she's a victim. I know Dad has preyed on her weaknesses, like he's done with mine, but I never remember her fighting back. Not even when he struck me for the first time. I was six, and I cried my eyes out, calling for my mommy, begging her to make it stop, but she just stared at me with this blank look on her face, like she did every time after that until I got old enough to understand she was incapable of coming to my rescue.

You saved yourself.

Jimmy's words resurrect in my mind, and I feel the truth of them deep in my bones. I have had some help, but he's correct. I am the only person who can save me, and I'm not out of the woods yet. It's a work in progress, and I won't be able to say I'm safe and free until I'm out from under my father's clutches. But I'm in the home stretch, and I just need to hang in there a little longer.

"You're taking Gayle Turner on a date tomorrow night," Dad says, yanking me from my head.

"What?" I splutter because that is literally the last thing I was expecting to come out of his mouth.

"You heard me. It's all arranged. You'll pick her up at eight, and I had my secretary make a reservation for you at Chelle's Steakhouse."

"Why the fuck did you do that?"

He clenches his hand around his tumbler. "Your language is appalling. You can't show up at Yale speaking like that." He waves a hand in my direction, and his lips pull into a grimace as he scrutinizes the additional ink on my arms and my neck. "It's bad enough you look like that. Lawyers don't look like thugs."

"Taken a look in the mirror lately, Pops?" I snap, cutting across him. "You might not have my ink or use my appalling language, but you're a thug all the same." Dad has climbed his way to the top using any and all means necessary. Rumors are rife within legal circles about his association with shady characters and criminal enterprises, so he's far from a saint.

My tats and piercings might make me look like a thug, to some people, but there's only one gangster in this family, and it ain't me.

True to form, he ignores me as if I haven't spoken. "I have told you, time and time again, to stop with the ink. Don't make me take it out on your mother. This is your last warning. Clean up your act, Vander, or I will make you."

"I'd like to see you try."

He throws his glass over my head with a loud bellow, and I duck down in time to avoid it. It slams into the wall, shattering upon impact.

"That was my daddy's," Mom says, in a dazed voice, staring straight ahead. It's a miracle she even noticed. She's kicked off her shoes, and her knees are tucked into her chest as she swigs from the vodka bottle.

"Do I look like I give a fuck about your daddy's precious Waterford Crystal?"

"You gave a fuck when you married Mom for her father's connections," I spit out.

Dad only married Mom because her father was a judge and he used his influence to land Dad a prestigious job with a top law firm the second he graduated from Yale Law. My grandparents are both dead now and not here to see the way things have turned out for Mom and me. I doubt they would've been so supportive of the marriage if they knew how he has cheated, lied, bribed, and stolen to get to where he is. He's even swindled Mom out of her inheritance, ensuring she has no independent wealth to fall back on so she's eternally tied to him.

I bet it kills him he couldn't stop me from claiming the inheritance they left for me. I got the cash the day I turned eighteen, and he couldn't do a damn thing about it. That money is all I have to use as leverage when I try to convince Mom to leave him. There is just enough to set her up in an apartment, free of his clutches, and pay for my first couple of years at Yale.

He points his gun at my head. "Don't fucking tempt me."

I bark out a laugh. "We both know you won't shoot me. You're arrogant enough to want your legacy to continue, and I'm your only option."

"Unfortunately." He fully loosens his tie and rips it off his neck while keeping the gun pointed at me. "God knows I fucked enough women in an attempt to spawn another heir because I didn't want to be saddled with you."

Mom doesn't even flinch at his words. She is long past the point of caring about his ongoing infidelity.

"That makes two of us. What a pity you only shoot blanks." A smug grin spreads over my mouth as his fingers curl around the trigger of the gun, and I bet he wishes he could put a bullet in my skull now.

"I fathered you, didn't I?" he snaps.

Yeah, but it took years and plenty of miscarriages before Mom bore him a child.

"It's possibly hereditary. You should be careful before you throw shade."

I shrug. *Who gives a shit?* I'm not even sure I want kids. It's not something I have given much thought to. I just want this meeting over and done with, so I return to the matter at hand. "I don't care what's set up. I'm not dating Gayle Turner. She's a pain in the ass."

"I don't give a shit what you think." He slides the gun back into his desk drawer, and I wonder why he bothers waving that thing around anymore. It's an idle threat and we both know it. "Her father is a potential new client. Winning the Turner Media account will enhance my portfolio and my reputation and guarantee Leland signs the papers agreeing to sell Bentley Law to me when he retires."

Always Meant to Be

"What the fuck does me taking Gayle out have to do with that?"

"Her father asked it of me. Apparently, she's been trying to get your attention for months, but you're ignoring her. She's hurt and asked her daddy to make it happen."

I snort out a laugh. "Of course, she did. The conniving little bitch." I pin him with a sharp look. "I won't let you pimp me out. I'm not doing it."

"Yes, you are." He stands and smirks. "I don't see the problem. I've met her, and she's just crying out for dick. She's a hot piece of ass with big fuckable tits. Take one for the team. It's not like it's a hardship."

Acid churns in my gut at his lecherous grin. "You take her out then."

"She wants *your* dick. God only knows why." He rounds the desk. "When she kicks you to the curb, I'll happily take her for a ride." His smirk expands. "Show her what it's like to be fucked by a real man."

I keep a neutral expression on my face as his insult wafts over my head. I lost my virginity at fourteen to an older girl, and we had a steamy three-month affair. She taught me how to please a woman and turned me onto the addictive joys of sex. I've been sexually active ever since, and I have added to my repertoire over the years. I have fucked enough women to be confident in my bedroom skills. I've had zero complaints with most women begging me for a repeat performance. Unlike my dad, who I'm sure is a selfish prick in bed. I bet he'd need a compass to locate a clit and it's all about his satisfaction.

"Find some other way of schmoozing her dad," I say, standing as he approaches. "Organize one of your infamous orgies. Strippers, coke, and booze should suffice."

In a lightning-fast move, one I didn't think him capable of, he darts around me, grabs the back of Mom's neck, and slams her face-first into the desk, repeating the motion a couple of times as she howls and I attempt to pull him back. The vodka rolls to the floor, spilling everywhere. Dad rams his elbow back, shoving it into my ribs, and I stagger back, momentarily winded.

"I can keep this up all night. You know it turns me on," he says, grinning at me over his shoulder as he continues banging Mom's face into the desk.

"Stop. All right," I huff out, wincing as I struggle to draw a breath. "I'll do it. I'll take Gayle out tomorrow, but it's one date and one date only."

Dad slams Mom into the desk one final time before releasing her. Her body slumps to the ground as she passes out, her bloody face landing in the puddle of vodka pooling on the floor. "You'll take her out as often as is necessary until I sign Turner Media." He prods his finger in my chest. "Remember your place. You are my puppet. You do whatever the fuck I say. Continue to bait me, and your mother will pay the price."

Chapter Fourteen

Kendall

"You're looking a little tired there, Van," West says, smirking at his best friend across the dining room table. "Late one last night?" He flashes him a grin, showcasing the perfect white smile we paid a small fortune for, before shoveling a forkful of roast beef in his mouth. It's the second Sunday in a row Vander has joined us for dinner, and I'm torn over it. One part of me is happy he's here while another part wants to keep my distance so I avoid temptation.

"Okay, I'll bite." Stella leans forward, angling her head and staring at Vander. "What did you do last night?"

"Who, more like," West murmurs, hiding his inappropriate comment behind a cough so his younger brother doesn't hear.

But I did. I hadn't much of an appetite to start with, and now it's vanquished.

"Shut up," Van hisses under his breath, glaring at my eldest son.

"Oh, this is good. Now, I'm intrigued." Stella waggles her brows. "Tell me who you were with."

"It was nothing," Van says. "West just likes stirring shit."

"That's enough," Curtis says, his tone as biting as the look he gives Vander. "You are a guest in our house, Vander, and cursing is not permitted at the table. We have innocent ears."

Vander ignores Curtis, turning his face to mine. "I apologize, Kendall. It won't happen again."

I nod and briefly smile before averting my eyes. I'm on edge with him here. Afraid one of us will give something away without meaning to. Which is ridiculous, because it's not like we've done anything.

Yet. A little devil whispers gleefully in my ear. With invisible hands, I swat it away.

"West says shit and fuck all the time," Ridge, unhelpfully, supplies. "And Stella is always saying cock on the phone with her friends."

Stella splutters, almost spilling her water down the front of her shirt.

"That kind of language is not becoming," I tell my youngest son. "I don't want to hear you saying those words again. Understood?" Ridge is nine, so I reckon I have three, maybe four, years tops, before he enters that phase.

Curtis narrows his eyes at our eldest children. "You need to watch what you say around your brother."

I work hard not to roll my eyes. Curtis has been known to drop expletives on a regular basis, and I find it laughable he's attempting to parent. He's usually the fun, reckless one while I'm the boring disciplinarian. I drill him with a look. "That goes for you, too," I say because I can't help it.

"Relax, Dad," West says while a muscle clenches in my husband's jaw. He has never liked me reprimanding him in front of the children. "It's not like we go around cussing all the time. I bet he hears worse in school."

"I can't be held accountable for his eavesdropping," Stella says, pointing her finger at Ridge. "No listening in on my phone calls or I won't let you stay up late when I'm babysitting."

Ridge scowls, and a flash of fear crosses his face. I know he has his sister wrapped around his little finger, so Stella's threats are empty, but if it helps to stop my baby from cursing, I'm all for it.

"Now, quit deflecting, Van. Who were you out with last night?" Stella waggles her brows.

"He was on a dinner date with Gayle Turner," West supplies when it's clear Vander is not going to say anything.

Pain spreads across my chest, and I dig my nails into my thighs. I know who she is. She was all over him at his birthday party, thrusting her big boobs in his face any opportunity she got. He didn't seem interested, but maybe I was mistaken.

Why does the thought of them together send my stomach pitching to my feet and cause nausea to swim up my throat? He's young, free, and single, and I have no claim on him or right to the jealous envy twisting my insides into knots. I hop up. "I'm going to get dessert." Swiping my plate, I head out to the kitchen to compose myself.

I dump my half-eaten food into the trash, rinse my plate, and place it in the dishwasher while trying to ignore the pressure sitting on my chest and the dagger-like pain stabbing me through the heart. Gripping the edge of the counter, I hunch over, drawing exaggerated breaths as I silently lie to myself.

"I didn't want to take her out," Vander says, and a squeal rips from my throat at his unexpected presence. He walks toward me. "My father made me do it."

"What?" I lift my head and push off the counter as he sets a bunch of dirty plates down on the island unit. "What do you mean?"

He walks confidently toward me. "He's trying to land the Turner Media account. Her dad asked mine to do this." He steps close, and the tips of his sneakers brush against my ballet flats. "It meant nothing." He leans down, and notes of sandalwood and orange tickle my nose as his cologne swirls around me. He presses his mouth to my ear, and my heart gallops behind my chest. "I didn't even kiss her though it wasn't for lack of trying on her part."

I'll bet. I knew girls like Gayle in high school. If she has set her sights on Vander, she will be tough to shake. The thought settles in my gut like a rock, and I have to remind myself—*again*—that he's not mine. He's a free agent. He can date whomever he likes. It doesn't matter if we have feelings for one another. Nothing can happen, and it's better if he dates because maybe he'll put all notions of an *us* aside.

Vander pulls his head back, staring at me, and I hold my breath as he peers into my face. Having him this close is disconcerting. He could be a model with his big, mesmerizing green eyes framed by thick black lashes, and his sharp jawline, strong nose, perfectly proportioned thick lips, and the tempting layer of stubble on his chin and cheeks. His broad body encases my smaller one, and he makes me feel feminine and protected yet empowered at the same time. It's insane how safe I feel just being around him. I don't ever remember feeling like this around Curtis.

"I like that you're jealous," he says, his lips tipping up at the corners. "It shows you care."

"Vander." I narrow my eyes in warning before sidestepping him. "You can't say stuff like that to me."

"Sorry." He cocks his head to one side, looking completely unapologetic. "I can't control the things that come out of my mouth when I'm around you."

My fingers brush the discolored skin on his cheekbone. "How did you get this bruise?"

His smile fades. Shoving his hands in his pockets, he steps

Always Meant to Be

back. "Don't ask." He looks down at his feet as tension tightens his jaw.

Rage swirls through my veins unbidden. "He hit you?" Closing the gap between us, I tip his chin up, forcing his eyes to mine. Sometimes, when I look into Vander's eyes, he seems *so old*. He has always carried the weight of the world on his shoulders, but staring into his eyes is like looking at an ancient battle-weary soul, and I hate that for him. "I thought the boxing put a stop to that."

I called child services once after he showed up at my place with a cut and bruised face. That asshole Gregory made it go away, and he used his fists to deliver a brutal punishment to his wife and his son. It was a lesson learned the hard way, and I didn't bother reporting him again. Instead, I found the boxing club, and Vander learned how to defend himself.

"It has," he says, wrapping his fingers around my wrist. "But that doesn't mean things are good."

I know this. I have tried my best to be there for him, and I know West supports him, but he shouldn't have to live like this. I already know the answer to this question, but I'm going to ask it anyway. "You're eighteen now, Vander, and you have your future all mapped out. Why do you still stay there? You have the inheritance from your grandparents, and you'll get into Yale to study art, so why don't you just leave?" If my home life wasn't such a mess, and I didn't have such confusing feelings for him, I would offer him one of the guest bedrooms. But it's out of the question.

He straightens up, and some of his usual confidence returns. "We can't talk about this here." He glances over his shoulder. "We need privacy, and there's something I need to say to you. I know a place we can go. Meet me there in a while."

I bite the inside of my cheek as I open the oven door and remove the apple and berry crumble. "You know I can't," I whisper. I set the crumble on top of the stove before walking to the refrigerator in search of the whipped cream.

Vander stays silent for a few beats, reaching into the overhead cupboard, easily removing the bowls. He sets them down on the counter, and I open the refrigerator door. My heart accelerates when I hear his quiet footsteps approach as I grab the whipped cream. "Please, Kendall." Heat rolls off his body in waves as he stands close behind me. I shut the refrigerator door and concentrate on breathing because I appear to have lost the ability. "I have a place I go to in Palmer Park when I need to think. It's completely sheltered, and no one will see us there. Tell *him* you're going for your usual walk, and meet me there."

I won't need to tell Curtis anything because he's apparently playing golf after dinner. A likely excuse.

"We can't do this," I whisper, not moving a muscle.

He leans in, pressing his chest against my back, inciting a riot of illicit feelings inside me. His warm breath blows across my ear and delicious tremors skate over my skin. "I just want to talk. Four o'clock. I'll text you the coordinates."

Chapter Fifteen

Kendall

"This is such a bad idea, Kendall," I mumble to myself as I head toward Vander's spot, clutching my phone, using Google Maps to guide my path. It's almost four thirty. I'm late, and it will be dark soon. I spent the last hour trying to talk myself out of doing this, yet here I am. It seems I'm incapable of saying no to him, and that's troubling.

"I'd just about given up on you," he says, stepping out from behind a tree.

My heart lodges in my throat, and I almost trip over my sneakered feet. "Jesus, Vander. Don't sneak up on me like that! You scared the shit out of me."

"Sorry." This time, his apology is sincere. Without asking, he takes my hand, jerking his head to the side. "My hideout is just around the corner. Come on. I'm dying to show you."

Instead of pulling my hand away, my fingers thread through his, and a soothing warmth sinks beneath my skin.

"I'm glad you dressed warm," he adds as he guides the way. "It can get real cold up here this time of year." He tightens his grip on my hand as we navigate over rough, bumpy terrain, heading around a large boulder and descending a few feet along the rockface. Maneuvering around a few trees, I suck in a gasp as we come to a stop beside a little secluded area. It's set a few feet back from the edge, bordered on both sides by high jagged tan sandstone. A plaid blanket lays across the space with two cushions. Vander's black backpack rests against the side. "You can't see this spot from the path, so no one will know we are here."

"Is this where you bring all your girls?" I stupidly blurt before engaging my brain. "Forget I said that," I murmur, sitting down on one of the cushions. I stretch my legs out, wiping some dirt off my yoga pants.

He drops effortlessly down beside me despite his broad body and long legs. His eyes dance in amusement as he stares at me. "I don't take girls anywhere, and you're the first person I've brought here."

I blink at him in a stupor. "No one else has come here with you? Why?"

Reaching into his bag, he removes a matching plaid blanket and drapes it over our laps and our legs. "This is where I come when I need to be alone." He holds my gaze captive as he adds, "I have never felt the need to share it with anyone until now."

The air shifts with the gravity of that admission. These kinds of gestures have the most power over me. "Thank you for showing it to me," I croak when I eventually find my voice. "I'm honored you would trust me with this."

"I trust you completely," he quietly says, handing me a bottle of water. "I have coffee too, but I thought you might like water first after the walk."

"You are always so thoughtful."

He shrugs. "I try."

We lean back against the rock, drinking our water in companionable silence for a few minutes.

Always Meant to Be

"The view is stunning. I can see why you come up here. It's like there is no one else in the world but us. It's quiet and peaceful. Perfect for contemplation. I love it." While I passed plenty of walkers and joggers on my way, the crowd thinned out the higher I went. It's also getting dark, it's a weekend night, and the park closes in a couple hours.

"It's one of my favorite places to draw too." He offers me an apple.

I shake my head because my appetite is still shot to shit. "I'd love to see more of your work."

"You can come by any time. I've been working on some oil paintings in my studio."

"I didn't know you used oil paints."

"I'm trying different things. Expanding my horizons. Challenging myself. My art teacher says showing versatility might help with Yale."

"You'll get in." I smile at him. "There is no doubt in my mind."

His eyes glue mine in place, and I'm back to not breathing. The wind ruffles his hair, blowing dark strands over his brow and into his eyes. His face is drowning in emotion, and I see it all because he doesn't hide from me, and I seriously love that. "Thank you for believing in me, Kendall. I'm not sure you fully understand how much it means to me."

Without stopping to think about it, I reach out and link our fingers. "It's easy to believe in you because you are so talented and such a good person." He barks out a harsh laugh, and I sense the agony underscoring it. A stabbing pain spreads across my chest, and I hurt for him. "They don't deserve you."

"I know." Picking up a loose stone, he lets it fly. It soars over the edge, disappearing into the abyss. "But I can't leave." He turns to face me. "At least not yet." I squeeze his hand. "I need to put my Yale plan into place and then try to persuade Mom to leave him."

"And if she won't?" I softly ask.

"Then I'm done." He throws his head back and closes his eyes, gripping my hand more tightly.

"You have done more than most sons would do."

He angles his head to the side, opens his eyes, and looks straight at me. "You don't think West would go to the ends of the earth for you?" He arches a brow. "Because I'm telling you now," he adds, without waiting for me to reply, "he would. He would do everything I have done and more."

"As I would for him. Stella and Ridge too. They are the most precious things to me in this world, and I would do anything for them."

"Like stay with your cheating husband?"

I don't confirm or deny it, but I'm sure my silence says enough.

He moves his position, sliding closer and his knee brushes against my thigh. I look up into his solemn face. "Why won't you talk to me? I know there is more to it than you have said. You can confide in me. I won't tell anyone."

Pain whips me from all sides. Gently, I cup one side of his face because it's too hard not to touch him when we're this close. "And that's exactly why I can't. You are West's best friend, Vander. I don't want you keeping secrets from him. This already feels like a big one."

Silence bleeds into the air, and I watch all manner of emotions flit across his face. He leans into my palm while his hand lands on my knee. "I love West like a brother. He's been there for me, and I would do anything for him." His tongue darts out, wetting his lips, and my eyes track the motion of their own accord. Tension bleeds into the air, and his face burns against my palm while heat seeps into my leg, through the blan-

Always Meant to Be

ket, from his hand. "But what I feel for you surpasses that. I feel so fucking guilty for even voicing it, but it's the truth."

"Don't do that." I lower my hand from his face and bend my knees so his hand falls away. "Don't make this a choice."

"That's not what I'm saying." He kneels before me, pinning me with a pleading expression. He is shielding absolutely nothing, and I sense the same warring emotions flowing through his veins. "I hate I can't spend time with you, and time with him, and be open about it. But I'm not stupid. I know what people would think."

"Not just *people*. I'm talking about West. Stella too. They wouldn't understand."

"I wish I was older." He emits a weary sigh. "This wouldn't be an issue then."

"I'd still be married."

"Why, Kendall? Why are you staying with him? He isn't worthy to be your husband."

"I know, but it's complicated."

A wry laugh rips from his mouth. "Isn't everything."

Steely determination washes over his face as his eyes lock on mine again. "I'm not making a choice, but I don't see why I can't be friends with West and friends with you, and we keep things separate, like I do with my boxing buddies and my friends from school."

"It's not that simple."

"It can be."

"Beginning a friendship when we have admitted we have feelings for one another is a disaster in the making."

"We wouldn't be beginning anything, Kendall." His eyes flash with tenacity. "We've been friends all along. Maybe it wasn't conventional, but that's what we were to one another until I fucked everything up at the party. I just want that back. I need you in my life."

Right now, he looks every bit his age, and he might as well have reached out and squeezed a hand around my heart. I have never been able to abandon him when he's needed me, and I don't think I can do it now. *But how do we do this? How do we keep it platonic and not cross a line? And can I spend time with him while keeping it a secret because no one would understand?*

I don't have any answers, but I'd challenge anyone to look at his gorgeous, pleading face and to listen to his heartfelt tone, and turn him down. I don't know that I can.

"I was wrong before," he says. "I shouldn't have pushed for more. I should have been more understanding of your situation, but I get it now. I won't ask about him. I won't pry, but please, please, just don't shut me out. I need you as my friend, and I think you need me as yours too."

Chapter Sixteen

Vander

"Bowie says we're not hanging at your place tonight," West supplies when we meet at our lockers at the end of a fucking long school week. "What's up with that? Friday nights at Vander's is practically legendary."

"I told you yesterday I have plans with Crusher tonight." I grab the books I'll need for studying over the weekend from my locker and stuff them into my bag. "And I got some work done this week. The place is a mess." I'm planning to spend the weekend painting the carriage house and fixing it up nicer. I need something to distract me from thinking about Kendall. Despite our friendship pact, I haven't seen her all week, and I'm antsy.

He scratches the back of his head, frowning. "When did you tell me that?"

I roll my eyes. "When you were groping your girlfriend in the parking lot, dipshit. I should've known better than to talk to you then."

He grins. "I'm not going to apologize for letting my woman distract me. Hazel is the best distraction ever." West slings his gym bag over his shoulder, glancing behind me with a grimace, before eyeballing me. "Incoming."

Shutting my locker, I slowly turn around just as a girl with a sickeningly sweet voice says, "Hey, sexy."

I close my eyes for a nanosecond, praying for patience that is in limited supply these days. Schooling my features into a neutral expression, I look at Gayle, wondering what the fuck she wants now. The girl is legit driving me insane. Her hands land on my chest, uninvited, as she presses herself up against me. "Want to hang out?" She bats her eyelashes and licks her lips, and I'm sure she thinks she's seductive, but all it does is irritate the hell out of me. I want to tell her to get lost, but Mom's battered face resurrects in my mind, and I stuff the words back down.

Without altering my expression, I remove her hands from my chest and say, "I have plans."

Her lip juts out in a pout, and she puts her hands on her hips and thrusts her chest forward. "Plans with who?" Her eyes narrow in suspicion, and I don't like her tone or what it implies.

"None of your business," I say, signaling West with a look as I move around her.

"You're going to make this up to me!" she calls out as West and I stride away from her.

I rub at my throbbing temples, praying Dad signs the account soon. I can't put up with this for much longer.

"What's up with that?" my buddy asks as we stalk along the hallway toward the gym and changing areas.

"I told you my dad made me take her out. I have zero interest. Like zilch. I had a fucking headache after our last date because the girl does. Not. Stop. Talking." We round the corner, heading in the opposite direction of the masses. I should have left through the front doors, but I know Gayle would follow me like an annoying yapping puppy. I do everything to

Always Meant to Be

avoid spending time in her presence, so I'll slip out the rear doors and walk around the side of the football field, taking the long route to the parking lot. "Don't even get me started on how she kept trying to grab my dick under the table."

"Everyone can see she's hot for you."

"She's in it alone. My cock shrivels up the second I'm in her company."

West chuckles. "You've done your duty now. Just tell her to fuck off."

"I wish it was that simple."

"Wait." West slams to a halt. "Are you saying the psycho is making you take her out again?"

I nod. "Until he secures the Turner Media account."

"Start dating other girls at school. A different one every night. Let her see she means nothing to you, and she'll get the message."

"If I did that, she'd run to her daddy claiming I'm disrespecting her or some shit." I drag a hand through my hair, sighing in frustration. "I have no choice but to see this through to the end."

"Just when I think I couldn't hate your father any more than I already do." West shakes his head, stopping in front of the entrance to the male locker room. Coach's booming voice can be heard through the door, even if we can't make out what he is saying.

"You should go." I grab the strap of my bag and prepare to walk off.

"Mom's organizing my eighteenth birthday party for December third. My place. Eight o'clock. Make sure you're there."

"You know I will be." I jerk my head up. "Later, dude."

A few hours later, I'm parked a couple houses down from Kendall's house, hoping she doesn't spot me when she returns from work. She must be working late as it's almost eight and she's still not home. The dickhead's car is parked in the driveway, and I'm guessing he's waiting for his wife to return before he heads out. I know there is no proof, but my gut tells me he has a new fuck buddy.

The passenger door opens, and Crusher dumps a paper bag on my lap before climbing into my truck. He's dressed head to toe in black, and he has a ballcap pulled down low over his face. "Did you forget the dress code?" he asks, waggling his finger in my direction as he shuts the door.

"There's a dress code?" I cast a glance over my gray Henley, faded, ripped jeans, and boots, wondering what the fuck the dude is on about.

"We're undercover, duh."

"Dude, I have tinted windows. No one will even know it's us let alone see what we're wearing." Heat seeps into my thigh from the bag, and I toss it back at my buddy as he sets two coffees in the cupholders. "You're late."

"Sorry." He smirks, rustling the bag as he rummages in it. "Ran into a girl on the way out. She blew me in the alley behind my apartment building and I lost track of time." Removing a paper box, he hands it to me. "Peace offering."

I open the lid, inspecting the grease-laden burger. "No, thanks." I pass it back to him, gesturing at myself. "This body is a temple, and I don't infect it with that coronary-inducing shit." I'm careful what I eat, and I work hard to maintain a certain level of fitness. A healthy body helps to fuel a healthy mind. There are many things I can't control about my life, but I can control this.

"Suit yourself, asshole. More for me."

"Didn't you eat earlier?" I headed to the boxing club

straight from school, and I know Crusher went to the diner with a few of the others after their workouts.

"Pussy doesn't count." He flashes me a grin before taking a massive chunk of his burger. I return my attention to the Hawthorne residence, watching as Kendall's red SUV comes into view at the end of the road. Grabbing a coffee, I gulp back a mouthful, instantly grimacing as the semi-warm bitter taste hits the back of my throat. Crusher chuckles. "We can't conduct a stakeout without nasty coffee and greasy burgers. You always see cops doing that in shows."

"You're an idiot." There is no heat in my tone because Crusher is one of the good guys, even if he is a bit of a clown at times. Kendall pulls into her driveway, alongside her husband's brand-spanking-new Mercedes, and kills the engine. "Remind me again why I asked you to do this with me?"

"Because you need backup and I'm just that awesome," he says before stuffing half the burger in his mouth.

My heart beats erratically in my chest as she climbs out of her car. She looks fucking beautiful, as usual, and desire surges through my veins. Normally, she wears her long, blonde hair loose and wavy—it's my favorite look on her. But she styles her hair differently for the office, either wearing it in a high ponytail or an elegant chignon, like she's sporting now, and her confident businesswoman persona turns me on like you wouldn't believe. Her fitted pink wool coat hugs her soft curves, and the belt tied around her middle emphasizes her slender waist. The hem of her pencil skirt is just visible under the coat. Slim, shapely legs are encased in sheer pantyhose and she's wearing glossy black high heels.

She's my every fantasy come to life, and my heart aches to be with her.

Opening the back door, she bends over, retrieving a bulging briefcase and her purse.

Crusher whistles under his breath as he watches her. "That is one hot sexy mama. I'd do her."

I jerk my elbow into his ribs, and he almost chokes mid-bite. "Watch it. That's my best friend's mom." *And the woman I'm obsessing over. The one I'm madly, stupidly in love with.*

"No way, man." His eyes almost bug out of his head as he leans forward in his seat. "That's the woman the dude is cheating on?"

I nod tersely.

"Is he blind or insane? Who in their right mind would cheat on a woman like that?"

My sentiments exactly. "He's a stupid prick, but it will be his loss, not hers."

"Does West know we're doing this?" he asks after Kendall has disappeared through the front door of her house.

I shake my head. "Like I said, I don't want to involve him. If what I suspect is true, this will kill him."

"It sucks, man," he says, after finishing his burger. He dabs sauce from the corner of his mouth with a paper napkin before wiping his oily fingers. "What'll you do if we find evidence of cheating?"

I glance over my shoulder to the back seat, where my Nikon camera rests. "Document it and then consider my next move." I'm unsure where to go from there. I only just got Kendall to agree to be friends and I promised I wouldn't interfere or mention her marriage. So, I can't turn around and explain how I spied on her husband and found confirmation he's cheating. I suspect she already knows. If she does, then I'm not sure this will make any difference, but I have to try. She wouldn't approve of me doing this, but I've got to do something. Maybe looking at the physical proof of his betrayal will spur her into action. Thinking of her remaining married to that asshole ignites a tidal wave of rage I usually only feel for my father.

"Is that the douche?" Crusher asks, kicking his booted feet up on the dash, as Curtis emerges from the house.

"That's him," I growl, clenching my fists. I start up the engine as he climbs behind the wheel of his Merc.

"He looks like a slimeball."

"I have always thought so." Tugging my ballcap down lower over my head, out of habit more than necessity, I wait a few seconds before pulling out onto the road behind West's dad.

Crusher turns the radio on low as we trail Curtis for twenty minutes. He pulls up in front of a three-story townhouse a couple of miles from the UCCS campus, parking at the curb, directly underneath a street lamp.

"Shit." Crusher presses his nose to the tinted window as the front door of the townhouse opens and three brunettes walk out. "I think I know one of them."

"Which one?" I ask, snatching my camera from the back seat as Curtis exits the car and heads toward the women.

"The girl at the back with the shorter hair. I might have fucked her one time in the bathroom at TJ's."

"You might have?" I arch a brow as I remove the lens cover from my camera.

He grins. "I'm in my last year of college. Fucked a lot of pussy since I rocked up here, and I mean *a lot*. Can't expect me to remember every broad."

"Charming. I bet the girls would love to hear that."

Bringing the camera to my face, I snap a succession of pics as Curtis leans in to kiss one of the women on the cheek. His arm slides around her waist as he escorts her to the car. Her two friends trail behind them. I continue snapping away, snarling as the girl grins up at him, sliding her hand up his chest. Curtis opens the passenger door, and I get a good look at her under the glow of the light before she slides inside.

"She's a looker," Crusher says. "It's like he went out of his way to find someone who looks the complete opposite of his wife." I'd just thought the same thing. The girl has long poker-straight black hair, and her skin looks pale against her bright red lips. She is poured into a teeny black dress, which leaves little to the imagination. Ample cleavage threatens to spill out of the front of her lowcut dress. It dips at her narrow waist before flaring over wide hips. She's shorter than Kendall by a few inches. "She's much younger than him." Crusher states the obvious.

I let them pull away from the curb before following. "This is student land. If they live here, they must go to UCCS." Which means she is most likely in her early twenties.

We trail them to TJ's Sports Bar & Grill, one of our favorite haunts, and follow them inside. It's crazy busy tonight, and all the booths and barstools are occupied. Curtis leads the ladies through the crowd, finding an empty high table with one stool, which he claims for the brunette with the red lips. He flags a waitress and orders drinks while we hang back, just out of sight.

"He's her sugar daddy." Crusher states the obvious again. "She probably sees the car and the flashy clothes and thinks she's onto a good thing."

"He's fucking pathetic." I cast a quick glance around the packed bar. "Look at this place, and then look at him. He sticks out like a sore thumb in his chinos and polo shirt."

"You want a beer?" Crusher asks as I fix my eyes on Curtis and the girl with their heads bent together, deep in conversation.

I shake my head. "I'll have a water, and we're not staying long." I don't want him to see me, but I need some evidence. A kiss on the cheek and a hand around her back isn't much to go on, even if it's clear by the blatant eye fucking they are more than friends.

Always Meant to Be

I pretend to mess with my phone while I keep an eye on the dickhead and his little friend. Crusher returns with a beer for him and a water for me, and we move spots over to the side, pressed in against the wall. I have a better angle here to take pics, and it's more private.

The girl flings her arms around Curtis, pulling his face down to hers and smashing her lips against his. His hands gravitate to her hips, and she spreads her legs, leaving room for him to stand between them. Thank fuck, there's a decent camera on my phone because I just hit the jackpot. Grabbing handfuls of his hair, she presses herself up against him while he devours her mouth, like he's not in public. Her legs wrap around his waist, as he thrusts against her, neither of them caring they are drawing attention.

He clearly doesn't give a flying fuck if he gets caught, and it enrages me. How dare he treat the sweetest woman I know like this. It's like the ultimate slap in the face for everything Kendall has done for him. *And this asshole claims he's a family man?* What a fucking joke. He lied to his kids' faces when he promised he was going to make things right with their mom when he clearly has no intention of fixing his marriage.

A part of me rejoices at that thought until I think about the devastation this will do to Kendall. Curtis is a selfish prick, and I wouldn't put it past him to remain married to her while continuing to fuck around behind her back. I'm so glad I didn't bring West into my confidence. Seeing his dad like this would kill him. And Kendall would be so hurt if she witnessed this. It's bad enough he's cheating, but to do it on her doorstep, in such a disrespectful manner, indicates how little he thinks of her.

I catch it all on video and grab a few pics, and then I've had enough. I can't watch this another second before I do something I might regret. The urge to drag the asshole outside and beat him bloody is riding me hard. While I'd love to slap him around, I'm not convinced I'd be able to stop before killing the jerk, and he's not worth risking jailtime. "I'm leaving." I chug back the rest of my water. "Are you coming or staying?"

"A couple of guys from my class are here. Why don't I stick around and get some more footage? He doesn't know me from Adam, and I'll be discreet."

I clamp a hand on his shoulder. "Thanks, man."

"If I can remember that chick's name, I might be able to infiltrate their little gang and find out what he's been saying."

"That's not a bad idea."

"I'll work my legendary charm." He puffs out his chest, and I bark out a laugh. He's so cheesy. Sometimes I wonder how he gets so many women—until I see the way they eye up his muscles and his tattoos. Every woman likes to think she can tame the quintessential bad boy, and Crusher works that to the max.

"Remember no one can know," I remind him.

Before we came out tonight, I thought about whether I should confront Curtis or let him see me so he knows I know. I decided that wouldn't work to my advantage. Knowledge is power, and this intel gives me some leverage. I'm not sure how I'll use it, but having it in my back pocket, to whip out when needed, is of most value. Ensuring he doesn't know I'm onto him works best for now.

"I won't breathe a word of it to anyone, and I'll ensure no one sees what I'm doing."

Chapter Seventeen

Kendall

"I need to tell you something," Shirley says as we speed-walk around one of the less busy trails in the park. Usually, I help out at the retirement home on Saturday afternoons, but today I was asked to come at eight a.m., and I finished at midday, so I was home when Shirley knocked on my door thirty minutes ago asking if I was up for a walk. She slows down, gesturing toward a bench on my right. "I think we should sit for this."

"Okay." Nerves prickle the back of my neck as I take a seat beside my neighbor. I unscrew the cap on my bottle of water and knock some back. Shirley knots her hands on her lap and audibly gulps. "Whatever it is, just tell me." I have a sixth sense I already know.

"There is no easy way to say this, and the last thing I want to do is hurt you, but I can't keep this to myself any longer."

"This is about Curtis," I say, sure of it now.

Shock splays across her face. "You know?"

I drink another mouthful of water. "That he's cheating on me? Yeah."

"Oh, Kendall. I'm so sorry." She rests her gloved hand on my arm.

"How do you know?"

"Adrian and I were out for dinner at Chelle's Steakhouse, and we saw him having dinner with another woman. It was clear it was a date."

I tilt my head to the side. "Don't sugarcoat it, Shirl. What did you see?"

She steeples her fingers against her chin. "They were all over one another. It was blatantly obvious and really inappropriate." Sympathy dances across her face. "It sickened both of us so much we got our dinner to go and left."

"Did he see you?"

She shakes her head. "He was too engrossed in the woman. We considered confronting him, but Adrian felt we shouldn't interfere. He's disgusted with Curtis and wants nothing to do with him now."

Adrian and Shirley are thirteen years older than us, and they've been married for twenty-five years. They don't have any kids—by choice—and they are completely devoted to one another. I can say, with complete confidence, that Adrian would never cheat on his wife.

"When was this?"

"Last month," she admits a little sheepishly. I guess now I understand her questioning me on psychic night.

"Don't feel bad for not telling me straightaway. I get it, and I really appreciate you telling me this now even though I already knew."

"How did you find out?"

"He told me." I proceed to give her the Cliff Notes version of what's been going on, and she listens attentively.

"I wouldn't have believed Curtis capable of such treachery and deception if I hadn't seen it myself."

Always Meant to Be

"That makes two of us." I twist the bottle cap between my fingers. "Though my shock, hurt, and humiliation are gradually giving way to extreme anger. The instant West and Stella are gone and Ridge is in bed, he leaves, like he can't stand to be around me. I'd get it if I was the one who had cheated on him, but I'm the injured party here."

"He's an asshole," she seethes. "I don't know how you can bear to look at him let alone have him touch you in fake PDAs. I would curl into a ball and die if Adrian did that to me."

"I don't have that luxury. I need to keep it together for the kids."

"You have such inner strength."

A harsh laugh spills from my mouth. "I really don't feel terribly strong right now. I'm clinging to my sanity by my fingernails."

"What are you going to do, and how can I help?"

My heart swells, and I reach out and hug her. "I'm not sure, on both counts, but knowing you know comforts me."

"I'm here for you. Whatever you need. You only have to ask."

"I need you to keep it confidential. I can't risk the kids finding out. It would hurt them so much."

"No one will hear it from us," she assures me, and I know it's the truth. She's not the type to gossip. "But if Curtis continues parading his mistress all over town, someone else is going to see. Keeping it a secret from West and Stella may not be possible."

"I can't believe he's being so reckless! Especially when he's the one who insisted we play this charade until Stella graduates."

"He's a pig. You can't possibly be considering going along with his plans." She shakes her head.

I sigh. "I only agreed for the kids, but I'm not putting up

with this. He thinks he calls all the shots, but he's going to get a rude awakening."

Her eyes glimmer. "What do you have planned?"

"I'm not going to sit back and let him play me for a fool. I have a few ways I can take back control. I met with a great divorce attorney this week, and she gave me some food for thought. There are things I can do to be smart. To cover myself when the time comes to divorce, and I intend to protect myself and the kids as much as I can." I already have my own bank account, and my wages go directly in there. I transfer a set amount into our joint account on a monthly basis as Curtis does. He pays more as he earns more, and we both have access to our savings account. I'm going to start siphoning as much money as I can and buying anything I might need later when everything is divided up with the divorce.

I'm not as emotional this week, and hearing this new information helps to focus my anger in the right direction. I need that internal rage to spur me into action, and I know just where to start.

"What's she like?" I know I shouldn't ask, but I can't help it.

Her features soften. "Are you sure you want to know?" I nod. "She's young. College age if I had to guess. Dark hair. Big eyes."

"Sexy and beautiful, right?" I tilt my head to the side. "You can say it. I know Curtis wouldn't pick anyone who wasn't gorgeous."

"She's not as gorgeous as you, and he's a fool." She scoffs. "No older man snags a pretty younger woman unless she's after his money."

"Curtis is flashy, but he has a lot less money than she might think."

"Even less after you divorce." She grins. "I hope you take him to the cleaners."

"I have a full-time job, so the finances will be split accordingly. I'll get the house as the primary caregiver, and there won't be any issue with joint custody. The attorney said she can negotiate it as part of the settlement that Curtis has to pay for college for the kids. Those are my priorities."

"Maybe you should quit your job so he has to support you after you divorce. Put the squeeze on his finances so he doesn't have the cash to wine and dine his floozies."

"I need my job now more than ever. I want Curtis out of my life, and I want to be able to support myself independently. I don't want to be beholden to him any more than I have to be." I have already resigned myself to the fact I won't be able to apply for part-time hours again after Christmas. Even if I get a generous settlement in the divorce—part of which will be compensation for the years I stayed home with the kids so he could advance at work—and Curtis will have to pay child support, it most likely won't be enough to maintain the standard of living I'm accustomed to unless I keep working.

Also, I enjoy the confidence I glean from my work and the sense of personal satisfaction I get from working outside the home. I know I'm a good mom. I love my kids, and taking care of them comes naturally, and it's something that gives me enormous enjoyment. Watching my children grow and develop into the amazing humans they are is one of life's greatest rewards. They are my greatest achievement, and nothing Curtis can do will ever take that from me.

But it's more than that. For me, having outside interests keeps me stimulated and happy and allows me to channel it into my home life. My kids are at school, and I would quickly grow frustrated if I was at home all day with no job to keep me busy. I am not knocking it, and I enjoyed the time I spent with the kids when they were little and I wasn't working, but it's different now. I discussed options with my attorney, and while I could get more alimony if I wasn't working and was solely financially dependent on Curtis, I don't want to lose my independence.

Glancing at my watch, I notice the time and rise to my feet. "I need to head back." The asshole is taking Ridge on an overnight camping trip with his Little League team, and they will be leaving shortly. I want to say goodbye to my son before they go. "Thank you for telling me," I say, as we walk toward the park exit at a more leisurely place.

"I'm sorry I hesitated. I should have told you immediately."

"No apologies are necessary."

"I can only imagine what you are going through, Kendall, and my heart breaks for you, but I know what I'd do if I was in your shoes." I arch a brow, urging her to continue, as we walk through the park gates. "I'd find myself a hot young lover. Why should Curtis be the only one to have fun?"

I'm still mulling over Shirley's words as I walk toward Vander's place a few hours later. Curtis and Ridge have gone camping overnight. Stella is having a sleepover at a friend's house, and West has gone to dinner and the movies with Hazel. Viola asked me if I wanted to come over to her place, but Vander had already texted me asking me to come for dinner, and I didn't turn him down.

I agreed to his friendship suggestion last weekend even if I'm not one hundred percent confident we can pull it off. The butterflies cartwheeling inside my chest attest to that. I'm excited to spend the evening with him, and that's all kinds of wrong. Which brings me back to Shirley's parting statement. A

Always Meant to Be

fling with a sexy younger guy could be just the thing I need to give me a confidence boost and get through these next couple of years. Hearing about Curtis's pretty girlfriend has thrown me for a loop even if I'm glad I know what I'm dealing with now. A young girl is not going to want to play stepmom to three kids. Especially when two of them are closer in age to her than the man she's screwing. I can't bear the thought of anyone else occupying a mothering role in my kids' lives, so maybe it's a blessing she's young.

Perhaps I should throw caution to the wind and take a young lover. I've been told on many occasions that I look young for my age, and I had no shortage of admirers when I was in school even though everyone knew I was going steady with Curtis. I know I look good for my age, and if I put myself out there, I'm sure I would find someone to have some fun with. But the prospect is daunting. Online dating is the norm these days, and I wouldn't have a clue where to start. The thought of it gives me goose bumps.

Vander would seem like the obvious choice except he's West's best friend and he's got his own problems to worry about. *And* we have decided to be friends.

I look up, startled to find I'm already at the gates to the carriage house Vander calls home. I was so lost in my head I didn't even notice the walk here. I send him a quick text, letting him know I'm outside, and the gate opens a few seconds later.

"Hey." Vander stands just inside the gate, waiting for me with a large smile on his face. "I was half expecting you to chicken out."

"Me too," I truthfully admit, handing over the bag with the dessert I made.

"I'm glad you didn't." His hand moves to my lower back as we walk toward the open doorway. The gate eases closed behind us. "After you." Vander steps back, letting me enter the house first.

I notice the changes instantly. "You've been busy. The place looks great." I spin around, taking it all in, as I remove my coat.

I hear the smile in his voice as he shuts and locks the door. "I'm glad you like it. I wanted to make it homier so you'd feel comfortable when you're here."

My heart does a twisty jump in my chest. "Are you saying you did this for me?"

He nods, depositing the bag with the lemon cake and whipped cream on the small kitchen counter. "I had a contractor here this week, and he built the feature wall, installed the electric fireplace, and fitted a tub in the bathroom, but I sanded and varnished the floors and painted the wall myself. Tomorrow, I'm going to paint the kitchen cupboards. I went to that furniture store on Main Street and bought everything else you see."

The old leather couches have been replaced with a larger sleeker contemporary gray leather sectional, positioned in front of the new fireplace. Painted a rich navy blue, the feature wall has been built around the electric fireplace currently flickering with vibrant purple-blue flames. The feature wall contrasts beautifully with the original rustic stone walls, helping to give the space a modern yet traditional feel. A colorful patterned rug adorns the hardwood floor in front of the fire. Inviting plump cushions in shades of blue, white, and gray adorn the sectional. The new distressed coffee table is perched on top of the rug, matching the new end tables on either side of the couch. Stunning colored-glass lamps with large white shades reside on both.

But it's the massive canvas hanging on the rear wall, over the couch, that really makes the room. "My God, Vander, this is incredible." After dropping my coat and purse on the couch, I walk toward his painting with an awestruck look on my face. "It's both intricate and simple," I rasp as my gaze wanders over the myriad of colorful lines. They swirl across the canvas in different directions and shapes, and at first look, it would appear to be haphazard in design. Until you look closer and see how uniquely brilliant it is. "You're not just talented. You're intelligent with your gift," I whisper as my finger traces over the shape of a face embedded into the lines. Within the larger face are more faces, all cleverly incorporated into the painting. I spin around with tears in my eyes. "I am lost for words. This steals my breath, Vander. And I know this is only a fraction of what you can do."

His face glows at my praise, and I silently scream at his parents for not seeing how truly amazing he is. "Do you really like it?"

I vigorously nod. "Does it have particular significance?" I ask, whipping my head back around to the painting. "All the faces within must mean something," I murmur. I'm no art expert, but Vander puts thought into everything he does.

"I wanted to capture how we all wear different faces and have different sides to our personalities. How so many different parts go into making a person whole."

He comes up beside me, and I stare at him with emotion blistering in my eyes. There is so much sentiment behind those words and that drawing. He's magnificent. A god among gods. He has never stood taller or appeared more luminous than he does to me right now.

Curtis never unraveled the essence of who I am inside, showing no interest in the things that make me the person I am or the part of me that challenges my drive for understanding and enlightenment. He couldn't understand why I like to question and analyze the things we can't explain in our world.

But Vander gets it.

He shares the same passion for knowledge about the things we can't easily explain or see. I've always seen that in him. I know why he's questioned it too, but he has the ability to look beyond his personal quest, and that makes him light years ahead of Curtis in maturity. I hoped giving him a copy of *Meditations* for his birthday would coax him to probe deeper within himself for the answers he sought, but I never expected this.

In this moment, I believe every word Dee told me. I believe our souls are harmoniously aligned, existing in perfect synchronization, and dancing to the same beat.

Vander's emerald-green eyes peer into my face with so much intensity it almost knocks me off my feet. I should look away, because it's wholly intimate, but I can't. I'm enraptured by him. Everything about him speaks to me on an innate level, and I wonder why I'm denying this bond we share when it feels like I will die if I don't feel his lips on my lips, his hands on my body, his naked skin against mine.

Right now, I don't care about his age or the other obstacles blocking our path. All that exists is us and this profound connection drawing us closer and closer until it feels like my soul is bursting, my heart is swollen, and my body is on fire.

My heart skids around my chest, thumping wildly, as I step closer to him.

I want nothing more, in this moment, than to kiss him. From the hungry look in his eyes, and the way his gaze drops to my mouth, I know I'm not in this alone.

Chapter Eighteen

Kendall

"That's so profound. I love it," I murmur, still staring into his eyes. Internally, the angel on one of my shoulders is screaming at the devil on the other, and I'm conflicted. I know what I want. I want his mouth on mine, and it feels like I will die if I don't get to taste his lips. But a sliver of doubt slides into my mind, and the angel's voice grows louder, attempting to drown out the demonic voice urging me to do it.

Vander opens and closes his mouth in quick succession, and I know what he was about to say. His emerald eyes lower to my mouth, and I barely remember to breathe. We stare at one another, suspended in time, and electricity crackles in the space around us. His gaze darkens as his eyes remain glued to my lips, and I can't stop looking at his mouth either. I'm twisted into knots. Tempted to grab his shirt and pull him to me, but I'm equally terrified of propelling fate into motion. Indecision comingles with anticipation in the air. We both know we're hanging on the edge of a precipice, and if we fall, there can be no undoing it.

That thought drags me back to reality. I step away from him and avert my gaze, sucking long breaths deep into my lungs. I stride toward the kitchenette to put some physical distance between us. "The whipped cream needs to go into the refrigerator," I say, hoping he can't hear the tremble in my voice or see the shaking in my hands as I remove the container from the bag.

He clears his throat as I open the small refrigerator door and pop the whipped cream inside. "Dinner is almost ready. Go sit down, and I'll get you a glass of wine," he says.

My heart accelerates as he draws near, and I slam the refrigerator door shut and spin around, clinging to it as he purposely slides sideways to avoid brushing against me. Everything is suddenly awkward, and I can't stand the forlorn look on his face. "Maybe I should go," I whisper.

He shakes his head. "Don't go." He drags a hand through his messy damp hair as air spills from his mouth. "We had a moment, but it doesn't need to ruin our night." Pleading eyes pin me in place. "Please, Kendall. I've been looking forward to seeing you all week."

I can't refuse him when he looks at me like this. "Okay."

His shoulders visibly relax. "Good."

I take a seat on the new leather sectional as music filters through the speakers on low. Thankfully, it's not rap or that loud heavy metal West listens to sometimes. "Is this Halsey?" I inquire as Vander looms over me.

He hands me a wineglass while nodding. "It's her new album. It's awesome. I think you'll like it. Listen to the lyrics."

"Okay." I smile up at him as I lift the glass to my lips.

"Do you want to eat at the counter or eat here?" He points at the coffee table, looking adorably uncertain.

"I'm good with here. Viola and I have coffee-table eating

Always Meant to Be

nailed at this point." Slipping my shoes off, I grab two cushions, placing them on the rug on the floor. "There. Perfect." Leaning down, he presses his lips to my hair, and my heart almost jumps out of my chest it's beating so fast. "Like you," he whispers before leaving me to return to the kitchen. Gulping over the messy ball of emotion nestling in my throat, I grab my wine and sit down on one of the cushions.

Vander approaches a couple minutes later with two plates. "Do you have placemats?" I ask before he sets the plate down in front of me. He shakes his head, so I grab two magazines from the shelf under the table to use instead. No point in risking damage to his new table. Putting the food down, he walks off to grab water and silverware. He drops down on the cushion beside me and hands me a knife and fork. "I hope you like it."

I lean over the heaping bowl of chicken and chorizo pasta, and my belly rumbles appreciatively. "It smells delicious." I wrap the spaghetti around my fork and take a bite, groaning as the garlicky-tomato flavor hits my tongue. "Tastes delicious too," I say after I have swallowed. He visibly melts under my praise, and I'm instantly reminded of how much that's been lacking in his life. "Where did you learn to cook like this?"

He finishes a mouthful of pasta before answering. "We used to have full-time housekeepers who cooked for us, but they all kept leaving. Dad either hit on them or they saw how he treated his wife and kid, got scared, and left. Then Dad stopped hiring staff when Mom got really bad. Mom can't cook for shit, and she's only interested in a liquid diet. I lived on takeout for a while. When I got into boxing, I didn't want to eat crap anymore, so I taught myself to cook from videos. Keaton Kennedy has a great online cooking show. He focuses on healthy meals with a specific emphasis on athletes, so it's perfect for me."

I bob my head. "I've watched a few episodes. He's good.

Austen Hayes—the wide receiver for the Baltimore Ravens—is his husband and he's from Golden. Colorado has pretty much claimed Keaton as one of their own. They are a beautiful couple, and Keaton is a great chef. I have a couple of his cookbooks at home. I'll loan them to you, if you like?"

"Cool. Thanks."

"You're just full of surprises, Vander." I mean it as a compliment.

He shrugs, like he's not one of the most resilient people I've ever encountered. "I actually like cooking," he says, staring into space while I eat. "I find it therapeutic."

"I'm the same," I admit before taking a drink of my water. "If I've had a bad day or I'm stressed about something, you will always find me in the kitchen cooking up a storm."

"I cook for my mom too," he adds, and we continue talking in between eating. "If I didn't feed her, she'd waste away."

I almost lose my appetite at his words. "You're a good son, Vander," I quietly admit.

"It's still not enough."

I rest my hand on top of his, needing to offer him comfort. His eyes meet mine. "You're more than enough." We smile at one another, and I remove my hand before my fingers get ideas.

"Speaking of food, what are you doing for Thanksgiving?" It's only five days away, and I doubt his mother has organized anything.

"It'll just be Mom and me. Dad is spending it in the city." A dark look crosses his face, but he doesn't elaborate. He doesn't need to. "I'm going to cook."

"You should come to our house. Both of you. There will be more than enough food." It's a spontaneous offer, but I can't regret it even if it will make the day more torturous for me. Pretending to play the happy couple with Curtis in front of the kids and his parents will be horrendous. Having Vander there

Always Meant to Be

will only add to my misery, but in another way, his presence will soothe me. And I can't bear to think of him all alone, rattling around that big house with his semi-comatose mother.

"I don't know." He scrubs a hand along his prickly jawline.

I know why he hesitates. "There will be no judgment in my home. Besides, your mom knows how to conduct herself in public." It's another reason I despise Diana Henley, but a part of me feels for her too. She can turn the charm on in public and appear like a functioning human when the need arises. Yet, she can't do that for her son. At home, she lets him see the true extent of her addiction. Forces him to care for her, and I have zero respect for her because of it.

Curtis will probably hate I invited her, but oh well.

"I will ask her. She'll probably say no."

I won't ask him to ditch his mother on Thanksgiving, so I only say, "Just let me know either way."

We chat about less stressful things as we finish dinner, and I help him to clean up. Then we sit on opposite ends of the couch, listening to more of Halsey's new album, in between talking, as I sip a glass of crisp Sancerre while Vander drinks a beer. "Are you still attending your philosophy class on Monday nights?" he asks, swiping my empty glass and getting up to refill it.

"Yes. It's the highlight of my week." Vander returns, swinging his legs up onto the couch. I follow suit, tucking my legs underneath me and covering my knees with my dress to ensure I'm not flashing anything I shouldn't be.

"What's the hot topic this time?" he inquires, handing me a fresh glass of wine. Our fingers brush in the exchange, but I forcibly ignore the tingles shooting up my arm.

"Um…reincarnation." My cheeks heat as I stumble over the word. Ever since Dee said the things she said, I have been struggling to wrap my head around it. It's one thing being open-minded and believing in the abstract and quite another when it potentially becomes a reality. Truthfully? I don't know what to think.

His eyes light up. "Interesting subject. What's your view on it?" It almost appears like he's holding his breath while he waits for me to reply.

I bite down on my lip as I contemplate my response. "What's yours?"

"Answering a question with a question. Hmm." He toys with his lips, and my eyes are like heat-seeking missiles latching on to a target as I watch him pluck his plump lips with long, lean fingers. "Classic deflection maneuver there." His lips curl up at the corners in a teasing manner.

He's not wrong, but I'm rethinking everything right now, so I go for another tried-and-tested deflection technique. "Most Buddhists believe in reincarnation, and a report we looked at in class said one in four Americans believe reincarnation exists."

"I find that fascinating, but I'm interested in what *you* think." Gawd, he's like a dog with a bone. He stretches his legs out, and his bare toes brush against my dress-covered knees because his legs are just that long. "Sorry." He pulls himself upright against the armrest so his feet aren't touching me anymore.

"There is enough anecdotal evidence to suggest it's real," I truthfully admit. "I'm with John Locke and similar mindsets. I believe personal identity is tied to having the same consciousness, we retain the memories from consciousness to consciousness, and it's nothing to do with the body we occupy."

He bobs his head. "It's the soul that is reincarnated, not the physical body. Though I have read some of the teachings of Lamaistic belief and it makes a compelling case for reincarnation of the body."

"We discussed the Dalai Lama too. Each Dalai Lama

Always Meant to Be

believes their spirit is reincarnated in the body of their successor and that person is born at the moment of his death. It's interesting, but how is it compelling?" I'm on a high in this moment, thrilled I can have these kinds of conversations with him, knowing he's not just paying me lip service when he says he shares my passion for philosophy. He reads and studies it too. *How many eighteen-year-olds do that?*

"They take precautions to ensure the holy succession, and there have been witness reports going back for hundreds of years that attest to things that can only be explained by reincarnation."

"Like what?" I sit up closer and lean toward him, taking a mouthful of my wine as I eagerly wait for him to answer. We only started this subject at the end of class last week, so this is new to me, and perhaps it's something I can raise at our next session.

"Like there was a rainbow over the house where the baby was born. His birth was indicated in a vision. The child could tell holy visitors' identities even when they tried to disguise it. Some recognized previous belongings like rosary beads, and others were readily able to repeat the Buddhist mantra. All of this while only a young child. That can't be faked. How do you—"

The front door handle rattles, violently, unexpectedly, cutting Vander off mid-sentence. My eyes pop wide in alarm, and my heart lurches to my throat. Anxiety prickles the back of my neck, and acid churns in my gut. Fists pound on the door. "Van! Open up!" West shouts, his impatient raps growing more insistent.

"Shit." Vander curses under his breath while I go into full-on-panic mode. *My son cannot find me here! How the hell would I ever explain it?*

Vander jumps up, grabbing my glass of wine, my shoes, my

coat, and my purse. His eyes dart around the room. "Give me a sec," he roars while taking my elbow and yanking me up from the couch. "Hide in the bedroom," he whispers, guiding me toward the room at the back with urgency.

"Oh my God," I splutter. "This isn't happening."

He throws my purse and shoes on the bed and sets my wineglass down on his bedside table. "Kendall." He clasps my face in his large palms. "Calm down. I will handle this." He presses a kiss to my brow. "Trust me, sweetheart." He tips my face up. "It's going to be okay."

"He can't know I'm here." I fist his shirt as the pounding starts up again on the door.

"He won't." He kisses the top of my head. "Just stay here, and keep quiet. I'll get rid of him as quick as I can." We both wince at his words. I nod, and he leaves, closing the door behind him.

The urge to tug on my hair and pace the floor is riding me hard, but I can't risk West hearing. Only a wall and a thin door separate the rooms, and the noise could carry.

"Shit, man. What's wrong?" Vander asks, and my panic instantly transforms to fear for my son. *Has something happened?* Tiptoeing to the door, I press my ear against the wood.

"I just had the biggest argument with Hazel. I think we might have broken up. Ugh."

West's frustrated groan contains an undercurrent of pain, and I long to wrap my arms around him and comfort him. But I can't. It's not something life-threatening, thank God. Stress lifts from my shoulders, and I step away from the door. Padding softly toward the bed, I reach for my purse to grab my AirPods. I don't want to hear their conversation because I don't want to breach my son's privacy. He came here to talk to his best friend, not confide in his mother.

Always Meant to Be

It's bad enough I'm keeping my friendship with Vander a secret.

I don't want to add to my list of sins.

Sitting on the edge of the bed, I shove my AirPods in and pull up one of my playlists, drowning out their voices before I hear something I shouldn't. I take a large swig of wine while hoping whatever has happened between West and Hazel blows over. I like his girlfriend. She's sweet and loyal, and she's brought out a different side to my son.

Needing further distraction, I pick up the battered copy of *Meditations* resting on top of a pile of books by Vander's bed, smiling despite my predicament. I thumb through it, my smile expanding as I spot the highlights and notes. I get such a kick out of knowing we have a common interest and that he's not just blowing hot air up my ass. Vander is genuinely interested, and it gives me a warm and cozy feeling. Setting *Meditations* down, I pick up the next book. *The 48 Laws of Power* by Robert Greene. I tried to read that one time, but I found it heavy going. Vander has a bookmark in the middle of the book, so he's making better progress than I did. I'm putting it back when an envelope slides out from underneath the back cover.

Reaching to the floor to retrieve it, I almost have a coronary when I spot the photo peeking out from the top of the open envelope. Curtis's side profile has more than piqued my curiosity, so I don't feel bad when I pull the photos out and spread them on the bed.

My entire body shakes as I skim my eyes over every picture. It is one thing to know my husband is cheating and quite another to see the evidence of it laid out before me. Mounting horror consumes me as I grapple to accept what's in front of me. Tears well in my eyes, and pain pierces my chest as I stare at the photos of him with his girlfriend.

She's young and beautiful. Just like Shirley said. Neither of them cares they are in a crowded public place as they practically dry hump one another. I slam a hand over my mouth as nausea swims up my throat, and the worst pain imaginable is tearing me to shreds on the inside.

I don't love my husband anymore.

I haven't for a long time.

But the pain of his betrayal and his complete and utter disregard for my feelings really fucking hurts.

So much for wanting to protect our children from the truth.

My hurt ebbs a little to make room for anger. And it's not all reserved for my scumbag of a cheating husband. *Why the hell does Vander have these pictures? I told him not to interfere, so why has he involved himself?*

Chapter Nineteen

Kendall

"It's safe to come out now," Vander says, opening the door twenty minutes later.

I'm sitting on the end of the bed, still seething. Lifting my head, I glare at him as I stand and thrust the photos into his chest. "Want to explain how these are in your possession?"

His gaze lowers to the pictures before his brows climb to his hairline. Picking his head up, he fixes me with an unapologetic look. "I followed the asshole and took the photos myself."

"Jesus Christ." I had suspected as much, and I suppose it's better than him getting someone else to spy on my cheating husband and his sidepiece.

He claws a hand through his hair. "You're mad."

No shit, Sherlock. "Mad doesn't begin to cover what I'm feeling right now."

"I knew there was more you weren't saying, and I had to know."

"I didn't tell you for a reason!" I shout, losing the hold on my tenuous emotions. "I didn't want you keeping secrets from

West, and now you'll have to." I push at his shoulders, and the photos fall to the floor, surrounding us. "You're an accessory now. And, so help me God, Vander, if you breathe one word of this to my son, I will never speak to you again."

"You think I'd show him these? You think I'd want to hurt him like that?" He folds his arms in front of his chest and stares at me. Incredulity bleeds into his tone and his expression. "What kind of fucking friend do you think I am?"

"A shitty one!" I blurt. "I specifically asked you to butt out, and you ignored me!"

Grabbing my stuff, I push past him, needing to get out of here before I say something I won't be able to take back. I'm angry with Vander for going behind my back and doing something I asked him not to do, but I'm well aware the person I'm furious with is Curtis, and I don't want to vent that rage on anyone but him. I'm also hugely embarrassed Vander witnessed that. *What does it say about me as a wife that my husband continuously has affairs?* It's basically broadcasting the fact I can't keep him happy or satisfied, and I don't want Vander thinking that about me. It's humiliating.

"I'm not going to apologize for my actions," he says, as I walk toward the door. "I will never apologize for trying to protect you."

"Protect me?" I swing around, struggling to keep my emotions in check. "How does that protect me?" I point in the direction of his bedroom as my voice breaks. "Have you any idea what it does to me to see those images?" Tears well in my eyes, and they are a mix of anger and hurt.

"I never intended for you to see them." He moves cautiously toward me. Pain and sympathy shimmer in his eyes. "I'm sorry you found them." He lifts his arm, his fingers aiming for my hair, but I jerk back, out of his reach. Hurt flares across his face.

"What did you intend to do with them?" I ask while I put my coat on and sling my purse over my shoulder.

He shrugs and schools his features into a neutral line, attempting to mask his emotions. "I wasn't sure, but it can't hurt to have evidence that might be useful later."

"You had no right, Vander." All the anger flees from my tone as exhaustion sets in, seeping deep into my bones and my psyche. "I know your intentions came from a good place, but you can't ignore my wishes and go behind my back again. This doesn't involve you, and you need to stay out of it before you get hurt. I'm carrying the weight of so much responsibility on my shoulders right now, and I don't want to add you to it."

Hurt splays across his features again. "I'm a *responsibility*?"

"Right now, you're a *liability*, and I can't handle that on top of everything else." I turn to go, hating how such a wonderful night turned so ugly. With my fingers curled around the door handle, I look over my shoulder at him. "Thank you for dinner. It was a nice night up until it wasn't." I don't wait for his reply, opening the door and walking outside.

I'm waiting in the hall, just inside the door the following morning, ready to accost my vile husband the second he returns from his camping trip with our youngest. I barely slept a wink all night after learning what I did. Hurt still simmers in my veins, but red-hot rage is the prominent emotion consuming me, and I can't wait to take it out on the source of my anger.

"Mom!" Ridge bursts through the door, wearing a smile and yawning. "I had the best time! It was awesome!"

"That's great, honey." I lean down and hug him, squeezing him close. "I'm glad you enjoyed it. Where's Daddy?"

"He's putting the camping gear in the garage. Then he said he had to go out."

Over my dead body will he leave before I have said what I need to say. "I made chocolate chip cookies. They should still be warm. There's a plate in the kitchen and a glass of milk with your name on it." I know that's all the incentive he needs.

"I'm starving! Thanks, Mom." He kisses my cheek before racing down the hallway. A smile ghosts over my mouth as I watch my youngest, but it quickly fades. What is going to have to happen will upset him, and I hate that for all my kids. Fuck Curtis. This is all his fault. Wrenching the door open, I storm outside, in search of my errant husband.

"Where'd you think you're going?" I snap as Curtis strides from the garage toward his Mercedes. He took West's truck camping last night, but clearly that's not good enough for his whore.

"None of your business." He shoves past me and climbs into his car.

Pulling the photo I kept from Vander's stash out of the back pocket of my skinny jeans, I slap it against the driver's side window before he can take off.

His nostrils flare as he stares at the picture, but it does the trick. Killing the engine, he gets out. "Where the hell did you get that?" he snarls. No apology. No excuses. No consideration for how it must have felt to see that.

"I'm not doing this out here," I say, glancing around. A couple of our neighbors are mowing their front lawns, and some are out walking and biking with their kids. They aren't paying us attention yet, and I would like to keep it that way. "Your study. Now."

I stomp back inside with his heavy footsteps following behind me.

After he steps foot in the study, I close and lock the door. I

Always Meant to Be

whirl around and accost him. "I agreed to this farce for the kids because I thought we decided it would derail West and Stella to discover the truth when they're at such pivotal moments in their lives." I shove the photo in his face. "This is *not* protecting our children!" I work hard to keep my voice low. It's not easy when I want to shout and scream and slap the shit out of his remorseless face. He pushes my hand away, and I crumple the photo in my fist. "Neither is taking your whore to dinner in our fucking town where you were spotted!" Crossing my arms over my chest, I glare at him. "I'm not having West and Stella find out like this. I'm filing for divorce in the morning."

"No." He shakes his head. "I'm not messing up West's chance of a college football career and potentially an NFL one."

"You should've thought of that before you practically fucked your slut in public!"

"She's not a slut or a whore. She's actually a really nice girl."

"Good for her. I don't give a flying fuck."

He smirks, and I want to grab the framed wedding photo from his desk and smash it into his smug face. "Jealousy is very unbecoming on you, Kendall."

I flip him the middle finger, beyond enraged. "News flash, asshole. I'm not jealous. She is welcome to your disloyal ass. All I care about is protecting my children. You should want that too." I unfurl the crumpled photo, thrusting it in his face again. "Do you think your kids would want anything to do with you if they saw that?"

Fear flashes across his face for an instant before he hides it. "You wouldn't hurt them like that."

Arrogant jerk. The truth is, I will never show my kids those photos. It would devastate them, but Curtis doesn't need to know that. "I will hurt them if it's for their own good. I won't have you make a fool of me or them by flaunting your current fuck buddy around town in front of everyone." I prod my finger in his chest. "This is how it's going to go down. We'll keep up this charade for Thanksgiving and West's birthday, and then we'll tell them we are divorcing. You can move out the morning after West's party."

He barks out a laugh. "You don't get to call the shots, and I'm not leaving my kids."

Has he always been this stupid, or is this development new? "You're the one who wanted to wait to divorce. I agreed because I thought we were on the same page. This is not acceptable to me, and I won't put up with it. You either do as I ask, or I'll tell West and Stella the truth. The kids won't want anything to do with you if they see these photos. You heard what they said." I wave the crumpled picture in his face, knowing it will irritate him. "I have more where this came from, and I *will* show them to the kids if you even attempt to cross me."

Vander was right after all—they have come in useful.

"They will hate you for life, and I won't lift a damn finger to change their minds," I add.

"You agreed divorcing now would derail their futures, so how is showing them those photos any different?" he yells. "Let's just stick to our agreement. I'll be discreet. I won't go out in town. They won't find out."

Unbelievable. He won't even end it for his kids. I have always known Curtis was prone to selfishness, but this proves it unconditionally. I narrow my eyes to slits. "Don't you fucking shout at me or try to feed me lies, you deceitful prick! The only person you care about is yourself. If you truly cared about protecting your kids, you would cut that slut loose."

"This has got nothing to do with Ingrid, and I'm not ending things. It's serious."

His words hurt, which I'm sure was the intention. All it does is strengthen my resolve. "There's no way I can pretend when I hate your fucking guts. I can't even look at you, and your touch makes my skin crawl. We can't put on a show. It won't work. The kids will see straight through it, and that will only hurt them worse in the long run." I have been thinking about the things June said, and she's right. Staying with Curtis —and attempting to live a lie—will only hurt them more. I firmly believe this is the better route to take. No matter what way we do it, there will never be a right time to tell our children we are getting a divorce. "I refuse to lie to them," I continue. "We will just get through the next week, and then we'll tell them."

"I don't agree to this." He glowers at me.

"I don't care." I smirk in his direction. "And you can't stop me. We are getting divorced now, and you are moving out. If you refuse to play ball, I'll be forced to use these photos."

"You won't. You're bluffing."

He's right. I am. I would die before I let the kids see those pictures. As much as I hate Curtis, he is still their father, and I won't interfere in their relationship with him. There are lots of challenging times ahead, but that is one of the biggest challenges—keeping my personal opinions to myself and not letting how I feel about him influence how my kids handle things. "Am I?" My brows lift. "You underestimate how much I loathe you, Curtis. Go ahead. Call my bluff. You're the one who'll suffer the consequences."

"You're such a fucking bitch! How I managed to stay married to you this long is a fucking miracle."

"Touché, darling." Sarcasm drips from my tone.

A muscle grinds in his jaw, and it feels good to have the upper hand. "Fine. You've made your point. We'll do it your way, but if you even think about showing those photos to the kids, I will make it my goal to ruin your life. I will come after you with everything and leave you with nothing." I'm sure he wishes he could do that, but it isn't the way the law works. He stalks off, stopping at the door to glare at me again. "I'm on a business trip Monday and Tuesday, but I think I'll get an early start."

"What a super idea!" I say, letting my grin run free. "Good riddance!" I add when he wrangles the door open, almost yanking it off the hinges. "Tell your little girlfriend I wish her good luck because she's going to need it."

Chapter Twenty

Kendall

I take some vacation time from work this week, making the best use of it while Curtis is away, transforming the master bedroom into my ideal sanctuary. I completely gut the room, replacing all the furniture, repainting the walls a dusky pink, and installing the plush gray carpet I have always wanted. My new four-poster bed has flimsy white curtains and six-hundred-thread-count Egyptian cotton bed linen. The dazzling white sheets and pillowcases have a thin gray border running around the edge, and it's crisp, fresh, and sophisticated. A myriad of pink, gray, and white cushions adorn the bed, contrasting beautifully with the gray-patterned drapes covering the window.

In the corner, I replaced the couch with a large white leather recliner and stacked white bookshelves around it. A tall reading lamp, some patterned cushions, and a mini refrigerator complete my new reading nook. Inspirational quotes in silver frames line the side wall, but I have purposely left the other wall free because I plan to buy one of Vander's paintings to hang there.

I have plans to remodel the closet, and I want to install a dressing table with an LED mirror, but that will have to wait until after the holidays because I couldn't find any contractors available to complete the job on such short notice, no matter how much of Curtis's money I offered them.

A thick padlock is secured to the inside of the bedroom door, and I moved all of Curtis's things to the guest bedroom. He can sleep there until he moves out next week. When Stella asked what was going on, I lied and said her daddy's snoring was keeping me up at night and it's best if we slept apart for now. I'm not sure if she bought it, and I hate lying to her, but my friends are right—there is no way I can continue to share a bed with a man I despise. I'm liable to strangle him in his sleep, and I'd rather not spend the rest of my life behind bars because Curtis Hawthorne isn't worth it.

An evil grin creeps over my mouth every time I think of Curtis's reaction when he returns home and sees what I have done. I am clinging to my anger now and using it to propel me into action. My despicable husband is not playing me any longer, and it's time to redress the balance.

The results of my medical screening came back, and thankfully, I'm clean. It was so humiliating completing the form at my ob-gyn's, especially since Dr. Leo is the doctor I went to when I was pregnant with Ridge. But I had to put my embarrassment aside and remember I'm not the one who looks like a piece of shit in this scenario. I won't take any risks with my health, period, and I needed to know if Curtis had passed any diseases to me. At least that is one less thing to worry about.

The front door slams; there's a loud thud in the hall and then the sounds of racing footsteps bounding up the stairs. Wiping my hands down the front of my apron, I check that I set the timer on the stove before stepping out into the hallway to investigate. Schools end early today because it's Thanksgiving

Always Meant to Be

tomorrow and the start of a four-day, long weekend. I collected Ridge earlier, and I know he's up in his bedroom playing X-box, so it's either West or Stella who just came in. Spying the duffel bag dumped in the hall, I confirm it's my son. He's been in a bad mood all week, and I've been feeling guilty because of Saturday night. This is the exact scenario I was trying to avoid.

Vander has sent me a few text messages I haven't replied to because I would rather speak to him in person. I half expected him to show up here, but he hasn't. Things weren't left on the best of terms with us, and I regret I was so angry with him. He shouldn't have gone behind my back, and I was right to be mad at him for blatantly ignoring my wishes, but the photos were a game changer. They gave me some bargaining power, and he's the reason I was able to instruct my attorney to draw up the divorce papers on Monday.

Pushing thoughts of Vander aside, for now, I head up the stairs to talk to my eldest son. "Knock, knock," I say, peeking my head through his door. West is sprawled out on his bed, on his stomach, with a pillow over his head. Entering his room, I close the door and walk over to him. He removes the pillow from his head as I perch on the edge of the bed. I ruffle his hair as he twists onto his side, looking at me with a helpless expression. "You know I'm here if you want to talk, and a problem shared—"

"Is a problem halved," he finishes for me. "Grandma Reed was a smart woman. I wish I got the chance to know her."

My mom died when West was three, and he doesn't remember her or my father, who passed a year later. My parents had me when they were in their forties, and I was their only child. Growing up a rebellious teenager in that household was a strange experience, but Mom was always full of wisdom and never quick to judge. I miss her every day. "Me too, son. She would have loved you." My parents would have been in their late seventies now if Mom hadn't died of breast cancer and a drunk driver hadn't mowed my father down and killed him.

"Women are so confusing." West sighs, flopping on his back and staring at the ceiling.

"Tell me what's troubling you." I pull my legs up onto the bed and prop my back against the headrest.

West pulls himself upright to sit alongside me, and I wait for him to continue. "Hazel and I had a fight."

I hate I have to pretend I didn't know. "Do you want to tell me about it?"

He angles his head, and his big blue eyes stare at me. "Promise not to get mad?"

I cup his handsome face, brushing wayward strands of his dirty-blond hair off his forehead. "When have you known me to get mad at you?" I work hard to never lose my temper with the kids or ever raise my voice. I'm not saying I'm a saint. There have been occasions where I've lost it, but it's not the norm.

"You flipped out that time I was hitting golf balls in the backyard and broke the kitchen window."

"You scared the shit out of me, West. If I hadn't ducked in time, it could have seriously injured me."

"True." A mischievous grin dances across his mouth.

I smile as I remember him as a little boy. He was constantly getting into mischief, and I could always tell by the naughty grin on his face. "If you need to discuss something serious, we can discuss it like adults." I rub his cheek before dropping my hand to my lap. "You're going to be eighteen next week." Tears stab my eyes, but they are happy, nostalgic tears this time. "I can't believe you're all grown up." Leaning in, I kiss his brow. "I hope you know how proud I am of you. Every day, I count my blessings I have you for a son."

"Ditto, Mom." He wraps his arms around me. "I always

Always Meant to Be

knew you were the best, but when I look at what Van has to deal with, I know it for sure."

"Yeah." I sigh as we ease out of our embrace. "Poor Vander doesn't have it easy."

"Oh, by the way, he told me to tell you they'll be here tomorrow. Him and Diana."

I had assumed when I didn't hear anything it meant they weren't coming. I will have more than enough food, so it's not that big of a deal, but I don't want things to be awkward. Things are already going to be tense as hell without adding another source of tension. I decide to go over and see him tonight to make amends. "Oh, good."

"Thank you for inviting them." West rests his head back and takes my hand in his. "I see how you have tried to help him over the years, and that speaks volumes about the kind of person you are." He eyeballs me with a glint in his eye. "Does Dad know Diana will be joining us?"

"I'll tell him when he gets home later." He won't be in the best mood after getting served with divorce papers today and then discovering I've moved all of his things to one of the spare bedrooms. He can't stand Diana Henley, and I can't wait to bury the knife in deeper. "Now, tell me what's going on. Is everything okay with you and Hazel?"

His Adam's apple jumps in his throat. He bites on his lower lip as he stares at me. "We had a pregnancy scare."

My heart lurches to my toes and back up to my head before going for another spin. I'm not sure what he sees on my face, but it's enough to warrant reassurance.

He squeezes my hand. "It's okay. It was a false alarm. Hazel isn't pregnant."

I am relieved. She is only seventeen, and West is just turning eighteen. I don't want history repeating itself even if that sounds hypocritical. I know Hazel wants to be a vet and

West has his football dream. I want them to be able to pursue their dreams, not be forced to abandon them. "But she thought she was."

He nods. "We were scared, and I was fucking ecstatic when the test was negative. But she freaked out when I admitted it, and now she won't talk to me."

That doesn't sound like Hazel. "What exactly did you say?"

He scratches the back of his head with his free hand. "I might have cursed a bit and then said I was glad it hadn't ruined my football career before it had begun."

Yeah, that'll do it. "What did Hazel say?"

"That football was all I cared about and I was selfish not to consider how it would've impacted her plans. She also said she wouldn't have been unhappy if the test had been positive but, clearly, I would have. According to her, that shows how temporary I consider us to be." His brow puckers as he stares at me. "I tried to backtrack, but she didn't want to hear it, and now she's ignoring my texts, and she won't speak to me in class. I went over to her house after school, and she refused to see me. I know I put my foot in it, but she's completely overreacting."

Definitely, but emotions are heightened when you're a teen, and I remember plenty of times where I overanalyzed things that didn't warrant such scrutiny. "Hazel loves you. She adores you." I see the way they look at one another, and it warms my heart. "She will come around. She just needs time. I suggest you back off for a few days. Maybe send her a text and let her know you love her and you're going to give her some space. Ask her to call you when she feels up to talking." I kiss his cheek and slide off the bed.

"Should I send her flowers?" West asks, peering up at me. "Van suggested it, but I don't know if Hazel would even appreciate the gesture. I can't seem to say or do anything right."

I crouch down so I'm looking at his face. "I'll let you in on a secret. Every woman loves flowers. Any girl who says she doesn't is lying. You can never go wrong with flowers. I think Van knows what he's doing."

"Huh." West grabs his cell off his bedside table. "Weird for a guy who doesn't do relationships."

Weird indeed.

"Kendall, wait up!"

I slam to a halt as Vander's deep voice washes over me like a security blanket. Shoving my hands into the pockets of my windbreaker, I turn around, stepping off the path to the side so I'm not in anyone's way. The park is quieter than usual this afternoon with only a handful of joggers and people out walking. I expect most families are at home getting ready for tomorrow. I bounce on my feet to keep warm as I watch Van approach with his long-legged stride and fierce determination etched on his face.

Sweatpants manufacturers should approach him to model their product because he's rocking the hell out of the black sweatpants and matching hoodie he is wearing. He has the hood pulled up over his messy dark hair, and his hands are hidden in the pockets of his pants. Black-and-white Nike high tops complete his effortless look.

He is so hot, and I honestly don't know how I'm the one who has caught his eye.

"Hey." His eyes quickly sweep over my body when he stops in front of me. "Cute yoga pants." His lips twitch as he takes in the multicolored stretchy leggings I'm wearing.

"They were a birthday gift from Stella," I admit, lifting one shoulder. "Walk with me?" He falls into step beside me. "I'm glad you caught me. I wanted to talk to you before tomorrow." I look up at him. "We need to clear the air."

"I know you were pissed, and you had every right to be, but I was only trying to help."

I don't know what he hoped to achieve with the stunt, but I can't be mad at him any longer. "I know you were, and I was too harsh. I shouldn't have said some of the things I said. I'm sorry if I hurt your feelings." I glance up at him. "I was angry and embarrassed, but that's not on you."

"You have nothing to be embarrassed about. He's the embarrassment. He doesn't realize how lucky he is."

I don't think Curtis ever felt like that, but that's neither here nor there, and I'm done discussing my husband. "Things are going to be difficult over the next few months, and I need you to promise me you won't interfere. I also need you to promise you won't ever tell West what you saw." It's going to be hard enough for the kids as it is. They don't need to know all the seedy details.

"I don't want to tell him, but I don't want him finding out the hard way or discovering I knew and said nothing. If the tables were turned, I'd want him to tell me."

"I agree with all of that, but I need you to trust I'm handling it the best way I can."

His eyes penetrate mine. "What don't I know?"

I swing my arms at my sides as I pick up my pace. "Things are in motion." I'm being vague on purpose because I can't tell him I'm divorcing Curtis before I tell my kids. Vander is already hiding enough from West. "I can't tell you yet, and I hate that I have to ask you to lie to your best friend. You are already keeping one big secret from him, and now this."

"No offense, Kendall, but that's my call to make, not yours. I'm not planning on saying anything to West about his dad, but

Always Meant to Be

I can't promise that will always be the case. Haven't we already been over this? What's the point in repeating ourselves?"

I jerk to a halt. "The point is, I can't spend time with you if you won't butt out!"

His eyes widen, and a big-ass smile materializes on his face. "You still want to spend time with me?"

I chew on the inside of my mouth as I start walking again. "We shouldn't. What happened Saturday night proves us hanging out is risky."

"But you were enjoying yourself, right?" He takes my elbow, forcing me to stop. "I didn't just imagine it. We had a good time."

Since Saturday night, I have been trying to convince myself to let him go. Believing the West incident was a sign that continuing this friendship will only end in disaster. But, for reasons even I don't understand, I can't let him go.

I should, but I can't.

"We did," I reluctantly admit. "But West almost caught us. What would you have told him if he did discover us together?"

"The truth." He tucks a stray piece of my hair back into my ponytail. "That nothing happened. I cooked you dinner, and we talked about philosophy over a glass of wine and a beer." He shoves his hand back in the pocket of his sweats. "He wouldn't have read any more into it. His brain would never go there. You're making this out to be something more than it is."

I arch a brow because come on. He knows I know he still wants more than friendship, and we have admitted our feelings are stronger than that. I honestly don't know what I'm doing or why I can't just shut this down—whatever the hell *this* is.

His lips twitch. "Focus on the facts, Kendall. Nothing has happened. It's innocent."

Brushing his lips against mine was hardly innocent

although it stopped short of a kiss. "Let's not kid ourselves. We both know our feelings for one another are far from innocent."

He leans down, pressing his mouth up against my ear. "But we haven't acted on those feelings," he whispers, and I shiver all over. "*Yet*." He straightens up and flashes me a grin. "Whenever you change your mind, I'll be more than happy to act out my every fantasy with you."

My jaw slackens, and my mouth drops open. He chuckles before waggling his fingers and jogging away, leaving me dumbstruck and tingling with anticipation in the middle of the park.

Chapter Twenty-One

Vander

"Are you out of the doghouse yet?" I ask West as we sit on the large deck that wraps around the rear of his house, drinking beer, while Stella, Kendall, my mom, and West's grandmother put the finishing touches to our Thanksgiving dinner. Ridge is watching TV in the game room, and Curtis is with his father in the study, smoking cigars and drinking bourbon. It'll be a miracle if I get through this dinner without ramming my fist in his face, but I promised Kendall I wouldn't interfere, and I'm determined to keep the promise this time.

"Not fully, but I think it'll be okay." He takes a swig from his bottle. "You were right. The flowers helped."

I grin. "Told ya." I went all out and gave Kendall the biggest bouquet of pink and purple flowers. It's Thanksgiving, so I can get away with it. The look on Curtis's face was priceless, but he had to suck it up as his parents were watching. I asked Mom to hand Kendall the champagne and chocolates so it didn't look too obvious. "Women love flowers."

"That's what Mom said. Anyway, Hazel called to thank me

for them. She said she loved me and she was just all up in her feelings. We're going to hang out tomorrow."

"Good. I'm sick of looking at your mopey, heartbroken face."

He thumps me in the arm. "I missed her like crazy. It kills me to go more than a few hours without seeing her, holding her, or talking to her. Honestly, this past week, it has felt like I was missing a part of my heart."

"I know the feeling," I blurt without thinking.

He sits up straighter, eyeing me curiously. "You do?"

Goddamn it, Vander. I'm a fucking moron. I can't backpedal, so I'll have to make a joke of it instead. "Of course, I don't!" I punch him in the arm. "I'm just messing with ya. What the hell would I know about missing a girl?"

I could write the book on it.

"Truth, dude." He smirks before taking a swig of his beer. "One of these days, you'll know, and then you'll get it."

I shrug, drinking my beer and keeping my mouth shut before I put my foot in it again.

"Things aren't good at home," he adds, lowering his tone and glancing around. "My parents had a blazing argument last night, and I think they're going to split up. Things have been super tense since our conversation, and I'm beginning to think my dad fed me a pile of horseshit."

I wish I could confirm he did, but I can't involve myself without losing Kendall. And I meant what I said—I couldn't hurt my friend like that either. Unless there is no other option. West will find out in time, and when he does, I'll be there to support him through it. I still don't understand why Kendall hasn't kicked Curtis's cheating ass to the curb because she's no pushover. But I know she has an agenda and I need to be patient. "What was the fight about?" I probe.

"I'm not sure, but Stella thinks it's because she kicked him

Always Meant to Be

out of the bedroom and moved all of his things to the guest bedroom."

I silently fist pump the air and cheer Kendall on. I don't know what she has planned, but I pray she executes it fast because it will mean one less hurdle to jump in convincing her she belongs with me.

Dinner was bearable but only just. Kendall and Curtis put on a show, which seemed obvious to me, but I'm the only one around the table in the know. Mom behaved, but I knew she would. She has mastered the art of looking sober while alcohol sluices through her veins, and she's had enough practice making small talk at my father's social events to sail through dinner without raising eyebrows. I notice Curtis giving both of us the stink eye when he thinks no one is looking, and I get an enormous thrill out of knowing I bug him.

It's not the first time I've met his parents—West's grandparents and Kendall's in-laws—and they are nice people. They are always pleasant and take the time to talk with me. I have no clue how they managed to produce such a disappointing offspring. I bet they'll be disgusted when they find out what he's done.

Per the house rules, West, Ridge, and I do the cleanup. His grandpa helps to clear the table, but Curtis doesn't lift a finger, which is typical.

I'm in the kitchen alone, scrubbing the last pot, when Kendall walks in. I guess sending out juju vibes to the universe worked after all. I finish washing the pot and set it on the drainboard, before turning around. "I was hoping to catch you alone," she says, smiling as she removes something from one of the drawers. "This is for you." She hands me a gold-wrapped package.

"What is it?"

"Open it and see." Her tinkling laughter is music to my ears. I eagerly tear at the paper, extracting the two cookbooks. "I was going to loan you mine, but I figured you could use your own set. Those are the two most recent Keaton Kennedy releases. I skimmed through them, and there are some great recipes in there."

I can hardly speak over the messy ball of emotion clogging my throat. "Thank you," I croak, setting the books down on the counter.

"Hey." She casts a quick glance over her shoulder at the closed door before stepping up to me. Her fingers brush against my cheek. "What's wrong?"

"Nothing." I hold her hand against my face. "Absolutely nothing. I'm just overwhelmed you got these for me." Her features soften, and if I'm not mistaken, that's adoration I see written on her face.

"It's only a couple of books."

"It's the thought behind the purchase that counts most." God, I want to kiss her so badly in this moment. She has no idea how much she means to me because the words don't exist to adequately describe it. "You listen to me. You see me. You support my passions. You make my life better."

"Vander." Her breathy tone sends all the blood rushing south in my body, and I'm already semi-hard. Tears glisten in her eyes. "I could say the same of you."

We stare at one another, conveying everything we can't say with our eyes. The craving to hold her is almost more than I can bear. Every part of me strains to connect with her. I don't know how much longer I can restrain myself. Not when every cell in my body is screaming for her touch. "You belong with me," I whisper, clasping her hand tight to my face, unwilling to let her go.

"You belong with someone your own age," she counters after a few intense beats. She pulls her hand away from my face and averts her gaze. "You deserve to find someone young and pretty without any complications. I want you to be happy. I want that for you so much."

"My happy place is you." I reel her into my body, clamping my hands on her lower back to stop her from wriggling free. "*You* make me happy. I don't want any other girl. I never have, and I never will. I only want you."

"Vander, please." Tipping her chin up, she stares at me with tears in her eyes. "Please forget about me and find someone else."

I shake my head. "It won't happen. I can't tell my heart how to feel." Taking her hand, I place it over my chest, hoping she can feel the steady thrumming of my heart. "This is yours, Kendall, whether you want it or not. It doesn't matter if you don't claim it, it will always beat only for you."

"I wish so many things were different," she whispers as a tear rolls down her face. "I wish I could be everything you want me to be, but I don't see how it's possible." She shucks out of my hold, circling her arms around herself.

"Let's not set any parameters. Let's just see where things take us. I'm here for you. As your friend or more. You call the shots, and I'm right here." I slide the keyring out of my pocket. "I have something for you too." Taking her hand, I place the keyring on her palm and curl her fingers around it. "That's a key fob to open the back gate and a key to the carriage house. I want you to be able to come and go freely. If you need a place to escape to, come to me."

She stares at me intently, worrying her lower lip between her teeth before releasing it. She opens her mouth to say something when the door swings open, and I instantly remove my hand from hers. Curtis steps into the room, his gaze narrowing suspiciously as he looks from me to her. "Why is the door closed?"

"We were just finishing the cleanup," Kendall says, spinning around to face her husband. "If you were finally getting your lazy ass in gear, you're too late to help. It's all done now."

I see red when he walks up and slides his arm around her shoulder, pulling her into his side. "I love this newfound sense of humor." He swats her ass, and I'm seconds away from punching his lights out. Pressing his mouth to her ear, he says in a tone that's clearly audible, "It turns me on like you wouldn't believe."

"Curtis!" Shock mixes with rage as she steps out from under her husband's arm. "We have company. Behave yourself."

I can't watch this shit go down. I need to get out of here. Ignoring Curtis, I smile at his wife as I grab the cookbooks from the counter. "Thanks for the books and for dinner, Kendall. It was delicious, like always."

"Thank you for coming, and thanks again for the gifts."

"It's the least we could do after all the effort you went to." I stare pointedly at Curtis, who has yet to offer one word of gratitude to his wife for everything she did to ensure we all had a great Thanksgiving. "I'll get Mom, and we'll be on our way."

"I'd offer to give you a bottle of wine to take home," Curtis says, "but your mom drank us dry." A sneering laugh accompanies his spiteful words, but I ignore him and stride out of the kitchen, needing to put as much distance between us before I do something I'll regret.

Always Meant to Be

"What are you doing here?" I ask later that night when my bedroom door swings open and my father steps inside my room. He said he was spending the holidays in Denver, so we weren't expecting to see him at all this weekend. I planned on sleeping at the main house, to keep an eye on Mom, and now I'm glad I did. I don't trust my father in the same house as my mother. It's not like he has any real incentive to keep her alive. *Why else does he support her addiction by keeping a fully stocked liquor cabinet and a doctor on call to fill repeat prescriptions when needed?* It's like he wants her to drink herself into an early grave or OD on prescription meds.

"Need I remind you I live here every time I set foot in my own goddamn house?" he barks.

Setting my sketch pad aside, I climb to my feet and stand, loving that I'm taller than him by a few inches. It always makes me feel superior to look down at him, and I know it irritates him to no end that I'm taller, broader, stronger, and hotter. "What do you want?"

"Miles Turner phoned to invite us to dinner at his house tomorrow night. I told him we'd be there at eight."

Ah, so that's why he came home. "I'm not going." I would rather remove all my teeth with pliers than subject myself to Gayle Turner and her pompous parents.

"Where is your mother?" he asks, purposely cracking his knuckles as he drills me with a pointed look.

And there's the reminder as to why he keeps Mom alive. If she dies or he divorces her, he has nothing to hold over me. Familiar helplessness thunders through my veins. I badly need to hit something or someone. It seems I'm truly being tested today. "Fine," I grit out. "I'll go."

He chuckles, and I shoot daggers at him. "Pleasure doing business with you, son."

I throw my sneaker at the door after he leaves, emitting an

exasperated roar as I strip out of my clothes and change into my running gear. I need to let off steam before I self-combust.

I head out into the dark streets and pound the roads, only returning after I've expended all my pent-up aggravations and my legs are close to collapsing. I'm dripping with sweat as I climb into the shower and attempt to wash away the frustrations of the day. After I have changed into clean sweats, I slip my slides on and go in search of Mom.

I find her in the theater room, passed out on one of the reclining chairs with her fingers still clutching a near-empty vodka bottle. Prying it from her clutches, I set it down on the ground and grab her cell phone before scooping her into my arms. I carry her to her bedroom, hating how light she feels in my arms. At least she had a good home-cooked meal today, and I watched to ensure she ate a decent amount.

I slide her under the comforter in her dress and pantyhose, tucking the covers around her, before I head back downstairs to fetch her a glass of water and some pain pills.

I leave them on her bedside table, and I'm just about to exit her room when her cell vibrates with an incoming call, drawing my attention. Snatching it up, I swipe Mom's finger across the screen and answer the call from her one and only friend. "Dana," I whisper as I creep out of Mom's room. "It's Vander. Mom's sleeping."

"Hey, Van. I am glad you answered. I've been calling your mom for days."

Dana was Mom's best friend in college, and she's the only one she has kept in contact with over the years. Last I heard, she was living in Europe with her second husband, and Mom hasn't seen her in years. "I'll get her to call you back tomorrow."

"Please do. I wanted to let her know I got divorced and I'm back in the US. I bought a house in Vermont, and I was hoping she would come and visit me. We have a lot of catching up to do."

An idea forms in my mind. If I can get Mom away from Dad for a while, he can't force me to date Gayle Turner while he works to win her father's account. "That sounds like a great idea, Dana," I say. "Mom could use a vacation. Send me the details, and I'll organize everything. I'll message you with the time her plane lands."

Chapter Twenty-Two

Vander

"Why aren't you dressed?" Dad asks, his nostrils flaring as he barges his way into my room the following night. I'm sitting at my desk in jeans and a hoodie, anticipating the moment he'd come looking for me. "And where is your mother? We can't be late."

"Mom's on vacation," I say, smothering a smile as I stand. "And I'm not going. You can tell Miles Turner to go fuck himself." I straighten up Dad's tie before he can stop me. "You should bring your latest whore. Give her as a peace offering to Gayle's dad. I'm sure that'll soothe his ruffled feathers."

Dad shoves me away, and I laugh. "What did you do, you little punk?" His hands reach to wrap around my neck, but I grab him by the wrists with one hand while I land a solid punch to his solar plexus with the other. A strangled sound rips from his throat as he doubles over, clutching his stomach.

"I swear it's like you want me to give you another black eye," I taunt. "Your last one has only just healed."

"Where. Is. Your. Mother?" he growls, straightening up and rubbing his stomach. His carefully styled dark hair is all messed up, and his freshly pressed white shirt is wrinkled. I get an inordinate thrill from seeing him disheveled, knowing it will piss him off.

"Someplace you won't find her." I made sure of it. I enlisted Jimmy to hire the private jet in his name, and West paid for it, using funds I wired to his bank account. I had to dip into my inheritance to cover the plane cost and to transfer money to Dana so Mom has enough to live on. I cut up all of Mom's cards and made her promise not to go near her normal bank account. Dana is going to set her up with a new one on Monday.

I took a risk and filled Mom's friend in on everything during our hour-long phone conversation last night. It seems Mom has confided some things in her over the years, but Dana didn't realize it was this bad. Her first husband was abusive, so she has some experience she can relate to. I didn't hold back in explaining how bad Mom's addiction is, and she has promised to talk to Mom and try to get her to agree to go to rehab. Dana said Mom could stay with her for as long as she needs, and I'm hoping she'll stay in Vermont until it's time for me to leave for Connecticut. After that, it's up to Mom. For now, this is the best thing I can do to help her.

Maybe Dana will be able to get through to her where I have failed.

"That's what you think." Dad sneers as he pulls out his cell phone.

"You won't be able to locate her through her cell. She left it behind." I smashed it to shit and gave her a burner cell instead because I have always suspected Dad had a tracking device on it. I bought myself a burner too, purely so I can use it to call Mom. I'm keeping it hidden under one of the floorboards at the carriage house. Protecting Mom's location is of paramount importance because I don't trust Dad won't kill her for this even though I'm the one who forced her to leave.

Always Meant to Be

If looks could kill, I'd be dead a hundred times by now. My father is bristling with rage. His entire body is shaking with anger as he glares at me. He knows he can't do anything about it. If he comes at me, I will beat the shit out of his abusive ass. If he tries to retaliate, he knows he will push me away for good and all of his future plans for the legal practice will go up in flames. Perhaps it's ill-advised to push him like this when I don't have an offer from Yale yet, but the opportunity presented itself to get Mom out of state, and I jumped on it.

I have six months until I graduate, so I just need to ride it out until then.

"You'll regret this, boy," Dad says, waving his finger at me. "No one gets the better of Gregory Henley, especially not my own flesh and blood." He stalks out of my room, and I watch him leave ten minutes later, from the living room, glad Mom is out of his reach but scared I may have poked a beast I have no chance of caging.

I return from the boxing club late on Saturday night and park my truck alongside the carriage house, peeking at the bright lights in my upper floor studio with a lump in my throat. I know I didn't leave the lights on before I went out, which means I have an intruder. It could be Kendall. I gave her a key so she could come over anytime, and I wouldn't have an issue with her being in my studio, but I don't think she would enter it alone. Which means it's my father.

I scramble out of the truck as that thought lodges in my brain and burst into the house. Dumping my bag on the floor, I take the stairs two at a time up to the second level.

After we moved here and I discovered this place, I claimed it for my own and converted the entire second floor into one large workspace where I can paint and draw to my heart's content.

I slam to a halt at the sight of Kendall—sitting on the floor, in the center of my art studio, surrounded by tons of canvases, in various stages of completion, some hanging on the walls and others propped against it—with the most awestruck expression on her face.

Hearing my footsteps, she looks up at me. Her eyes are swimming in emotion, and my heart slows down when I realize there is no threat and speeds up as I acknowledge what she now knows. "Vander," she rasps, her throat clogged with emotion. "Why didn't you tell me?"

I drop down on the floor beside her, mirroring her cross-legged position. I gulp over my nerves. "I didn't want to scare you."

Her gaze flits to the paintings hanging around the walls.

Every single one is of her.

"They are all of me," she whispers, like it's a secret. And I suppose it is. Only it's our secret now.

"You're my muse, Kendall," I truthfully admit. "You inspire me like no one else ever has or ever will." My fingers wind through her long hair as she tips her chin up to look at me. She is shielding nothing from me now, and I let everything show on my face.

I love her so much, and I am tired of denying it.

"But it's more than that," I continue. "You are all I see." My fingers move from her hair to her face as I cup her cheek. "Every time I take a new canvas out, your face is the first image that springs to mind." I emit a deep chuckle. "If I didn't need a diverse portfolio, and to expand my skill set for Yale, every painting in this room would be of you."

"Who else has seen these?"

"No one." I know why she asked. "I keep my studio locked

most times. Even when I'm using it, and I never let any of my friends up here." To be fair, they rarely ask. West is the only exception. He cares about me, and he knows how much is resting on my acceptance to Yale, so he has asked to see my work a few times, but I always put him off. "You're the only other person who has a key."

"I'm so sorry, Vander. I shouldn't have come up here without asking you first. It's just I was hoping to buy one of your pictures to hang on my bedroom wall, and temptation got the best of me when I was waiting for you to come home."

"You don't need to apologize. That rule doesn't apply to you." I stroke her cheek with my thumb. "I don't want there to be any secrets between us."

"Me either." Scrambling to her feet, she takes my hand and pulls me up. "Which is why I want to know about this one," she says, dragging me toward the picture that replicates the vision I see in my dreams. Her fingers thread through mine as we both stare at the drawing. It's the biggest canvas I have ever painted —a long, rectangular one that gave me enough scope to depict the Egyptian river, the pyramid in the background, and the town built along one side of the riverbank.

With her free hand, she reaches out, tracing over the couple embracing in the water. "This is going to sound insane," she softly admits, her gaze glued to the painting as she speaks. "But this scene looks familiar." Her words send a jolt straight through my heart, buoyed by a fresh layer of hope. Her brow scrunches in concentration as her fingers move over the picture in a slow sweep. "My heart beat like crazy when I first saw it, and I swear images flashed in my mind." She glances up at me, showcasing a faint blush on her cheeks.

"What images?" I squeeze her hand as butterflies swoop low in my belly.

"That man," she whispers, stepping closer to me. "I saw his

face. Felt the warmth of his adoration and the intensity of his love." Her cheeks darken from pink to red. "Looking at his face was like looking into a mirror of my soul." She slams a hand over her heart. "He is the other part of me. I just know it. A lifetime of memories flooded my mind out of nowhere." She shakes her head, sending waves of soft blonde hair cascading over her shoulders. "I felt him in here. Like he's ingrained inside me, but —" Tears well in her eyes, and I clutch her waist as she lowers her gaze to the floor.

I am scarcely breathing, wound tight in anticipation. "What, Kendall? What else did you see and feel?"

"This is nuts," she whispers, peering up at me as she presses her body up against mine and grabs a handful of my shirt. I'm not even sure if she's aware she's doing it. I'm glad I showered at the club today. That I don't smell like ass.

"Say it." My hands slide around her waist and palm her lower back as I press her tight against me. "Tell me."

Her eyes probe mine for a few seconds, and I wait with bated breath for her to reveal what I have figured out these past few months. "It was you," she finally admits. "He didn't look like you, but it was you."

"It *was* me. It *is* me, and she is you."

"What's going on, Vander?" Her fist tightens in my shirt, and we're pressed so close she must feel my hard-on nudging her stomach.

"We never got to finish our conversation about reincarnation the other night, but I believe in it. I believe in it because I have been dreaming of that river and us for years without having any understanding of what it meant until recently."

Shock splays across her features. "The psychic saw you," she murmurs, staring deep into my eyes like I hold all the answers to the unexplainable.

I frown. "What?"

Always Meant to Be

"At the psychic night at Shirley's house, she told me she saw you. That she saw you from the first moment she met me. Dee said in every lifetime we find one another because the bond is so strong. Apparently, we always have to overcome obstacles to be together." A startled laugh bursts from her lips as a lone tear sneaks out of one eye. "This is insane, Vander. I'm an open-minded person. I'm fascinated by the things we can't explain, but this is on a whole other level. It can't be true, can it?"

I brush her tear away and rest my forehead against hers. "Is it insane?" I whisper over her lips as we stare deep into one another's eyes. "Is it really that hard to believe? I feel it, Kendall. I feel this immense draw to you. I always have. I couldn't understand it when I was a kid, but I do now."

"I feel it too."

Her breath wafts over my lips, and I'm inching past the point of no return. "I told you we were always meant to be." I remind her. "It's what I believe with everything I am."

"I'm so confused, yet I'm not at the same time." She lifts her forehead from mine while tightening her hold on my shirt. There isn't an inch of space between our bodies, and I'd challenge anyone to pry us apart in this moment. "It's the maddest feeling."

"I have this inner peace when I'm with you that is absent in all other aspects of my life. I trust in that feeling. I know it sounds nuts, but I believe it all. You are mine, and I am yours, and not even time can separate us."

"I know one way we can determine this," she says, pulling my face down closer to hers. Her blue eyes flare with heat and intent as her gaze roams from my eyes to my lips and back up again. "Kiss me, Vander. Kiss me, and prove you're my soul mate."

Chapter Twenty-Three

Vander

My heart races around my chest like a cheetah on skates as I contemplate how I'm seconds away from something my heart has desired for so long. Nervous adrenaline mixes with liquid lust as excitement builds inside me. I want to cherish this moment and never forget a single second of it.

Growing impatient, Kendall takes matters into her own hands, pulling me down as she stretches up on her tiptoes to press her lips to mine. The instant her lips glide against mine, something buried deep, deep inside me springs to life, like a dormant volcano that has suddenly erupted, gushing forth lava with gleeful enthusiasm after centuries of being restrained. It's like some inner switch has been flicked and everything that has come before is inconsequential. Nothing else matters in my world, only the woman kissing me with the same need and devotion I feel.

My arms wrap around Kendall, hauling her up off her feet as I angle my head to let her deepen the kiss. I hold her up, pressed flush against me, as we give in to our desire. Her lips are like molten chocolate moving against mine, and I want to eat them up and drink them down, gorging and feasting as if I have never eaten or drank before. Lust burns a path along my skin in every place where she's pressed against me, and I can barely control myself. My flesh is blistering, oozing with potent need, and she's the only remedy to temper the flames. I lift her up my body, and her legs automatically encircle my waist as I walk us toward the wall. Our mouths are devouring one another, our tongues dueling, and our mutual moans are dripping down our throats.

I push her against the wall and grind my erection into her pelvis as a growl rumbles from deep within me. She whimpers into my mouth, her nails digging into my scalp, as she clings to me. I nip, suck, and bite at her lips while thrusting my tongue into her mouth and rocking my hips against hers as we kiss. She's clawing at me everywhere she can reach. Fisting handfuls of my hair, dragging her fingers across my scalp, burying her nails in my shoulders, and grabbing my back through my shirt. Lifting her hips, she pivots against me, and my dick jerks behind my sweatpants, leaking precum from the tip.

Using my body to keep her flush to the wall, I move one hand lower, brushing against the soft curves and dips of her gorgeous body. I'm internally rejoicing at the way she shivers and moans at my touch. The whole time, we're kissing and kissing like we can't get enough. I know I can't. I'm terrified to stop in case it's all been a dream and I'm going to wake up and cry. Slipping my hand under the hem of her dress, I trail a path along her thigh, almost coming undone at the feel of her silky-smooth skin against my rough fingertips. My fingers brush against her panties, and she goes rigidly still underneath me.

She shoves at my shoulders, urging me to stop, and I remove my hand from under her dress as I reluctantly tear my lips from hers. "What's wrong?" I ask, reading her body language and carefully setting her feet on the ground. I might be an asshole for loving how swollen and bruised her lips look after my demanding kisses, but I can't help the surge of pride I feel.

"I can't do this." Tears leak from her eyes as she ducks down and slides out from under me. "I need to go home." She races toward the stairs, and I give chase.

"Kendall, wait. Let's talk about this. Don't run away."

"I can't do this now, Vander," she calls out, over a sob, as she flies down the stairs.

"Kendall, please. Baby, please don't leave like this," I say, hot on her heels.

She whirls around at my front door, and pain stabs me through my chest at her tear-sodden face. "This is all too much."

I move toward her, but she shakes her head and holds up a palm. "I can't make sense of any of this," she sobs, and it's killing me she won't let me comfort her. "I need time. Space to process everything." She swipes at the tears rolling down her face as she yanks the door open. "Please give me that."

Giving her time to convince herself what we just shared wasn't real isn't the best course of action, but I promised myself I wouldn't push her, and I meant it. "Okay. Take whatever time you need, but you know what's in your heart is the truth. You can't keep running from it." I can't let her go without confirming what she means to me. I need her to have no doubts in relation to where I stand. Stepping toward her, I cup her face in my hands before she can stop me. "You can't keep running from me. I love you, Kendall. I love you so fucking much. You are my entire world, and I will never give up on you." I press a fierce kiss to her lips before stepping back even though it physically pains me to do so. "If you need me, you know where to find me. I'll be waiting."

It's been one week since Kendall and I kissed and she bailed on me, and I haven't heard a peep out of her. Remaining true to my word has been torturous, but I'm giving her the space she asked for and praying she doesn't deny what we share or find other reasons not to move forward with our relationship.

Now that I have tasted her, there is no going back.

My blood is on fire.

My body is weak with need.

And my heart feels hollow without its missing part.

I crave her with a need that is possessive and instinctual, and it honestly feels like I'm going out of my mind.

Kendall has got to be feeling it too because I know I'm not alone in this.

I can't concentrate for shit this week, and West has been pestering me almost daily to tell him what's wrong. My knuckles are aching from pounding the punching bag so fiercely, but nothing takes the edge off this restlessness. My mind and body thrum with excessive energy like I've been woken from a deep slumber, and now I'm bursting with vitality. I can't shut it off, and I have barely been sleeping because I can't switch my thoughts off. Jerking off multiple times a day—always to visions of Kendall—is not enough to sate this boundless, twitchy hunger consuming me from the inside out.

I talked with Jimmy, updating him on the latest with Kendall, and he cautioned me to bide my time. To give her the space she needs to come to terms with everything. But that's easier said than done.

I need her.

I need her.

I need her.

I love her.

I love her.
I love her.

Butterflies careen around my chest as I walk toward West's house to attend his eighteenth birthday party. I'm excited to see Kendall, but I'm on edge too because I know Curtis will be here, and I'm barely holding it together as it is. My hands twitch at my sides, and I don't know how I will stop myself from reaching for her when every part of me is dying to touch her.

Here goes nothing, I think as I rap on the front door. It opens instantly, and I try not to be disappointed when I see who is greeting me. "You made it!" Stella throws herself at me, wrapping her arms around my neck and planting a loud kiss on my cheek. "West was about to send out a search party," she adds, pulling back and leaving space for me to step into the hallway. "You're the last to arrive."

"I got caught up in my studio," I truthfully admit. All week, I have been painting up a storm and adding to my considerable Kendall collection. "Lost track of time."

"You're here now. The party boy will be happy." She loops her arm through mine and drags me through the house and out to the backyard.

Kendall rented a large marquee for the night, and the party is already in full swing. Several heaters are dotted around the space, and it's warm. A band is entertaining the crowd, and the dance floor is packed with boys and girls from school throwing questionable moves. Circular tables and chairs occupy most of the rest of the space. On the left, a hot buffet is spread out along a rectangular table, and people are helping themselves to food and drink.

"Stay here for a sec," Stella says, disappearing for a short while. When she returns, she hands me a can of Dr. Pepper. "It's actually beer." She winks. "The only drinks officially on offer are water or soda because my parents aren't as cool as yours."

I stare at her like she's grown an extra head. *Is she for real?*

"Mom did go all out on the food though," she continues, babbling away. "Anyway, we got creative and replaced some soda cans with beer, and we have more booze stashed in the garden for when the oldies retire for the night." She waggles her brows. "That's when the party will really get started." She grabs my arm and pulls me forward. "Come on. West and Hazel are over here." I let her haul me toward a table at the top of the room, just at the edge of the dancing area, while I surreptitiously scan the marquee for Kendall.

"I found him," Stella says, shoving me down into an empty chair beside my best buddy. Hazel is perched on West's lap, with her arms around his neck, looking all loved up.

"It's about time, man." West lifts his arm for a knuckle touch. "It's not like you to be late."

"Gayle has only asked us about ten million times when you were getting here," Hazel adds, and I groan, swallowing a healthy mouthful of beer. I will need it to deal with her tonight.

Eyes burn into the side of my head, and I look around, my gaze instantly finding Kendall's. She's seated at the table next to us with some friends. Viola is on one side of her and June on the other. Shirley and her husband Adrian are sitting beside Viola, and all of them appear to be purposely ignoring the dickhead at the other end of the table. Curtis is talking to a couple of other neighbors, throwing back his head and laughing, like he hasn't a care in the world. I visualize slicing his head off his shoulders, and it helps to take the edge off the rage bubbling underneath the surface of my skin, but only marginally.

Kendall stares at me for a few beats before getting up and walking in my direction. She is stunning in a lacy blue dress that is fitted on top with straps that crisscross over the shoulders and a skirt that flares out from the waist, ending just at her knee. She has silver sandals on her feet, and her hair is in some kind of braided design with soft blonde waves framing her beautiful face and hanging down her back. She looks pretty and young and elegant yet sexy, in an understated way.

"Your mom is definitely a MILF," Bowie says, uncaring Kendall is in earshot. "How old was she when she had you? Like ten or something?" From the glazed look in his eyes, I can tell he's already smashed. Otherwise, he would know to keep his stupid mouth shut. "She does *not* look old enough to have an eighteen-year-old son."

"Shut the fuck up," West snaps, pointing his finger in our friend's face. "Show some respect."

"West, language," Kendall says, coming up behind me.

"You'd say worse if you heard what Bowie said," West grumbles.

"It's good to see you Vander." She leans over the back of my chair, and it takes colossal willpower not to stare down the front of her dress. "West was worried you were going to be a no-show."

I can tell from the look in her eyes she was worried about that too. Terrified what happened last week has driven me from my best friend. "I was in my studio and forgot the time. I would never miss West's birthday." I gesture around the room. "You did an awesome job. Everything looks great."

"Wait until you see the cake," Hazel says. "It's freaking awesome." She smiles over my head at Kendall. "I still can't believe you baked it. You are so talented. You should open a bakery."

Kendall's warm smile is genuine as she beams at West's suck-up of a girlfriend. "I love baking and cooking, but I have zero desire to open my own place. I don't think I could handle the stress of it. I'm content with it being a hobby."

"Speaking of cakes," Curtis says, coming up behind her. "Should we cut it now?" He slides his arm around his wife and pulls her back against his body. Kendall is stiff in his arms, but I'm probably the only one who notices.

"People are still eating. We should wait for another half hour." Her voice is clipped, strain underpinning her tone.

"Okay." He eyeballs me as he brushes some of her hair aside to kiss her neck. I want to cut his lips from his face so he never touches her with his mouth again.

West watches his parents with curious eyes while I quietly seethe when Kendall brings her hands up over Curtis's at her waist and holds on to him. She avoids looking at me, and that only pisses me off even more. I grip the edge of my chair and count to ten in my head. Anything to stop myself from lunging at him and ripping him off the woman who is *mine*.

Chapter Twenty-Four

Kendall

I don't know what Curtis is playing at, but I am going to fucking kill him for this. While he refuses to rush the divorce through, he has agreed to speak with the children tomorrow to tell them we are separating and he is moving out. He wants them to get used to the idea of us splitting up before formalizing the divorce. I know from speaking with my attorney and what I have seen of cases at work it will take months to finalize everything, but if he thinks I'm going to let him drag his heels indefinitely, he has another think coming.

I would've thought he'd want to be free of me as quickly as possible so he can be with his "serious" girlfriend. Perhaps she's not as keen on the baggage he brings to the relationship and he wants more time to nail her down before dropping the bomb about the divorce. I don't know. I have no clue what goes through his brain anymore, and I have no desire to decipher it. I don't care about him. I just want him out of my life. Getting myself and the kids through it is my priority, as well as figuring out what to do about my feelings for Vander.

I have been a complete wreck all week. Unable to sleep, hardly able to eat, and barely functioning at the office. I can't get him out of my head, and I'm still struggling to process the things he told me. The dream. Dee's assertions. My beliefs on reincarnation and the memories flitting through my mind. Seeing Vander's painting unlocked something inside me, and now I'm being deluged with images of a previous lifetime, and I'm so confused. It's pretty freaking scary too. I wish I could talk to someone about this. I have been tempted to confide in June, but I'm terrified she'll think I'm crazy and recommend a trip to the loony bin. So, I left a message with Dee, and I'm hoping she can fit me in for a private session soon.

"Darling." Curtis approaches me as I stand, lost in thought, at the top of the marquee beside the cake, watching Vander entertain Gayle Turner with a growing pain in my heart. Vander is angry. That much I can tell. Though I don't know if he's angry because I ran out on him, stayed away from him all week, or if he buys into Curtis's performance and thinks I have forgiven him. "Are we ready to do this?" he asks, sliding his arm around my back and gripping my hip with his hand.

"What are you doing?" I hiss, forcing my lips to smile instead of snarling at my soon-to-be ex-husband.

"Acting like your husband. Which I still am, I might add."

I narrow my gaze as I look up at him, itching to remove his hand from my hip, but we have several eyes on us, and I don't want to make it obvious that I loathe my husband with the intensity of a thousand suns and his touch makes my skin itch. "I don't know what game you're playing, Curtis, but you need to cut it out. This is West's eighteenth birthday. A night he will remember forever. I don't want him looking back on it and believing the entire night was fabricated. We agreed to be civil to one another and to smile. We didn't agree to grabby hands and fake PDAs."

Always Meant to Be

It's crazy, but standing here like this, knowing Vander is watching, feels like the biggest betrayal. Memories of our heated make-out session have been replaying in a loop on my mind all week, and my little electric friend has been getting a vigorous workout after months of minimal use. My body tingles every time I remember how incredible it felt to have Vander's touch all over me.

I panicked when his fingers brushed against my panties because I knew if I let him touch me there we wouldn't stop, and I couldn't let it go that far. Not while I'm still officially married to Curtis and not until I've had time to think about everything and whether I'm ready to take a giant step and start something with my son's eighteen-year-old friend. Knowing what I know now, it's hard to think of him as eighteen. If his soul is the other half of mine, then age really doesn't matter.

When we kissed, it was both familiar and new, but it didn't feel wrong. Nothing has ever felt more right, and it terrifies me. I'm on the cusp of something life-changing, and I don't know if I'm brave enough to take that leap of faith.

"You need to learn to relax," Curtis says, squeezing my hip as he gestures for West, Stella, and Ridge to come forward. "Or you need to get laid." Before I can stop him, he swoops in and plants a hard kiss on my mouth. "I can take one for the team tonight, for old time's sake. What do you say?"

My entire body shakes with rage and not being able to release it makes me want to scream. "I say you're fucking crazy and hell will freeze over before I ever have sex with you again."

"I know you've got to be gagging for it," he says, smiling as our kids approach. "Consider it my last act as your husband."

I dig my fingers into his hand, uncaring at this point if the kids see. "Unless you want me to stab you with the cake knife, take your fucking hands off me and keep your disgusting offer to yourself."

"Mom." West's brow creases as he steps in front of me. "Are you okay?"

I force a wide smile on my face. "I'm fine, honey." I loop my arm through his and hold him close as Ridge sidles up to me, and I tuck him into my other side. My youngest yawns, and I reach down, kissing his cheek. He's exhausted, but I know I'll most likely have a fight on my hands when the time comes to leave. Curtis wraps his arm around Stella, beaming at the crowd as they gather around us, like he isn't the son of Satan.

Pain tightens my chest as my gaze locks on Vander's. His cold green eyes are devoid of emotion as he stares at me while cradling Gayle against his front, her back to his chest. His arms are encircling her waist, and she's clinging to his muscular forearms and beaming like she's just won an Oscar.

I look away, focusing on West as he thanks everyone for coming before thanking me and Curtis for hosting the party. He calls Hazel forward, and I step to the side to let him hug his girlfriend. She beams up at him as he makes a wish and blows out the candles. After, I make myself scarce cutting up the cake and placing it onto plates so I don't have to watch Gayle fawning all over Vander from her new seat on his lap. The more time that passes, the angrier I am getting. I thought Vander was more mature, but if this is some kind of game, he can play it alone.

I am done with men trying to manipulate me.

Viola, Shirley, and June help to distribute the cake, but I insist on serving my son's table because I want to make a point. "Cake for the birthday boy and his girl," I say, sliding plates in front of West and Hazel.

"Thanks, Mom."

Hazel squeals, immediately grabbing her fork and diving in. "I've been looking forward to eating this all night."

"How about you, Vander?" I ask, plastering a smile on my

face as I turn to face him. "Would you like to have your cake and eat it too?"

Gayle's brows knit together, and she giggles. "As opposed to what?" She eyes me with clear amusement.

"As opposed to having your cake and not eating it," West mumbles, around a mouthful of sugary goodness, rolling his eyes.

"Or not having cake and therefore not eating it," Hazel adds, swirling her tongue around the frosted icing on her fork.

"It's an idiom," I calmly explain although Vander gets exactly what I'm saying. "Can I get you some cake, Gayle?"

"Oh, God, no." She stares at Hazel in horror. Hazel is too busy shoveling cake in her mouth to notice her derision. Gayle pats her flat stomach. "I'm careful about what I eat, and that thing—" she points at my son's plate "—is a dieter's worst nightmare." She shudders as if my cake has personally affronted her. I'm tempted to grab West's half-eaten slice and smash it into her whiny face.

But that would be catty and immature, and I'm a grown-ass woman who would never resort to such childish behavior.

"Sugar is the enemy, you know," she continues, in an annoying high-pitched superior tone. Leaning back, she snuggles into Vander while running her hand up and down his arm. "It's just another thing we have in common, babe," she tells him, pressing a kiss to the underside of his jaw. Vander stares at me with a blank expression, and I work hard to shield my emotions. "Besides," she says, turning her face back around to me. "I'm too sweet as it is." She giggles at her own joke, and I'm done.

"That you are, Gayle." I smooth a hand down the front of my dress and deliver my most serene smile. "Well, if no one else wants cake, my work here is done."

"I'll have cake," Vander says, removing Gayle's hand from

his arm. "You know I can't resist your desserts." He says it deadpan, with no show of emotion on his face, but I hear the double entendre, and I'm fuming. With him for playing such stupid games and me for not being strong enough to stay away from him before it got to this point.

"Count me in too."

I turn toward the owner of the deep voice. Bowie rakes his gaze over me slowly, and I'm instantly uncomfortable with his attention.

"I'll always accept whatever you're offering, Mrs. H, if you know what I mean."

Oh, dear God. Cake is totally a euphemism, and rather than feeling flattered, I am seriously embarrassed and a little grossed out. Bowie waggles his brows, and I spot the glazed look in his eyes. He is totally trashed, and I am going to murder whoever smuggled booze into the party. My money is on Stella, but who am I kidding? I know most kids drink before they are legal—we did—but I was very firm with the kids about tonight. Their friends' parents are trusting us to safeguard their children, and sending them home drunk does not sit well with me.

"You're a fucking asshole!" West jumps up and races around the table with murderous intent in his eyes. "You take that back!" he yells as I swing around, blocking Bowie with my body and keeping my son at bay. Out of the corner of my eye, I notice Vander glaring at Bowie while gripping the edge of his seat. "You can't hit on my mom, you fucking perv!" West shouts.

"What's going on here?" Curtis asks, materializing at my side and getting the timing right for once.

"I think Bowie has had too much to drink," I say under my breath. "Can you arrange a ride home for him and calm West down. I'm going to put Ridge to bed."

Curtis nods. "I've got this. Go."

I walk off without looking back, pleased when my sleepy nine-year-old doesn't mount any protest and willingly takes my hand. I am ready for this night to be over.

Chapter Twenty-Five

Kendall

After changing Ridge into his pajamas and tucking him into bed, I head to my bedroom to take a breather. Standing in front of the mirror in my en suite bathroom, I stare at my reflection, wondering how my life got to this point. I attend to business, wash my hands, and brush my teeth before touching up my makeup. I plan to go back outside to say my goodbyes, and then I'm calling it a night.

When I walk into my bedroom, I almost scream in fright as Vander steps out in front of me. "You can't be in here. You need to leave," I say when my blood pressure has regulated.

"We need to talk."

"There is nothing to say. Go back to your date." I'm pleased I sound calm and not like the jealous shrew who is hiding inside me, waiting to show her claws.

I don't know what I was thinking, believing he could be into me.

It's so stupid to imagine I would hold his attention when he's surrounded by the Gayles of this world. I have nurtured three babies in my womb, and I have the stretch marks to prove it. My body isn't some blank canvas for him to paint with his mouth and his hands. My body reflects my life experiences, and I don't compare favorably to girls his own age with their flawless faces, supple skin, and desirable bodies. What happened tonight is inevitable, and it's best I realize it now before I'm even more invested.

"She's not my date. She's just..." Air whooshes out of his mouth as he runs a hand through his gorgeous messy dark hair. He looks good tonight, but I have tried not to notice. Dark jeans hug his muscular thighs and legs, and his black fitted shirt clings to his broad shoulders, taut chest, and sculpted biceps. He has the shirt rolled up to the elbows, highlighting the impressive ink on his arms.

I won't be distracted by his looks, and I'm in a pissy mood after his behavior tonight. "Someone to make me jealous?" I surmise.

His eyes burn into mine. "Did it work?"

"Oh, it worked like a charm, Vander." I fold my arms across my chest and fix him with a sharp look. "It proved you are more like my husband than you would care to admit. You have shown me you are manipulative and a lot less mature than I gave you credit for." Harsh? Maybe, but I'm mad, and I'm confused, and I hate feeling like this. Like I'm a teenager again vying with nasty bitches at school over a man. I left all of that behind me, and I won't do this. I thought Vander was different, but it seems like I was wrong. "There are plenty of obstacles in our way without adding immature games into the mix, so thank you for making this easier for me." I point between us. "This ends now."

"The hell it does!" he snaps.

"Lower your voice!" I hiss. "Ridge is sleeping in the next room."

Always Meant to Be

He rubs at a spot between his brows. "What's the problem, Kendall? You can't hack it when someone gives you a taste of your own medicine?"

Anger burns through me, and I am holding onto my sanity by my fingernails. How dare he try to turn this back around on me. I count to ten in my head before I am composed enough to reply. "If you are suggesting I have been using Curtis, a man who is my husband, by the way, to make you jealous, you are very much mistaken."

He harrumphs, and I grind my teeth, wanting to scream in sheer frustration. "I know what I saw! He has been all over you all night, and you've let him!"

"Because I didn't want to make a scene at my son's party by forcibly removing my wayward husband's hands! If you think I enjoyed it, think again. Tonight has been an exercise in restraint, and I'm about to blow a gasket, so I suggest you get the hell away from me, Vander, before I take it all out on you."

"You hurt me," he says, letting his guard down as his anger fades. "You ran away from me, and you haven't reached out all week, and then I show up here, and you're playing happy family with that asshole who is cheating on you. What the hell am I supposed to think?"

"You're supposed to trust me," I say, working hard to lower my tone. I don't want to react in anger, but he is making it difficult. "You told me you did, but clearly you don't."

"I do." He steps toward me, and I shake my head in warning, but he ignores me, grabbing me at the waist and reeling me into his body. "I do trust you, Kendall. I just saw red. His hands were all over you, and I wanted to kill him."

I slide out of his embrace. "I had no choice but to play along. It's West's birthday, and I didn't want to do anything to upset him. But you had a choice, and you chose to flirt up a storm with Gayle Turner and let her paw at you, knowing what it would do to me. You purposely chose to hurt me, so you don't get to turn around and accuse me of hurting you. It wasn't intentional, but your actions were."

He closes his eyes momentarily and wrings his hands together. "You're right." His eyes blink open. "I was so fucking jealous, and I didn't stop to think. I'm sorry. You know she means nothing to me. I was only using her to get back at you."

"That is all kinds of wrong, Vander. I know you don't like her, but she likes you, and it's a pretty shitty way to repay her devotion. I don't care if she's a whiny bitch. She doesn't deserve that. No one does."

"I will apologize to her, but right now, I don't want to talk about Gayle. I want to talk about us."

"Well, I don't, and you need to leave before someone comes up here and finds you in my bedroom." I walk toward the door as he wraps his hand around my elbow, pulling me back into his chest.

"I'm sorry for being an asshole. I swear it's not who I am. You have been driving me crazy all week," he says as his strong arm circles my waist from behind. My back is pressed up against his front, and heat rolls off him in waves. "It feels like I'm going insane. I can't live like this, Kendall. I can't live without a part of my soul. Not knowing how you are feeling is literally making me nuts. I'm sleep-deprived and Kendall-deprived, and I can't function when I'm running on fumes. I was wrong to do what I did, and I promise it won't happen again."

I exhale heavily as I sink into his warmth, unable to avoid temptation. It's so hard to stay mad at Vander, and to resist him, when he lays his heart on the line and he holds me like this. "I know this is hard for you," I say, turning around in his arms so I'm facing him. "It's hard for me too, but I'm trying to do the right thing, and you're not making it easy."

Always Meant to Be

"I can't bear the thought of you living with him. I can't stand to think of him putting his hands on you. I have never felt the intensity of the feelings I have for you, and I'm struggling to deal with all the uncertainty."

I can relate to that. A sigh escapes my lips as I rest my head on his chest. "God, we are making such a mess of this."

He sets his chin on my head while his fingers tangle in my hair. "We were warned it wouldn't be easy."

I bark out a dry laugh. "That's an understatement." Lifting my head, I look up at him, instantly magnetized by the hypnotic depths of his big green eyes. "I should be the adult in this situation, but I'm clueless. I'm struggling as much as you are."

"I'm an adult too, Kendall, and you don't have to shoulder it alone. But I don't know how to handle this when Curtis is in the way."

I trail my hand up his chest, needing the solidity of his body to ground me. "I'm divorcing Curtis, Vander," I admit because there doesn't seem to be much point in keeping it a secret for the sake of a few hours. "We are telling West, Stella, and Ridge tomorrow, and I was planning on telling you then. He's moving out tomorrow night."

His eyes light up, and I can practically see a layer of stress lift from his shoulders. He clasps my face in his hands. "I know this must be tough for you, and I know West is going to be upset, but I won't lie and say this doesn't make me happy, because it does."

"I can't promise you anything yet."

He leans in and kisses my lips. "That's okay."

"My children will need me, and my head is pretty much a mess."

"Mine too." His mouth glides against mine again, and I grab his shirt. "We can figure it out as we go along."

"Vander, I—" He cuts me off with a long, slow, passionate kiss, and I stop protesting, giving in to him as he bands his arms around me and holds me close. He angles my head so he can take the kiss deeper, and I willingly open for him when his tongue slides along the seam of my mouth. I moan into his mouth as his tongue plunges inside, stroking mine and ramping my desire up a couple of notches. His erection digs into my stomach as he moves us back until my spine hits the wall. Grabbing my thigh, he pulls my leg up around his waist, and I gasp as his hard length presses against my pussy through my flimsy dress. My panties are wet, my core pulsing with abject need as the kiss turns heated and we grind against one another, groping and caressing through our clothes, and I'm slowly losing control.

We are on the verge of taking it to the next level when a pounding sounds on my door. We jump apart as my heart somersaults in my chest and blood rushes to my head. "Mom," Stella calls out. "Are you in there?"

I almost collapse against the wall as I look at the door, noticing Vander locked it. Thank fuck, I got a new deadbolt. If Stella had walked in on this, I don't know how I would have explained it. "Give me a minute, sweetheart," I call out.

I point at the bathroom and shove Vander in that direction while lifting a finger to my lips to urge him to be silent. Lowering his head, he plants a quick soft kiss on my lips while I slap him away and push him into the bathroom, quietly closing the door. There isn't time to check if I'm presentable, so I quickly straighten up my clothes and rub around my lips to catch any errant lipstick before smoothing my hair back and striding toward the door.

The second I unlock it, my daughter falls into the room, and I barely manage to catch her. I narrow my eyes at her as she straightens up. "Have you been drinking?"

She giggles. "A little."

"Damn it, Stella. Your grandparents are here. They'll throw a hissy fit if they see you're drunk." Curtis's parents are lovely, but a bit straitlaced.

"Gram and Gramps are gone." Stella yawns and flops down on my bed. "I came up to see if you were okay. West and Bowie had a massive argument in front of everyone." For God's sake. I told Curtis to take care of it. Honestly, he can't be trusted to do a damn thing. "And then Shepherd hit Bowie," Stella continues, "when Gayle revealed Bowie has a bit of a thing for older women and, apparently, he fucked Shep's mom last year."

I wonder if that is what this is for Vander. A desire to sample an older woman before he gets it out of his system and returns to dating girls his own age. Shaking those disturbing thoughts aside, I refocus on my inebriated daughter. "Welp, it wouldn't be a party without some drama, I suppose," I say, taking Stella's hand and pulling her up. I need to get her out of here so I can get Vander out of my bedroom before someone sees. Hiding him in my bathroom has me all kinds of nervous.

Stella cocks her head to the side, studying me curiously. "Are you feeling okay? You look flushed, and you have a rash all over your chest." She laughs as she toys with my hair. "Were you rolling around in the garden or something? Your hair is all messed up."

"I'm not the one you should be worrying about, missy. You're swaying on your feet."

"I'm fi—" Her eyes startle wide as she clamps a hand over her mouth.

I can only watch in horror as she races toward the bathroom door and yanks it open. Panic slams into me, nausea swims up my throat, and my knees almost go out from underneath me. The sounds of vomiting reach my ears, and I force my shaky limbs to move. When I step into the bathroom, my daughter is bent over the toilet bowl, puking her guts up, but there is no sign of Vander. A light wind lifts strands of my hair, and I glance at the window, noticing it is open.

Oh my God. He must be outside, hiding in the tree that butts up against this side of the house. I hope he's okay because there is nothing I can do until Stella stops getting sick. Needing to do something to distract my jangled nerves, I wet a damp cloth and attend to my daughter, wiping her brow and pushing hair out of her eyes while she expels the contents of her stomach.

After, I help her to her room, telling her to get changed and that I'll be back with some water. Then I dash back into my bedroom, closing and locking the door before racing to the bathroom. I'm just in time to see Vander climbing back through the window. "Are you crazy? I hiss. "You could have fallen and seriously injured yourself!" I help him to maneuver his body inside. He barely fits through the window, and it's a miracle he managed to get outside before Stella caught him.

"I had no choice. There was nowhere else to hide, and I couldn't risk Stella finding me." He jumps down and straightens up. "That was a close call," he adds, grinning and visibly shivering.

I rub my hands up and down his arms and over his body to help warm him up. "Too close." First West, and now Stella. I'm not cut out for this, at all, and I feel so guilty for hiding something as big as this from my kids.

"Don't read into it," he says as if he has a hotline to my thoughts.

"It's hard not to."

"I love you, and you love me. That is all that counts."

If only it were that simple, and I don't remember telling him I loved him. "We can't talk about this now. You need to leave so I can return to Stella."

Always Meant to Be

"Just promise me you'll come see me tomorrow night. I don't care how late it is. I can't go another day without seeing you."

"I can't promise anything, Vander, but I will do my best."

Chapter Twenty-Six

Vander

When I return from a run the following afternoon, West is waiting for me. He's sitting on his butt on the dirty ground outside the gate to the carriage house with his legs bent and his face buried in his knees.

"Hey, man." I open the gates and clamp a hand on his shoulder. "Come on in."

Without uttering a word, he scrambles to his feet and follows me inside. I know why he's here, and I need a couple of minutes to compose myself so I can be the friend he needs right now. "I'm gonna grab a quick shower. I have beer or there's tequila in the cupboard. Help yourself."

He nods, making a beeline for the refrigerator. His shoulders are tense, his back stiff, and he's not carrying himself with the usual confidence. I feel for him, I really do, but I'm also pleased she went through with it. I barely slept all night worrying Kendall would change her mind or Curtis would try to talk her out of it. Guilt jumps up and bites me as I think these thoughts, and I feel like the absolute shittiest friend on the planet.

Leaving West to his beer, I head into the shower to get my head on straight. Compartmentalizing my feelings is something I have become good at, and I need to do that now. I can't be thinking of Kendall or selfishly thinking of myself when my buddy needs me.

West is on his second beer when I emerge from my bedroom ten minutes later. Grabbing a cold one from the refrigerator, I join him on the couch. "What's up?"

A muscle clenches in his jaw, and he tightens his grip on his bottle before answering me. "My parents are getting divorced."

I squeeze his shoulder. "I'm sorry for what you're going through."

"My dad is an asshole. I hate him." He drains half his beer, and a thunderous look washes over his face. "Everything he said was lies stacked upon lies." He turns to face me with red-rimmed eyes. "He's having another affair, and he wasn't even going to tell us." He knocks back more beer. "Mom had to basically force him to admit it although she did agree they have been drifting apart for the past few years and splitting up was inevitable." Grabbing one of my new cushions, he throws it at the wall. "It's such bullshit, and now everything is changing."

"What can I do?"

"Distract me." He runs shaky fingers through his hair. "Hazel is at her grandparents' house all afternoon, and she's got some volleyball team night out to go to later. I don't want to return home until that asshole is all moved out."

"Where is he moving to?"

"An apartment in Denver owned by his employer. It's only temporary until he finds his own place. He says he's going to stay local, and he promised he'd still be at all of my games and around to take Ridge to Little League and camping, but I don't buy it. He'll be too busy fucking his slut to care about his kids."

Always Meant to Be

He waves his bottle in my face. "Mark my words. Just wait and see."

For West's sake, I hope he's wrong. I hate Curtis Hawthorne, but he's still his dad, and he supports his son in a way my father never has.

"How did Stella and Ridge take the news?"

"Stella is pissed, like me. Ridge burst out crying, and he was hugging Dad begging him not to go."

"Shit." I rub a hand across the back of my neck. "That must've been hard to watch."

"It was. He's too young to understand Dad is a piece of shit who betrayed Mom." He drains the rest of his beer and leans his head back, closing his eyes.

"Want to head to the club and go a few rounds in the ring?" I suggest even though I have just showered and Sundays are my day off. West needs to physically express his emotions, and there is no better place.

He slowly nods. "Yeah, I think I do."

I text Kendall later that night to tell her West is with me and not to come over. After a couple of hours in the ring, we came back to my place and called in reinforcements. It's a somber affair with some of our closest buddies, a few beers, and copious games of *Call of Duty*. I think West is imagining his dad every time he annihilates the enemy. I know I am. I hate seeing him so upset, and I'm kinda pissed at Hazel. She could've ditched her plans for tonight to comfort her boyfriend because I really think he needs her.

A knock at the door pulls me out of my head, and I go to answer it, reeling back when I see Bowie on my doorstep. Shoving him away, I close the door and square up to him.

"What the fuck, dude? You can't be here." He's sporting a nasty bruise on one cheek and a cut on his lip. "The last thing West needs is to see you, and Shep isn't exactly your biggest fan either." I heard what Stella told Kendall last night, and the news his mom slept with his crush must be killing Shepherd. He's as melancholy as West tonight.

"I fucked up, but I don't think I deserve to be blackballed."

"No one is saying that, but you need to lay low for a while."

His features harden. "You're not letting me in? Seriously?"

He's twitchy and struggling to maintain eye contact, and I'm pretty sure he's on something. "Go home, Bowie. Let this blow over."

His mouth pulls into a sneer. "I hear West isn't the only one who needs consoling. Perhaps I'll pay Mrs. H a visit. Stella too if she's up for a threesome."

My arm juts out before I have processed the motion, and I punch him hard in the face. He goes down fast, clutching his nose and cursing. The door opens behind me and a couple of guys who are on the football team with Bowie and West step outside. "Get him out of here before I kill the motherfucker." Pun *not* intended. I shake out my sore fist, seething on the inside.

"Fuck you, asshole." Bowie climbs to his feet, using his fingers to mop up the blood spilling from his nose. "I'm done with you."

"I don't know what's going on with you, but this isn't the way to handle it. Keep pissing off your friends, and you'll find you have none left." I don't wait for his reply, leaving the jocks to take care of the douche as I head back inside to look after my buddy.

Always Meant to Be

"Where did you disappear to Saturday night?" Gayle asks, slinking up beside me as I retrieve my books from my locker. I'm a bit hungover this morning after staying up until midnight drinking with West. I asked him if he wanted to sleep on my couch, but he insisted on going home. I think he felt guilty for abandoning his family all day, but he needed space to process everything.

"I went home," I say, stuffing a couple of books in my bag and shutting my locker.

"You're no fun." She pouts, running her hands up my chest. "I was hoping to receive an invite to your place." She presses herself up against me and curls her hands around my neck. "I'm free tonight if you want to hang out." She licks her lips and lowers her eyes to my mouth. "I can stay over too. I know my daddy won't mind."

This is what I get for using her to get back at Kendall. Something I have been beating myself up over continuously since Saturday night. Kendall was right when she called me out on my behavior, and I'm ashamed I stooped so low and let jealousy get the best of me. Kendall has enough on her plate without dealing with my petty shit. I still don't know where we stand, and I may have ruined things before they have even begun.

Removing Gayle's arms from around my neck, I step back, creating some distance between us. "I'm sorry if I misled you, Gayle, but I'm not interested in hanging out with you anymore."

"What?" She laughs, closing the gap between us. "You're a funny guy."

I hold her wrists aloft before she can touch me again. "I'm not joking. I'm not interested in dating. I don't have the time."

She waggles her brows and grins. "Who said anything about dating?"

Eh, you did. When you ran to your daddy to force me to take you out. I'm tempted to say it, but I just want to drive my point home and get this over and done with.

In an unexpected move, she slams me back against the lockers and pins my body with hers. "I want you, and I see the way you look at me. I know you're feeling this too. We can forget about dating for the moment. As long as we're fucking, I don't mind." I slide out from under her hold, failing to disguise the full-body shudder that overtakes me. Gayle being Gayle, she completely misinterprets it. "See, you are literally shivering from my touch." She visibly gloats, and it's not attractive.

"I assure you it's not in a good way."

A frown puckers her brow. "Don't lie to me, Vander. I know when a guy wants me, and you want me."

"You know shit, Gayle." I'm done being Mr. Nice Guy. The only way of getting through to someone as delusional as her is to pull no punches. "I only took you out because my father forced me into it. I have no interest in you, Gayle. Zero, zilch, nada. I don't want you. I would rather boil my balls than take you to bed. There will be no dating, no fucking, no anything." I grab hold of the strap of my bag. "Don't fucking come near me again. I don't want to talk to you or even see your face. Are we clear?"

"You are such an asshole." Her façade drops for a second, highlighting her hurt, and I feel like the biggest dick.

"I am. You'd do well to remember it."

"No one turns me down and doesn't end up regretting it. You'll see," she shouts after me as I hightail it to homeroom before I pick up a tardy slip.

Always Meant to Be

"What the hell, man?" West says, coming up behind me in the student parking lot. It's the end of a long day, and I could really do without this shit. "That's going to cost a lot to fix," he adds, tracing his finger along the jagged scrapes etched into my truck on both sides.

"I want to wring Gayle's scrawny neck," I say, opening the back door and tossing my book bag inside.

His eyes pop wide. "Gayle keyed your truck? Damn."

"She's the only one I've pissed off who would do something like this." Bowie currently hates my guts, but I'm not the only one. Something is up with him, but this isn't the way to handle it. He didn't sit at the jock table at lunch, and I don't understand why he seems intent on ostracizing everyone. Still, I know this isn't his style. If he wants to get back at me, he'd come at me the old-fashioned way—with his fists.

"You should report her. That's criminal damage."

"Nah. That would only add fuel to the fire."

"That's the point." He swipes his duffel bag off the ground and slings it over his shoulder. "I bet her daddy would sign with a different legal firm if you reported his daughter to the police. You'd get her off your back once and for all, and it would stick it to your dad too. I know that's what I'd do if I was in your shoes." West is in anti-father mode right now, so I'm not surprised he has suggested this plan of action.

"My dad has been laying low, and it's the way I prefer it. I have already done enough to tarnish the deal with Turner Media. If I deliberately sabotage it, he might actually kill me or expend more effort trying to find Mom. Tempting as it is, I think it's best to leave it alone. Gayle appears to have gotten the message, and if this is the price I have to pay, I'm cool with it." Besides, there are no cameras out here, and I have no proof. The police wouldn't be able to do much and I doubt they'd even care. "Do you want to hang out tonight?" I ask, wanting to offer him as much support as I can.

"I can't. Mom wants us to have dinner together and watch a movie. She was hella emotional this morning. She's upset we are all upset. I didn't think how much my disappearing act yesterday would hurt her. I need to spend some time with my family right now."

"Of course. You know where I am if you need me."

West drags me into a hug and thumps my back. "Thanks for being there for me yesterday."

"You have been there for me through all my shit. I've always got your back."

I don't see Kendall the rest of the week, and I only talk to West at school, because they are hunkering down as a family and trying to get their lives back on track. Most everyone has heard the news by now, and Kendall's friends are rallying around her. I want to be the one to support her, but my needs must take a back seat. We are texting every day, but I still have no clue where I stand with her or if she has any room in her life for me.

It's depressing, and it feels like my life is on hold because it is so much duller without her in it. I try to keep myself busy with schoolwork, taking my truck to the garage to be repaired, putting in extra sessions at the gym, and painting. I submitted my college applications early, so I don't have that as a distraction anymore, but I focus on searching for suitable apartments near Yale and investigating the various financial supports on offer. Supporting Mom has made a considerable dent in my inheritance, and by my calculation, I will have enough to put myself through two years of college before it runs out. I could live in the dorms and save a bit of cash, but I want to have my own place so Kendall can visit. We haven't discussed what will happen next year when I leave, and we're not even in a relationship, but I want to ensure there is always room for her in my life because I cannot contemplate Kendall not being in it.

I am walking to my truck after my session at the boxing club when my cell pings with a message from her. My bad mood instantly lifts, and I don't need to look in the mirror to know I'm grinning like a loon. She wants to hang out tomorrow night, and I'm already starting a countdown. I tap out a reply, telling her not to eat and that we'll get takeout.

I am halfway home when my cell rings; my father's name flashes on the screen. I ignore him, cranking the volume up louder on my stereo, but he refuses to go away, calling me incessantly, until I give in and answer. "What?" I snap, irritated he's ruining my buzz.

"You think you're so clever. You think you can do whatever you want and there won't be a price to pay, but I don't bow down to anyone, especially not my flesh and blood. You took something from me, and now I'm going to take something from you too." A menacing laugh filters through the phone, sending icy chills down my spine.

"If this is about Mom, get over it already." I know he has tried to find her, but she's safe and out of his reach. Dana talked Mom into giving rehab a shot, and she's at a remote private center, enrolled under a fake name, and he'll never find her. It's costing me a small fortune, but if it saves Mom, it'll be worth it.

"I lost the Turner Media account because of you, and I won't forget that anytime soon."

"Get real, Dad. Your shady reputation cost you that account. It wasn't because of anything I did or didn't do." You don't build a multimillion-dollar corporation by making business decisions based on emotions. If Miles Turner chose a different legal firm to represent him, it was for reasons outside of me and his daughter. I'd stake my life on it.

"I'll enjoy breaking you down, Vander," he replies, refusing to accept the truth, because he's just that egotistical. "And when you are lying in a heap at my feet, I will build you back up exactly the way I want you to be. By the time I'm through with you, your life will not be your own. It will be mine, and you'll have no choice but to do what I say."

The line goes dead, and it feels ominous.

I drive home with an eerie sense of dread, hoping my father's threat is all hot air but terrified it's not.

Chapter Twenty-Seven

Kendall

"**M**om!" West's urgent shout reaches me in the kitchen where I'm cleaning up after dinner. "I need your help!"

"What's going on?" I hear Stella ask as I jog across the kitchen toward the hallway. "Oh my God. What happened to your face?" she asks.

I race out into the hallway with my heart in my mouth, but nothing could prepare me for the scene that lies in wait. West has his arm around Vander's back, and Vander is leaning against my son, clearly injured and on the verge of collapsing.

"What happened?" I ask, working hard to keep the panic from my tone as I approach them. I slide up on Vander's other side, taking his arm and draping it over my shoulders.

"You should see the other guy." Vander attempts to lighten the tone, but I'm not amused.

"Let's get him to the bathroom," I tell West before turning my attention to my daughter. "Grab the first aid kit from the kitchen and bring it to me."

Stella runs off to retrieve it. Propping Vander up between

us, West and I get him to the downstairs bathroom. Vander eases down onto the closed toilet seat, wincing and clutching his ribs. "My paintings," he pants as West and I share a look. "I need to go back for them." He moves to get up, but I shake my head.

"I need to check your injuries, and you aren't in any shape to go anywhere right now."

"Please." Pain-stricken eyes latch on mine. "He burned at least half of them before I stopped him. I don't want him to finish the job."

"Van, your dad was passed out when we left. I doubt he's getting up anytime soon."

My head whips between West and Vander. "Your father did this?" I know he has hit him in the past and they have gotten into it when Vander shot up, bulked up, and learned how to use his fists, but this is on a whole other scale. "How did he even get a chance to do it? I know you are stronger and capable of overpowering him."

Vander's eyes darken with rage. "I came home from the gym, and he was in the garden burning my artwork." A bitter laugh bubbles up his throat. "It was like I was thirteen all over again." His Adam's apple bobs in his throat. "I was in a panic, trying to save my paintings, so I didn't see him approaching with a baseball bat. He was going crazy, even more so than usual, and he really came at me, caught me off guard. He got a few hits in before I gained the upper hand and gave it back to him and then some."

"He's a prick," West hisses. "All fathers are pricks," he adds, snarling.

West refuses to speak to Curtis, proclaiming he wants nothing more to do with him. While I was relieved when Curtis moved out, it means I'm the one left to pick up the pieces. However, I prefer it that way because I don't trust

Curtis with my children's' fragile emotions. He's too selfish to ever put them first. My kids are suffering, and I'm doing my best to support them as they grapple with their feelings.

"Why did he do this now?" I ask, feeling guilty I haven't had much time for Vander lately.

"He lost the Turner Media account." Vander peers at me through his swollen left eye. He has bruises all over his face, dried blood on his nose, and a cut on his lip.

"I heard about that. Greg has been like a demon at work all week, but what has that got to do with you?" *Surely, Greg isn't blaming Vander?* He took Gayle Turner out on a date purely to appease both fathers, so he played his part.

"He blames me."

"That is ridiculous, and I am going to tell him so. He can't take his aggravations out on you!"

"No." Van shakes his head as Stella comes into the room. "You can't get involved, Kendall. You don't know how far he's prepared to take things. He's pissed I got Mom away from him, and he's determined to fuck up my life. He has declared war, and this is just the start. You can't put yourself in the middle of it." I didn't know anything had happened with Diana, and guilt rears its ugly head again.

"Van is right, Mom," West says. "He's a fucking psycho, and I want you nowhere near him."

"I can't believe your father did this to you." Stella hands me the first aid kit as she pins compassionate eyes on Vander. "He should be locked up."

He should, but I tried that route before and ran into a solid wall.

"If you want to beat Gregory Henley, you have to play him at his own game," Vander says.

"How do you do that?" West asks.

"I don't know yet." Vander shifts on the toilet seat,

grimacing in pain. "But I'll figure it out."

"Okay. I need to check Vander's injuries," I say, putting my practical hat on. "West, go clear out one side of the garage to create space so we can temporarily move Vander's paintings in there." I will have to go and get them myself because they'll need to be covered so it's not obvious most of them are of me. "Stella, go change the bed linen in the spare bedroom. The blue one," I add, not wanting to put him in the bedroom Curtis was sleeping in. I glance down at Vander as I pop the lid off the medical kit. "I don't want you going back there tonight. You can stay here."

"I'll grab a few of the guys and head over to the carriage house to get your stuff," West offers.

"No," Vander and I say in unison.

"You said yourself Greg is a psycho." I set the kit on the window ledge beside me. "I want you nowhere near there. I will organize something. For now, just clear out the garage, please."

West opens his mouth to protest, but Vander shakes his head. "Your mom is right. It's not safe. I'll ask Jimmy to get a couple of the older guys from the boxing club to go over later. They can get my paintings and my stuff."

"Okay." West skims his eyes over his best friend. "Maybe I shouldn't have pulled you off him. Maybe I should've let you finish the job."

I'm not touching that. "I'm glad you got there when you did." My gaze swings to Vander. "Should we be worried about your father pressing charges? Maybe you should report this."

"He won't press charges." Vander gingerly lifts his T-shirt up. "He'd never do that."

"We should at least take pictures," I say. "That way, if he tries to do anything, we have evidence of your injuries."

Vander nods as West helps him to fully remove his shirt. I

suck in a horrified gasp at the sight of the bruising on one side of his chest and along his rib cage. "I'm going to get ice for those ribs," West says. "They're going to hurt like a bitch." He should know. He's suffered his fair share of bruised ribs over the years, thanks to football.

When we are alone, I crouch down and tenderly cup Vander's face. "How much pain are you in, and don't lie to me."

"It's about a five," he says, softly poking his ribs and biting down on his lower lip. "I have suffered worse."

"I hate that you have," I whisper, battling a sudden rush of emotion.

"Kendall." Vander grips my wrist. "I'm okay. Trust me when I say he's hurting far worse than me."

"You didn't kill him, did you?" I have to ask. Not because I care about that piece of shit—because I care about Vander.

"West checked. He was still breathing. Just out cold." He brings my wrist to his mouth, pressing a soft kiss to my skin. "I've missed you," he whispers.

"I've missed you too," I whisper. "I'm sorry I didn't have any time for you this week."

"Don't do that." He shakes his head, reluctantly letting my hand go. "Don't apologize. I know this was a stressful week for you, and you had to prioritize your family. I could never resent you for that. I reminded myself hourly when the need to see you was almost too great."

I stand and tilt his face up. "I'll look after you now. You're safe here, but you can't stay for long." The temptation will be too great.

"I know." His tired eyes lock on mine.

"Your beautiful face," I say, softly examining the bruising on his cheeks and jawline.

"It'll heal." He shrugs, like it's no biggie, and I hate that it probably isn't for him.

Before I patch him up, I take several pictures with my cell, ensuring I capture every mark, bruise, and cut. He spreads his thighs so I can step between them as I tend to his face first. West returns with ice packs, which Vander holds to his ribs as I clean his face and apply arnica cream to the bruises and antiseptic cream on his cut lip. Vander asks West to grab his gym bag and cell from his truck so he can call Jimmy.

"You might need an X-ray for those ribs," I say, afraid to even touch them.

"Nah. They're only bruised."

"Are you sure?"

He nods. "Dad cracked a couple of my ribs one time before. I know what it feels like."

"I hate him," I blurt. "Perhaps I should start putting poison in his coffee at work."

Vander looks up at me with an amused grin. "You'd do that for me?"

"I would," I reply without hesitation. "If I thought I could get away with it."

"I appreciate the sentiment, but he's my problem to take care of."

"Be careful," I whisper. "Your future is on the line."

"He's going to try to take that from me," he calmly replies. "But I'm not going to let him."

"You should hear from Yale in early January. As long as you get an offer, he can't take that from you."

"I wouldn't be so sure," Vander replies. "He's an alumnus, and he has contacts. He can pretty much do whatever he wants. I wouldn't be surprised if he already knows I didn't submit an application for Yale Law."

"The deadline for submissions isn't until February. He doesn't need to know you submitted an early application for the art program."

Always Meant to Be

Vander shrugs, and a grimace sweeps over his face. I frown. Any movement that shifts his ribs seems to hurt, and he needs to remain still. "He'll be on alert after discovering my art studio today."

Glancing over my shoulder, I check the coast is clear before I thread my fingers through his hair. "He will have seen the pictures of me."

"I know." Air expels from his mouth. "Why do you think I want you to stay away from him? The paintings and drawings prove nothing except I'm a little obsessed with you. He won't read any more into it unless you start getting all up in his business, and then he'll suspect it's more than a one-sided crush. I don't want him using you to get back at me."

Greg will attempt to use me to hurt his son. Of that, I'm in no doubt. But fuck him. He can try, but he won't succeed. I am done with assholes trying to push me around and underestimating me. I don't know how I can rescue Vander's future, but I'm damn well going to try. "I'll stay out of his way," I promise. "As much as I can when we work in the same law firm."

"I'm glad Mom is in rehab and he can't use her for a punching bag."

He just used you instead. "Diana is in rehab?" I ask, and he nods. "That's great, Vander. I hope she sticks it out and it helps."

"Me too."

We sink into silence because there is nothing more to be said. Taking one of the ice packs, I hold it to his swollen eye as we stare at one another, tension building in the small bathroom until it feels like it might explode. With my free hand, I stroke his arm, up and down, in what I hope is a comforting gesture. Vander's hand moves to the back of my leg, and I lean a little closer, careful not to press against his sore ribs.

We pull apart when we hear footsteps approaching. Stella

confirms the guest room is ready, and we help Vander upstairs, getting him settled into the bed. Vander phones Jimmy while I go to the kitchen to grab some water and pain pills and to heat up a plate of lasagna because I'm pretty sure he hasn't eaten.

"Jimmy, Crusher, and a couple of the other guys are en route to the carriage house to box up my stuff and salvage whatever is left of my studio," he says when I walk in carrying a tray table. "They know to bubble wrap the shit out of the paintings. I'll call the local storage facility in the morning and rent one of their units."

"There is no rush. We have empty space in the garage now Curtis is gone, taking his car and his tools with him." I unfold the tray legs and position it over Vander's lap.

"How are you holding up?" he asks, tucking my hair behind my ear.

"I'm fine. Just worried about the kids." I'm going through a whole host of emotions, but I'm not sorry Curtis is gone. I'm relieved he's out of my hair. His parents are devastated and disappointed in their son, but they were quick to offer me their support, which means a lot. My friends have been rallying around me too, and though I'm struggling to sleep and eat, and concerned about the future, I know this is just a transitional phase. My life has altered almost overnight, and I need to rethink everything I thought I had mapped out for the future. Uncertainty is unsettling, but I know I'll be fine in time.

"West is taking it hard," Vander admits, confirming something I already know.

"Stella is too, but she's better at keeping up a front. Ridge cries himself to sleep every night and it's heartbreaking."

"I want to be here for you, but I don't know how," he says, picking up a fork.

"Just continue being there for West. That's the best way you can help me right now."

Chapter Twenty-Eight

Vander

I spend an uncomfortable night at Kendall's house. Every time I turn over in my sleep, pain stabs me along my side, crushing my lungs and making breathing difficult. I wake gasping for air with sweat plastering hair to my brow. There is no question of me attending school even though I hate the absence on my record. "Mom called the principal," West confirms when he stops into the room to check on me before he leaves. "And she's taken a personal day from work to take care of you. I offered to stay home, but she wouldn't let me."

"I don't want anyone taking time off work or school. I can take care of myself. It's not like I'm completely incapacitated."

"You know my mom. She'd never leave you alone in that state."

"It looks worse than it is."

West chuckles. "Bullshit, but I get it. I fucking hate getting injured and having to limit what I can do."

"Begone with you." Kendall appears in the hallway behind West. "You're going to be late if you don't leave now."

"I'm going." West pulls his mom into a hug. "Thanks for taking care of Vander. You're one in a million, Mom."

Kendall is quiet as she steps into the room, carrying a tray. "I have breakfast." She rounds the bed just as the front door slams. Setting the tray on the floor, she helps me to sit upright in the bed. I try to push her away, but I'm in considerable pain, and she's having none of it. "Stop resisting. You're hurt, and you need to let me take care of you."

"I don't want you doing that." I snatch her hand, and she sits on the edge of the bed. "I don't want to be a burden or a responsibility. I'm not one of your kids." She flinches, and it's probably not the best choice of words, but I need to get this off my chest. "I want to be your best friend, your confidant, your lover, your *everything*. But never a burden."

"Vander." She gently cups my cheek. "You could never be a burden, and it's not like that. Not at all. It'd be easier if I did consider you like one of my kids, but my thoughts about you are the complete opposite." Her hand lowers from my cheek, and her face contorts. "Honestly, you even saying that grosses me out."

I emit a quiet chuckle. "I just want to ensure we're on the same page."

"I'm looking after you because that's what you do when someone you care about needs help."

I'm not going to lie. Her use of the word care instead of love hurts, but I can't make this about me any more than it already is. And I am grateful for everything she's doing to help me. "Thank you."

"I like having you here." She lifts the tray table, placing it over my lap. "Though it's not conducive to a good night's sleep." A rosy hue blooms on her cheeks. "It was hard to think about anything else but you being in the room just down the hall."

"I know the feeling. Even the pain couldn't stop those thoughts from entering my mind."

"Eat." She lifts a fork, placing it in my hand. Her soft hand caresses my skin as she curls my fingers around the handle, sending warmth shooting up my arm. "Then you can take more pain pills, and I will run you a bath. I'll put some Epsom salts in it. That should help with healing."

"Thank you." I cut up my omelet and shovel a piece in my mouth. "This is delicious," I say when I have finished chewing. "Aren't you having any?"

"I ate with the kids. I'm just going to clean up and then I'll come back to check on you." Tentatively, she leans down, pressing a lingering kiss to my brow. "I'm glad you're all right, Vander. I was really worried."

"I'm stronger than you think, and I'll be back on my feet in no time."

Kendall returns when I have finished every morsel on my plate and swallowed my pain meds. She helps me into the main bathroom where the tub is already filled and ready for me. I may have played up my inability to walk unaided so I could feel her lithe body against mine and the touch of her arm around my bare back. "Uh, do you need any help undressing?" she asks, her cheeks staining with a blush again.

I could probably do it, gritting my teeth through the pain, but this is too good of an opportunity to waste.

I said I wouldn't push Kendall.

That doesn't mean I won't give her a nudge here and there.

"Yeah. I don't think I can pull my shorts down without it hurting." West helped me out of my sweats last night, giving me a pair of his training shorts to wear as they were more comfortable to sleep in.

Her tongue darts out, wetting her tempting lips as she eyeballs me. "No funny business, Vander."

I shoot her my most innocent smile. "Me? As if." My smile expands, and I can almost hear her heart beating furiously in her chest.

"Brace a hand on the sink to steady yourself," she says, purposely moving behind me. I suck in a gasp the second her warm hands move to the waistband of my shorts, her fingers skimming against the skin on my lower back.

"That's a big tattoo." She trails her fingers up my spine to the words inked in a curve along the top of my back, from one shoulder blade to the other. "You become what you love." The tips of her fingers trace along the words as she reads them, and her touch has the usual effect on me. I'm tingling all over, barely feeling any pain, except in my dick, which is hard as a rock and throbbing. "Is that Marcus Aurelius?"

"Yes," I croak, struggling to breathe over the riot of sensations her touch ignites in my body.

"You really liked the book."

"I do. So much of what he says resonates with me."

"I love that, and I love this quote. It's perfect. Did it hurt?" She continues to run her fingers lightly across the tattoo.

"Not really. This will make me sound like a masochist, but I love the feel of the needle on my skin when I'm getting inked. The pain confirms I'm alive, and getting my own designs etched on my skin reminds me I'm the one in control of me. I'm responsible for this pain, and it's freeing. It's a powerful feeling. I'm probably not explaining it right—just it's a surreal experience getting tattooed. There's this kind of...reverence about the entire thing. I feel at peace when I'm there. It's quiet, except for the sound of the machine and my own thoughts, and I enjoy it."

There's a pregnant pause before she speaks. "Wow, that was very eloquent." Her warm breath fans across my upper back as her fingers go on the move. "I have never thought about it like that. I used to talk about getting a tattoo, but Curtis didn't approve, so I forgot about the idea. But now." She moves to my side, her fingers grazing up my arm as she examines the ink there. "Now, I might reconsider."

"You should." I twist my head to look at her. "Let me design something for you."

Her eyes lift to mine, and a familiar magnetic charge fills the space between us. We stare at one another, and it's like looking into the mirror of my soul. Her fingers are stationary on my arm, and her touch feels like a permanent brand on my flesh. "Okay," she whispers. "I'd like that."

I didn't expect her to agree, and my heart swells with love and pride that she's prepared to let me design something so intimate. "Do you have any specific requirements?"

She shakes her head, smiling. "No. Surprise me."

"I will." We grin at one another, and the air sparks with that same electrical current.

Kendall gulps, tearing her gaze away first, returning to the ink on my arms. We are silent as she explores the tattoos on both my arms, my upper chest, and my neck. I have all manner of stuff etched on my skin. Ancient Greek and Egyptian symbols, swords, snakes, dragons, knives, and quotes that speak to me. "These are amazing, Vander," she says, inspecting each design carefully. "Every single piece is exemplary. I can tell how much thought and effort went into it."

"I am never flippant about what I put in or on my body. My skin is the ultimate canvas, and I never want to treat it with anything less than the respect it deserves. I put huge thought into every design. Every tattoo has meaning to me."

Her gaze trails up my neck and onto my face as she moves directly in front of me. "I am never more attracted to you than moments where you show me your heart and soul. It's beautiful, Vander." Her hands palm my face. "You're beautiful." She steps in closer, and I know the second she feels my hard-on nudging her stomach because her eyes pop wide, and she goes rigidly still.

"*You're* beautiful," I whisper, my gaze dropping to her lips and back up again. "And now you know what you do to me."

Anticipation hovers in the air, and I'm dying to kiss her, but I can't be the one to do it. We're in her house, and I won't overstep the boundaries. *Challenge them?* Hell yeah, but I won't take that final step. Air whistles from her mouth as she holds herself very still, her eyes lowering to my lips. I hold my breath, wondering what she'll do. Stumbling back, she removes her hands from my face, taking all the warmth with her. A red flush creeps up her chest onto her neck, and I'm glad to see she gets as hot and bothered as me. "We can't cross a line in my house, Vander."

"I understand."

Her features soften. "You make it so hard to resist."

"Then don't." I wind my fingers through her hair. "I know this isn't the time, but when I have found a new place, tell me you'll spend the night. I need to be with you."

"I can't make any promises, Vander. You know that."

Dejection seeps into my veins, and I'm not sure what she sees, but it's enough for her to reassure me. "I want you too, but it terrifies me. We both know if we cross that line there is no coming back."

I nod. "You're the end of the line for me, Kendall. I don't need us to cross over it to know that truth."

"Are you always this intense with girls?" she asks, moving around to my back.

"Never before you."

"You make me feel special," she whispers, her fingers returning to the waistband of my shorts.

"You are special, Kendall, and I hate you can't see it." That asshole has really done a number on her. Her self-confidence is pretty low, and I vow to do everything in my power to help her to reclaim it.

"You need to get into the bath before the water turns cold." She purposely ends the conversation, and that's okay. I have a bit more patience. I can wait a little longer.

"You're the one stalling," I tease. "Get rid of my shorts."

She grabs the top of my shorts and rips them down my legs in one fast move. A startled gasp escapes her mouth when she realizes I'm not wearing any boxers. "Oh my God, Vander!" she squeals. "You're naked."

Slowly, I turn around, incapable of shielding my massive grin and the massive appendage proudly jutting out from my body. "One has to be naked to take a bath," I tease as my cock salutes her.

She squeals again, covering her face with her hands, and I'm not having it. "Don't be shy, sweetheart. Drink your fill because this beast is all yours." Gently, I pry her fingers from her face and brush my thumb against her lower lip. "Look," I command. "Look at what you do to me."

Her chest heaves, and panic mixed with excitement flits across her face. She is so adorably cute, and I am so gone for this woman. "Look or I'll make you touch it," I whisper while devouring her mouth with my gaze.

Without any further hesitation, she drops her gaze down my body, over my broad chest and curved abs, and along the V-indent at the side of my hips before she hits the jackpot. Her brows climb to her hairline, and her mouth opens into an O shape. "Oh my...holy wow."

Brushing hair over her shoulder, I press my mouth to her ear, grinning like an idiot. "Do you like your cock?" I whisper. "Are you imagining your lips around it or the way it will feel moving inside your hot little pussy?"

A strangled sound rips from her lips, but she continues

staring at my dick, and I fucking love it. My cock jerks, loving the adoration, and I decide to push a little more. "If I put my fingers inside you now, how wet would you be?" She thrusts her arm out, gripping the side of the sink to keep herself upright. Her cheeks are flushed, her breathing is heavy, and her hard nipples are poking at the front of her flimsy blouse. I know she's as turned on as me, and liquid lust is a rampaging beast charging through my veins demanding I take what is mine. I want to bury myself balls deep inside her and stamp my mark all over her body. I want to erase every man who has come before me so all she sees is me. I need her to know we are destined to be together and I will never walk away, because she is my fate and I am hers.

A bead of precum leaks from the tip of my cock as she continues feasting on me with her big blue eyes. I want to push her to her knees and make her taste me, but I will never force any part of myself on her. She has to do it willingly, and this isn't the time or the place.

"I don't need you to answer, sweetheart, because I already know." Leaning down, I press a featherlight kiss to her neck. She shivers and closes her eyes, biting down on her lip, and I am so in love with her. "Open your eyes," I whisper, gliding my mouth along her neck before stepping back. I grab my junk and give it a few slow pumps. Her hand flies to her chest as she watches, as if in a daze. "This is all yours, Kendall. When you're ready to take what you own, there will be no turning back. Unless that time is now, I suggest you leave before I lose all sense of control and do something you won't be able to resist."

Her eyes fly to my face, and without uttering a word, she races past me out of the bathroom, leaving me alone with my cold bath.

Chapter Twenty-Nine

Kendall

"Be careful with that!" I call out as Crusher and West struggle to maneuver the large couch through the narrow front door of Vander's new apartment.

"Let me help." Vander moves toward them, but I shoot him a warning look that halts him mid-step.

"Don't even think about it. You're still healing." I point at the bench that runs along the wall on the inside of his new dining table. "Sit your ass down, and leave the heavy lifting to someone else for a change."

My words hold double meaning, and I know he gets it. It's been difficult for Vander to take a back seat while everyone else has busted a gut to get his new apartment ready for him to move into before Christmas. It's directly above the boxing club, and it was a gift from Jimmy. The large industrial-type space comprises two main areas. One side is being kept for Vander's new art studio, and the other side is his living space. It hasn't been used as an apartment in a long time, but it still had a small kitchen and separate bathroom, both desperately in need of renovation.

The space was largely lying vacant, and Jimmy didn't hesitate to offer it to Vander in his time of need. He owns the building, and he's refusing to take rent, and honestly, I could kiss the man. He's the father Vander never had, and I can tell from the interactions between them that Jimmy loves him like a son.

We have spent the past ten days stripping the place and getting it ready for Vander to move into. I found a contractor to replace the old kitchen and bathroom with new ones and a guy to sand and varnish the original hardwood floors. Stella, West, Ridge, and I came over every night after dinner to paint the walls, and it's actually been a fun bonding time. It allows all of us to forget our problems and just enjoy doing something to help Vander.

Vander has been moody and grumpy all week because I wouldn't let him help. His ribs are still sore, and he needs to heal. I suspect part of his moodiness stems from sexual frustration. Something I can relate to. Ever since he bared his naked body to me, I have been unable to forget how freaking sexy he is. His toned ass. That carved six-pack that almost looks painted on. His enticing big dick. My little electric friend was getting so much use it died, and now I'm reliant on my fingers to get me off every night. It's becoming problematic because I cannot get him out of my head. Every night, when I lie in bed and close my eyes, he is all I see.

Vander's cock is beautiful. I never thought I would say that about any man's cock, but it's the truth. He is long and thick and straight with a soft purple head and manicured pubic hair. Not that I'm an expert. I only have Curtis to compare him to, but there *is* no comparison. I feel like I've been stuck with a cheap, inferior Costco dick for years while now I'm being offered the Whole Foods Market experience which comes at considerable cost but it's worth paying the extra for the increase in quality and service.

Always Meant to Be

"Mom!" Stella tugs on my elbow, yanking me out of the way as Crusher and West carry the couch into the room. "You were miles away." She peers at me. "Are you feeling okay? You're very red in the face."

I turn even redder at her words. "I'm fine." I wave my hands in the air. "It's just warm in here," I lie.

"Mom, it's fucking freezing. We only just turned the heating on," West unhelpfully supplies.

Vander is sporting the biggest grin on his face, and I swear he always seems to know where my mind has wandered to.

"Must be your hormones," Stella quips. "Though you're far too young to be getting hot flashes."

"Stella!" I shriek, absolutely mortified at the turn of this conversation. "Just stop," I hiss, and she giggles.

Leaving the guys to retrieve the rest of the furniture and boxes from the moving van, I head to the kitchen to make something for dinner. Anything to distract me from that embarrassing conversation. I dropped by the grocery store on my way home from work and came straight here to put everything away. Stella drove Ridge over while West and Vander drove the U-Haul rental, and Crusher came in Vander's truck. Removing the chicken and vegetables from the refrigerator, I set them on the counter. I am stretching up to the overhead cabinet when Vander appears behind me.

"I'll get it." He reaches over me. "What do you need?"

"The white rectangular dish."

He places it on the counter, beside the chicken and vegetables, squinting as he studies it. "I don't remember owning this."

"Because you didn't," I say, selecting a few jars of herbs from the rack fixed to the wall. "I bought you new stuff." Biting on the inside of my cheek, I admit something we have been keeping from him. "Your dad trashed the carriage house after the guys collected your paintings, clothes, personal belongings, and furniture. They didn't think to pack up the kitchen."

His jaw pulls into a tight line. "You should have told me."

"I didn't want you to worry. Besides, you have a brand-spanking-new kitchen, and it deserves all new stuff."

"Let me pay you for it."

"Consider it a housewarming gift." I smile at him as I turn the oven on.

Discreetly, he hooks his pinkie around mine. His eyes are shining with emotion when he looks down at me. "I can't thank you enough for everything you've done for me."

I can think of plenty of ways you can repay me.

I swat that annoying inner devil aside as Vander's mouth tugs up at the corners and he fixes me with a knowing look. *Gah, how does he do that?!* "People care about you, and we all want to keep you safe."

The smile slips off his face. "Did the psycho return to work yet?"

I shake my head as I extract a wooden spoon and chef's knife from the drawer and place them on the chopping board. "He didn't show up all week. Apparently, he has a viral infection that is contagious, so he canceled all of his face-to-face client meetings and worked from home."

He harrumphs. "A likely story. At least it keeps him away from you."

I know he's worried about retaliation. "I'm not going to let him do anything to me. Try not to worry," I say as I place chicken breasts into the oven dish.

"Give me something to do," he says as the guys carry his TV inside.

"You can chop these." I hand him the knife, the yellow squash, and a zucchini.

"Have you thought any more about my suggestion?" he

Always Meant to Be

asks, while removing another knife from the drawer and handing it to me.

I get to work on chopping the red onion, bell peppers, broccoli, garlic, and tomatoes while we talk. "I'll do it," I confirm as we work side by side. "Learning self-defense is a no-brainer, and Jimmy assured me he had no issue with you teaching me in the gym."

"Cool." He smiles warmly at me, and I get lost in his gorgeous face for a couple seconds.

"Mom." Stella stalks toward us, and I quickly drag my gaze from Vander. "Ridge is bored, so I'm going to take him downstairs to the boxing club to show him around. Jimmy said I could."

"Good idea, but be back in thirty minutes to help set the table for dinner."

"Aye, aye, captain." She salutes me before grabbing Ridge into a chokehold and wrangling him out the door.

Vander laughs. "Stella is a spitfire. The guys in school are nuts about her. They are all vying for her attention."

I groan. "Please don't tell me that." Stella has been the strongest of my kids since the separation, but that doesn't mean she's not feeling the emotional upheaval. She is just better at hiding it, which concerns me. I would rather she let it all out, but I suspect she's trying to put a brave face on for me. West is crazy emotional and super angry all the time. Ridge is sad at times when he's not distracted by school or sports or his friends.

Curtis took Ridge to his apartment in Denver last Friday night and kept him until Saturday evening. That is part of the interim agreement we have in place until we hash out the full details of the divorce. However, he is already breaking it. He texted me yesterday to say he couldn't take him tonight, but he'd take him Saturday night instead. He just expects I have no plans and it's okay to treat his son badly to accommodate his girlfriend. Not that he mentioned her, but I'm pretty sure she is the reason he switched the nights around.

"You don't need to worry about Stella, Kendall." Vander swipes some tomatoes from my board when he is finished cutting up his vegetables. "She knows how to handle herself. She might be a bit wild, but she's smart. Besides, West has them all terrified. If anyone even thought of doing her wrong, they have to answer to us."

That comforts me. I often wonder if I'd had a big brother would he have warned Curtis to treat me right or cautioned me against going out with him? "I'm glad Stella has people who care about her welfare."

"You do too." He looks over his shoulder, checking the coast is clear before he leans his face into mine. "Please say you'll come over tomorrow night. We really need to talk. Curtis has Ridge, and I used my injury to bail on the party West and Stella will be attending at Shep's house."

"I'll make you a deal."

He props one hip against the counter and smiles at me. "Let's hear it."

"If you come with me to the retirement home tomorrow, I'll come over here after."

"What's happening at the retirement home?"

I smother a giggle. "We're throwing the old folks a Christmas party, and one of the volunteers had to bow out at the last minute."

He shrugs. "Sure. I can do that if you promise you're mine for the night."

His wolfish grin does twisty things to my insides, and his eyes heat with dark promise. I want to give in to the amazing chemistry we share, but I'm not ready to rush into anything yet. I have loved having Vander stay with us, but it's been torturous too because I had to keep it strictly PG, and the temptation was almost too much to bear. "We can spend time together, but I *will* be going home." I subtly squeeze my thighs as my core throbs, and the devil in my ear screams at me for being a coward. "I'm coming over to talk, Vander. Nothing else."

"Okay." His impish grin pins me in place.

"Vander." My tone contains censure.

"What?" His grin widens as he holds his hands in the air. "We're only going to talk. It's not like you're hot for my body and afraid to admit it or anything."

Before I can retaliate, West pops his head in the door and the moment is over.

"You have got to be kidding me," Vander huffs, slanting narrowed eyes in my direction. "When you asked me to help, you failed to mention it would involve this!" He holds up the red and white Santa Claus costume and scowls at it.

"Where's your Christmas spirit?" I struggle to contain the giggle that wants to break free. "It's for a good cause, and I think you'll make an excellent Father Christmas."

"I think this deserves a reward." He waggles his brows and licks his lips suggestively. "I'll do it if you let me feast on your pussy after." His eyes glimmer with dark intent, and my nipples instantly harden as desire coils in my belly. "Or you could always get on your knees." His grin is downright wicked, and I'm throbbing down below, my neglected pussy rejoicing at the promise of some real action.

Jesus. I am so out of my depth with Vander. Curtis never spoke to me like this, and I didn't think I'd like it. But I do. I really do. I'm still not giving in though. "Nice try, but no."

"Say yes, baby, and you've got a deal." He nuzzles his nose

in my neck, and I shove him off before I do something reckless—like agree.

"We already have a deal, and I know you're a man of your word, so prove it." I thrust the fake belly into his chest. "You're going to need that, and don't forget to wear the beard," I add, backtracking out of the room.

"The least you could do is help me to get dressed." He clutches his side and bends over. "I'm still sore."

His pout is adorable, and I burst out laughing. "You have been dressing yourself for school all week. I think you'll manage." The bruising on his face is barely noticeable now, and his black eye is fading. It's nothing a little bit of makeup won't hide today. I know his ribs will be sore for another few weeks, but he's managing with a heating pad, anti-inflammatory gel, and pain meds, so he can't pull the wool over this gal's eyes.

His eyes flash with intent as he stalks toward me and reels me into his chest. "I know you've been daydreaming about your cock. Don't you want to see it again?" He thrusts his hips at me, confirming he's hard, and my legs almost go out from under me. "Touch it?" he purrs, grabbing my ass and pulling me firmly into his erection.

He is definitely getting braver, and I am falling harder.

He nips at my earlobe, and his warm breath sweeps over my cheek as he whispers, "I bet we could lock this door and grab some privacy." He pivots his hips, rocking into me again. "It won't take long. After almost two weeks in your house and not being able to touch you, I'm liable to explode the second you wrap those pretty fingers around my dick."

"Oh my." A quivering voice accompanies the words, and I shuck out of Vander's hold like I've been electrocuted, glaring at him for putting me in such a spot. "Aren't you quite the catch?" The older woman in the doorway swoons at Vander as she deliberately rakes her gaze over him from head to toe. "You're a lucky woman, Kendall." She waggles her brows at me, and it's a surreal moment. "Tell me, lovely. How do I get me one of those?" She points at Vander and grins.

Beverly is at least seventy, and while her brain is sharp, her body is letting her down. She had a stroke two years ago, which left her paralyzed from the waist down, which is when she moved into the retirement home. She wheels herself into the room, stopping her wheelchair directly in front of Vander so she can get a better look at him. She is brazen and bold, and I kind of idolize her.

"Beverly." I smooth a hand down the front of my dress and clear my throat. "I didn't see you there."

"I wouldn't have noticed either if I had the attention of this young stud."

Vander chuckles, extending his arm. "The name's Vander though young stud works too." He shakes her hand, laughing louder when she refuses to give it back.

"You have really big hands." She looks down at his feet. "Big feet too." Mischief dances in her eyes. "You know what they say about men with big feet and hands, don't you?" Her playful gaze dances from Vander to me and back again.

"I'll bite, Beverly," Vander says, still holding her hand. "What do they say?"

"Van!" I hiss. "Don't encourage her."

"That they also have big dicks," she blurts, and I feel another giggle building at the back of my throat. Finally releasing Vander's hand, she spins around on her chair to face me. "So, is it true? Does he have a big schlong?"

Vander bursts out laughing, and there are tears rolling out of his eyes. I glare at him and then Beverly.

"Don't ask Kendall to tell you," Vander says when he has composed himself. "She won't go near it."

"It's not for his lack of trying," I mumble, not expecting Beverly to have sharp hearing too.

"Well, if Kendall isn't interested, I am." Beverly turns her wheelchair around so she's facing Vander again. "Whip it out, young stud, and I'll tell you if the rumor is true."

Chapter Thirty

Vander

My cell vibrates with a succession of notifications, and I inwardly groan, already knowing what I'm going to see. I skim over the group chat comments as we exit the retirement home and walk toward Kendall's SUV, shaking my head. "I can't believe you sent photos to West. He shared them with everyone, and this afternoon will live on for eternity now. Thanks a bunch." There is zero heat in my tone because I'm not even the slightest bit mad, but I like teasing her. Ensuring no one is looking, I slap her ass as I lean down and nibble on her ear.

She shrieks, collapsing into giggles again. It was worth sweating under the heavy costume and enduring the way the too tight pants were strangling my balls just to hear Kendall laugh. All afternoon, she's had the biggest smile on her face, and I love it. I'd walk barefoot on hot coals if it meant she forgot her troubles and had a little fun. "I didn't know he would share them. I swear."

Reaching the car in the darkened visitor parking lot, I press her up against it and cage her in with my arms. "It's okay. You're going to make it up to me." I let a wolfish grin loose.

"I am, am I?" She arches a brow while raising the stakes.

"You know it, babe." I lean down to kiss her, but she twists her head to the side, so my lips graze her cheek instead of reaching the intended target.

"What are you doing?! Anyone could see!" Her tone borders on hysterical.

"Relax, sweetheart. This place is deserted, and it's dark." Without giving her a further out, I press my lips to hers and kiss her like I've been dying to do all afternoon. She caves instantly, snaking her arms around my neck and pressing her hot, tight body up against me. That's all it takes to elevate my desire to an all-time high. I growl into her mouth as I feast on her, devouring her lips as months of pent-up need run free. She whimpers against my lips as I grab her ass and pull her into me, leaving her in no doubt how much she turns me on.

Fuck, I want her. I want her bad.

"Vander," she pants, pushing me away and then pulling me back in close. "We need to stop."

I dip my mouth to her neck. "Promise me we can pick this up when we get home, and I'll let you go now. Otherwise, all bets are off." I suction my lips to her neck, nipping, licking, and kissing her soft skin as I inhale the scent that is uniquely her—sweetly floral and wickedly spicy.

"Fuck," she whispers, clutching the back of my shirt as I nuzzle that sensitive place between her neck and her collarbone.

Hearing her curse cranks my arousal up a few notches, and I'm painfully hard behind my jeans.

"Your mouth should be outlawed, Vander. It makes me lose all semblance of control," she admits in a raspy tone, arching her head back and moaning.

"Imagine what my cock will do to you." Reluctantly, I tear my lips from her body. Although the parking lot is empty, I won't take uncalculated risks with her. She blushes, and it's too fucking cute for words. "I'm partial to this color on your cheeks." I feather my fingers across her creamy skin.

"You make me feel like an inexperienced horny teenager." She stares deep into my eyes. "It's unnerving and exciting."

"I *am* a horny teenager, and trust me when I say no one has ever made me feel the way you do." I purposely leave the inexperienced bit out because I won't lie. Although, I am younger, I'm pretty sure I have had more sexual partners than Kendall. West mentioned one time how his parents were high-school sweethearts, so I doubt Kendall has had many lovers.

"It's embarrassing to admit I'm the same."

"That's not embarrassing, babe." I haul her into my arms and hold her tight. "It's called fate." She shivers against me, and I'm reminded we're outside on a cold, dark December night. "Let's get you inside the car, and then I'll take you home and warm you up."

"I don't mind cooking," Kendall says as I pull her SUV into a vacant spot in the parking lot of the strip mall a few blocks from my apartment.

I suggested we get takeout because I want her all to myself tonight. Killing the engine, I turn to face her. "I know you don't, but you work too hard, and you deserve to relax and chill out. Also, I'm needy and selfish. I don't want you wasting a second in the kitchen when I can have you in my arms instead."

She visibly melts as she leans across the console to plant a soft kiss on my lips. A guy could really get used to this. "You say the sweetest things."

"It's no lie." I wind my fingers in her hair. "I'm addicted to you, Kendall. Every minute I'm not with you is spent longing for you. Our time together is limited, so I always want to make the most of it."

"Well, come on then." She pulls back, grinning as she opens the door. "Let's not waste another second."

After we have placed our order at the Thai place, we head to the liquor store to pick up some beer and wine. We are returning to collect our order when Kendall slows in front of a housewares store and peers at the display in the window. "Do you want to go in?" I ask, leaning against the side of the door. "We have a few minutes to kill."

"You don't mind?"

I shake my head, frowning slightly. "Why would I mind?"

She opens her mouth to say something but clamps it shut again. "Okay." She beams up at me. "Come on."

I trail her around the store as she looks at everything, her eyes lighting up as she leans down to smell a candle or when she runs her fingers across one of the soft throws. "This store has the prettiest things," she says, smiling at the woman behind the cash register.

"Let me buy you something." I shove my hands in the pockets of my jeans to avoid taking her hand. Although my apartment is on the outskirts of town and it's unlikely we will run into anyone she knows, I automatically understand she doesn't want to be seen in any kind of romantic or compromising position with me in public. It sucks, but as long as I get to touch her in private, I can live with it.

"You don't need to do that. I earn my own money. I can afford to buy things for myself."

"I know you can," I say, taking the candle from her hand and picking up the pink throw she's eyeing lovingly. "But I want to get you something for your new bedroom. You have done so much for me, and I want to show my appreciation." Taking a risk, I lean down and whisper in her ear. "But mainly it's because I love you. I want to spoil you and take care of you. That's what soul mates do."

"Oh, Vander." Emotion pools in her eyes as she stares up at me with complete adoration. I freeze frame the moment because I never want to forget it.

"I fucking love you so much, Kendall. I wish I could shout it from the rooftops."

She subtly squeezes my hand. "We should go," she says in a low tone, glancing over my shoulder. "Before I throw all caution to the wind and kiss you right here."

The biggest grin graces my mouth. "I would have zero issue with that."

Her tinkling laughter swirls around me, and I don't think I have ever felt this happy.

Grabbing a second candle—to keep at my place for her—I walk to the counter and pay for all three items. Then we collect our takeout and head to my apartment.

"We should talk," Kendall says after we have eaten, put the leftovers in the refrigerator, and stacked the dirty dishes in the dishwasher.

"We should make out," I coolly reply, winking as I hand her a chilled glass of Sancerre. I kick off my sneakers and flop down on the couch beside her, slinging my arm around her shoulders and pulling her into my body as I take a sip of my beer.

"You're incorrigible." She rolls her eyes, but she's smiling as she snuggles into me.

"When it comes to you, absolutely." I tweak her nose and tug her closer.

She straightens up a little, twisting around so we're facing one another with my arm loosely draped over her shoulders. "What are we doing, Vander?"

"Talking, it would appear." I sigh before knocking back a mouthful of beer. I have a feeling I'll need it for this conversation.

"What do you want from me?"

I quirk a brow and slant her with a lustful look. "Everything, sweetheart. I want everything with you. Your present. Your future. Your heart. Your soul. Your body." I stop short of saying your hand in marriage because I don't want to completely terrorize her, but that thought doesn't scare me. Leaning in, I brush my thumb against her lower lip. "I just want *you*, Kendall. I can't breathe if I don't have you in my life."

"I come with so much baggage, Vander." She takes a sip of her wine while maintaining eye contact with me. "I'm a mess. My life is a mess. I don't want to drag you into my crap."

"You're not dragging me into anything I don't want to be dragged into, and I could say the same about my life. The only thing that makes any sense is you and me." I link our fingers and stare into her beautiful blue eyes. "I know what I want, Kendall. I want you."

"You can't mean that. It would be so much easier for you to date someone your own age. Someone without baggage."

I set my beer down on the end table and cup her face. I thought we had already settled this, but it's clear she needs more reassurance. "Baby, I don't want someone my own age. High-school girls have never appealed to me. They are all about the drama, and it's so hard to have a meaningful conversation with teenage girls." I don't want to generalize because it's not true of every girl, but I need to get my point across. "I have always gravitated toward older women, but even coeds are immature. I don't know how to make you understand me more clearly. I'm attracted to you on so many levels, Kendall. We have this undeniable chemistry, this electric connection, and you *get* me. I love talking with you, and I feel like I can tell you anything. We have deep conversations about the meaning of life, and you never judge. You listen and support. Everything about you fascinates me, and the more I learn about you, the harder I fall. Nothing you can say is going to change that. You can cut me out of your life, and it won't make any difference. I will always love you. It will always be you."

She gulps, and her eyes turn glassy. "You say that now, but you are still young. How do you know what you feel now is how you'll feel a year from now? Ten years from now?"

She has really put thought into this. "I have felt like this for hundreds, maybe thousands, of years, Kendall." I press a kiss to her brow as my fingers tangle in her hair. "I know my heart. I know what I am feeling will never change. You're the only one having trouble accepting this."

"I don't want to ruin your life. You have so much to look forward to."

"That's an impossibility, and I can still achieve my goals while in a relationship with you."

"Is that really what you want?"

I have to remember she's vulnerable because Curtis has done a lot of damage. While I feel like I have said this over and over and it's a little bit frustrating when I just want to be with her, I understand her concern. At least she seems to have accepted the concept of an us, and she has moved past the denial stage, which is progress. "It is. There is nothing you can say that will sway my mind."

"What about West?"

I dot kisses all over her face to buy myself some time before I reply. "I know my best friend, and I won't lie. He'll be pissed. He'll get angry and lash out. But, in time, he'll come around to the idea of us. As long as he sees that I'm treating you right, he'll be happy for us." I have given it a lot of thought, and I fully believe that. It won't be easy. West is stubborn, and he *will* freak out, but I know it won't be forever.

"We can't tell him now." She rests her head on my chest, and I fold my arms around her back. "He's so angry about his father and the divorce. I can't drop this on him too."

"The timing isn't right," I agree, tilting her head back. "Why don't we agree to keep our relationship a secret until graduation. The dust should've settled by then, you'll be divorced, and West will be looking forward to college. We can talk to him at that point and explain. He'll have all summer to come to terms with it and to see how good we are for one another."

"He'll hate us for going behind his back. He may never forgive us for that."

"He will. He's my best friend, and you're his mom. He loves you. He is prone to emotional reactions, but he's not unreasonable. As long as you're happy, he'll be fine. He *will* come around."

She doesn't look fully convinced as she shucks out of my arms and straightens up. "What's the point of even starting something now? You'll be gone in six months."

"Me leaving for college won't change how I feel about you or alter what I want to build with you. We'll do the long-distance thing. I'm renting an apartment off campus so you can come visit me some weekends, or I can come home. It's only a four-hour flight."

Her mouth hangs open. "You seriously want to remain in a relationship with me while you're in college?"

I nod without hesitation. "Like I said, I know what I want, and I want a life with you. I have never been surer about anything."

Always Meant to Be

"Those are the best years of your life, Vander. You don't want to be tied down to a divorced woman with three kids and a truckload of self-doubt."

"Don't sell yourself short, and I do. College, for me, is all about art and building the kind of career I have dreamed of. I have no interest in girls, and that won't change whether we are in a relationship or not. The only woman for me is you." She knocks back a large mouthful of her wine while I close the distance she created. I place my hands on her hips. "How about this? We agree to see each other from now until I graduate, and then we can talk about the future?" I won't change my mind, but I think I need to ease Kendall into this. Her self-confidence has been dealt a blow by her cheating ex, and she can't comprehend the depth of my feelings for her.

I have just under six months to prove to her I'm sincere and to convince her she belongs with me.

Challenge accepted.

Chapter Thirty-One

Kendall

I rap on Vander's door, four nights after Christmas, trying not to fidget, but my rapidly beating heart is making it difficult to concentrate on anything but him—the man who has stolen my heart and all sense of reason along with it. I have reached a decision about us, and it's a big step for me. I know that after tonight everything will change, and I'm incredibly nervous. More than I was the first time I had sex with Curtis and on my wedding day.

Not sure what that says about me.

"Where is your key?" Vander asks when he swings the door open.

"In my bag," I admit as he pulls me inside, closes and locks the door, and immediately folds me into his warm protective arms.

"What's it doing there?" His voice is muffled as he buries his face in my hair. "I gave it to you so you could come and go as you please."

I lift my head to peer up at him. I haven't seen him since Christmas day when he joined West, Stella, Ridge, and me for dinner. Curtis had begged me to let him share the day with us, but I refused. West is still not speaking to him, Stella has the bare minimum to do with her father, and although Ridge wanted him there, it's best he gets used to the new arrangement that will see us splitting up the holidays and spending time separately with the kids.

Vander stares at me expectantly, awaiting a response.

"We haven't resolved anything yet, and I didn't want to be presumptuous." We had a big heart-to-heart the Saturday before Christmas, and I left his apartment that night having given both of us a lot to think about.

"You know how I feel about you, and it won't change. The key is as much symbolic as it is practical," he says, pulling me over to the couch. The place is toasty warm, and he has a bottle of champagne resting in an ice bucket on the table along with two flutes and a bowl of chocolate strawberries.

"What's all this?" I ask, unbuttoning my coat.

"A celebration to mark the beginning of us." He smirks as I reach the last button on my coat. "How's that for presumptuous?"

I laugh as I slip the coat off my shoulders and hand it to him.

"Holy fuck." His eyes are out on stalks as his gaze roams me from head to toe, drinking in my fitted, lacy, strapless, black dress, sheer pantyhose, and skyscraper stilettos. He tosses my coat on the end of the leather sectional and reels me into his arms. "You are so fucking sexy," he murmurs, lowering his mouth to my neck. "Stay the night, Kendall. Let me make you mine."

I close my eyes as he plants a slew of drugging kisses up and down my neck. Shivers dance over my skin, and my legs almost buckle. His touch does the most amazing things to me. His hands mold against my ass as he pulls me in flush against the hard length of his erection. Even if I hadn't decided to give his six-month proposal a go, I would be hard-pressed to deny him anything right now. *Pun intended.* He turns me on like you wouldn't believe, and I'm like a dog in heat. It's so embarrassing, but it's the truth. "Okay," I whisper, and he stalls, lifting his head and gaping at me with shock splayed across his face.

"Okay?" Excitement blends with hope in his eyes.

"I'm tired of fighting my feelings for you," I admit, taking his hand and pulling him down onto the couch with me. "I want to give the six months a try, but I can't promise anything after that, Vander." He vigorously nods his head, still looking shell-shocked, like he can't believe I agreed. "And we've got to keep this between us. It means we can only meet here. We can't risk going out in public. If you want to do this, it has to be on those terms."

"I will take you however I can get you," he says, sounding dazed. "Holy shit, Kendall." He reels me into a huge hug. "I didn't think you'd agree."

"I almost didn't," I truthfully admit as we ease back with our arms still loosely in an embrace.

"What changed your mind?"

"June."

He raises a brow, urging me to continue.

"I spoke to her the day after Christmas. I needed to confide in someone."

"I thought you would've gone to Viola."

"I don't think Viola would understand." I run my fingers through the five-o'clock shadow on his jawline, loving the tingly feel of his bristle against my skin.

"You already knew what you were going to do." He palms one side of my face.

Slowly, I nod, not surprised he gets it. Vander has a high

level of emotional intelligence. "I just wanted someone to tell me it was okay to take something for myself."

"Remind me to thank June when I see her next."

"For someone who doesn't like cock, she sure was excited for me." I giggle as I recall our conversation. "I had barely gotten the words out of my mouth when she was dancing around the room, screaming and shouting and telling me to go for it." I hold back on telling him exactly what she said. It made me blush, and it would only stroke Vander's ego.

June is into women and happily engaged to her fiancée, Carly, but she didn't hold back in her gushing about Vander. It seems I'm not the only older woman who has noticed how hot he is.

"I knew I liked her for a reason." Vander scoops me up and deposits me on his lap until I'm straddling him. My short dress rides up my thighs, and I'm flashing a lot of skin. His eyes darken, and a shudder works its way through me. My new panties are already wet, and he hasn't even touched me.

Adrenaline courses through my veins, comingling with trepidation. "I'm scared," I admit, placing my hands on his shoulders.

"Scared of what, baby?" He rubs his nose up and down my neck as his hands land low on my back. "You know I'll take care of you."

"Scared of everything." I want to say this last piece and then move forward with my decision. "Scared my kids will hate me if they find out. Scared of ruining your life when you have your entire future ahead of you. Scared of losing you when you discover I'm not everything you make me out to be." I toy with the hairs on the nape of his neck. "Scared of loving you so much I forget myself all over again." *Scared of getting naked with a guy who looks as perfect as you do, knowing I won't compare to the girls who have come before.* I hold the thought back because that insecurity is best left unspoken.

"It wouldn't be worth the risk unless there was something to lose, and it's completely understandable to be scared." He lifts my hand, pressing a soft kiss to the underside of my wrist. "I'm scared of getting everything my heart desires and not being able to hold on to it."

"It's not too late to back out," I say, hating how those words feel like a dagger slicing through my heart. I am already so invested in him. Deep down, I've been denying how I feel, hiding behind all the obstacles and clinging to them instead of facing my reality. I am already half in love with Vander, and I don't think it will take long to give him the rest of my heart.

"We both know it is." He brushes a soft kiss on the corner of my mouth. "There is nothing you or I could do to fight this. We are meant to be." He kisses the other corner of my mouth.

"I'm so selfish," I whisper. "I used to think I was a good mom, but a good mom doesn't sneak around with her son's best friend behind his back, especially knowing the risks."

"Your being with me doesn't make you a bad mom, Kendall. There is nothing wrong with taking happiness for yourself." His lips glide briefly against mine, and a contented whimper flies from my mouth. "This feels good, feels right, because you and I were written in the stars, babe." He wraps me up in a huge hug with his face buried against my chest. "Don't feel guilty for being with me when it was always our destiny." His warm breath ghosts over the exposed skin of my cleavage, hardening my nipples to sharp points.

"I will try," I truthfully say because it's not like this guilt is going to evaporate in a puff of air.

"I can't deal with uncertainty." He pulls back and stares up at me. "If you are giving me six months, I need you to fully commit to it, Kendall. Anything less will only mess with my head."

"I'm committing to you," I say without hesitation. "That won't change. I'm just explaining I will have periods where I have doubts and I'm consumed with self-loathing and guilt. You need to prepare yourself for that."

"We can work through it as long as we are together."

"Let's do this then," I say, leaning down to kiss him. "Let's be wild and reckless together."

Chapter Thirty-Two

Kendall

Vander immediately takes control of the kiss, angling his head and gorging on my mouth with urgent, impatient lips. We devour one another, and I groan when his tongue slips between my lips, exploring the inside of my mouth. His hands clamp down on my ass, and I slide down his body until my dress has ridden to my upper thighs and I'm sitting directly on top of his erection.

I don't know who moves first, but it heats up fast. We are frantically thrusting against one another in a desperate quest to get closer, and it's still not enough. Grabbing fistfuls of his hair, I rock my hips against the bulge straining beneath his sweatpants, grinding myself along his hard length as every nerve ending in my body comes alive. He bites down on my lower lip, before soothing it with his tongue, while his fingers creep under the hem of my dress from behind. I moan into his mouth as he kneads my ass through my flimsy lace panties. Liquid lust gushes from my core as his fingers brush against my bare flesh, and I'm about ready to erupt from my skin.

My nipples ache behind my dress as I thrust my body

against his while he eats my mouth with a savagery I love. "Wrap your legs around my waist and hold on tight," he demands when he pauses to draw a breath. I do as I'm told, clinging to him as he stands and walks toward the bed tucked into the alcove just inside the window. He continues kissing me, and it helps to steady my nerves.

Very carefully, he lowers me to the center of the bed on my back before climbing over me. Keeping himself propped up by his elbows, he peers into my eyes, his expression serious and full of longing. "Please tell me you want this." He traces the tip of his finger across my collarbone, eliciting a rake of fiery shivers along my skin.

"I want this," I say in a husky voice. "But I'm nervous." He's used to nubile, flawless bodies, and that's not me. I know I'm in good shape for my age, and I'm not immune to the way men look at me, but I'm no pretty young thing with a bag of sexual tricks up her sleeve.

"Don't be nervous. I will take good care of you." He kisses me softly, which is at huge odds with how he was devouring me on the couch. "I know how to make it good for you, but I won't lie. I'm primed to explode, and I can't be gentle the first time. I need to fuck you, Kendall. I need to fuck you hard so your body understands you're mine now."

Jesus Christ. I truly am out of my depth with him, but I'm looking forward to getting schooled. "I want you to fuck me hard. Don't hold back, Vander. Give it all to me."

My words ignite something inside both of us, and it's like a race to strip out of our clothing.

"You're so fucking beautiful," he says when we are down to our underwear. "Sexy too," he adds, skimming his fingers over the front of my lacy, strapless, black bra. He lowers his head and trails his lips along the swells of my B-cup breasts as his hands roam freely over the bare skin of my stomach. I flinch a little when his fingers ghost over my stretchmarks, and he notices because he bends his head, dropping feather-soft kisses along the puckered skin, making me feel cherished and helping to settle my nerves. "You're perfect," he murmurs, licking a line across my lower belly as he eyeballs me. "Never believe anything less."

Every drag of his tongue has my core pulsing with need, and I run my fingers over his shoulders, exploring the toned muscles of his back as he worships my body with a reverence that I'm unused to. He moves back up my body, planting a passionate kiss on my lips, and I practically melt into the bed. Reaching around, he unclips my bra as he stares deep into my eyes. "I love you." He flings the bra aside, exposing my bare breasts to him for the first time. I have to fight the urge to cover myself, and I'm sure he can see how I'm trembling.

Lying on his side, he trails his fingers up my body as his eyes fixate on my chest, and he drinks his fill. "Don't be nervous. You're so fucking gorgeous." He cups one of my breasts. Lowering his mouth to my other breast, he flicks his tongue over the hard peak of my nipple. "These are perfect." He lavishes attention on both breasts with his mouth and his fingers, alternating between them until I'm a writhing mess on the bed. Every time he sucks on my nipple or squeezes my flesh, I feel it down below, and my panties are drenched, such is my need for him.

I'm close to coming before he's even touched my pussy. His hard-on is hot and heavy through his boxers against my leg as he diverts his attention from my chest and moves lower. He leaves a fiery path in his wake as he kisses and caresses his way down my body until his mouth is hovering over my lace-covered mound.

Pushing my legs apart, he repositions himself in between my thighs and dips his head until he's eye level with my vagina.

I'm on fire. Panting and sweating and tingling with need. All lingering trace of nerves evaporates when he presses his mouth over my core and looks up at me. "It's time to feast on my pussy," he purrs, lifting my ass with both hands as he tugs on my panties with his teeth. Losing patience quickly, he drops my ass and rips my panties on either side, shoving the scraps of lace aside as he lowers his mouth to my crotch and dives in.

I'm grateful for my recent spa trip and the neat landing strip I'm now sporting. It's been a while since I've had to bother with grooming down there, and I'm glad I had the foresight to get waxed everywhere. I also had a mani, pedi, and a facial because I wanted to look as good as possible knowing this moment was approaching.

I almost fall off the bed with the first swipe of his tongue against my slit. My hands curl into the comforter as he parts my folds and proceeds to eat me with his lips and his tongue. "Oh, God," I moan, closing my eyes and giving myself over to the new sensation. I cry out when his tongue thrusts inside me and his fingers begin circling my clit. He applies the right kind of pressure to my sensitive bundle of nerves as his fingers pick up their pace, rubbing me harder and faster.

"Oh, God, Vander." I shove my pussy in his face when I feel my climax building, too turned on to be ashamed of how I'm wantonly rubbing myself all over him. "Don't stop. Please, don't stop." I blink my eyes open when he pinches my clit, and I climb higher, almost reaching a peak. I'm jerking my hips into his face as his eyes latch on to mine while he eats me alive.

We maintain eye contact, and it's one of the hottest moments of my life. He rubs harder, thrusting his tongue into me deeper, and I explode into a million bright lights when he pinches my clit for a second time, and my orgasm rockets through me like a powerful tornado.

I come undone in a way I never have before, thrashing and

moaning and repeating his name, as he continues to work me until he has sated every last drop of my orgasm. I vaguely feel him move over me and open the drawer of the nightstand while I try to return to Earth from my heavenly high.

When I refocus my vision, he is kneeling between my spent thighs, his erection hard and straining and fully sheathed. "Ready, babe?" he asks, leaning down to kiss me.

Tasting myself on his lips is a first. It seems so dirty, but it cranks my arousal to dizzy heights and supercharges my bravery. "Fuck me, Vander. Please."

Holding his cock, he guides it to my opening, gluing his eyes to mine as he nudges my entrance before he slams into me in one hard thrust. I scream, instantly wrapping my legs around his waist as he starts pumping in and out of me like a man on a mission. Yanking my hips up, he urges my legs to hold on tighter. I tilt my pelvis, clinging to his body as he thrusts into mine, hitting places inside me I have never felt before. He bends down to kiss me while he fondles my breast. I claw at his shoulders and his back, arching my head and granting him access to my neck as he plunders me, working my body like a finely tuned instrument, evoking a host of sensations that are wholly new.

In one powerful move, he surges upright, taking me with him as one muscular arm bands around my back holding me on his lap while he fucks me. My arms wind around his neck as his mouth covers my breasts, his tongue darting out to flick my over-sensitized nipples as I bounce up and down on his cock, and he grinds up into me. I grab his hair, whimpering and moaning while he palms my ass, worships my breasts, and rams his big dick inside me.

"I need to go deeper," he grunts, removing his mouth from my chest. "Get on all fours, babe." He slaps my ass, hard, before I scramble off him and get into position. With his leg, he shoves my thighs wider apart before driving his erection into me from behind. We both hiss as we reconnect, and then he digs his hands into my hips while pressing my head into the pillow. I cling to the bed as he ruts into me like a wild animal, shoving his dick so far inside me it feels like he's penetrating my womb.

The grunts slipping from his mouth are primal and raw, and I'm cresting the wave of another orgasm while he pounds into me, and I slam back into him as we create a natural rhythm. The only sounds in the room are skin slapping against skin and our mutual groaning. "Fuck, Kendall. You feel so damn good," he pants in between thrusts. "I'm not going to last much longer." Covering me with his body, his fingers find my clit again, and he rubs me in sync with the movements of his hips as we both chase our climaxes. Pressure is building inside me, quicker than I thought possible after my last orgasm, and tears of joy prick my eyes when I fall off the cliff, and seconds later, he joins me.

We continue moving our hips until we are both sated, and then we collapse onto the bed in a tangle of sweaty limbs. Emotion has swollen my chest to bursting point, and I'm struggling to contain it when he spoons me from behind, wrapping his arms tightly around my waist, holding me close, and kissing my neck, like he just can't get enough. The tender way he's cuddling with me is the opposite of the possessive way he took me, and I'm a mess as so many emotions lay siege to me.

I burst into tears as I cling to his arms, wondering how I got so lucky and praying I'm enough to hold on to him. Because now I know what it's like to be with him, I don't ever want to let him go.

Chapter Thirty-Three

Vander

Her sobs gut me, and the thought I might have hurt her devastates me. "What's wrong? Why are you crying?" I turn her around in my arms. Her face is blotchy, and her lower lip wobbles as tears cling to her lashes. Her hair is a knotty mess from my hands, and her lips are swollen from my kisses, yet she has never looked more beautiful to me. "Did I hurt you?" That was the best sex of my life, and the thought it might not have been the same for her is agonizing.

"What?" She shakes her head as her eyes pop wide. "No. Of course not." She audibly gulps while struggling to compose her emotions. She cups my cheek as she stares lovingly into my eyes. "Sex has never been like that for me, Vander. I've never orgasmed from penetration, and no man has ever gone down on me. I didn't know it could be so good. I'm a little overwhelmed." Two red dots bloom on her cheeks before she buries her head in my chest.

Shock renders me speechless for a few seconds before I

clear my throat. "Kendall." Gently, I angle her head so we are eye to eye. "Are you for real right now?"

She nods. "I would never lie about that."

It's risky asking this, but I need to know what I'm dealing with. "How many men have you slept with?"

"Only my husband," she whispers as she draws circles on my chest with her finger. A little laugh leaks from her lips. "Pathetic, right?"

Wow. Just wow. "The only pathetic one is Curtis." Anger burns inside me as I consider all the ways he has neglected his wife. "What a fucking selfish asshole."

"I never had anyone to compare him to, but you're right. He was lazy and completely selfish in bed. It was only ever about his needs."

I want to strangle the life from that prick, more so now than ever. What a cunt. On the plus side, it means I can claim a lot of firsts I thought were lost to me. "I can't believe he never made you come during sex."

"Try ever," she whispers. "He has never made me come."

If she wasn't clinging to me, I think I would've fallen off the bed. "I'm going to enjoy giving you pleasure and showing you what you've been missing," I say when I have recovered from the shock. I am done talking about that jackass. "Was I too rough?" We probably should've talked about sex before we went there. I just assumed because she'd been married for a long time it wasn't necessary.

She shakes her head, her blush expanding as she smiles. "Not at all. I liked it. I liked it a lot."

I kiss her softly. "That was incredible, and I'm dying to do it again." Taking her fingers, I curl them around my cock so she feels how ready I am for round two. I kiss her again, harder this time, before purposely withdrawing. There is something I'm dying to show her, and it can't wait a second longer. "But first, I want to give you a gift."

"You already gave me a gift." Her fingers close around the Tiffany chain hanging around her neck.

"I have something else for you. Something I couldn't give you at Christmas." Prying her fingers from my dick, I climb out of the bed. She pouts, and it's adorable. Chuckling, I bend down to kiss her. "Don't worry, babe. The night is young, and I am far from finished with you." I give her tits a quick squeeze. "Let me grab my sketch pad."

I race to the dining room table and snatch my pad before returning to the bed. Kendall is sitting up against the headrest with the covers pulled up under her arms. I get in beside her and set the pad on my lap. Turning to face her, I yank the covers down to her waist. "Let's get one thing straight, sweetheart. When you're in my bed, you don't cover up. You'll be naked and proud." I let my heated gaze roam her body while I force her hand to my dick so she feels how it jerks and twitches while my eyes feast on her gorgeous body. "Do you feel what you do to me?" She nods. "Use your words, Kendall."

"I feel it," she croaks.

"Feel what?" I envelop my hand around her hand on my dick.

"I feel how much I turn you on."

I peck her lips. "Good girl." I clasp her face in my hands. "I know you're nervous and suffering with doubts, so I will keep repeating myself until you understand. I love you. I want you. I desire you. You're beautiful. You're perfect. You never have to hide from me. Okay?"

"Okay." A dazzling smile spreads across her lush mouth, and I'm entranced. "You're so good for my ego."

"I'm good for you. Period." I pin her with a cocky look as I lower my hands to my sketch pad.

"You are." She leans her head on my shoulder, glancing down as I flick through pages until I come to the one I want.

She gasps and lifts her head. "Is that...?"

"Your tattoo," I confirm, moving the sketch pad onto her lap so she can inspect the butterfly drawing in more detail.

"Oh, Vander. It's stunning." She skims her fingers over the design with an awestruck expression on her face. The butterfly's wings are open, as if in flight, and I colored them a vibrant blue with brown-rimmed tips. A myriad of twinkling white lights extends over the wings and above, giving it an ethereal quality. "I love these lights, and it's so pretty. This quote is perfect too." Her eyes are dancing as she raises them to mine. "Aurelius?"

I nod, sliding my arm around her shoulders and pressing my lips to her temple. "I found a couple of quotes that would work, but this one fit best."

"The past is the doorway to the future," she reads in a reverent tone.

"That's a blue morpho butterfly," I explain. "Butterflies have many meanings within different cultures, usually symbolizing life, love, change, and rebirth." I track a path up and down her arm with the tip of my finger as I talk. "Many believe butterflies represent a person's essence or soul, and the color blue represents joy or a change in luck. Some say the morpho butterfly is a wish granter." I peer deep into her big blue eyes. "I wanted to design a tattoo that had meaning for us and was something that represented who you are as a person too. I wanted something feminine and pretty just like you. And I love that it matches the color of your eyes."

Setting the sketch pad aside, she climbs onto my lap and smashes her lips against mine. Elation seeps from her mouth to mine as she kisses me passionately, and I want a lifetime of kisses like this. When we finally break for air, we are both panting, and I'm hard as a rock underneath her ass. "I have never met anyone who gets me the way you do or anyone more thoughtful." Her eyes fill up. "You make it impossible not to fall, Vander. I can't believe you are mine. It's surreal."

"Believe it, babe." Reaching over, I pull the drawer open on my nightstand and grab a few condoms before tossing them on the bed. "Because I *am* yours. Now and always."

Her eyes are drowning in love, and she doesn't need to say it for me to know. Perhaps she hasn't realized it herself yet, but I see it, and that's good enough for now. "I already asked Boner if he'd do your ink, and he agreed."

"Boner?" Her eyes widen. "Do I even want to know?"

I chuckle. "Probably not. He's one of my friends from the boxing club. He's the one who did my ink, and he's a true artist. Honestly, I wouldn't trust anyone else with you."

Her fingers skate over my ink. "I wondered how you managed to get inked before you were eighteen because I know your father wouldn't have consented."

"He didn't. I forged his signature on the paperwork." I shrug, chuckling at her disapproving expression. "Boner knew. He didn't care as long as he had something on file."

"You'd better hope Gregory doesn't find out."

"I'm not worried. Even the psycho wouldn't cross Boner." I grab her ass in both my hands as my tongue darts out, and I lick between the valley of her tits. "He looks scary, but he's a gentle giant, and I promise you're in good hands."

"Will you go with me?" she asks, grinding slowly on top of me.

"It's not optional." A moan slips from my lips as she moves over my erection. Stars burst behind my eyes as her bare pussy slides along the length of my cock. Goddamn. I really want to fuck her without any barriers. "Babe." I clamp my hands on her hips, stalling her movement so I can look her in the eyes. "Are you on birth control?"

She nods as she drags her fingers through my hair. "I'm clean too. Got tested recently."

"I have always used condoms, but I don't want to with you. I want to feel all of you."

"I would like that too." She nips at my ear. "But I don't think we should get used to it. The pill isn't infallible, and we should still use condoms most of the time."

I swat the condoms off the bed onto the floor. "Okay." I'd agree to just about anything while she rubs her pussy back and forth along my dick. "Ride me, baby." I tug on her lower lip, dragging it gently between my teeth. "Claim your cock, and do to it what you like."

That alluring blush creeps up her neck and onto her cheeks as she reaches back, grips my cock, and holds it steady while she positions herself over me. I watch her chest heave as she slowly lowers herself onto my dick, until I'm fully situated, and I wonder if this is another first. Her eyes lock on mine while she holds herself still, letting both of us acclimate. Grabbing her face, I pull her lips to mine and ravish her mouth as my cock pulses inside her warm inner walls. "Jesus, Kendall," I whisper over her skin as I nip at her jaw before trailing kisses along her neck. "You feel incredible. Nothing compares to this, but I need you to move, baby."

She bounces up and down on me, and pleasure zips up my spine as her channel squeezes me with every thrust of her hips. Her tits jiggle when she picks up speed, and I bury my face in her chest while grabbing handfuls of her ass. I jerk her up and down on me as I suck, lick, and bite her tits and her nipples. She is writhing and moaning on top of me, and she has never looked hotter. Moving my hands to her hips, I control her movements, slamming her up and down on my dick, but it's not

Always Meant to Be

enough. I need more. I need to impale myself inside her so I leave an indelible mark.

Without warning, I swing my legs over the side of the bed and stand, keeping her latched on to my cock, until I reposition us at the edge of the bed. Lowering her on her back, I thrust her legs over my shoulders before bending my knees until I reach the right angle to drive into her. I ram into her like a madman, pushing all the way in and pulling back out. I keep up a punishing pace because I can't control my hormones or the possessive need to own her completely. Her body jostles up and down on the bed as I pound into her, tilting her hips up so I can drive even deeper. But it's still not deep enough.

Bending down over her, with her legs still hanging off my shoulders, I plant my hands on either side of her head as I fuck her into the bed, grunting as I push myself in farther and farther, fueled by this relentless need to bury myself deep, deep, deep. My mouth collides with hers in a desperate marriage of lips, teeth, and tongue, and I swallow her cries as I feel a familiar tingle building at the base of my spine and my balls tightening. I know I can't hold back for much longer, so I push up off the bed and maneuver us around until we're lying vertically across the middle.

Rearing up onto my knees, I latch her legs around my waist and move my fingers to her clit while I slam in and out of her. "I'm almost there," I pant as a line of sweat glides down my spine. Little beads of sweat dampen her forehead, plastering strands of golden hair to her brow. "Come with me." I flick at her nub as I plow into her with my cock, holding a little back in an attempt to delay the inevitable. I won't let loose until she's ready to soar with me. With my free hand, I explore her body, running my fingers over her hips, her stomach, and up to her tits.

When I tweak her nipples, she lets out a primitive moan,

and her back arches off the bed. Her hips buck, her breathing speeds up, and a flush spreads over her pretty skin, and I know she's close. Pressing down on her clit, I rut into her harder and faster, and I can't stop my orgasm.

I let out a roar as I come, rubbing her tight bundle of nerves, and then she's flying with me, and the sounds bouncing off the walls of my apartment are almost inhuman.

I collapse on top of her before rolling to the side and taking her with me. Pushing her hair out of her eyes, I carefully examine her face. There are no tears this time, only the biggest smile. She laughs, scraping her fingers through my hair in a way that has me purring like a cat. "I have a feeling you're going to exhaust me, Vander." She leans in and kisses me. "Is sex with you always a full-body workout?" she teases, dropping kisses on my chest while I recalibrate my breathing.

"Yes, and yes," I pant, grabbing fistfuls of her hair and angling her head so she's looking at me. "I love you."

Her features soften. "I know." She places her hand over my heart before dipping her head and kissing my chest.

"I won't ever get tired of showing you how much." My fingers creep down her spine, and my palm flattens on her ass. I knead her flesh, and a little squeal escapes her mouth. I smirk, dusting kisses all over her face. "Give me three minutes, and I'll be ready to prove it to you again."

Chapter Thirty-Four

Kendall

"Someone seems happy," June says, popping her head in the door of my office on Monday.

"That is one way of putting it." I grin at her like a loon because I can't stop smiling. I have been floating on a cloud since Saturday-night-slash-Sunday-morning. "Want to go out for lunch?"

"Abso-fucking-lutely." She winks. "I want all the juicy details!"

I stand and grab my coat. "I think that can be arranged."

"Okay, spill, chica. Please tell me the reason you're walking a little funny is because you got the best dicking of your life over the weekend," June says, occupying one of the seats at the corner table of the coffee place around the block from the office.

I stare at my friend with my mouth hanging open as I

deposit the tray with our wraps and coffees on the table. "Wow. Way to just put it out there."

"I'm calling it like I see it." She grabs her wrap and takes a sip of her coffee as I claim the seat opposite her.

"Am I really walking funny?" I won't deny I'm sore or every time I sit I still feel Vander inside me, but I didn't think it was noticeable.

"Only to the discernible eye."

That just means her. "Okay, good, because I can't have people figuring out what's going on."

"What happened?" She pins eager eyes on me as she bites into her wrap.

My cheeks heat as I unwrap my lunch. "I did it," I say, looking around to ensure no one from work is here. "I committed to him for six months, and we had sex." My lips curve at the corners. "For hours. Over and over again. In all manner of positions. All of Saturday night and again on Sunday morning."

She claps her hands in glee and squeals, like she's five. "That is freaking awesome, and I don't need to ask if it was good because no one fucks for hours if it isn't."

I lower my voice and lean toward her. "He's a fucking god in the bedroom. Like, he seriously blew my mind. I never knew sex could be so amazing. I haven't been able to stop thinking about it, and I'm on a countdown until we can do it again." I let a wide grin loose. "I think I'm addicted to sex with him." I shrug, still grinning. "I think I'm just addicted to him, period." I bite into my wrap, basking in the afterglow and letting my excitement bubble to the surface. "He's incredible, June. So thoughtful and attentive, and I just love spending time with him."

Her mouth makes an O shape. "Oh, wow. You're in love with him."

"I'm not ready to admit that to myself," I truthfully reply because I'm the queen of denial lately. "He tells me he loves me all the time, but I won't say it until I'm sure what I'm feeling is love."

"Bullshit." June dabs sauce from the corner of her mouth with a napkin. "You know what you're feeling. You're just terrified to admit it, and that's okay, Ken. You should go at your own pace, and don't feel pressured to do or say anything you don't want to."

"He doesn't pressure me. Not at all. He's letting me set the pace, yet he totally took charge too, and it was so freaking hot." I squeeze my thighs together as liquid heat gushes to my core when I remember all the ways he commanded my body. Glancing around again to ensure no one is listening, I strain toward her over the table. "He gave me five orgasms! Five in one night!" A giggle rips from my mouth. "Curtis never gave me one, and I was married to him for over seventeen years."

June almost falls off her chair. "What the actual fuck?"

"I know." I take another bite of my wrap. "I can't believe I was so complacent. That I accepted it and didn't demand more." I take a sip of my coffee. "Vander has really opened my eyes. I totally settled with Curtis, in all aspects of our lives together. Why did I do that?"

Sympathy splays across her face. "You were young when you met, and then you were busy with the kids and your career. You put your own needs on the back burner. You're only realizing it now because you've had no choice but to confront it."

"I feel like I've been wasting my life. Not my kids, obviously. They're my world. But why didn't I divorce Curtis years ago? Even before his first affair came to light?" I shake my head. "I'm annoyed at myself for letting myself be treated like this for years. For fooling myself into thinking I had a happy marriage and a loving partner." I tear off a big lump of my wrap, chewing slowly as June waits for me to continue. "Vander is only eighteen," I whisper. "We have only just begun, and already he's making me feel cherished and adored in a way Curtis never did. I've been so stupid."

"You're doing something about it now, and you are exactly where you should be in life. Don't look back and regret what's come before because you might not have found Vander if things had panned out differently. I think that's the only way you can look at it."

It's so simple when she puts it like that. "You're right, and it's not like I can change my past, so dwelling on it will get me nowhere."

The door swings open as I search through my bag for my keys. Vander pulls me into his apartment and pushes me up against the wall. His lips crash down on mine in a demanding kiss, and my bag drops to the floor as I encircle my arms around his neck and drive my fingers into his hair. I love how much he wants me and how he's not afraid to show it. This is all so new, but I am loving it, and I can't get enough of him either. Our kissing quickly escalates, turning frenzied as we grope each other through our clothes, desperate for one another.

I don't protest when he shoves my skirt up to my hips, pushes my panties aside, and plunges two fingers inside me. "Fuck, baby. You're so wet," he mumbles against my neck as his lips glide over my overheated skin. "Are you sore?" he inquires, tenderly pumping his digits in and out of me.

"No," I semi-lie. "I want you, and you don't need to be gentle."

"Thank fuck." Using his free hand, he shoves his sweatpants down his thighs, and his cock springs out, long, thick, hard, and all mine for the taking.

Licking my lips, I swipe my thumb across the precum beading the crown of his dick while smiling. "Going commando?"

"It's my new thing," he confirms, adding a third digit and roughly thrusting his fingers inside me while his thumb rubs circles on my clit. "Our time is precious. I want to be ready to take advantage of every opportunity." He winks, and I'd laugh, only he chooses that moment to press down hard on my clit and my legs turn to Jell-O. I already feel my climax building, and I'm amazed at how quickly he gets me there. "We don't have much time," he says, removing his fingers and lifting my leg. He fastens it around his hip. "This will be hard and fast, baby, so hold on tight."

I shriek as he slides an arm around my back and coaxes my other leg up until I'm wrapped around him and he's holding me up. With skill, he guides his cock to my entrance and pushes inside me. A guttural moan trickles from my mouth as he fucks me, hard and fast—as promised—against the wall. I cling to him, kissing him repeatedly as he thrusts into me while holding me up between him and the wall like I weigh nothing. His fingers move down between our bodies, and he resumes playing with my clit as he speeds up, pivoting his hips and drilling into me while I hold on for dear life.

We come within seconds of each other, and I can hardly feel my legs as he slowly lowers them to the ground. I hold on to him because I don't trust myself to remain standing if he lets go. His lips move softly against mine, and I'm so gone for him. He already means so much to me. "I could get used to that greeting," I quip, sweeping my fingers over his gorgeous face.

"Good." He kisses the end of my nose. "Because there's plenty more where that came from." He bundles me into a hug, holding me tight. "I can't stop thinking about you or reliving last weekend. My bed feels empty waking up without you in it."

"I know the feeling." I rest my cheek on his shoulder and savor the feeling of being in his arms. "I have never had this before, Vander," I admit, playing with the ends of his hair. "I imagine this is what it feels like to be high."

"I'm your drug." He lifts his head, and even if I didn't see his massive grin, I hear it in his tone. "And you're most definitely mine." He rubs his nose against mine, and I melt. *How is someone young so romantic yet sexy and hot at the same time?* It's not like he had any role model to live up to. It's clearly intrinsic. Born of years and years of loving me in the past. The more we are together, the more I truly believe that because it feels so natural being with him like this.

"Drugs aren't healthy," I remind him.

"Not all drugs are bad," he whispers, suctioning his lips to my neck. "Some are life-sustaining."

There he goes being all perfect again. "That they are." I dust kisses all over his handsome face before gently pushing him away. "I told Stella I'd be home by eight." I hate we don't get many opportunities to be together, but he doesn't complain.

Taking my hand, he lifts it to his lips before planting a kiss on my palm. "Okay." He pulls up his sweats and lowers my skirt over my hips. "Get changed, and we'll head downstairs together."

"Everyone is staring," I murmur, sticking close to Vander's side as we walk through the boxing club, heading toward the area at the back with the mats.

Always Meant to Be

"Ignore them." He shoves his middle finger up at a guy who is blatantly checking out my ass. "They're all nosy bastards."

"What do they think this is?" I whisper.

"Exactly what it is. I'm teaching my buddy's mom self-defense because she's recently separated, hot as fuck, and she needs to learn how to defend herself from assholes and perverts."

I roll my eyes and crick my neck from side to side to loosen some of the tension. Vander drops my bag on the ground, beside the mats, as Jimmy approaches.

"Kendall." He gives me a quick hug. "It's good to see you."

"You too, Jimmy. Thanks for letting us do this here."

"Not a problem. In fact, I was wondering if we shouldn't maybe make this a regular thing. Invite other women to sign up."

"That's a freaking awesome idea," Crusher says, lifting me up as he wraps me in a hug. "How's it hanging, Ken?"

Vander yanks me out of his arms and glares at his buddy. "Stop manhandling her."

Crusher chuckles before lowering his voice. "Unless you want everyone to know you've got a hard-on for your buddy's mom, it's probably best not to get so territorial."

All the blood drains from my face, and I whip my head around to Vander's. He promised we would keep this a secret, and I will lose my shit if he hasn't kept his word.

Vander flips him the bird. "It's called respect, douche."

"Okay. Enough." Jimmy steps in between them. "Crusher, go warm up in the ring, and let Kendall and Vander get started." Vander frowns when he spots my glare. Jimmy smiles softly while shaking his head. "I'm the only one who knows, Kendall, and I will never tell. Crusher is just being Crusher." Jimmy turns his attention to Vander. "Keep it strictly professional, son."

"I fully intend to." A muscle clenches in Vander's jaw as he watches Jimmy walk away. "I swear I didn't say anything to Crusher," he says, stretching his arms up over his head. "He's just making assumptions."

"We can't ever let our guard drop." I chew on the inside of my mouth as I feel eyeballs on my back. "Maybe we should do this upstairs from now on."

Vander smothers a grin. "Then we wouldn't get anything done."

I cough to disguise my laugh. "True."

"Come on. Let's warm up, and then I'll run through some basic techniques with you."

By the time I leave an hour later, I'm sweating profusely, I ache all over, and I realize I'd be utterly useless if anyone came at me. I wasn't able to block any of Vander's moves, and he overpowered me every single time. It was also difficult concentrating with him touching me so much. But there is no denying I need it, and I intend to talk to Viola and June to suggest they get some training too.

"Got a minute?" I ask June the following Monday as I lounge against the door to her office. Her head is buried in her laptop, and she has a look of fierce concentration on her face.

"Of course. Come in."

I step inside and shut the door behind me. "I need a favor."

She leans back in her chair and sets her pen down. "What's up?"

"Does Carly's friend still work in the administration office at Yale?"

She nods. "She does. She recently got promoted too."

Good. That might come in handy. "Do you think you could

arrange a phone call? I want to talk to her about financial aid for Vander."

June arches a brow. "He got in?"

I smile. "He got early acceptance." I'm not surprised. I knew he would be offered a place. "West got into OU too on a football scholarship."

"That's amazing news. You must be so proud."

"I am, but I'm worried about Vander. His finances aren't great, but the financial aid options at Yale are based on ability to pay, and his father's wealth could be a big issue. I want to find out how we can submit a special case for him." Vander doesn't know I'm doing this or that I saw the papers spread out on his coffee table over the weekend. I wasn't snooping, per se, because his budget calculation was in plain sight. He is paying for his mother's rehab, and it isn't cheap. He'll be lucky if he can afford one year of Yale. I saw applications for student loans, but if he can get financial aid from the college, it'll save him racking up a ton of student debt. I want to help if I can.

"I'll talk to Carly tonight and see if she can give Della a call. I'm sure she'd be willing to talk to you."

"Great, thanks."

I stop by the printing room on my way back to my desk to copy a few files, inwardly groaning when I walk inside and find Greg there. He's standing at one of the copiers, loading papers into the document feeder. He only returned to work recently, and I have managed to avoid seeing him until now.

"Kendall." He jerks his head in acknowledgment as I walk by.

"Gregory." It takes effort to sound civil.

Tension bleeds into the air as I walk to the farthest copier, putting as much distance between me and Vander's father as possible. I do my best to ignore him as I remove papers from the first file and put them into the document feeder. The whooshing of the copiers is the only sound in the room as we purposely ignore one another. I wet my dry mouth and focus on the task at hand, wanting to get in and out as fast as possible.

My heart rate accelerates when I spy Greg walking toward me, out of the corner of my eye. Bypassing me, he crouches down just behind me, searching for something on the supplies shelf. My hands shake as I reach for my second file, inserting more paper into the document feeder as I lean over and collect the copies of the first file along with the originals.

Something brushes against my leg, and I turn rigidly still. My heart jackhammers behind my rib cage as a tickling sensation creeps up the inside of my leg. Blood rushes to my head, and panic sluices through my veins as fingers brush along my inner thigh. I stumble to the side, gripping the copier for support as I swallow over the bile collecting in my throat. "What are you doing?" I stare at Greg as he straightens up.

He flashes me a blinding smile while waving a wad of envelopes at me. "Dropped these. Oops," he lies.

I narrow my eyes. "Don't touch me again."

He steps forward, putting himself all up in my space. "Or what?" The amused look on his face irritates me to no end, and I straighten up and glare at him.

"Or I'll report you to human resources."

He chuckles, but it's a low menacing sound. "Do you honestly think Paul Cummings would give a shit?" He backs me up, against the printer, trapping me in the corner with no way out. I wish I could remember any of the moves Vander showed me last week, but my brain is mush as terror does a number on me.

"I bill millions of dollars every year, honey." He runs his fingers down my cheek, and I move to swat his hand away when he grabs my wrist and squeezes it. "I could bend you over this copier and fuck your brains out, and no one would give a damn." He thrusts his pelvis into me, and acid churns in my gut as I feel the evidence of his arousal pressing against my stomach. His fingers sweep down my neck. "We should try that sometime." Leaning in, he licks up my neck, and it's a miracle I don't puke all over him. "Now that we're both spouseless and free as a bird."

"You couldn't pay me to touch you, and if you don't get away from me, I'll scream."

He steps back, holding his hands up like he wasn't just groping me against my will, chuckling again. "This is going to be fun. I am really going to enjoy it." He blows me a kiss as he backs toward the door. "Until next time, sexy."

Chapter Thirty-Five

Vander

"Senior year is shit," Shep grumbles as we make our way out of school on Friday afternoon.

"It's nearly over." I remind him while we walk toward the parking lot. "We are already into February, so there are only three more months of school before we graduate. I thought you were happy with your college acceptance."

"I am. I just thought this year would be more fun. It's our last year together before everything changes. We should be enjoying it, but we can't hang at your place anymore, West is a grumpy motherfucker, and Bowie is still being an asshole. It sucks."

"We can hang out at my new place sometimes, but we can't party like before. I promised Jimmy I wouldn't piss off the neighbors." There are apartments over most of the business premises adjacent to the boxing club, and I don't want to cause issues for Jimmy when he has helped me so much. Also, I want to keep my weekends free so I can see Kendall. We don't have much time together, and with Curtis being a dick over the divorce and constantly switching the days he takes Ridge, I need to be fluid with my weekend planning.

I reach my truck just as Gayle Turner slides behind the wheel of her BMW a few cars down. She revs the engine, scowling as she flips me the bird through the window before she peels out of the parking lot.

Shep laughs. "She really hates your guts now."

"Thank fuck." I unlock my truck and throw my book bag in the back alongside my gym bag. I just about have time for a quick training session before I'm picking up Kendall to get her tattoo. "Took her long enough." I climb into the driver seat and roll down the window. "Later, dude." We touch knuckles through the window, and then I floor it out of there.

"Hey, Van." Stella greets me at the door to Kendall's house a few hours later. "The Sulk is up in his room."

"The Sulk?" I quirk a brow as I step into the hallway.

"It fits West to a T right now. He is so freaking moody all the time."

I don't disagree. "You know why."

She sighs and runs her fingers through her long dark hair. "Yeah. He's taking the impending divorce really hard."

"You seem to have accepted it," I say as she closes the door behind me.

She shrugs. "Not much we can do. It's happening whether we like it or not, and honestly, Mom is way happier now Dad is gone. According to Ridge, Dad is happier too. Maybe it's for the best."

Stella is thirteen months younger than West, but in a lot of ways, she acts like the older sibling. Not that I begrudge my buddy his feelings. He is entitled to them, but Stella is taking a more pragmatic approach while West is succumbing to anger, and he can't see much of anything else right now. Kendall is worried, and so am I. He's skipped a few classes and gotten into trouble with Coach for showing up late to training, and he seems to be constantly arguing with Hazel these days.

I like hearing Kendall is happier, and I'd like to think part of that is due to me. "Sounds like it," I reply, purely to not appear rude. "Is your mom ready?" I add.

Stella frowns, before her features smooth out when realization dawns. "Oh, right. You're here for Mom." She giggles. "I can't believe she's getting a tattoo, but good for her."

Kendall and I have agreed we'll be as honest as we can with the people in our lives. I know she hates lying to her kids about where she is on those weekend nights when she's with me. Ridge is none the wiser because he's with Curtis, but Stella and West think she stays over with June, and I know the guilt is killing my love. "I think it will be incredible."

"It will." Stella nods. "It's a stunning design. Mom loves it. You did good." She thumps me in the upper arm.

"If you ever want me to design something for you, let me know, and the guy who does my ink, the one who's doing your mom's ink, is a good friend. I can hook you up with an appointment any time."

"I definitely want ink, but I'll probably wait until I'm eighteen. Dad would never consent, and I don't think Mom would either. I think she'd prefer for me to wait and properly think about it."

"Think about what?" Kendall asks, descending the stairs and stepping foot in the hallway.

"Getting a tattoo."

"Is that something you want?" she inquires, coming to a halt alongside her daughter.

Kendall looks gorgeous in a floaty red-patterned dress that

drapes seductively off her shoulders, molds to her cleavage, and flows outward from under her tits to her ankles. My dick approves, instantly hardening behind the zipper of my jeans. Thank fuck, I've got a hoodie on, and it covers the evidence of my all-consuming need for her.

"I haven't given it a lot of thought, but probably someday, yeah."

"We can talk about it when I get back," Kendall says. "Wish me luck."

"You should do a few shots to numb the pain," Stella suggests as Kendall grabs a black jacket from the coat stand.

Kendall grins at her daughter. "I have delivered three babies, Stella. I think I can handle one small tattoo."

"Holy fuck." Kendall grips my arm with her free hand as Boner works on her ink on the inside of her wrist. "That hurts more than I was expecting it to."

"The wrist is a sensitive area," Boner explains, not looking up from the design. "The skin is thinner, so you feel it more."

"That's why I suggested your upper arm." I remind her of the conversation we had in the truck on the way here.

"It's a pretty design, and I wanted to put it in a place where I could show it off when I wanted to and hide it when I need to." She doesn't want anyone in the office to see it, and it will be covered by the sleeves of her suit jacket.

"I think it'll look cool here." Boner lifts his head, flashing her a mouthful of gold teeth. He's a scary-looking motherfucker. Over six feet tall. More than two hundred and fifty pounds of sheer muscle with bulging biceps and thick thighs. His head is bald, contrasting sharply with his long, straggly brown beard. Add in the ink covering most every part of exposed skin, and the numerous piercings, and he sends some women running in the opposite direction. But the guy has the biggest heart. He would do anything for anyone and he's a kickass tattooist. "It's a good choice."

"Thanks, Boner. I really appreciate you doing this."

Boner chuckles. "So you've said."

I cock my head to the side and smirk. "At least four times in the twenty minutes we've been here."

"It never hurts to be gracious," she replies, narrowing her eyes at me.

"Yes, ma'am." Boner smiles warmly at her, and I can tell he likes her. It's hard not to. After two seconds in Kendall's company, anyone can see what kind of a woman she is. Good. Sweet. Kind. Compassionate. Caring. Smart. Thoughtful. Loving. I could go on. "Good manners are underrated these days and hard to come by," he says.

"That is very true," Kendall says before hissing and gripping my arm tighter.

"Do you want to see my tattoo?" I ask, knowing she needs a distraction.

"You're getting more ink?"

"Yep." I slide my small sketch pad out of the back pocket of my jeans and pull the stool up closer to her chair. I flip through the pad until I come to the page I want. "I'm getting this done over my chest."

Her brow creases in concentration as she inspects my drawing of the circular snake eating its own tail. I've drawn it in the same blue as her butterfly with some contrasting gold elements. "It's an Ouroboros," I explain. "It's from ancient Greek and Egyptian mythology, and it symbolizes death and rebirth." Her eyes whip to mine. "In the seventeenth and eighteenth centuries, they were often carved on gravestones as a symbol of reincarnation."

"I love it." Her eyes fill up with emotion, and I'm glad Boner is busy with her tattoo so he can't see the way we are staring at each other. There's no disguising our feelings when we can't tear our eyes away from one another like this. "It's perfect." She brushes her hand against my fingers, and I feel her touch all the way through to my toes. "The path to your future is buried deep in your past." She reads the quotation I'm getting inked under the snake, and it's closely aligned to the one currently being etched onto her skin. I like the idea of us having different tattoos that mean the same thing and a permanent reminder of the bond we share.

No one else will understand the intimacy or the significance, which is perfect.

This is something we are doing for us.

"Aurelius?" she mouths, and I nod. Her eyes glisten with happy tears, and I wish I could kiss her. I probably could, and Boner wouldn't say anything, but I made a promise to Kendall, and I intend to stick to it.

"I love you," I mouth at the same time Boner speaks.

"Are you two fixated on reincarnation or something?" He chuckles.

"Or something," I mumble.

"I find it fascinating," he says, and we get into a deep conversation about life and death, Kendall's philosophy class, and MGK and Megan Fox.

"Are you happy you got it done?" I ask her ninety minutes later when we leave Boner's ink shop with new tattoos.

"It hurt more than I thought, but I don't regret it." She walks close beside me as we head to my truck. "Not at all." She beams up at me. "I love it. Thank you."

"I like that this is our secret even if it's out in the open."

She nods, as I open the door and help her up into my truck. I race around the hood and climb inside, stretching across the console the second my door is shut. My lips meld against hers, and I grab her face as I kiss the shit out of her. Thank fuck for tinted windows, because I seriously would have gone insane if I didn't get to do this now. "I've been dying to do that," I admit, feathering kisses all over her gorgeous face.

She laces her hands behind my neck. "I wanted to kiss you so badly in there. When you were explaining about your tattoo." She scrapes her nails along my scalp, knowing what it does to me.

"Keep that up, and you're getting fucked," I warn, nipping at her lower lip as I grab her boobs through her dress.

"I wish we had time."

A devilish glint appears in my eyes as I lift her over the console and dump her in my lap. "Who says we don't?" I push my seat back and recline it as I grab the hem of her dress and gather it up. "Unzip me, babe, and impale yourself on my dick. Right fucking now."

A pretty flush climbs up her chest and onto her neck. "What are you doing to me, Vander?" She bites down on her lip in a way that is incredibly sexy before making quick work of my jeans and freeing my erect cock. "Are you constantly hard?"

I love the way she's staring at my dick like she wants to devour it. My cock pulses, leaking precum, because I cannot get enough of her. I have sex with Kendall on the brain twenty-four-seven. "When I'm with you or thinking about you? Abso-fucking-lutely yes." I lift my hips so she can tug my jeans down a bit more, and then I lift her by the waist, positioning her over me as I hold her dress up. "Slide your panties to the side and climb on, baby."

She giggles, leaning down to kiss me as she maneuvers into

position. "You're popping my car-sex cherry," she purrs against my mouth as she lowers her pussy over my erection.

I hiss, through gritted teeth, at the feel of her warm flesh coating mine. Sex really doesn't get any better than this. "I'm glad your ex was such a lazy, unimaginative, unadventurous fucker," I say, thrusting up into her as she starts rocking on top of me. "It won't take long to erase all memory of him from your mind."

"You're already doing a stellar job, Vander," she moans, grinding on top of my dick. "And I never want to stop doing this with you."

Chapter Thirty-Six

Kendall

"I've been doing some research," I say, as I stir the homemade pepper sauce in the pan, the following night in Vander's apartment.

"What kind of research?" he asks, sliding his hands around my waist from behind. Sweeping my hair away from my neck, he presses his lips to my skin and plants a slew of open-mouthed kisses along my hot flesh. I close my eyes and shiver as my pussy aches for his cock.

I'm still mesmerized at how insatiable I've become, as it's completely new. Even when I first started having sex, I never remember being this desperate for Curtis or feeling like I would die if I couldn't have his hands on me. Vander already fucked me over the couch when I arrived an hour ago, but I want him again. My carnal need for him is at an all-time high, and I'm like a horny teenage boy with sex constantly on my mind.

"Research of the kinky kind?" he adds when I don't reply. Lowering his hand, he cups my pussy through my dress.

"You know I'm happy to leave that up to you." I trust Vander with my body one hundred percent, and he always makes me feel so damn good. I love leaving my pleasure in his magical hands, and he never disappoints me. He's got mad skills, and I can't get enough. I'm a born-again slut and I freaking love it.

"I love that you're up to try anything," he murmurs, rubbing me through my dress.

Reluctantly, I remove his hands from my body because I didn't plan this belated celebratory dinner only to burn it. Reducing the heat on the stove, I turn around and circle my arms around his neck. "I love that you're bringing out a side of me I haven't explored." I bite down on my lip as I contemplate how to make my next request. "You know how you said previously you wanted me to pose for you?" He nods, and his eyes instantly spark to life. "I thought we could do that after dinner."

"Hell yeah." He grabs my hips and yanks me into his hard body, kissing me passionately.

We break apart, smiling as we continue to cling to one another. "Good." My smile brightens as I think about his face when I tell him my idea. I think he'll love it. But first things first. "Dinner is ready. Go pour the champagne, and sit down."

"This looks delicious," he says, salivating over the chargrilled steak, dauphinoise potatoes, green beans, and pepper sauce.

"I'm sorry we didn't get to do this last weekend." Fucking Curtis screwed my plans up at the last minute. He is stalling on the divorce and backtracking on things he promised me, and I'm running out of patience. I can't wait to be officially and legally free of him. I'm not impressed with his lack of commitment to our temporary agreement or how he now appears to be contesting everything. It's almost like he resents me for not being miserable now we're apart. Like a punishment for daring to be happier without him, so he's determined to mess with me and ruin my good mood.

Always Meant to Be

"Don't apologize. It's not your fault that asshole fucked with our plans." He cuts a piece of steak and pops it in his mouth, instantly groaning. "This is so damn good." Leaning across the table, he plants his mouth on mine. "Thanks, sweetheart. You're spoiling me."

"I like spoiling you, and you do it enough for me." He is so incredibly good to me—bringing me flowers every Sunday when he comes over for dinner, invoking huge amounts of patience trying to teach me self-defense, texting me every morning and every night to let me know he's thinking of me, helping me with my philosophy homework, running me a bath when I arrive on Saturdays worn out after a busy week—and he's even returned to the retirement center with me a few times and helped out. We spend as much time together as we can out in the open, without having to sneak around, because he knows how hard that is for me. He sees the guilt I'm carrying and how I hate lying to West and Stella about where I stay over every week.

But it's more than that. Vander makes me laugh. He listens to me and seeks out my advice. He shares my beliefs and encourages my passions. He worships me and makes me feel desirable. He's teaching me how to ask for and give pleasure in the bedroom, and he's the reason I have a permanent smile on my face and a constant spring in my step. He's giving me my confidence back, and I can't put a price on that.

"You never told me about your research," he says in between mouthfuls of dinner.

"I looked up Machine Gun Kelly and Megan Fox after our conversation with Boner last night, and he was right. They seem to have a very spiritual relationship, and they fully believe they are soul mates." I take a sip of my wine in between mouthfuls of the sumptuous steak and the melt-in-the-mouth potatoes. "Like us, they felt the connection straightaway. She said they are twin flames. I like that, and I love them. They are so hot for one another, so in love, and the things they post about each other online are just beautiful." It's possibly a little cheesy, to some people, but they can get away with it. They are bringing the entertainment and the glamour back to rock and roll, and I think the world needs that right now.

"He carries a necklace with her blood in it," Vander says with a little glint in his eye. "To celebrate their recent engagement, they drank each other's blood." I blink at him as his lips curve up at the corners. "When we get engaged, we should totally do that too."

My mouth drops to the table, and he chuckles. "Is that too vampire-y for you?" He wolfs down more of his dinner.

"I don't think vampire-y is a word, although I could be mistaken, but it wasn't that part that had my jaw dropping, even if I draw the line at wearing or drinking blood." I gulp another mouthful of wine.

"Ah, I see." He leans back in his chair, all casual, smiling confidently across the table at me while popping another piece of steak in his mouth. He maintains eye contact as he chews, enjoying seeing me all flustered. The punk. "It's the engagement part."

I nod and guzzle more wine. He sits up straighter, losing the cocky grin, replacing it with a serious look as he slides his hand across the table and threads our fingers together. "I don't want to freak you out, but I'm not going to lie to you either. I want to marry you some day, Kendall. That's a promise. I already consider you my wife, in here." He thumps his fist over his heart. "In the only way that counts."

I get up and walk around to him, kneeling at his feet. My pulse is pounding, and my heart races as I take his hands and peer up at him. There will never be a more perfect moment to tell him how I feel. "I adore you." Emotion gathers in my throat as I press a kiss to his knuckles. "I crave you." I climb to my feet and crawl into his lap, tilting his face up to mine because I need to be looking into his eyes when I say this. "I love you."

Emotion shines in his eyes as he stares at me. "Say it again," he whispers, clasping my face in his large hands.

"I love you."

"Again."

I laugh as happy tears pool in my eyes. "I love you, Vander. I love you so damn much. It feels like I've been waiting for you to show up and infuse life in me." He kisses me softly, and the joy emanating from his soul is like a beacon of light illuminating his body in a golden halo.

"I love you, Kendall. You have breathed life into me and given me reason to hope."

"You are so romantic." I peck his lips as I drag my fingers through his hair. "Sexy too."

His pupils dilate, and his hands dig into my hips. "I need you," he says, his voice thick with lust and matching my own need. "I need to feel every part of you fused with every part of me."

Sliding off his lap, I push the remnants of our dinner to one side of the table before climbing up on the other. I lie back on the table as he stands, widening my legs so he can get into position. We don't even fully remove our clothes, only the parts that stand in the way of him burying his body deep inside mine.

"I'm making a new rule," Vander says as we sit on the floor, semi-naked, feeding one another cold leftovers. "Clothing is banned when we're together."

I lean back into his chest and giggle. "Considering we are naked more than not, I think it's a good rule. I approve." I never thought I would ever be this comfortable naked around a man, but everything comes so naturally with Vander that my nakedness barely registers anymore.

His muscular arms wrap around my waist as he nuzzles my neck. "I did some research too."

I lean back and look up at him as I shovel the last of the potatoes into his mouth. "You did?"

He nods, and I wait for him to finish eating before he replies. "I wanted to find out if there are other couples like us, and there are tons." Removing the fork from my fingers, he drops it on the empty plates and pushes them aside. "It's more common than you think."

"I know." I spin around in my underwear facing him. "Did you read about Juliet Mills and Maxwell Caulfield?" Reading about their love brought tears to my eyes. If any couple inspires me and offers hope, it's them.

He tweaks my nose. "I did. They seemed most similar to us. There's an eighteen-year difference between them, and they married a few months after meeting on the US tour of *The Elephant Man*. He was only twenty-one and she was thirty-nine with two failed marriages behind her. She had kids too. They've defied all their critics, and they've been happily married for thirty-eight years."

"It was love at first sight, and they believe in soul mates too," I add.

"Nothing is impossible." He brushes his fingers over my face and my neck, sweeping his hands across my collarbone, lighting an inferno in his wake.

"I'm not concerned about our age difference anymore," I truthfully explain. "It doesn't matter. Not when we connect on this level." I trace the tattoos on his upper chest with my finger, careful not to touch his Ouroboros because it's still raised and red-rimmed, like my own ink. "I don't even care what other people will say. Fuck them."

He rises, grinning as he pulls me to my feet. "We're knocking those barriers down, one by one." Taking my hand, he leads me to his studio.

"The only thing that matters is my children and how they will react. Especially West. That is all I'm worried about now."

Vander switches the light on in his studio as we enter that side of the apartment. "They will come around in time," he says, reeling me into his arms. I wrap my arms around his bare waist and press my lips to his chest. He tilts my chin up with his finger. "Does this mean you're in this for the long haul?"

"We said six months and then we'd reassess." I remind him, running my fingers over his gorgeous mouth. "But I don't need to wait six months. I know what I want, and it's you. It will always be you."

He envelops me in his arms, almost hugging me to death. "You make me so happy, Kendall," he whispers. "I want to dance in the rain with you, sleep out under the stars, and shout my love from the highest mountain so no one doubts the depth of my feelings for you."

"You make me happy too, and I want to explore the world with you. I want to visit the Parthenon in Athens, return to Egypt and find our river, freeze our butts off in Ireland, and watch the All Blacks perform the haka in New Zealand. I want to hold your hand as you build your dreams and paint rainbows in the sky."

Grabbing my face, he kisses me deeply and slowly, and I swoon against him. When we break for air, we stare at one another, communicating with our hearts and minds, not needing words to convey everything we are feeling. "This is insane," I whisper, planting my lips on the inside of his wrist. "But insanity has never felt so normal."

Chapter Thirty-Seven

Vander

"Draw me like one of your French girls," Kendall says, standing in front of me in her lacy, white underwear, dangling a silver necklace with a big blue heart locket from her finger.

"And how is that?" I ask though I have an inkling of what she means.

"Have you ever watched the movie *Titanic*?"

I shake my head. I'm seriously lacking on the chick-flick front because I've never had a girlfriend, I rarely date, and I don't have any sisters.

"Blasphemy," she jokes, walking slowly toward me, sashaying her hips in a way that has my cock jumping in my sweatpants. "We need to rectify that sometime, but right now, it means I want you to paint me wearing this." She jiggles the necklace still hanging from her finger as she bats her eyelashes at me. "And only this." She enunciates the words, and it's sexy as all get out. I'm two seconds away from ravishing her on the floor when she steps back, waggling her finger in my face. "Nuh-uh. No sex until after you draw me in the nude."

"Babe." I groan, rubbing my throbbing dick. "Don't torture me."

"You're a tortured artist. You need to suffer for your art," she purrs, pointing at the chaise longue at the back of my studio. "Pull that into the middle of the room."

As I comply with her demands, something occurs to me. "You made me buy this on purpose."

A satisfied grin curves over her mouth. "I did. I guess I should confess," she says, walking toward me and dropping a few coins in my hand. I stare at her in confusion. "For the portrait." She leans in and brushes her mouth against mine in a tantalizingly slow manner, leaving me panting like a dog. She unclips her bra and tosses it aside. "The instant you said you wanted me to pose for you, I thought of the scene in *Titanic*. It's so erotic and romantic, and every time I watch that movie, I wish it was me." Her cheeks stain a rosy-pink color as she shimmies her panties down her slim legs. She strides toward me, buck-ass naked, completely confident, and utterly regal. Her gorgeous blue eyes glisten with emotion as she steps up to me, placing her hand on my chest. "I never thought I'd get to do something like this. I never thought I'd have the balls to strip in front of any man, under the glare of spotlights, let alone pose for a drawing, but I'm not ashamed to do this." She kisses the corner of my mouth. "Because you are giving me back my confidence, Vander, and you make me feel beautiful."

"You *are* beautiful." I peruse her body slowly, loving what I see. "You're exquisite, Kendall. Like a delicate bloom flourishing and coming to life before my eyes. I can't take my eyes off you. You are all I see."

"I love you, painter boy." She kisses the other corner of my mouth before swatting my ass. "Now get to work." I watch as she crawls onto the chaise longue and props herself on her side with her head on the armrest, one arm thrown up behind her and her hand beside her face. "Put the necklace on me," she demands, and her bossy tone cranks my arousal to the max. It'll be a miracle if I can get my hands to stop shaking long enough to draw her.

I fix the necklace around her neck, positioning it in the crevice between her pretty tits. She swats my hand away when I cop a cheeky feel, warning me to keep my hands to myself. When I have her posed just right, I ask permission to snap a few pics to reference later when I'm finishing the painting. Kendall agrees, and after taking a few shots, I put some music on in the background, pull my chair over, and settle down to draw her.

Little puffs of air glide from her plump lips, and her chest inflates as I begin drawing her. "Relax, sweetheart," I murmur, my eyes moving from her naked body to my pad as I pencil in her outline, willing my hands to stop shaking. "Hold as still as you can."

"As you wish, painter boy." Her face is flushed, her eyes bright as she attempts to contain her nerves. I know this is a big deal for her, and it means so much that she trusts me to do this. As long as I live, I will never forget this moment.

Silence descends as I continue to draw her, filling in the curves on her body, while fire burns in my veins and my skin sizzles. Our chemistry sparks in the room, bouncing off the walls, adding an extra element to contend with. My hand trembles again, and she notices. "You're shaking."

I lift my eyes, immediately finding her gaze centered on me. "I'm nervous. I'm drawing the woman I love in a moment I have fantasized about for a long time. It's kind of surreal, and I want to capture your beauty perfectly. Not just what is visible on the outside but the beauty that radiates from within."

Her face softens. "I love you, Vander, and I trust you.

You're too talented to be nervous. I know it's going to be breathtaking."

"I think the day I'm not nervous about my talent is the day I've become complacent," I admit, forcing my gaze back to my pad. I could sit and stare at her for hours and never grow tired of the view.

"So, nerves are good?" The inflection in her voice poses the question.

"Some are. As long as it isn't debilitating." I raise my eyes and pin her in place. "Now, shush, woman. Let the maestro work."

Classical music wafts in the air as I settle into my work, perfecting her body on the page before I focus on her face. My fingers smudge the pencil, creating soft shadows that set the tone and warm contours that present her body in an almost ethereal way.

I inspect her face as my wrist tilts and I pencil in her features, marveling over the perfect symmetry, her cute button nose, her full mouth, the delicate smattering of freckles across the tops of her cheeks, and—the pièce de résistance—her stunning big blue eyes. Framed by thick, long, black lashes, they are the most unique violet-blue color I have ever seen. Kendall's eyes truly are the window to her soul, and when I look into them, I instantly fall into their vibrant depths, and it takes colossal willpower to drag my gaze away.

"Keep that up, and you're getting fucked," she murmurs, reciting my words back at me.

"Keep what up?" I feign innocence as I finish lining her lush mouth.

"Looking at me like that."

"I can't help it. You hypnotize me."

"Are you done yet?"

I chuckle. "Whatever happened to keeping my hands off

you?" I lick my lips as I skim my eyes over her body in a deliberately slow perusal.

Her thighs visibly tighten, and she squirms, forcing all the blood to rush to my dick, transforming the semi I've been sporting this past hour into a full hard-on. "I didn't think this would take so long or it would be so hard keeping still."

I'm proud of how well she did. It's not easy posing for any artist, especially naked and where there is strong sexual chemistry. Kendall is not the type of woman to sit still for long. She is always on the go. Always active, so I know it was a bit of a challenge. "You did amazing," I say, closing my pad, setting it and my pencil on the small table beside me. Dropping to my knees, I crawl toward her. "And I think you deserve a reward."

She bites down on her lips as I approach, and a pretty blush blooms on her chest. I pull up to my knees and lean over to kiss her. "I love you."

Her fingers tangle in my hair, and she tugs my head back, arching my neck so she can more easily reach my lips. Her tongue darts out, and she licks a line along my top lip and then my bottom one, and my cock tries to drive a hole through my pants. "I love you too." She plants a hard kiss on my lips. "That was one of the most erotic moments of my life, and I can't wait to see it."

Repositioning her so she's sitting in the center of the chaise longue, I part her thighs and move in between them. "It needs more work, and I don't want to show you until it's complete." I press a soft kiss to her inner thigh, and she shivers.

"That's fine by me," she rasps, gasping when I lift her leg and plant it over my shoulder, granting me better access to her softest place.

Parting her folds with my thumbs, I stare at her glistening pink pussy with a hunger that is endless. "Hold on, babe. I'm starving, and you're about to be devoured." Kendall grips the back of the chaise, and I dive in, feasting on her warm, soft flesh, using my fingers and my tongue to bring her to the brink of ecstasy, time and time again, until I take pity on her and finish the job.

Watching her fall apart, with my mouth on her most intimate parts, never ceases to amaze me. I never thought I'd have this with her, and now I know what it feels like, I never want to let her go.

Chapter Thirty-Eight

Vander

"That's better," I say, watching Kendall tilt forward at the waist, bend her elbow, and swing it back toward Crusher's face. He rears back, on instinct, and she gets free.

"That's how you get out of a hold if someone sneaks up on you from behind," I tell Viola and June. They joined our self-defense sessions these past couple of weeks, so I roped Crusher and Boner into helping. Not that it required much coercion. Especially on Boner's part because I'm pretty sure he has a giant-sized boner for Kendall's childhood friend. *Pun intended.* I've spotted Viola checking him out too, so I think the attraction is mutual. What a pity Kendall and I have to conduct our relationship in secret. We could have double-dated.

Man, if West could hear my thoughts, he'd give me such shit.

"Then you can deploy another move," Boner says, pulling me out of my head, "like a groin kick or the heel-palm strike to incapacitate your attacker so you can escape."

"Ladies." Jimmy strides across the floor like he means business. "I need you to go to my office and lock the door. No questions asked. Just do it." He slaps his keys into Kendall's palm. "Crusher will escort you and stay with you," he adds as Kendall's eyes flit to mine.

Alarm bells are ringing in my ears, but I keep my expression calm and nod at my love, silently conveying it's okay. June and Viola exchange worried looks with Kendall, but they do as they are told, quietly trailing Crusher out to the small hallway that leads to Jimmy's office. "What's going on?" I ask the second they are out of earshot.

"I spotted someone climbing up the fire escape toward your apartment."

"Who?" I ask, immediately racing toward the exit.

"It's too dark to tell," Jimmy says, running behind me with Boner in tow. The guys in the ring stop sparring to stare at us, but I ignore them, yanking the door open and sprinting outside.

"I bet this has something to do with my father," I say through gritted teeth as I take the stairs that lead to my apartment two at a time. He's been way too quiet lately, and that makes me nervous. It's not inconceivable to consider he has heard I've received, and accepted, an offer to attend the art program at Yale and I've submitted an application for financial aid.

Quickly opening the door to my apartment, I burst inside, just as I see a shadowy black figure escape out the window. I've got a split second to decide whether to go out the fire escape after him or try to catch him on the ground. Choosing the latter, I sprint past Jimmy and Boner and race back down the stairs, jogging past the boxing club and around the corner to the rear of the property and the parking lot. I arrive in time to see the guy jump on a motorcycle and kick-start the engine. Frantic, I look around for something, anything, I can throw at him to knock him off, but the lot is empty except for a few trucks and a couple of dumpsters.

The guy revs the engine, and I have to jump out of the way as he comes at me. I land on my side on the gravel-lined asphalt, narrowly missing being knocked down. "Vander!" Kendall screams, and I lift my head to see her leaning out the window of Jimmy's office. "Are you okay?"

I climb to my feet, brushing gravel off my training top and sweats. "I'm fine." I walk to the window. "Someone was in my apartment. I want to check it out, and I'll come back for you then."

Behind her, Viola and June look concerned while Crusher wears a "what the fuck" expression on his face.

I trudge back up the stairs, silently cursing myself for not following the guy out the fire escape. When I enter my place, Boner is placing a long sheet over my latest oil painting of Kendall. I finished the drawing, and Kendall loved it. It's definitely one of my best pieces, but it helps when I have intimate knowledge of the subject. It felt like a waste to confine her beauty to a page on a sketch pad, so I transferred it to a large canvas, and I've been working on it all week.

"I won't tell anyone," Boner says, looming in front of me and snapping me out of my head. "And it's not exactly a shock."

My brows climb to my hairline.

"I helped clear out your old place, and I saw the other paintings you had of her. When you were getting ink, I could tell you two were close. I saw the way you were looking at one another, and it all stacked up." He clamps a hand on my shoulder and smiles. "She's sweet and hot. Good for you, man."

"We have more pressing concerns," Jimmy says, walking through from the apartment side of the space. "I can't see anything out of place."

"He wasn't up here long enough to cause damage," I

surmise, stepping into my apartment and raking my gaze over my living space. "We disrupted him before he could do what he came to do." I spend a few minutes checking things, but it doesn't look like anything is missing.

"There have been a few break-ins in the area," Jimmy says as the front door opens and Kendall walks in. Concern is etched upon her face as she stalks toward me, her head darting sideways when she passes my studio, and lines furrow her brow.

"She wouldn't stay put," Crusher says, ambling in the door behind her, followed by Viola and June. "She was freaking out you were hurt."

"What's going on?" Kendall asks, skimming her gaze around the room.

"Jimmy spotted someone climbing the fire escape, and we came to investigate. The asshole got away, but it doesn't look like he took anything," I explain, wishing I could pull her into my arms and kiss her worries away.

"I'll install an alarm system and some security cameras," Jimmy says. "I've been meaning to get around to it. Now seems as good a time as any."

"I'll pay for them," I offer.

He shakes his head and waves his hand in my face. "I'll write it off as a business expense."

Now isn't the time to argue with him, so I drop the subject. But it's got me thinking, and I need to have a private conversation with Kendall. I glance over her shoulders at her two friends, who are quietly taking everything in. "We'll have to call it a night, and I need a word with Kendall."

"I'll see you tomorrow at the office," Kendall says, turning around and yanking June into a hug.

"I'll see you tomorrow at lunch," Viola says. They quickly embrace, and then everyone leaves.

Always Meant to Be

"Come here," I say when the front door is closed. She falls into my arms, and I hold her close. "I'm okay. Don't worry."

She fists my top as I smooth a hand down her hair. "But I do worry. Was it your dad?"

I exhale heavily as I steer us toward the couch. "I don't know. Could be, or it was a thief. Apparently, there have been some break-ins in the area."

"The security cameras are a good idea either way."

"I agree, which is why I want to install some at your house. An alarm system too." I settle her by my side on the couch.

She tucks her hair behind her ears before turning to face me. "That's a good idea. I'll take care of it this week."

I press a kiss into her hair. "Let me organize it. I'll have to do it for here anyway, and I can probably get a better deal for two properties."

"Fine. But I'm paying." She narrows her eyes, warning me not to disagree. "Curtis will have to pay half, and it will piss him off."

"It shouldn't," I bark, my mood souring like it always does anytime that prick comes up in conversation. "He should want to pay it to ensure his family is safe, and he should have suggested it before he left." *What man abandons his family without taking every precaution to ensure their safety?* I take deliberate, slow breaths, calming myself down. "I don't want to take any chances. What happened tonight might not be coincidental."

She cocks her head to the side. "Did something else happen with your dad I don't know about?"

"I spoke to my mom last night." I can't stop the smile forming on my face. "She's divorcing him, Kendall. As soon as she gets out of rehab, she's getting the paperwork drawn up."

"That is wonderful news. I'm happy for both of you."

"Reconnecting with Dana was the best thing for Mom. She

seems able to get through to her in a way I haven't. Rehab is going well, and she'll be out in five weeks." I trail my fingers along her face. "She asked me to come visit. Something about a family therapy session, sans the asshole, naturally."

"Are you going to go?"

I bob my head. "Yeah. I think it could be good. Painful, but good. I am thinking of going next month, at the start of spring break, and combining it with a trip to Yale. I would like to check out the campus and maybe view a few apartments." Wetting my lips, I peer into her eyes. "I was hoping you might come with me." She chews on her lip, and her brow scrunches up. "But it's totally fine if you can't." I rush to reassure her as my heart sinks.

It's not really fine. I want her with me so badly. I want her involved in the decisions I'm making about my future because it impacts her future too. Plus, I want to spend time with her in public without the fear of anyone seeing us. I want to take her out for dinner, and make out at the movies, and walk hand in hand along the beach without worrying we'll be caught. I want a taste of what it'll be like to love her freely, but I won't pressure her.

"I want to go with you." Her fingers trace through the growth on my chin and cheeks. "I want to explore Yale with you and help you to find a place to live. I want to enjoy spending time together without having to constantly look over our shoulders." Our thoughts are always so in sync. "Leave it with me." She leans in and kisses me. "I'll try to work something out."

Chapter Thirty-Nine

Kendall

"For the record, I think that is a really bad idea," June says as we exit Bentley Law out onto the sidewalk. "Like really, really bad."

"I have to do something," I say, loosening my scarf because it's not quite as cold as it was when I arrived at work this morning. For early March, the weather has been milder than usual. "I won't let Greg ruin everything Vander has been working towards."

"You *are* doing something," she says as we head in the direction of the restaurant where we're meeting Viola for lunch. "Both of you have new security systems, and you've set up a meeting with a Yale financial aid officer. Della told Carly she's pretty confident Vander will get full financial support. She said Yale's financial policy is strictly needs based and they support students' needs with no loans required."

"I'm encouraged to hear that," I truthfully admit. "And I'm confident he'll get full financial support, but it'll mean jack shit if his father uses his contacts to rescind his place on the art program. I know you think that's unlikely, but you don't know what that man is capable of."

She slams to a halt, tugging on my elbow and pulling me in to the wall, away from the busy street. "I know exactly what that asshole is capable of. I work with him too, and I've heard all the rumors. Why do you think I don't want you to go ahead with your plan? Baiting him is too risky, Kendall. You could lose everything and make things worse for Vander. Have you considered that?"

"Of course, I have." I rub at a tense spot between my brows. "But I can't sit back and let this play out how Gregory Henley expects it to play out. He has an agenda, and I'm not going to be a pawn in whatever sick game he is planning. He is not using me to get back at Vander, and I'm not letting any man manipulate me again."

She tugs on my elbow. "We better get a move on. Viola will bust our balls if we're late." We resume walking. "I understand where you're coming from. You love Vander, and you want to protect him. That's noble but not if you end up sacrificing your career for him. How will you support your kids if this backfires and you end up out of a job?"

"Doing this is the only way I can protect Vander *and* my job. If I sit back and do nothing, I may end up fired anyway. Look at what happened to Tania." I drill her with a look because she knows I am making sense.

We stop at the entrance to the restaurant. "I care about you, Kendall, and I don't want you to get hurt. If you won't tell Vander what his father is doing, you need to at least come clean with Vi. You need more than my opinion."

"Come clean about what?" Viola asks from directly behind us, and we yelp in fright.

Nerves fire at me as I turn around to face my best friend. I have been keeping my secret from her because I'm a chickenshit. I know she won't approve, and I don't want anyone bursting my bubble, but I can't keep lying to her now June has alluded to the truth. I have no choice but to fess up. "I'll tell you inside," I say, opening the door and walking to my doom.

"You have achieved the impossible, Ken," Viola says, twenty minutes later, after I have spilled my guts.

I have barely touched my salad while my two besties have almost finished theirs because I've been doing all the talking. Fessing up about my relationship with Vander and ending with the predicament I find myself in.

"You have truly shocked me." She sets her silverware down and takes a sip of her glass of water.

"Because I didn't tell you?"

"No. It doesn't surprise me you confided in June and chose to hide it from me. You went to the person you knew would encourage you over the person you knew would caution you to hold back."

"Hang on here a sec." June pushes her plate away and glares at Viola. "Don't make out like I flippantly pushed Ken into his arms as if I didn't have her best interests at heart or imply there is something wrong with her loving him. You have said yourself how much happier she's been these past three months. Vander is a huge part of that."

"I'm not denying that or begrudging you your happiness, Ken." Vi's features soften as she looks at me. "I'm shocked you have done something so reckless."

Her words sting. "This is why I didn't come to you." I push my uneaten salad away, losing my appetite. "I knew you would judge me."

"Now who's being unfair?" Viola leans across the table and takes my hand. "I'm not judging anything but your timing. I'm shocked you would do this behind West's back. That you didn't wait until the divorce was finalized and Vander had graduated to do this the right way." Her earnest eyes pierce mine. "Vander is a good guy. We all know that, and if he makes you happy, then I couldn't give a flying fuck about his age. But society will. Your family will. Your work colleagues may look at you differently. And hiding it from the start is a shit show in the making. That's what I object to, Kendall. I want you to be happy, but how will you retain that happiness when the lie is discovered and you risk losing everything and everyone you care for?"

"You're being overly dramatic," June says, and I can tell from the hostile expression on her face she regrets her words at the door because they set all of this in motion.

"You think I'm selfish." I yank my hand back and fold my arms around my chest.

"You are one of the most selfless people I know, but I think you rushed this decision, and now you're paying the price. You're caught in the middle of whatever is going on with Vander and his dad, and I'm worried about you." She angles her head, eyeballing June. "On that, we do agree."

"I don't have many options here, Vi, and I love him. He's my forever love." Shock splays across her face, and I can tell she doesn't buy it. But I don't care. I'm not here to convince her what we share is the real deal. If she's my friend, she'll support me, no matter what. "I won't stand on the sidelines and watch that asshole destroy his future."

"You say he's hit on you a few times now?" she asks, and I nod. "Then go to human resources. File a complaint. Do this legal and aboveboard."

"That is exactly what I intended to do until I remembered hearing the rumors about one of the girls who used to work on his team. I phoned Tania, and she was very frank with me. Told me he sexually harassed her, on several occasions, and she brought it to HR immediately. They refused to believe her without proof because it came down to her word against his, and of course, he denied it. Then he made her life a living hell until she was forced to resign. He ruined her reputation and refused to give her a letter of recommendation. She had to move out of state to get another job."

"Kendall suspects he has something on Paul Cummings, the VP of HR, and that he'll force him to turn a blind eye unless she has concrete proof of what he's doing," June supplies, lifting her mug for a refill when the waitress appears at our table.

I ask her to box my salad up, and she takes it away after refilling our coffees. "Tania said she doubts she was the first or I'll be the last. She told me she wished she'd thought of doing what I plan. She agrees that baiting him into doing something and recording it is the only way to beat him at his own game, and unless either of you can think of a better course of action, that's what I'm going to do."

"Hey, painter boy." I can't contain my grin as I greet my lover when he appears in front of me in the lobby of the hotel in Bridgeport.

"Baby. I missed you." Vander drops his weekend bag and picks me up, swinging me around, before planting my feet on the ground and passionately kissing me. When he breaks our lip-lock, he brushes hair out of my face and smiles as he keeps me bundled in his arms.

"How was the drive?" I ask, running my fingers through his hair.

"Smooth sailing, and I made it in under four hours."

Vander drove from Vermont while I flew directly to Connecticut. "How did the session go with your mom?"

"It was emotional but good." He kisses the tip of my nose.

"She has really turned a corner, and she's determined to stay sober and cut all ties with my father." He holds me closer. "She apologized and promised she's going to be there for me now."

I really hope she stays the course. "That's great, babe."

"I love it when you call me that." His smile expands, and he stares at me like he can't quite believe we are here. It's contagious, and I cling to his arms and giggle into his neck while surreptitiously scanning the people milling around the hotel lobby and reception area, watching for expressions of horror. But hardly anyone is paying attention to us. They are too busy going about their day to notice or care. Another couple walks by, heading for the exit and smiles at us. There is no shock, judgment, or disgust, and it feels so freeing. "I am so freaking happy you were able to come with me this weekend."

"Me too," I say, shucking out of his embrace and taking his hand. "Although I hate lying to my family." They think I'm gone for three nights on a work trip.

Vander slings his bag over one shoulder and leans down to kiss me. "I hate you had to do that too, but it won't be for much longer. It's only two months until graduation."

"West is still so angry," I admit as we walk toward the elevator. I flew to Hartford on the red-eye so I could attend my meeting with the Yale financial advisor first thing this morning. Then I drove my rental the twenty minutes to Bridgeport and wandered around for a few hours before checking in to our hotel. "I'm scared of how he's going to react." Truthfully, I don't know whether we will be able to fess up when they graduate. Though I know there is never going to be a good time to admit our relationship.

"He told me he didn't speak to Curtis the entire time you were at OU."

I spent last weekend in Oklahoma with Curtis and West, visiting the campus where my son will be attending college in

Always Meant to Be

the fall. I only saw Vander on Monday at our self-defense class, and we couldn't really talk with the others there. He flew to Vermont on Wednesday morning to see his mom, so we haven't had an opportunity to talk about last weekend. "He didn't. It was extremely awkward, even if a part of me loved how angry it made my ex." We're still not divorced or even close to an agreement, but I always refer to Curtis as my ex because he firmly occupies that space in my head. "It's not good though. I don't want West to hate his dad. He's the only one he's got."

We step into the elevator with another couple and a family. Vander pulls me into the back and slides his arm over my shoulders. I look up at him the same time he looks down at me, and we grin. We're like two kids let loose in Disneyland for the first time, and it makes me giggle. I bury my face in his chest to stifle my laughter.

We're still grinning like loons when we get out on our floor, and my euphoria expands when Vander pushes me up against the wall in the hallway and kisses the shit out of me. I moan into his mouth as my libido instantly kicks into gear. "I need you," I whimper against his lips. "But not here." I draw the line at exhibitionism too. Shoving at his shoulders, I force him to step back.

"I'm warning you now," he says, taking my hand as we stride toward the end of the corridor where our room is. "I won't be able to take my hands off you this weekend. We don't know when we'll get to do this again, so I'm going to overdo it to keep me going until this becomes our norm."

"I have no objection to that," I say, reaching into my bag for the key card.

Vander cages me in from behind as we stand in front of the door, leaning down to press a kiss to the underside of my jaw. "Thank you for being here, Kendall. It means everything to me."

I turn around and kiss the corner of his lips. "I want to support you. You're my everything, and I don't always get to demonstrate that the way I'd like."

Vander's eyes blaze with heated emotion as he swipes the key from my fingers, opens the door, and shoves me inside our room. Two minutes later, he's driving his cock into me as I stand facing the wall with my legs spread and my dress bunched up around my waist.

"Damn, babe." Vander hugs me tight, with his chest to my back, as we come down from our mutual high. "Sex with you gets better and better every time."

Angling my head, I lean back and kiss him. "It's because we're in love and you're taking the time to understand my body and teaching me how to understand yours."

"I love being your teacher," he says, moving us around so we're facing into our room. "Holy fuck, Kendall. What did you do?" His eyes are out on stalks as he takes in the lavish suite with separate bedroom and an outdoor balcony.

"I got offered an upgrade when checking in I couldn't turn down."

"I want to pay half," he immediately offers, like always. Vander is very generous and a stickler for paying his own way. I love that in a man even if I wish he was a bit more selfish. He needs every penny for college.

"Nope." I take his hand as I pull him over to the large floor-to-ceiling windows facing onto the gorgeous balcony. "I got a bonus at work, and it's my treat." I don't feel bad for my little white lie. I *did* get a bonus, but that's not how I'm paying for our upgrade. Vander got the invoice for the security systems made out to me, so I was able to take more money out of our savings account than I actually needed. I'm not sure Vander would appreciate that truth, but I get an enormous kick out of knowing my ex is partly paying for my weekend away with my new lover.

Take that and stuff it up your cheating ass, Curtis!

"I wish I was married to you already," he blurts. "Shit." He chuckles, spinning me around in his arms and fixing my dress down over my hips. "I didn't mean to get intense. I'm just excited to spend three days and nights with you." He brushes his nose against mine. "This is what it will be like for the rest of our forever."

Be still my heart. *How is he so romantic?* He slays me each and every time. "I can't wait." Although I'll have to because Vander is going to be at college for the next four years, and I don't know what will happen after that. Whether he will want to return to Colorado Springs or settle someplace else. I can't leave until Ridge has graduated, so it limits our options. My thoughts take the shine off my current euphoria, so I force them aside. There will be plenty of time to focus on the future in the coming weeks and months. Right now, I want to remain firmly grounded in the present because I don't want anything to ruin this weekend.

Chapter Forty

Kendall

"I don't want to go home tomorrow," I whine as we enter our suite after a gorgeous dinner in a Middle Eastern restaurant a short Uber ride from our hotel.

"Me either," he says, circling his arms around me from behind and pulling me back into his chest. "I legit feel like I could cry."

"This has been an amazing trip." A fruitful one too because the financial aid advisor confirmed—off the record—that Vander would get full financial support. I'm so excited, and I thought about telling him, but I don't want to get his hopes up until he receives the confirmation in the mail. I'm also not sure he'd approve of how I laid it all on the line, explaining in no uncertain terms the nature of his dysfunctional upbringing and the abusive hold his father has over him. She was shocked and sympathetic, offering reassurances his application would be reviewed on the basis of his own financial situation and not based on his father's considerable wealth. I turn around and hug him tight. "I have loved spending all this time with you."

As well as an official tour of Yale, we explored the town of

Bridgeport on foot and bicycles, made out at the movies, held hands walking along the shoreline at the Seaside Park Beach, swooned at the Housatonic Museum of Art, and fawned over one another every night at dinner like giddy newlyweds. When we weren't overdosing on PDAs, we were tangled in the sheets and if it's even possible, I'm more in love with him now.

Vander holds me close while tilting my head back so he can look at me. He peers deep into my eyes when he presses his lips to my wrist, igniting a flurry of delicious tremors across my skin. "I have loved going to sleep beside you every night and waking up with you in my arms."

"I love our morning sex." I rub my thumb across his lower lip. Waking up to Vander's hands and mouth all over my skin is another first, and it feels like the most natural thing in the world to open my legs and welcome him into my body. My core tightens as I recall the many different ways he has taken me this weekend, and I know it will take a long time before any experience tops this one.

"I love morning, all-day, and all-night sex." Snatching handfuls of my ass, he rocks his crotch against my stomach. "And speaking of." He pins me with a suggestive look as he picks me up and cradles me against his chest.

My legs and arms automatically curl around his body. "I love you." I dot kisses all over his gorgeous face as he walks us toward the bedroom.

"I love you too, and it'll never get old hearing you tell me that." He lays me down flat on the bed with tender loving care. "Stay still," he commands when I move to unzip my dress. "I want to undress you."

I prop myself against the pillows as I watch him remove my clothing, one painstaking piece at a time. His eyes leisurely stroll over my naked body as he strips his own clothes away, his gaze burning intensely as he roams every inch of my bare skin.

"Spread your legs and touch yourself," he instructs as he pops the button on his jeans. "I want to see how wet you are for me."

Without any hesitation or shame, I spread my thighs and run my fingers up and down my slit before pushing two inside my slippery channel. I'm soaked, but he always has this effect on me. I only have to look at him, and I'm instantly dripping with need.

"Show me." He kicks his jeans and boxers away.

Extracting my fingers, I hold them out for his inspection as he crawls up the bed and over my body. Taking my wrist, he drags my fingers under his nose, inhaling deeply as liquid warmth gushes between my legs.

Holy hell.

He is so dirty, and I cannot get enough.

"You smell like mine," he purrs before wrapping his hot mouth round my fingers and sucking hard. My hips arch off the bed as he licks the essence from my fingers while ravishing me with dark lust-charged eyes. "Taste like mine too." Bending down, he plants a long, slow, deep kiss on my lips. His hands cup my face as he breaks the kiss and kneels between my legs. "I love you, Kendall, and I can't wait to make you officially mine." He kisses me again, softly and sweetly, in a way that almost brings tears to my eyes, before he slides down my body and worships my other lips.

He brings me over the edge in a new record time, and my limbs are like mush on the mattress as he guides his throbbing cock to my entrance. "Be mine forever, Kendall," he whispers, easing carefully inside me, one measured inch at a time.

"I'm yours, Vander." I gasp as he tenderly fills me like we have all the time in the world. I hug his back as he covers me with his beautiful body, driving into me in languid, measured strokes that are the opposite of how he usually fucks me. Gone are the urgent thrusts and savage pounding as he takes his time, exploring every inch of my hot flesh with his lips and his hands while rocking into me carefully, driving slow and deep, until it feels like there is no him and me—only us.

My legs encircle his shapely waist as he makes love to me, and my fingers explore the toned curves and dips of his body while my mouth presses loving kisses to his lips. I have loved every time I've had sex with Vander, but this moment elevates the experience to a transcendental level.

We glide against one another in sensual, slow, deep motions, our bodies aligned with the synchronization of our hearts and souls. Time ceases to have meaning as we caress, kiss, and make love, and as long as I live, I will never forget how loved and desired I feel as Vander alters my world and shows me the light.

After, we lie in each other's arms, sweaty and sated, our hearts swollen with love and our souls replete. Resting my head on his chest, I trace his tattoos with the tip of my finger while he reads excerpts from *Existentialists and Mystics*, a book of writings on philosophy and literature by the acclaimed author and philosopher Iris Murdoch. We found the book in a local bookshop, and Vander insisted on buying it for me. The last semester of my philosophy class is focused on female influencers, and I already have books by Simone Weil, Hannah Arendt, and Simone de Beauvoir stacked on my nightstand at home.

Vander's dulcet tones lull me to sleep, and when I wake, in the early hours of the morning, it's to his lips on my lips and his hands all over my body.

"Working late again?" June asks, popping her head in my door as she buttons her coat.

"Yes. I want to take an extra few vacation days next week, so I'm working additional overtime hours." Easter is late this year, falling in the middle of April, and I can't believe how fast time is flying. It's been almost a month since Vander and I took our trip to Connecticut, and I'm suffering major withdrawal symptoms even though we are managing to snatch as much time together as we can.

"Okay, but don't stay too late. The asshole is still in the building. Make sure you leave with everyone else."

I'm not the only one burning the midnight oil in the run up to the holidays. "I will," I lie, forcing a smile on my face. "See you tomorrow."

My friends are going to kill me when they discover I'm going through with my plan after all. Viola and June thought they had talked me out of trapping Greg. To be fair, they *had*. Until the stakes were upped, and he's ready to make his move. I know he's coming for me, and I won't sit back and let him take the first potshot. I've got to take control and challenge him to do something I can use to get him fired and discredited. It's the only way to help Vander and safeguard my job.

Diana Henley served him with divorce papers on Monday, and Greg showed up at the boxing club, shouting insults and threats at his son, demanding he tell him where his wife is. Since then, he has shown up at his school and the apartment, demanding to be let in. Vander is holding firm in refusing to speak to him, and now that a temporary restraining order has been granted, Greg can't go near his son without risking arrest. He won't jeopardize his career or his reputation so foolishly, which is how I know he's plotting other ways to retaliate.

With her friend Dana's help, Diana hired an attorney in Colorado to handle the process on her behalf. As well as petitioning for divorce—with full alimony—she has begun civil proceedings to sue him for unlawfully stealing her inheritance, and she submitted a restraining order on the grounds of his constant abuse. Vander documented evidence over the years, which substantiates her claim, and it looks like Greg is not going to talk his way out of this. This time, his wife is not cowering in fear of his fists, and she's telling the truth about what went on in their marriage. It won't matter with the divorce petition, but it will impact the other proceedings against him.

The evidence is enough to seal her contact details, so all correspondence will go through the attorney, and it's killing Greg that he can't find where she is.

Honestly, if I was Diana Henley, I'd be scared for my life.

I haven't been able to sleep all week worrying about what Greg has planned next. If Diana succeeds, she won't need any more of Vander's money, and she has already told him she'll cover his college expenses. Greg can't get near his wife or his son with the TRO in place—which will become permanent in ten days—unless he contests it. He might, but he's smart enough to know the evidence will refute any excuses he might make, and I don't think he can risk attending the hearing. There are already rumblings within legal circles, and this doesn't look good for his career or his standing within the legal community.

Which means he's desperate to find other ways of forcing Vander and Diana to toe the line. Namely, me and Yale. Vander is scared shitless Greg is going to fuck up his place because he made that threat when he turned up at the boxing club, confirming he knows about his acceptance in the art program. I phoned Della and the financial aid advisor I spoke with at Yale and explained the situation. They tried to reassure me his place is secure, but none of us are naive. We know the way these things work. Greg Henley is a respected alumnus and a big donor to the university. Neither woman could guarantee Greg couldn't pull strings to mess things up for his son.

Vander once said in order to beat Greg you have to play him at his own game, so that's what I'm going to do. If I do nothing, Greg will come at me again, only this time it won't be subtle gropes and sleazy innuendos. He intends to use me to hurt his son, and I wouldn't put it past him to rape me. I'm not going to sit back and wait for him to attack me.

I'm taking control, and it needs to happen now.

Tonight.

I'm going to lure him into action and capture it on camera because I need irrefutable evidence to get him fired and disgraced. I'll ensure the news is plastered all over the media and the internet so he loses whatever clout he has with senior-level personnel at Yale.

Vander will be safe.

And more importantly, free.

Chapter Forty-One

Kendall

My palms are sweaty, and my heart rate is elevated as I watch the last employee walk out the doors of Bentley Law. It's almost nine p.m., and the only two people left in the building are me and Gregory Henley.

I have everything set up.

My cell is fully charged and sitting on my phone holder on the desk to the side of my filing tray, where it's not immediately noticeable but still at the perfect angle to video the scene how I expect it to go down. It's ready to record with an automatic backup to the cloud every ten seconds, in case anything goes awry. My desk is clutter-free with all files and paperwork safely locked away. A can of pepper spray and my keys are in the bottom of my filing tray should I need them. I changed out of my skirt suit into a short, tight, lowcut, red dress, and I have styled my hair and makeup as if I'm heading out for the night.

Nerves fire at me as I sip from a vodka cranberry can and attempt to calm down. I run over my newly learned self-defense techniques in my head while I wait for Vander's father to make an appearance. I know he will. I made a point of walking the hallways outside his office so he knows I'm still here. He won't pass up this opportunity.

A few minutes later, footsteps approach, and I know it's showtime. My hands shake as I press record on my cell and lean over my desk, hiking my ass in the air as I pretend to reach for something in the drawer. A cool breeze wafts over the backs of my exposed thighs as he enters my office, distorting the air. Hands grip my hips, and I shriek as he presses his body up against me. Blood pounds in my skull, and I'm trembling all over when he pushes his groin into my ass.

Reminding myself I'm in control and this is how I wanted it to go down, I swallow over the ball of nerves in my throat and play my part. My hands move back, and I angle my head, turning to glare at him as I attempt to pry his hands from my hips. "Get your hands off me, and step away."

Digging his nails into my hips, he thrusts the beginning of an erection into my ass, and I almost vomit. "Or what?" He leans his entire body down over me, nuzzling his nose into my neck.

"I'll scream!"

He chuckles before tugging on my earlobe with his teeth. "We're all alone here, darling, so go for it. All it'll do is turn me the fuck on." He pivots his hips against my ass and begins dry humping me. His body cages me against the desk, leaving me helpless to invoke any of the moves Vander taught me, and I can't access the pepper spray or my keys to attack him from this position either.

Panic crawls up my throat as I writhe underneath him, trying to buck him off, but he's too heavy, and he's crushing me. "I'll report you to Leland. You can't do this! I don't want this! Get off me!" I shout as he grips the hem of my dress with one hand, and his fingers inch up my thigh. Oh my God! *What was*

I thinking?! It wasn't supposed to go down like this, and now I'm genuinely terrified he's going to rape me.

"Leland doesn't give a fuck. All he cares about is money. Ask Leona Wallace and Janine Rindell. They tried going over my head, and they ended up without jobs and letters of recommendation."

All the blood drains from my face. I had no idea he'd tried this crap on anyone besides Tania. Maybe we need to partner up and go after him as a group.

"You broadcast your thoughts so loudly." He chuckles as his fingers move farther up my thigh, while he continues thrusting, and I continue trying to buck him off. "They both signed NDAs in exchange for a small cash lump sum. Neither will talk to you." In an unexpected move, he jerks back and flips me over so my spine is flat to the desk and I'm facing him. Before I can fight him, he pushes the muzzle of a gun into my thigh under my dress, and I turn rigidly still. "This is the way things are going down." Keeping the gun pressed to my flesh, he forces my legs apart and steps in between them. He bends down and presses his lips to my ear while a full-body shudder works its way through me. "You are going to do exactly as I say, or I will kill you."

"You won't get away with murder." I project my voice, wanting the recording to clearly hear me.

"I already have," he says, nibbling along my neck as I shiver and shake. "Several times."

I want to believe it's a lie, but I hear the truth in his tone. Lifting my arms over my head, he quickly secures my wrists with leather cuffs, hooking them to the edge of my desk so I can't move them. He straightens up and pulls my body to the edge of the desk, stretching my arms painfully and causing my skirt to ruck up a few inches. The hem barely covers my crotch, but it's enough to conceal what he's doing with the firearm under my dress.

I stifle a sob as he drags the muzzle of the gun up and down my lace-covered pussy while he unzips his pants and shoves them and his boxer briefs down his legs, and I contemplate the danger I'm in. Right now, being raped is the least of my concerns. He's holding me at gunpoint, and I already know he's a sick, psychotic bastard with little regard for women or human life.

He could kill me.

I was stupid to think I could pull one over on a man like Gregory Henley. It's clear he anticipated this, and I'm feeding his agenda. I need to extract myself from this mess I've made. I'm all out of threats, and the only thing I can do is appeal to any sliver of humanity that may be buried deep inside him. Ignoring how he is tugging on his disgusting dick and eyeing me like I'm his next meal, I fix a pleading expression on my face as I eyeball him. "Please don't kill me. My kids need me. You don't need to do this. Please remove the gun from under my dress." I want it noted on the video there is a gun because it's presently hidden from sight.

He lifts one of my legs over his shoulder while transferring the gun to the outside of my other thigh. Moving his hips, he begins thrusting in earnest, throwing back his head and moaning. When his eyes lower to mine, I swear I'm looking into the eyes of pure evil. "What about my son, Kendall? Doesn't he need you too?"

Air punches from my lungs at the smug expression on his face. *He knows. He knows about Vander and me.* "You leave Vander out of this." I hate how wobbly my voice sounds. "And you leave my kids out of it too." Bile collects at the back of my throat, but I force the next words out. "Do what you want with me, but you leave them alone."

Pinning me with a twisted grin, he continues thrusting against my crotch, and every time his erection nudges against me, I feel sick. I don't understand why he's dry humping me through my clothes, but it makes no difference. I am still being violated, and I can't stop the tears from welling in my eyes. He overpowered me so easily, and all my newfound self-confidence evaporates in a puff of air. Still, I manage to hold on to my tears because I know he'd enjoy seeing them, and I won't give him the satisfaction.

"I don't take my son's sloppy seconds," he says, running his right hand up and down my elevated leg as the cold steel of the gun prods the outside of my other thigh. My skin crawls at the feel of the roughened pads of his fingers, and nausea swims up my throat.

"Don't lie, Greg," Curtis says, sauntering into the room with a casual grin like his soon-to-be ex-wife isn't being assaulted on the desk in her office. "You'd fuck her in a heartbeat if I let you."

"Curtis?" My eyes widen in horror as he casts a derisory gaze over my body. "Why are you here? What's going on?"

Chapter Forty-Two

Kendall

"You look like a slut," Curtis says, coming up alongside Greg, who is still shoving his disgusting dick against my panty-covered vagina. "I should let him fuck you because you're asking for it in that dress."

Greg chuckles, amusement dancing in his eyes as he spots the confusion and horror in mine. "I don't usually accept my son's leftovers, but it'll add an authenticity to the proceedings, don't you think?" He grins at Curtis as he suddenly drops my leg and moves his hand underneath my dress.

"We got enough," Curtis cryptically replies. "It's believable without you fucking the bitch." He shakes his head, piercing me with a look full of disgust. "And trust me, she's a lousy lay. I wouldn't waste my spunk on her."

"Come now, Hawthorne." Greg slants him a sneering look. "You've seen the footage from Vander's apartment. She's far from a lousy lay."

Oh my God. They've been spying on us! I thought they hated one another, but it's clear they've obviously partnered up. "You had someone break in and plant a camera," I say as it slots into place. I know Vander and Jimmy searched the apartment for cameras and didn't find any, so I can't tell if they're bluffing or whomever they hired hid it someplace it wouldn't be found.

"You two made this so fucking easy." Greg chuckles as his fingers brush against the front of my panties.

Curtis wraps his hand around Greg's wrist, stalling his upward trajectory. "That's enough. You got what you needed. Let her go."

"Why do you care? You want rid of the bitch. I'm horny now, and I need to blow my load. Might as well fill her hole."

He's disgusting and repulsive, and if he does this, I don't think I'll ever recover.

"She's still the mother of my kids. If they found out I let you fuck her, I'd lose them forever."

"Rape, Curtis. The word you are looking for is *rape*, and you're damn right. They would cut you off forever if you let this happen." They'll cut him off when they find out he let Greg stage this, for reasons I'm still not privy to. It's on the tip of my tongue to spit that at my ex, but I shove the words back down, for fear he'd give his buddy the green light to proceed.

Curtis grabs the gun from Greg's hand and pushes him away from me. "I didn't agree to this." He brandishes the gun in Greg's face as the asshole pulls his boxer briefs and pants back up, and I heave a sigh of relief.

"I had to improvise. My son's been teaching her self-defense. How else was I supposed to ensure she shut up and played her part?"

Curtis frowns but doesn't reply as he yanks down my dress, unhooks the cuffs from the desk, and pulls me upright. I want to spit in his face or sideswipe his legs, but he's still holding the gun, and if he's desperate enough to buddy up with his enemy, then he's desperate enough to shoot me. *I know I'm a pawn in Greg's sick game, but how does this help Curtis?* If he thinks this will force me into accepting the terms of his latest divorce proposal, he can think again. When I'm done with him, he'll be languishing in a jail cell alongside Vander's father. "I don't know what you think you stand to gain here, Curtis, but you've just fucked everything up."

Leaning across me, Curtis swipes my cell from the holder and pauses the recording. "How dumb can one bitch be." He grips my chin painfully, his nails digging into my flesh. "I'm not the one who has fucked everything up."

I lurch for my cell, as he passes it to Greg, forgetting my wrists are still bound. Losing my balance, I take a tumble off the desk, but Curtis catches me before I face-plant the ground. Cursing under his breath, he plonks me in the chair in front of my desk, using his tie to bind one of my ankles to the leg. Greg absently loosens his tie and hands it to Curtis as he chuckles while watching the recording on my phone. "Great camera work, honey."

Internally, I flip him the bird.

"Just email yourself the file, and wipe it from her phone," Curtis instructs as he binds my other leg with Greg's tie. "I want to get this over and done with before security comes looking."

"I told you I handled that," Greg says, pressing buttons on my cell before he drops it on the desk. "No one will come near us."

Curtis grabs my wrists, scowling at my new ink. "This isn't you. It's crass. You're letting him change you."

I bark out a bitter laugh. "Vander *is* changing me. He's showing me how to appreciate my worth, something you did your best to destroy." I put my face all up in his. "Guess what? You didn't. And you get no say over what I put on or in my body. I'm free to do what I like and you can't stop me."

"Wanna bet?" He smirks, and I long to claw my fingernails

down his face and leave scars. Curtis walks over beside Greg, and both of them prop their butts against the edge of my desk, facing me. "In case it's not clear, you're not exactly in a position to make such assertions when we hold all the cards."

"You won't when I report you to the cops," I snap, glowering at both of them.

They trade wide grins, and all the blood drains from my body. "If anyone is reporting anything to the cops, it'll be me," Greg retorts.

"I haven't done anything, and you know it."

"The cops won't see it like that," Curtis says. "Show her." He eyeballs Greg while scrubbing a hand over his chin, showcasing his impatient nature.

"I warned my son, on several occasions, what would happen if he didn't play ball my way," Greg says, extracting his cell phone from the pocket of his pants.

"Like I warned you not to cross me," Curtis says, stretching his legs out and tucking one ankle over the other. "All you had to do was play happy family for a couple of years, and then we could have split up amicably, and none of this shit would be happening."

"On what planet would West and Stella ever be happy with you cheating on me because there's no way you'd ever have been able to keep that truth from them!"

"I had it all worked out, but you had to mess up my plans." He jabs his finger in my face as his lips pull into a sneer. "And then you go and screw a kid. You disgust me."

I bark out a laugh. "You're such a hypocrite. How old is your current fuck buddy? And how old was Lydia when you took her to bed?"

He fixes me with an arrogant grin, causing goose bumps to sprout along my arms. "They weren't sixteen."

My brow puckers. *What the hell is he talking about?* Vander is eighteen.

"You look confused, honey," Greg says. "Let me fill you in." He swipes the screen of his cell and sticks it in my face. "You and Vander made this simple for us. You were too busy screwing your brains out and making mushy declarations of love to notice what was going on around you."

I stare in horror as he flicks through images on his cell, showing pictures and videos of Vander and me, in various stages of intimacy. They don't just have footage from Vander's apartment either. Greg scrolls through tons of photos taken when we were in Bridgeport, and I am so glad Dana and Diana fled to Europe after she left rehab because he must have had someone following Vander all that week. *Or maybe the person was following me?*

"The texts were the cherry on top of the cake." Greg switches to a file containing hundreds of messages. "You really should be more careful with your cell phone around the office." He smirks, and I long to smash his face in.

"It's password protected!"

He scoffs. "Every phone is hackable. You just need the right people to show you how it's done."

Greg pulls up another file and dangles it in my face. "This video's my favorite. My son has really brought out your kinky side, hasn't he, darling?"

My cheeks burn in a combination of rage and humiliation as he plays a video showing me posing for Vander in the nude. "You had no right to invade our privacy, and it's illegal!"

Curtis snarls. "You have the nerve to call Ingrid a whore when you do that? You even let him take photos, you dumb bitch."

"Fuck you, Curtis. You're just pissed because Vander has

proven how shit you are in bed. He gave me more orgasms our first night than you gave me our entire marriage!"

Greg chuckles, looking highly amused.

Veins throb in Curtis's neck, and he looks like he wants to strangle me with his bare hands. He glares at me, and I glare right back. After a few heated seconds, he turns his venom in Greg's direction. "Your son's a dirty little punk. He's lucky you and I came to an agreement, or I might be tempted to put one of these bullets through his skull."

"Touch my son, and it'll be the last thing you do," Greg replies, quickly losing his amusement. He doesn't care about Vander except as something that belongs to him, and no one threatens what's his.

"You don't want me, but no one else can have me. Is that it, Curtis?" I snap.

"He's a fucking kid! I bet his balls haven't even dropped. Who the fuck is he to take something that still belongs to me?"

He's an insufferable arrogant ass. *How did I ever marry him? What the hell was I thinking?* Greg rolls his eyes as he repockets his phone, not pandering to Curtis's little temper tantrum. "Vander is more man than you'll ever be, and I can assure you his balls are fully grown. Along with every other part of him." I purposely trail my eyes up and down Curtis's body, lingering on his crotch as I snidely laugh.

My head whips back when he slaps me across the face, my neck jerking awkwardly. "I'll fucking kill you." He grabs my hair and twists it around his fist, yanking my head back. "I don't need much incentive."

"Focus," Greg says, sounding bored. "All this talk of balls reminds me I need to get laid. Let's finish this so we can leave."

Curtis slams his mouth down on me from above, and I instantly bite down hard on his lower lip. He roars, releasing my hair and slapping me across the face again. Pain darts across my cheekbone, and stars momentarily dazzle my eyes.

"I should have let him fuck you," Curtis hisses, dabbing at a bead of blood on his lip. "You deserve to be taught a lesson."

"That ship has sailed, Hawthorne. End this," Greg says in a clipped tone.

Curtis crouches in front of me, and I spit in his face. Wiping my saliva from his cheek with the back of his sleeve, he looks ready to rip my head from my shoulders. His hands fist into balls, and a muscle clenches in his jaw. "This is the deal, Kendall," he says in a lethal tone. "You will sign the new divorce papers giving me the house and half of the cash in our savings account. We'll share custody as agreed, and I'll pay half the college fees."

Our savings account has been decimated since we separated, and he knows I don't earn enough to get a mortgage to buy a house even remotely similar to our family home. He must think I was born yesterday. I raised my kids in that house, and I'm not giving it up without a fight. "No deal. The kids are living with me, so we stay in the house, and the only divorce papers I'm signing are the original ones."

"I need the house!" he shouts, and I narrow my eyes in suspicion.

"Why?"

He stands, looming over me with an evil grin. "Ingrid is pregnant, and I want my kid to grow up in the same house my other kids did."

I'm stunned into silence because this is going to devastate West and Stella. *Doesn't he see that? Or does he not care anymore now he's starting a new family?* "I don't care what you want, and no judge will rule in your favor when it comes to the family home. The kids are staying with me in that house. Find someplace else to raise your new family."

"You don't get a say in this," Greg says, cutting in because he's obviously run out of patience. "You will sign the divorce papers, end your relationship with my son, and agree to stay away from him and to stop meddling in his affairs."

"Why on earth would I ever agree to that?"

Greg comes to stand beside Curtis, and they tower over me, their legs brushing my knees as I remain trapped in the chair. "Because if you don't, we'll report you to the police for the statutory rape of a minor."

Chapter Forty-Three

Kendall

I bark out a laugh. "Are you two high or something?"

"You're right," Greg says, looking at Curtis. "She is a dumb bitch."

Curtis holds his palm out, drilling Greg with a sharp look. It seems it's okay for Curtis to insult me, but he takes offense if Greg goes there, which is interesting and maybe something I can use to play them off against one another. "Give me your phone," Curtis demands.

Greg opens his phone and hands it to his partner in crime. Curtis shoves it in my face. "Watch the time stamps," he snaps, scrolling through the videos and photos and texts.

I squint as I home in on the time stamps, and an icy chill creeps up my spine as I read the dates. They are all stamped two to three years ago. Slowly, the pieces are slotting into the puzzle, and I feel like I'm going to be sick. "What did you do?"

"I represent some clients with very particular interests," Greg says, taking back his phone and flicking through it. "I scratch their back, and they scratch mine. They can make just about anything go away or make anything happen, so I called in a favor. Doctoring files is like child's play to them. I sent them the recordings from Vander's apartment, the texts from your cell, and the photos the PI took last month in Connecticut. They had them back to me in less than forty-eight hours." He thrusts one in my face. "These guys are professionals. They didn't just alter the time stamps. They made sure the photos were appropriate for that time." He zooms in on the image of Vander, pointing at his neck and arms.

"They wiped his tattoos," I whisper as the true extent of my predicament becomes clear.

"They also used age software to wind back time. We just had to give them an image of both of you from a couple of years ago, and they worked their magic."

As I glance again at the photos, I see they have altered the settings too. While the video footage is from Vander's new apartment, they have superimposed it so it looks like it took place at the carriage house. "We'll tell the police the truth and no one will believe you. The hotel will confirm we stayed there recently, and I'll find an expert who can prove those images were doctored."

Both men laugh, and my cheeks inflame. "The hotel records have already been altered, and of course you'd both deny it. The cops will be expecting that," Curtis says.

"Don't consider bringing Viola or June or those thugs at the boxing gym into this," Greg warns. "Not unless you want to see all of them meet an untimely death." He folds his arms across his chest and grins. "And no one will go up against one of the biggest criminal organizations in Colorado. Anyone who attempts to discredit the evidence will be sent a clear message to back down."

I swing my gaze around to Curtis. "What are you even doing aligning yourself with him? You'll end up in jail, and your kids will hate you for life."

"The kids will hate *you* for life if this comes out." Curtis trails his fingers down the side of my face. "Imagine the abuse they'll endure in school if kids find out West's mom was fucking his best friend for years behind his back. Look how he's reacted to me, and I'm not fucking one of his school friends. He'll cut you out of his life in a heartbeat."

Pain tightens my chest, but I can't think about that now. I've got to stay in the present and try to find a way out of this nightmare. "He won't believe it," I whisper, twisting my head from side to side to shake off his vile touch. "I'll tell them what you've done. How you've set us up."

"You've been lying to them, Kendall. A part of me actually wants you to stubbornly refuse so you'll be arrested. You'll be the new villain, and I'll be the hero who swoops in to rescue them. It would be an easier path for me to tread. Even if you're not charged or you get off, the damage will be done. The kids won't want you. No court will give you custody or the house if you've been arrested for raping a minor. You'll lose your job, and no law firm will hire you. You'll be spat at in the street, and Vander won't want anything to do with you because you'll have ruined his life too. I could do that to you, but I'm giving you a way out because you're the mother of my children, and we both know they need you."

"Don't pretend you are doing this for anyone but yourself! Your new baby mama doesn't want to raise my kids. That's why you won't report me." We have come full circle, and I've called their bluff. They don't want to report me because it doesn't serve their aims. This is a threat to make me do things their way.

"West is off to Oklahoma in a few months, and Stella only has one more year before she'll fly the nest too. That only leaves Ridge. Ingrid will love Ridge because she loves me."

Laughter bubbles up my throat. "She loves your money,

you dumb fuck, and as soon as she has bled you dry, she'll leave you for a younger model, and I'll be cheering her on."

Curtis slaps me again. "You don't know her."

"I know enough to know you won't make a false report about me." I cock my head to the side. "You do know that's a crime, right?"

"*I'll* report you," Greg says. "If you won't agree to our terms, I'll do it, and I have the connections to make it stick. This only works for me if you break Vander's heart. I was going to go the Yale route first until I realized how obsessed he is with you. He'll be upset if I pull his place in the art program, but he'd get over it. He'll continue to deny me as long as he has you." He brushes his thumb against my lips, and I fight a fresh wave of nausea. "You're the key to all of this, Kendall. You're the only one who can give me what I want. Vander will never get over losing you."

"His soul mate." Curtis makes a gagging sound. "That boy would say anything to get into your panties."

"I don't expect a philistine to understand, or maybe it's your lower level of intelligence that means it all goes over your head. Either way, I couldn't care less what you think or what you believe. What Vander and I share is something neither of you will ever experience."

"What Vander and you share is dead in the water, honey." Greg pinches my lips. "You are going to break it off with him, I am going to drag that disloyal drunken slut of a wife home from Europe and chain her in my basement until Vander drops the art program and accepts a place at Yale Law."

Shock splays across my face as I realize he must have known where Diana is all along. Everything he has done, even turning up at Vander's apartment and making threats, has all been part of his play, and he was holding back, waiting to time it to perfection. I wouldn't be surprised if he has someone lined up to quash the restraining orders, but I don't see how he can make the domestic abuse stuff go away, not with the evidence Diana already submitted. *If she retracts it, surely the state can still prosecute him?* I don't know enough to say it with confidence though, and if anyone knows his way around the law, it's Gregory Henley.

Pressure settles on my chest as the reality of the situation dawns on me. Vander is never going to be free of this man. Not unless we kill him, and that's becoming more of a viable option. Right now, I need to buy myself some time because my brain is overloaded, and I can't think clearly. "You can't expect me to agree on the spot. I need time to think about it."

"I'm glad you see it our way," Greg says, grinning like the psychopath he is. I recoil as he kisses me, withdrawing his revolting mouth before I have time to bite his lip like I did with Curtis.

"Do you fucking mind?!" Curtis drags Greg away from me. "Hands fucking off."

Deep down, those two are still enemies and competitive as ever. Just because they have found common ground now, it doesn't mean it will always be that way. Whatever arrangement they have is tentative at best, and I wonder again how I might use that to my advantage. One thing is crystal clear. I need to get out of here so I can review my options.

Curtis removes the ties from my ankles as Greg unlocks the cuffs around my wrists. "You have twenty-four hours to break it off with Vander and instruct your attorney to accept the terms of your husband's agreement," Greg says, threading his fingers through my hair. I swat his hand away, and he grins.

"If you breathe a word of this to anyone, we will go straight to the cops and release one of those videos online," Curtis warns, striding toward the door.

"Choose wisely, Kendall," Greg says as they exit the room.

Chapter Forty-Four

Kendall

I crawl out of bed at five a.m., giving up on the illusion of sleep. My brain is going at a hundred miles an hour, and I can't switch it off. Since leaving the office last night, all I have been able to think about is the mess I'm in. I don't want to let Greg and Curtis win, but I can't have them reporting me to the police. Even if I can plead my case and get the charges dropped, the damage will already be done. It would devastate my kids, and Vander would murder his father and end up in jail for life.

No. I can't let that happen. No matter what, I need to protect Vander and my kids.

I wish I had someone to talk to about this, but I'm terrified to involve anyone because Greg seems to have eyes and ears everywhere, and he has more than proven how resourceful he is.

I honestly don't believe Curtis would let it get that far. From the way he reacted yesterday, I know he'd be furious if news got out about Vander and me because it'll make him look bad. The story would take on a life of its own, and the narrative would be he couldn't hold on to his wife and she was fucking a high-school kid because he couldn't fulfill her needs. He would be a laughingstock, and Ingrid might even kick him to the curb. And she's liable to do that if she's saddled with his kids.

Irrespective of what he said last night, he doesn't want the kids. Not really. He's making a new family, and that's all that's important to him now. He doesn't have a clue how to properly take care of them anyway, as he's always left most of the parenting to me, and he's far too busy enjoying life to even contemplate full custody. It's all a bluff. A means to an end to get what he wants.

Curtis is simple to figure out.

He wants the house, and he wants to be free of me and the kids. Having thought about it, I can give him that. While I have a lot of fond memories attached to our home, it's where we lived with Curtis, and I don't want reminders of him after we're divorced.

A clean break is exactly what's needed, and I've already come up with a plan.

Greg is the real villain.

He's the one I need to worry about. Curtis is only a pawn in Greg's game. Greg will do whatever it takes to get his way, and he has the connections to make it happen.

The way I see it, if I don't agree and I tell Vander, he'll either end up on a murder charge or go straight to his father and promise him everything he wants in exchange for setting me free. I won't let Vander ruin his future over me. However, if I do agree, it not only means breaking Vander's heart, but his future is still not his own. Greg is going to continue to harass him and use Diana to force Vander into giving up art school and following him into law. He'll be miserable, and he'll never get out from under his father's clutches. I won't facilitate that.

Which only leaves one other option. I have one bargaining chip, and I intend to use it to negotiate for Vander's freedom.

After waving the kids off to school, I phone work, explaining I need some personal time this morning and I'll be late arriving. Deciding to tackle the easier conversation first, I head to Denver to speak to Curtis. At least going into his place of work ensures I won't bump into Ingrid, and it should mean the conversation remains civil. I don't intend for it to take long.

I'm sitting in a small meeting room at the back of the reception area when Curtis arrives. He claims the seat across from me and leans back in his chair. "I hope you've made the right choice, Kendall. I really don't want to hurt my kids, but I'll do it if I have to."

"Cut the bullshit, Curtis. We both know you won't go there. You don't want it getting out about Vander because your ego is too fragile to handle it. I'd also wager Ingrid wouldn't be pleased, especially if you go to jail for fabricating evidence. Considering you're doing all this for her, you won't take that risk."

He opens his mouth to protest, but I hold up my palm. "Save it. I won't believe your lies, and I'm going to give you what you want—an expedited divorce and the house—but I have some conditions."

His mouth flies open again, and I drill him with a look. Surprisingly, he shuts up. "One, you give me my share of the house from your stock portfolio or your 401K and you agree to pay all the college fees." West has received a full scholarship, but Stella most likely won't, and she'll be starting college next year. I might not be in a financial position to support her, and while she can take out loans to put herself through college, I don't see why she should have to when her father can afford it. It's the least he can do seeing as he wants to cut us loose to focus on his new family. "Two, you give me full custody of the kids, and three, you agree to let me move out of state."

I can't stay here after this goes down. It will be virtually impossible to stay away from Vander after I have broken up with him, and I don't think my heart can withstand the pain of seeing him but not being able to be with him or even talk to him. I'm also doing it to protect my children, and I think a fresh start some place new is what's best for all of us. Moving out of our house to accommodate their dad and his pregnant mistress will kill them. I know how people gossip, and it will be unbearable.

Ridge will be upset because he loves his dad, and he won't really understand, but he's young, and he'll adjust. West is leaving in a couple months for Oklahoma, so my proposed move won't impact him. It's mostly Stella I'm concerned about. I don't want to force her to move or force her to live with her father as her only way to spend senior year with her friends, but I have limited choices, and I'm working toward the bigger picture. I hate the thought of leaving her behind, but I'll support whatever decision she makes. "There's just one caveat. If Stella wants to stay here, you let her live with you during senior year."

Curtis taps his fingers on the table as he stares at me while he thinks it through. It doesn't take long for him to decide, and I almost wish he had proved me wrong. "I agree, on condition you end things permanently with that punk."

He is such an asshole. It was okay for him to have multiple affairs, but as soon as I find someone, he gets pissy, as if he has any right to feel aggrieved. I don't bother making that point though because I'm done with him. I'm ready to draw a line under my marriage and move on. My chair scrapes across the floor as I stand. "You don't need to make that a condition, Curtis. It's already a condition, or were you not listening to anything Greg said last night?"

"I'm just making sure you stick to it." He stands and smiles, like he hasn't just tossed his own flesh and blood aside.

Looking at him now makes me sick. *What did I ever see him in?* He's a sorry excuse of a man, and I almost pity Ingrid. Or maybe she'll school him, and he'll finally get what's coming to him. I can only hope he does.

"Goodbye, Curtis." I stride to the door, pausing with my fingers curled around the door handle. I glance over my shoulder, looking at him for the final time, feeling nothing but relief our relationship is ending. I murmur under my breath, too low for him to hear. "One day, you're going to regret how easily you gave up your kids. I hope she's worth it."

Without wasting another second of my time or any further thoughts on this man, I walk out of his life for good.

After I leave Curtis, I head to my attorney's office to sign the modified divorce paperwork, feeling relieved to have that part concluded. Then I drive to Bentley Law and park in the employee parking lot for the last time. I expected to feel a little sad as I make my way up in the elevator for my meeting with the VP of HR, but I'm experiencing none of those emotions. I veer between elation at finally taking back control of my life and desolation at the prospect of what I'll need to do later, praying I'm strong enough to see this through.

I exit Paul Cummings' office immediately after tendering my resignation, smothering a smile at the look of outrage on the HR VP's face when I refused to work the period of my two weeks' notice and told him he'd be paying me for it along with the bonus I'm due and the paid vacation and sick time owed me. I also requested a letter of recommendation and demanded a letter confirming the noncompete clause in my contract is null and void as long as I don't work for any legal firms in Colorado.

I have no intention of returning to Colorado, and I'll need that letter to work in Lynette's legal practice when I move to Oregon. I'm so glad I arranged to meet my old high-school pal the last time she was back home and that Lynette had jokingly tried to convince me to move to Portland and work for her. When I called her last night, she didn't hesitate to offer me a job along with her assistance in finding an apartment to rent temporarily while I house hunt.

I'll work on closing out all open assignments and documenting a file with instructions for my replacement from home while I pack up my house. I resolutely refuse to spend another minute in this office, knowing Gregory Henley is down the hall. Even if my meeting with him doesn't go as planned, there's no way I can continue to work for Bentley Law after everything that has happened. Paul was apoplectic when I told him Leland would agree to my terms because I'm sure Greg will have no issue convincing him.

Stopping briefly outside Greg's office, I give myself a quick, silent pep talk, reminding myself I have leverage and promising I won't let him intimidate me. Checking to ensure my suit jacket is fully buttoned, I run a hand down over my jacket and onto my pants, smoothing out any wrinkles. I stopped in the bathroom after leaving Paul's office to brush my hair and fix my makeup. I'm a firm believer in looking the part, and I intend to kick ass today. Without knocking, I open the door and stride inside Greg's large, plush office.

Lifting his head, he drills me with a look as I close the door, and he hangs up the phone. "That was Paul," he says, waving his hand at one of the vacant seats in front of his desk. "He's seething." He flashes me a grin as I sit down, placing my purse on my lap.

"I want my terms met," I say, working hard to remain poised and calm, but my heart is slamming against my rib cage, and my palms are sweaty. I can barely look at Greg without remembering what he did to me last night. I almost puke every time I think about how close I came to being raped. Subtly, I grip the back of my purse and dig my nails into the soft leather. The motion helps to calm me.

"That all depends on what you're here to tell me." He rounds the desk, and I force myself not to cower as he approaches. "Give me your cell."

I narrow my eyes at him. "Why?"

"I need to know you're not recording this meeting."

"As do I." I arch a brow.

"You show me yours, and I'll show you mine." He chuckles, and I glare at him from under my lashes as I retrieve my cell from my purse. He truly is a sick, twisted bastard.

After we have examined each other's phones and are satisfied our conversation isn't being recorded, I grab my cell and my purse and stand. "Change of plans," I say, skimming my gaze around his room. "We'll discuss this outside on the sidewalk." I don't trust him not to have a camera in here, and I won't take any chances because he could try to construe my words and turn this back around on me. I need to dig us out of this hole not burrow a bigger one.

"I don't think so, darling."

"I think so." Opening up the video on my phone, I shove it in his face. "I have additional copies of this."

To give him credit, he barely reacts. I move to swipe it from his hands, but he grabs my wrist, warning me with dark eyes not to push it. I was hoping I could wing it and pretend I had the full recording backed up to the cloud, but deep down, I knew Greg would never fall for it. Thinking about ending things with Vander tears strips off my heart, and if I could find a way to fix this without breaking both our hearts, I would.

"Fine," he says, after watching the full recording. Even though it cuts out shortly after Curtis arrives in the room, he can see there is enough in there to warrant his concern. "We'll talk outside."

That rat bastard does have a camera in here!

"Leave your cell here," I tell him as I power mine off and hold it up for him to see.

He smirks. "Perhaps you're not as dumb as you look."

I don't even dignify that with a response, walking to the door without uttering a word. Grabbing his suit jacket off the back of the chair, he follows me out of his office and outside.

I stop at the corner of the building, checking there are no street cams in the vicinity.

"That recording is enough to go to the police and press charges against you for sexual assault."

He smirks. "I'm slightly impressed, but don't make yourself look stupid now. We both know I can make that go away." He pulls a cigar from his inside jacket pocket and lights it up. "You go near the cops, and I'll hang you out to dry."

"I already know that," I calmly reply. "Which is why I won't go to the cops." I stab him with a confident look even though I'm quaking on the inside. "I'll email that to every one of your clients, upload it onto social media, and send a copy to all the major media outlets. I'll ruin you before you'll have a chance to stop it."

"I'll return the favor and some," he replies, leveling me with a pointed look.

"Something I also know."

"What's your angle?"

Always Meant to Be

"We both have something on the other. Only one is real, but both have the potential to hurt us, so we make a new deal."

He puffs away on his cigar, giving little away with his expression. "Go on."

"I won't use this against you, and you won't use your *evidence* against me. We both hold on to our leverage, so if either one of us attempts to use it against the other, we each have a means to exact revenge. I'm giving Curtis what he wants, so he's no longer invested in this. The rest of your terms are now null and void. You let Vander and Diana off the hook, and I won't destroy you." In this scenario, I'm the winner, and I already know he'll never agree to that.

He barks out a laugh. "Nice try, honey, but no deal." He blows smoke clouds in my face, and I cough, waving my hands around to ward off the fumes. "You don't have that much leverage."

I was expecting this, and I'm prepared. "It's really quite simple, Gregory. You either care about your career, your reputation, and maintaining your wealthy lifestyle or you only care about exerting power over your son, no matter the consequences. You're an intelligent man. You've worked hard to build your reputation as one of the state's top attorneys. I know Leland is going to sell the business to you when he retires."

He quirks a brow.

"I'm office manager, Gregory. My team typed up the paperwork. It's a done deal, and you don't need Vander to run it with you. You never have, and you know he's never going to be what you want him to be. This was all just a game."

He shrugs. "I like fucking with him. He has never understood his place, and I'm not done teaching him life lessons."

"You're a sick bastard," I blurt, and he laughs.

"I'm beginning to see the attraction." He moves his hand

toward my head, and I stab him with a warning look while taking a step back.

"Do not touch me, or I'll send the emails I've already prepared to every one of your clients. All it'll take is a press of a button." I'm not lying. I have them all teed up.

He shrugs again, like I don't pose any threat. "Let me educate you, Kendall. In order to negotiate a deal, you need to offer something of value to the other party. You stand to lose very little in this deal while I'll lose my wife and son and the adrenaline rush I get from fucking with their heads. You need to meet me halfway." He stubs the butt of his cigar out on the wall behind him. "Make me the offer you came here to make me."

"I will end things with Vander and walk away from him if you relinquish your control on him. You agree not to interfere with his place in the Yale art program and not to use his mother to force him into doing your bidding. You will let him lead his life without interference from you, and you'll let Diana divorce you. You promise not to kill them or hurt them in any way. You will not hand that falsified evidence to the police or any authority figure or post any of it online or share any of it in the community. You will not show it to my kids or to Vander."

"That's still asking a lot."

"Is it?" I narrow my eyes to slits. "You were the one who said I was the key to all this. That Vander won't survive losing me, so I think this is more than enough."

He ponders my words for a few seconds before shaking his head. "I will agree on condition you stay away from him forever. That means no talking to him. No visiting him. No contact whatsoever, and you don't mention this deal when breaking up with him, or ever. This term is nonnegotiable and based on you ending the relationship tonight. If I discover you've breached this term, at any time, I will personally hand-deliver the evidence to the cops. There is no statute of limitations on rape of a minor in Colorado."

"Why do you hate him so much? Isn't it enough to tear me away from him now? Why would it matter if we reconnected in the future?"

"Because I want to break him fully, and this is the only option I have left. What good is splitting you up now if he can find his way back to you later?" He shoves his hands in the pockets of his pants. "Vander needs to learn you don't always get what you want in this life."

"I think he's already learned that lesson, and haven't you broken him enough? He didn't have a normal childhood, and you tried your best to break him over the years. He has suffered enough."

"He will never be done suffering." A look of pure malice washes over his face. "If I have to give up my plans and let him and that slut go, then this is the way it must be. Vander will never get over losing you. No matter how hard he tries, he will always be broken, and every day without you in his life will be a reminder of that."

Chapter Forty-Five

Kendall

I'm strung tight as a bow as I climb the stairs to Vander's apartment later that night. My heart is heavy as I contemplate what I'm about to do. I had no choice but to accept Greg's terms. My motivations going into the meeting were to ensure Vander is free, and he is. I know preserving my relationship with him was a long shot, and I was prepared to sacrifice it because I knew I had to offer something to Greg, and that's the only thing I could offer. He might think he has won, but I'm determined to take him down. This isn't the ending. It's only the beginning. And when I have put him behind bars, I will come for Vander and explain everything. I trust in our connection, and I know we will be together again when the timing is right.

Perhaps I'm delusional, but it's the only way I can reconcile this within myself.

After walking away from Greg earlier, I turned the corner and emptied the contents of my stomach on the sidewalk. I know my actions have saved Vander, and I don't regret the choice I have made, but it still feels like the biggest betrayal. I'll have to put on the performance of a lifetime now to get him to believe I am ending things with him to move away and focus on my kids. If he pushes me, as I expect he will, I'll have to lie. I'm going to have to tell him my feelings have changed, and I really don't want to do that. It will break his heart and pour acid on all of our memories, so I pray I can avoid it.

I've been calling and texting him since school got out, but he hasn't picked up. I stuck my head into the gym on my way up here, but Jimmy says he hasn't been by today, so I'm figuring he must be at home.

When I reach the top of the stairs, I stand outside his door and press my head to the wood. Tears prick my eyes, and I can scarcely swallow over the messy ball of emotion clogging my throat.

I love him so much, and this is killing me.

Breaking his heart and walking away without knowing how or when I will see him again will devastate me as much as him, but I can't bail now. If there had been any other way, I would have taken it. Straightening up, I swipe at the tears flowing from my eyes and remind myself of why I'm doing this. I'm protecting my kids and protecting the love of my life. My own feelings don't come into it. Removing my compact from my purse, I patch up my makeup and disguise my blotchy skin. Then I take a deep breath and use my key to open the door to Vander's apartment.

"Vander?" I shout in alarm, the instant I step foot into his place, gasping as I survey the devastation confronting me. His art studio is trashed. The chaise longue that holds such fond memories has been torn to shreds, and filler oozes from the ripped seating onto the floor. But it's the destruction of his paintings that hurts more. Someone has dragged a knife through some of his canvases and splashed red paint on others.

Forcing my feet to move, I call out for him again as I walk

into the living space, horrified to find it in a similar condition. The couch is overturned, the TV is smashed to smithereens, and someone has taken a knife to Vander's king-sized bed. Destroyed remnants of cushions, pillows, and bed linen coat the floors.

"Vander." Spotting him sitting cross-legged on the floor, in front of the window, with his shoulders hunched over, I rush to his side. "What happened? Are you hurt?" I gasp as I crouch down beside him, spotting his shredded knuckles. The skin is torn and oozing blood. Judging by that and the paint splatters on his shirt, I know Vander is responsible for the devastation to his apartment. I swear if Greg has double-crossed me, I will murder the motherfucker. Gingerly, I lift his hand, but he swats it away, causing me to lose my balance and fall to the floor on my butt.

"Don't fucking touch me," he snaps, slowly lifting his head. His eyes are puffy and red-rimmed, and his skin is blotchy.

Prickles of apprehension dance over my skin, lifting all the fine hairs on the back of my neck. "What's going on?"

"You tell me," he says in a gritted tone, sniffling as he stares at me with the most forlorn expression.

"What do you mean?" My voice cracks as dread slithers down my spine.

"Where were you last night, Kendall?"

I hug my knees to my chest. "Working late. You know that. I told you."

"You also told me you'd come by after, but you didn't, and you ghosted me until this afternoon. Why?"

Fuck! He knows something! How? My mind is spinning, and I don't know how to reply. I came here with a very specific purpose in mind. I had it all planned, and now I'm spiraling.

"Tell me it's not true." He lowers his voice as his eyes plead with mine. "Tell me you weren't with my father."

All the blood drains from my face, and every muscle in my body locks up as I realize what Greg has done.

"Oh my God." Vander drops his head, staring at the floor as his shoulders shake.

I'm frozen as I stare at him, wanting to refute it and craving to comfort him, but I'm mute, and my brain is muddled as conflicting voices scream at me to do something to make this right.

"I knew he'd use you to get to me," he says a couple of minutes later, breaking the tense silence. "I just never thought it'd be like this." Tears well in his eyes, and pain stretches across my chest making breathing difficult.

Vander pulls his cell from his pocket, swiping the shattered screen with his thumb and shoving it in my face. "He sent me that today. Emailed from an anonymous email, but I know it was him."

I stare in dazed realization as the video plays out on his phone. It's the scene from my office last night, but it's been doctored, and it comes off as a completely different situation. The sound has been muted, so the conversation can't be heard, and it looks so damn bad. It looks like we're consensually fucking. From the angle, you can't tell my hands are handcuffed, only that they are stretched over my head, like he put them there and I'm obeying. I didn't realize when I was trying to buck him off how it might look on camera. My back is arched, and my tits are thrust out with ample cleavage on view, thanks to the uncharacteristically slutty lowcut dress I'm wearing.

And...holy fuck.

I slap a hand over my mouth as I stare at my face on the screen with mounting horror. It looks like I'm enjoying it because that bastard has superimposed my face with footage from one of my lovemaking sessions with Vander. It's been cleverly done. I only know it's the truth because I know damn well the expression on my face was one of revulsion and terror.

A tear slips out of my eye before I can stop it. I can't stop shaking, and I can't speak over the lump wedged in my throat. I'm on the verge of a meltdown, and I don't know what to do. I bury my head in my knees to buy myself some time before I completely lose it. That fucking double-crossing prick. I am going to end him. I don't know how, but I will not rest until that man is either behind bars or buried six feet under.

How could he do this to his son? Was it not enough I was going to break his heart by walking away from him? Fuck that asshole. Fuck him to hell and back.

"Kendall." Vander's voice spears through me like an arrow, and the urge to throw myself into his arms and tell him it's all a lie is riding me hard. "Look at me." His tone is sharper and more confident. Slowly, I lift my head, peering straight into his eyes. I hug my knees tighter as I try to hold it together. "If there is something else going on here, if there is anything I need to know, now is the time to tell me." His eyes delve into mine, in that intense way of his, and I know what he's doing. He's trying to use our connection to seek the truth, and I can't give it to him. I can only give him the lie. If I tell him what he wants me to say—that his father sexually assaulted me and he's blackmailing me with the threat of reporting me for statutory rape—he'll walk out of here like a madman and commit murder. He won't care about the consequences. He will just want that man dead.

I love him enough to willingly sacrifice any prospect of an us if it means I get to keep him safe and out of jail. Pulling myself together, I lift my chin up and stab him straight in the eye. "I'm so sorry, Vander. I never meant for it to happen; it just did."

"Is that the truth?"

I nod, and it kills me to maintain eye contact, but I do.

He blinks successively, staring at me in shock, and his façade drops, showcasing the true extent of the pain I'm inflicting. I want to kill myself for ever putting that look on his face, but I can't lose sight of the big picture. "You fucked my father?" he whispers. "You willingly fucked that psycho?"

I nod. "I was coming here to tell you it's over. I didn't know he was going to send that to you. I never wanted you to find out like that."

He rubs at his chest, and the pain in his eyes mirrors the pain in my heart. "I don't believe this." He lifts his tear-filled eyes to mine. "How could you do this to me? Was everything a lie? Did everything we shared mean so little to you? Did *I* mean nothing to you?" His voice elevates at the end, and his features transform from sadness to rage.

I don't know how I get these words out, but I somehow do. "We had fun, Vander, and I do care about you, but it was never going to work. It was always going to be temporary." I shrug, like my heart isn't splintering into millions of jagged pieces inside my chest. Like it doesn't feel as if my soul is dying.

"Get out." He seethes, piercing me with dark, angry eyes. "Get out and never come back."

I scramble awkwardly to my feet, struggling to breathe over the agonizing pain ripping me apart on the inside. "I'm so sorry, Vander."

"I said get out!" he roars, and I jump at the hostility in his tone. "Get the fuck out, Kendall! I never want to see your face again."

I stumble from his apartment on shaky limbs, slamming against the wall as I tumble down the stairs with tears streaming down my face. Pushing out through the door, I stagger along the sidewalk like a drunk person, clutching my arms around my body as if that will hold me together. My feet slip over the gravel as I make my way to the parking lot behind the boxing club, and a sob bursts from my mouth when I can no longer keep my heartbreak inside.

Crashing against the corner of the building, I fall to pieces, sliding to the ground on my butt, not even feeling the rough asphalt underneath me. I'm so cold, and I can't breathe. I double over, dry heaving as my stomach attempts to expel its contents. Nothing comes out except bile and a strangled kind of howl that sounds like an animal in pain.

Huge wracking sobs are birthed straight from my soul, and I know I need to get out of here, but I can't force my limbs to move. I gasp and cry and scream as all pent-up emotions flow through me. My surroundings disappear as I give in to the darkness emanating from deep within me while it threatens to swallow me whole.

"Kendall, sweetheart. Look at me." A cold hand touches my cheek, and I flinch.

Swiping at my blurry eyes, I focus on the figure crouched in front of me.

"You're scaring me, sweetheart," Jimmy says. "Should I get Vander?"

"No!" The word erupts from my mouth as my eyes widen in alarm. "No." I shake my head and try to compose myself.

Jimmy says nothing as he hands me a tissue and watches while I dab at my eyes and try to resemble something human. "What's going on?" he asks, extending his hand and pulling me to my feet.

Yanking my hand back, I wrap my arms around my torso as if that will ward off the chill penetrating every molecule of my body. My lower lip wobbles as I caution myself to get a grip. "I'm glad I bumped into you," I say, wincing at the hoarse sound of my voice. "I need you to do something for me."

He nods, encouraging me to go on with a concerned expression on his face. "Vander and I broke up." Tears pool in my eyes again, and I want to attach a suction to my eye ducts until all the tears are sucked dry.

"I know he wouldn't do that, and you're clearly distraught, so why did this happen, Kendall?"

"I can't tell you." My head whips around, my eyes scanning the area for evidence of any cameras or spies. I wouldn't put it past that asshole to have sicced his PI on me again.

"Are you in trouble?"

Am I? I honestly don't know. What I do know is if I tell Jimmy anything he could die. I won't take risks with his life or anyone's. "Vander can never know about this. You didn't see me here."

"Let me help. Just tell me—"

I shake my head. "I can't, but you *can* help. Vander is going to tell you what's happened, and you're going to sympathize with him and support him, but under no circumstances are you to tell him to fight for me, or come after me, or read anything more into it."

His brow puckers, and I reach out, taking a hold of his hand. "Do you believe I love Vander? Do you believe in the connection we share?"

"Without a shadow of a doubt."

"Then trust me when I say I'm doing this because I love him so much I would break his heart—and mine—if it means I get to save him."

Slowly, he nods. "Are you sure I can't help?"

I shake my head again. "I've done the best I can, but it all hinges on Vander staying away from me. I need you to promise me you'll do whatever you can to ensure that happens. Promise me, Jimmy." I tighten my grip on his hand.

"I promise, Kendall."

A layer of stress lifts from my shoulders. "Look out for him, please. Remind him who he is, and make sure he doesn't lose himself or lose focus of his goals. I don't want this to derail his future, or else, it'll all have been in vain."

"You know I will."

I press a kiss to his cheek. "You're a good man, Jimmy. Thank you for caring about him and for not asking questions I can't give you answers to."

"He won't take this well."

"I know." How I manage to smile through my tears is unfathomable. "I don't know how I can go on without him, but this is how it has to be, for now."

"Aw, sweetheart." When he pulls me into a hug, I collapse against him, dissolving into tears again as I soak his shirt. When I ease back, he hands me a fresh tissue.

I blow my nose and wipe my damp face. "Two more things. Greg knows where Diana is. You need to find a way of telling Vander so he can warn her. And there is a camera somewhere in his apartment." I hate that Greg will see the devastation he has wrought with his game playing, but that is the last time he will spy on his son. "Don't tell Vander. Just find it and destroy it."

He bobs his head. "Consider it done."

"Thanks, Jimmy." I give him a quick hug before I make my way to my SUV.

"Kendall, you mind yourself, and trust that I'll look after our boy."

"Thanks, Jimmy. That means a lot to me."

I stay parked a few blocks from my house for hours, giving in to my grief and my loss, until I'm exhausted and physically incapable of shedding any more tears. Then I call Greg and scream abuse at him down the phone.

"Are you done?" he says when I pause to draw a breath.

"Not even close," I snarl, already conjuring up ways of ending the bastard.

"This needed to happen to ensure you followed through with it."

"The hell it did! I was going there to break off our relationship. You didn't have to do that! You lied to me. You've already reneged on our deal. How the fuck can I ever trust you?"

"You can't. Just like I can't trust you. That's the only way this deal works, but I give you my word I won't do anything else. I will stick to my end of the bargain as long as you do what you said and stay away from my son."

"Your word means jack shit after what you've just done."

"You should be thanking me!" he yells. "I made that easy on you. He hates you now, and he won't come looking for you."

"Don't pretend like you were doing me any favors. You did that for you."

He chuckles, and I have an urge to slam my face repeatedly into the wheel. "I might have done that for the entertainment value, but it definitely killed two birds with one stone. Did you see his face when you told him it was true?" His vile laughter has me reconsidering my plans, and I'm close to buying a gun and putting a bullet in his skull. "You broke his little heart, and now he's drowning his sorrows in beer and weed, and I'm betting it won't take him long to sink his dick into some young pussy."

I squeeze my eyes tight as the horrid visual dances before my mind's eye. I'm guessing that was the intent.

"Curtis got a kick out of it too."

I'm sure he did, but I couldn't care less about him now.

"You're a horrible human, and one day you'll get what's coming to you. Karma is going to bite your ass big-time."

"Stop your sniveling, Kendall, and woman up. Quit getting on my case. Go home, pack your shit, and leave this fucking town. If there's one thing I agree on with my son, it's that I never want to see your face again."

Chapter Forty-Six

Vander

I spend the weekend in a dazed state of numbness, but it does nothing to diminish the anger searing through my veins like molten lava. The only time I sleep is when I pass out, stoned or drunk or a combination of the two. Every other time I close my eyes, all I see is my dad fucking Kendall, and I want to murder him in cold blood.

West kept me company the first night, and I threw a party last night that bled into Saturday morning. When Jimmy showed up at my door a few hours ago, I expected he was here to rip me a new one, but he said nothing about the state of the place or the stragglers snoring and leaking drool on the floor.

His only concern was me.

I couldn't tell him. I can't force those words from my mouth.

West wanted to know what's wrong, and for a few seconds, I was tempted to tell him, but he's hurting enough, and I won't add to his pain. I won't use him to hurt *her*—even if she deserves it. Kendall is gone from my life, taking our secret with her.

"Thanks for your help," I tell Hazel a few hours later when my place has been put right. I'm standing outside my studio, staring at the only canvas left intact, wondering why I am incapable of destroying it. It's hidden behind a layer of bubble wrap and brown paper packaging because I can't bear to look at it.

Can't get rid of it.

Can't tolerate looking at it either.

Painting Kendall that night was the culmination of my every fantasy come to life, and I know it's my best work to date. I couldn't throw it away, so now I'm putting it into storage, and maybe someday I'll be able to uncover it and remember that night, and her, without this constant stabbing pain in my heart.

"No problem, Van. Your friend said someone will be here within the hour to remove the damaged stuff."

Jimmy arranged for a buddy of his to collect the trashed furniture, and I'll be sleeping on the couch from now on. No point in buying a new mattress when I'll be leaving in five weeks, and I have already called Mom to tell her I'll be joining her next week for Easter after all. I had planned on sticking around for the holidays and spending the summer here, to maximize time with Kendall, but now I can't get out of Colorado Springs fast enough.

Hazel pins me with sad eyes and squeezes my hand. "I hope whatever is wrong gets resolved soon."

I don't think there's any cure for a decimated heart, but I appreciate the sentiment and her willingness to help. She's my buddy's girl, but we're not close, so her showing up with West today meant a lot. I nod and force a smile before West leaves to walk her to her car.

When he returns a few minutes later, I'm parked on the couch with my feet on the coffee table and a beer in my hand. West sinks onto the couch beside me, kicking off his sneakers and swinging his legs up. He raises his beer bottle to his lips, eyeing me with concern. At least my falling apart has distracted him from his own troubles. "You ready to talk about it yet?"

"Nope." I guzzle beer and stare out the window at the dark night sky.

"I know this has something to do with your dad."

"Drop it, West," I say through gritted teeth. I wish I could tell him. I want to vent to my buddy, but I can't. It's bad enough I'm letting him keep me company after what I've done and when he's in the dark. I'm a shitty friend but too selfish to force him to leave.

Strained silence bleeds into the air, and I wish I hadn't trashed my TV. Watching some mindless show or playing *Call of Duty* sounds about perfect right now.

"My parents finalized their divorce," he says after a few awkward beats. "Mom is giving him the house and moving to Oregon. She got a job with an old high-school friend of hers."

Wow. She must have been planning that all along, and she mentioned nothing to me. She really played me for a fool. Rage burns at the back of my throat, and I drain the rest of my beer. I'm tempted to throw the bottle at the wall, but we only just cleaned up the mess. I know I should say something, but I don't trust myself to speak.

"Ridge is upset. He doesn't want to leave the asshole or his friends or his Little League team, but I get the sense Dad doesn't want to be shackled with a young kid because he only asked Stella if she wanted to stay with him."

Curtis is a fucking prick, and I still hate his guts. Of course, he doesn't want Ridge. It would mess up his plans. He's enjoying the single life, and a ten-year-old would curtail his freedom and hold him back.

"Stella is conflicted," West continues, single-handedly carrying the conversation. "She doesn't want to stay with Dad, but she's not sure she wants to complete her senior year in a new school."

"Stella will go with your mom," I say, not looking at him. "She won't want to be separated from Ridge either."

Air huffs from his mouth. "I think you're right."

"What about you?" I turn to face him. "What are your plans? You won't be leaving for Oklahoma until the end of June." The football team starts training early before classes commence.

"I'll go with Mom after graduation, to help her get settled, but I'm coming back then. I want to spend as much time with Hazel before I have to leave for college." Hazel is a year below us, and I wonder if their relationship will survive the separation. "There's no fucking way I'm staying with Dad and his slut though." He scrubs a hand over his prickly jawline. "I was going to ask if I could crash here, but you're leaving straight after graduation now, so that's out of the question."

"I'm sure Jimmy would let you stay here for a few weeks. I'll ask him."

"That would be cool. Thanks, man."

I nod. It's the least I can do for him after how I've been sneaking around with his mom behind his back for months.

Pain lances across my chest as Kendall's image resurrects in my mind, and I'm striding across the room to the refrigerator before I've even processed the motion. I return with two more beers, handing one to my buddy even though he hasn't finished his first beer yet. I pop the lid and glug a healthy mouthful. West eyes me with concern. "I know you don't want to talk about it, but what about last night?" His brows kick up. "Do you want—"

"Nope." I shake my head as acid churns in my gut. I do not want to think about *that*.

My fists pound into the bag, and sweat drips down my brow, as I go at it full throttle the next evening at the gym downstairs. Tomorrow is our last day of school before the holidays, and I'm looking forward to getting out of here. Mom and Dana are in Canada for Easter, staying with friends of Dana's. After what Jimmy told me yesterday, I'm glad they left Europe. I don't know how my father discovered where she was staying, but I'm not too concerned. Mom phoned this morning, confirming Dad signed the divorce papers, and I eased a sigh of relief until I heard he insisted the restraining orders were quashed and she dropped the civil suit as part of the deal. Mom assures me it's only because of the damage it will do to his reputation. He has agreed to give her back her inheritance plus an extra million if she lets it go. He has also promised to stay away from me and not interfere with my plans to attend Yale Art.

He'd better hope he stays the hell away from me because I will fucking kill him if he ever darkens my door again. I've been tempted to confront him. To unleash all this rage on his body, but he'd only like that. I refuse to give him the satisfaction of knowing he's achieved what he set out to do—he has stolen the only woman who matters and broken me in the process.

Mission accomplished, Dad. You sick predatory fuck.

I slam my fists into the bag, imagining it's Dad's face. I can't bring myself to imagine it's Kendall even though I'm furious and disappointed in her.

The front doors crash open, banging against the wall, and in an angry voice, someone shouts, "Where is he?"

Grabbing the bag, I steady it as I rip off my gloves and walk toward my buddy. "What's wrong?"

West storms across the room, like a deadly tornado hellbent on mass destruction, and rams his fist into my face. I stagger back, caught off guard by the punch and the look of rage on his face. There can be only one reason for that look, so I don't retreat when he swings at me again. "You fucking bastard! How could you?! She's my *mom*, you sick fuck."

I stand rooted to the spot as he throws several more punches at my face and upper body. Out of the corner of my eye, I see Crusher, Boner, and Jimmy approaching, but I shake my head, cautioning them to hold back.

I don't retaliate. I let West vent his anger on my face and my body. He isn't a trained fighter like me, and though his punches lack strength, they still hurt.

"Let's go to my place and talk about this," I say when he's stopped using me for target practice.

He stands before me, panting and red in the face, his fists clenching and unclenching. "I'm not going anywhere with you, you stupid prick. We'll do this here." He shoves my shoulders. "This is why you've been on a rampage these past few days? Because you're moping over my *mother?*" He grabs fistfuls of his hair and lets out a strangled roar. "How could you let me console you? How could you *fuck* my mother?" He lands a sturdy punch to my solar plexus, but I don't make a sound, almost welcoming the pain, because it was shitty of me. "You fucked my mother. Jesus, do you even realize how fucking wrong that is? She's old enough to be *your* mother!" He punches me in the nose, and blood spurts from my nostrils.

Jimmy inches in between us. "I think that's enough. Take this to my office."

"Screw you, Jimmy." West's nostrils flare, and he looks close to lashing out at Jimmy too.

"Leave us. This is between me and him."

Jimmy eyeballs me. "You don't have to take this."

"I know." We silently communicate and he nods, grabbing

Crusher and Boner and stepping out of the main room, leaving West and me alone.

"How did you find out?" I ask.

One side of his mouth curls into a snarl. "I got into an argument with my dad. I hit him." His dry chuckle sounds louder in the empty room. "His way of hitting me back was to inform me you were having an affair with my mom." His Adam's apple jumps in his throat, and the anger retreats for a second, replaced with deep-seated hurt.

"I'm not going to apologize for being with her, only for going behind your back. We didn't mean to hurt you. It's one of the reasons we kept it a secret. The plan was to tell you after graduation. I see now we should've come clean at the start. We were wrong to hide it."

"Ya think?" He glares at me before slumping to the ground with his back against the side of the ring. I sit beside him, biting back a wince as pain spreads across my ribs and stomach as I lower myself down. "I told you things about my parents' marriage in confidence, and you used that to take advantage of my mother when she was vulnerable." He rubs at his temples. "I knew you two were close, and it struck me as odd at times, but I figured she was the mother you never had." Disgust washes over his face. "But that wasn't it at all. You were preying on her, waiting to swoop in at the first opportunity and indulge whatever twisted mommy fantasies you harbor in that sick head of yours."

"That's not how it happened," I coolly reply. "Or how I see her. I love her, West. She's it for me." It hurts to admit, but it's still true.

He barks out another laugh. "Sure, you do. That's why you had Gayle's lips wrapped around your dick as soon as my mom came to her senses and dropped your manipulative ass."

"That isn't my finest moment. I was trashed and I regretted

it instantly." I feel sick thinking about it, but I was blinded by rage, and my senses were impaired. At the time, it felt like I was getting revenge on Kendall because I remember how jealous she was of Gayle at West's party. But it was dumb, and all it did was make me feel worse. *How ridiculous is it that I feel like I've betrayed Kendall when she was the one who cheated on me?* We're broken up now, and I'm free to fuck around with whomever I want. *I have no reason to feel guilty, so why the fuck do I?*

Because I can't forget the connection we share even if she has.

"Whatever." He climbs to his feet, and I stand. "I can't believe you did this. I can't believe I trusted you and you betrayed me like this. At a time when you know I've been struggling." He shakes his head, and hurt mixes with fury on his face. "My parents might've saved their marriage if you hadn't interfered. Did you ever think about that?"

I know I'm not the reason Kendall's marriage ended in divorce. West knows that too. He knows exactly why they split up, but I guess it's easier to paint me as the villain now. I say nothing, because I'm not going to argue with him. The truth is I *have* wronged him. If the tables were turned, and he was with my mom and they'd been lying to me for months, I'd be standing in his shoes, throwing punches, and lashing out with my words.

"You make me sick." He glares at me. "Stay the hell away from my mom, and stay away from me." He prods his finger in my chest. "You're dead to me now, and I want nothing more to do with you."

Chapter Forty-Seven

Vander

I spent another restless night, tossing and turning on the couch, wondering how one part of my life has gone the way I wanted but the other has crumpled to shit. I suppose I should be grateful Dad is out of our lives, Mom is on the mend, and I'm getting to pursue a career in art. But it all feels so hollow because I have lost my best friend and the woman I love in the worst possible way.

I will never get over Kendall's betrayal. Just like I know I'll never be able to evict her from my heart. I'm destined to dwell in this dark, depressing space for the rest of my life, and it's hard to feel excited for anything.

I can't stay here now. There is nothing left for me in Colorado. I want away from this toxic environment, and it can't wait until next month. I have enough credits to graduate early, so today will be my last day of high school. Then I'm heading home, packing my shit, and moving to be with Mom until it's time to leave for Yale.

I'm a little late as I enter the school building, startled to find the hallway still so busy. Usually, at least some students would have started heading toward their classes by now. The raucous laughter dies down as I walk toward my locker, conscious of the hushed whispers and finger-pointing going on behind my back.

"Motherfucker," some dickhead shouts at me as I pass by, and a chorus of laughter rings out.

All the blood drains from my face. *What the actual fuck? Has West told people about us?* I get him wanting to hurt me, but how could he do this to Kendall knowing it will damage her reputation and make her the subject of salacious gossip?

A muscle ticks in my jaw as people hurl taunts and accusations at me as I stalk toward my locker.

"Hey, Van. My mom just got divorced, and she's looking for a good time. Shall I pass on your number?"

"Fuck me, Mommy. Oh, yeah, just like that!"

"At least now we know why none of the girls at school were ever good enough. He prefers saggy tits, spare tires, and stretch marks."

"Kendall's a MILF. Now she's done with you, I'll give her my nine inches and really show her a good time."

I stop at that last one, slamming the meathead jock up against his locker and wrapping my hand around his throat. "Does West know you're spouting that shit about his mother?"

The asshole smirks. "He's too busy ripping all the nude photos off your locker to care."

Fuck. Dropping the jerk, I sprint toward my locker, and the crowd parts. I curse under my breath as I spot the mess awaiting me. Row upon row of posters is plastered to the lockers and adjacent walls down this end of the hallway, and West, Hazel, Stella, Shep, Bowie, and a couple of other buddies from the football team are frantically tearing them down.

"Get lost, Vander," West hisses, whipping his head up and snapping his teeth when he spots me. "You've done enough damage."

Ignoring him, I dump my bag on the floor and rip a poster from the wall. Someone has clearly superimposed my face and Kendall's face onto a couple of porn stars' naked bodies. My stomach twists at the way the woman is posed in the picture with her legs spread open, her pussy right there for everyone to see. The man stands behind her, fondling her large tits. As if that isn't bad enough, Kendall's cell phone number is written on the bottom along with "'Call Kendall Hawthorne for a good time. Teens are my jam."

"I'm going to fucking kill whoever did this." I'm seething as I tear down more pictures, wishing I was ripping into whoever did this instead.

"Get in line, asshole," West barks. "This is all your fault."

"Get to class!" the vice principal calls out in a shrill voice. She heads this way, blowing a whistle and shooing students out of the hallway. The security guard for the school is with her as they stride toward us.

Shock splays across her face when she comes to a standstill beside us. "Do you know who did this?" she asks, her gaze bouncing between all of us.

"No," Stella says, stepping forward. "But that's our mom." She points to Kendall's face, working hard to contain her emotion. "And that's her actual cell number. She's being bombarded with texts, messages, and rude pics." Tears well in her eyes, and her words have me feeling instant sympathy for Kendall. The urge to ditch school to go comfort her is riding me hard until I remember what she did.

"We will handle this," the vice principal says. "At school and with your mother. Go to class. All of you."

As I pick my bag up and sling it over my shoulder, I spot a familiar face up ahead, peeking around the corner that leads to the girls' bathroom. A look of childish glee is stretched across her wide mouth, and I see red. Gripping West's elbow, I subtly nudge my head in Gayle's direction. His eyes narrow to pinpricks when he sees her before she jerks back, realizing she's been caught.

West nods, and in this moment, we silently agree to put aside our differences and handle this our way. We walk away in the middle of the group, ducking around the corner unseen a minute later and storming into the female bathroom. The door slams against the wall before we lock it, dumping our bags on the ground. The bathroom is empty, but I know she's in here. She couldn't have escaped without us noticing.

"Get the fuck out here now, Gayle," West roars, shoving open stall doors in a rage.

"We know you did this," I add, working hard to keep my tone calm when I want to rip her to shreds.

"You have no proof," she says, emerging from the last stall with her arms folded across her chest and her chin pulled up.

"You're a spiteful little bitch." West stalks toward her. I don't know what expression she sees on his face, but it's enough for her to lose her bravado and back up into the wall.

"I have no beef with you, West," she blurts, pointing over his shoulder at me. "This is all Van's fault. I just wanted to even the score. This doesn't involve you."

She's insane. "You plastered fake pictures of his mother with her phone number over half the fucking hallway," I shout, losing the tenuous hold on my emotions. "Of course, it involves him!"

West is standing in front of her, visibly shaking and seething but not touching her. I have no such qualms. I'm out of here after today, and I've got zero fucks to give anymore.

"She deserves to suffer too! She stole you from me. She made me look like a fool!"

Grabbing her by the throat, I lift her off her feet and shove her aggressively into the wall. "Kendall had nothing to do with

Always Meant to Be

my lack of interest in you. I cannot stand you, Gayle. You're vacuous, irritating, and so damn ugly on the inside. My biggest regret is letting you anywhere near my dick because you're the last woman I would ever be attracted to. It only happened because I was trashed and vulnerable when you pounced." I have little recollection of it, thank fuck, except it was over fast. "You *are* a fool because I'm going to see you get expelled for this."

Her eyes pop wide, and her face turns blue as she struggles to get free of my hold. Her hand is gripping my arm, tugging on it while her legs wriggle in a fruitless attempt to escape.

"Van." West's warning goes over my head.

I squeeze her throat tighter. "Maybe I'll just strangle the bitch and do the world a favor."

Panic flares in her eyes, and she opens her mouth to speak, but only garbled sounds come out.

West shifts on his feet. "Van." He sends me another warning look as a dripping sound claims our attention. West bursts out laughing. "Oh my God. She's pissing herself."

Tears leak out of her eyes, and I let go before I accidentally kill her. She's not worth doing time for. She slumps to the ground, crying and gasping for air, landing in a puddle of her own urine. I take out my cell and calmly take a picture. I turn to West. "Strip her. Let's make a poster of our own. See how she likes her naked image being spread all over town."

West grins and bends down as Gayle scuttles away, wailing and screeching, with snot leaking from her nose. "Stop," she croaks, her voice cracked and hoarse. "I'm sorry."

"For what?" I demand, pressing record on my phone. "Confess or I'm exacting punishment my way."

She owns up to it all, explaining how she came by my place last night to ask me to go to prom with her. She happened to see West storming into the gym and followed him. She heard everything that went down. Enraged, she spent the night concocting a plan to get back at me and Kendall for making her look foolish.

As if either of us owed her anything.

As if what happened between us was any of her business.

She didn't stop to consider how damaging her actions would be. It wasn't even about getting revenge on me. Which it should have been. I didn't treat her right, and I wouldn't have blamed her if she took it out on me. But she didn't. This was done to humiliate Kendall because Gayle can't stand the thought I wanted her instead. She's a hot mess by the time she's finished, sniveling and whining, but I don't care. We have the proof we need. "You're pathetic." I pocket my cell. "You just couldn't let it go, and now you'll pay the price."

"I'll tell my daddy. He won't let you do this to me."

I chuckle as I retrieve my bag. "*You* did this to you. Not me. I just gave you a little incentive to come clean."

"You almost choked me." She starts crying. Normally, I'm moved by a woman's tears, but her tears have no impact on me. Irrespective of how I feel about Kendall now, I never wanted the news about us to come out or for the truth of our relationship to hurt her in any way. Curtis and Gayle have ruined that, but I'm going to get him back too. I know where he parks his Mercedes at night, and I plan to pay him a visit before I skip town. He helped set the match that has burned my world down, so it's only fair I repay the favor.

"You won't tell anyone because I'll instruct my father to sue you for slander if you do," I lie. "If your father attempts to come at me, please remind him who my father is. I'm pretty sure Miles knows my dad has criminal affiliations and what that would mean for anyone who crosses him or his family." No one outside my small inner circle knows about my fucked-up relationship with my father, so she'll buy this. I unlock the door as

West grabs his bag. "Prove you're not as foolish as we think," I say, opening the door. "Shut your mouth, accept responsibility, and walk away."

West drills her with a look. "This ends now."

Slowly, she nods, and we step out of the bathroom.

"This changes nothing," West says as we walk toward the vice principal's office to hand her the video.

"I know." I drag a hand through my hair. "I'm leaving tomorrow. You'll never have to see me again."

His face betrays no hint of shock or relief or any other emotion. He nods his head tersely. "Good."

As I walk out of the school gates for the last time an hour later, I can't wait to put hundreds of miles between me and Colorado.

Chapter Forty-Eight

Vander – 8 years later

I stand in front of the painting with my hands shoved into the pockets of my pants, staring at the woman who has held a recurring role in my dreams since the time I first met her when I was fifteen.

"She's beautiful," Mara says, materializing beside me.

"She is."

Out of the corner of my eye, I see her tilt her head and look at me with sad brown eyes. "She's the reason you don't date. Why you aren't interested in me."

Jesus, not this again. Turning to face her, I nod. "It's always been her. No other woman has ever interested me. Kendall is the reason I'm here."

She tucks strands of her jet-black hair behind her ear. "As in Portland or were you speaking metaphorically?"

"The answer is yes to both." It wasn't until my senior year I learned Kendall had visited Yale on the down low and organized for me to receive full financial support. That was the year I sold my first big NFT and I contacted the financial aid officer to stop my funding as I no longer needed it. Now, my digital art business is my main source of income, and I have opened galleries in three different locations purely for the joy of showcasing my paintings in my own space and granting opportunities to new artists to present their work. I have ambitious plans for expanding into other states, and I'm busy building a team around me who can help to deliver that goal.

Mom left me a sizable inheritance when she passed from lung cancer two years ago. One month ago, on the day my father was sentenced to life in prison, I sold my latest NFT for ten million dollars. I'm extremely fortunate I don't have to worry about money anymore. I have more than enough to last several lifetimes.

"We're not open yet." Mara calls out as footsteps resonate behind us. "The exhibition starts at eight. You can come back then."

"I was hoping to have a word with the artist in private," someone with a familiar voice says, and I whirl around, coming face to face with West for the first time in eight long years.

"That's out of the question." Mara's prickly voice confirms she's ready to go into full-on military mode.

"It's okay," I tell my assistant. "I know him."

West's gaze lands over my head as he walks toward me. He comes to a stop alongside me, staring at the painting of Kendall and me set in ancient times.

"That'll be all, Mara."

She purses her lips, and a scowl mars her forehead. Mara is very organized, and she has helped me to open three galleries in the space of three years, so she is very good at her job. But her personality leaves a lot to be desired at times. She doesn't like to be cut out of things, and she doesn't like to be told no. I have never given her any indication I am interested in her, yet she pursued me to the point I had to tell her to stop or I'd fire her. Tonight is the first time in six months she has broached the subject. I really hope I don't have to terminate her employment, but I will if she gets in the way of my plans.

Her heels clack on the tile floor as she walks away.

"You fucking her?" West coolly asks while his eyes remain glued to the painting.

"No. I have never touched her. She's my employee and nothing more."

His eyes drill into mine as we stare at one another. He looks the same yet changed. It's not just that his dirty-blond hair is a little darker than I remember it or he's a bit leaner than he was back in the day. It's the world-weary look in his eyes and the weight pressing down on his shoulders that make him seem older than his twenty-six years.

"Is my mom your muse?" he asks, breaking eye contact and returning his attention to the painting.

"Yes. She always has been."

"Even now?" He arches a brow. "After all this time? After everything that happened?"

I have a sense Mara is eavesdropping, and I really don't want to discuss this out in the open. I jerk my head toward the stairs off to the side. "We can talk in my office. It's more private there."

West follows me up the stairs to the large open-plan second floor that houses my office and my studio. Until I lay down permanent roots here, this is my only studio. I close the door behind him and flick the light on.

"It's good," he says as I walk toward the small seating area which separates my office from the painting side of the space.

I glance over my shoulder at him as I bend down to retrieve a couple of beers from the small drinks refrigerator I keep fully stocked.

"The painting," he clarifies, accepting the beer I offer him.

We sit down on the couch. "You've done well, Vander. You're living your dream."

I'm only living half my dream, and half a dream means nothing without the woman who inspired it—who helped to make it happen—by my side. "I'm sorry about your football career. I thought about reaching out to you at that time." West was in a bad car accident during his junior year in college. There was talk of him going into the draft early, but the injuries he sustained in the wreck ruined any NFL career and shattered his dream. He's a sports agent now, or so I read online.

"Why didn't you?" He raises the bottle to his lips.

"I didn't think you'd want to hear from me. You made your feelings crystal clear before I left."

"I was angry and hurt. First Dad, then Mom and you." He loosens his tie and pops the top button of his shirt. "I felt betrayed. Broken. Lost." He shrugs, picking at the label on the bottle. "I did for a long time."

"I'm sorry to hear that. I know what it's like to feel those things."

He drums his fingers on his knee, while piercing me with an earnest look. "She didn't cheat on you, Vander."

"I know."

His brows climb to his hairline. "If you know, why haven't you done anything about it?"

"I'm doing something now." I'm not getting into anything with him until I've shared everything with Kendall.

He blinks repeatedly while drilling me with a look. "Are you saying you're in Portland for Mom?"

I nod. "Not a day has gone by where I haven't missed her. Where I haven't woken up thinking of her. My soul aches for her, West. I know it's been eight years, but I couldn't come for her until that bastard was behind bars."

He nods while sipping his beer. "She's coming tonight."

My eyes widen. "She knows about my showing?"

"You weren't the only one keeping tabs or the only one pining. She has never forgotten you either, Van."

My heart soars at that revelation. I was planning on visiting her tomorrow, but I should've known fate would play a part. "Why are you here?"

Setting his half-empty beer bottle down, he leans forward, propping his elbows on his knees. "I don't want to see her hurt, any more than she has been. I wanted to let you know she was coming so you'd agree to speak with her. I thought I'd have to persuade you, but I clearly got some things wrong."

"You thought I hated her and her devotion was one-sided."

"Can you blame me?"

I shake my head before tipping it back and swallowing more beer. "Why is she coming to see me?"

He drains the rest of his beer and stands. "That's for Mom to tell you."

I rise to my feet. "It was good to see you, West, and you don't need to worry. I want to see Kendall. I need to talk to her too. I'm not here to hurt her. It's the opposite."

Air expels from his mouth and the tension on his face eases a little. "Good. Just keep an open mind, and let her explain everything, yeah?"

His cryptic comment has me intrigued, and now I can't wait for Kendall to show up.

"Van." West turns around when he reaches my door. "Not that you need it, but you have my permission. I won't stand in your way if Mom is who you want. I never would have. My main frustration back then was how you both kept it a secret. That hurt so damn much."

"You should know she hated that. She agonized over it and carried so much guilt. I did too."

He bobs his head. "I know. We talked about it a few years later when I finally took my head out from my ass."

"You were my best friend, and I hated sneaking around behind your back, but she is the love of my life. Her needs came first. Before mine. Before yours. I won't apologize for prioritizing her."

"I wouldn't have it any other way. I just want her to be happy. I want her to be treated right. I know we don't know each other anymore, but I know you're a good man."

"I'd like to rectify that." I walk toward him. "I'm planning to stick around town." It all depends on how things with Kendall go.

"I'd like that, but you need to talk to her first."

"I'd do anything for her, and I want the same things you do. I promise you I'll treat her like a queen, which is what she deserves."

"She does, and see that you do, Vander, because if you hurt her, you'll have me to answer to."

Chapter Forty-Nine

Kendall

"I think I'm going to be sick." I slam to a halt at the side of the building where Vander's Blue Morpho Gallery resides. It's the official opening of his Portland gallery, and I was praying the court case against Gregory Henley would have concluded before this night because I really wanted to attend.

It's been eight long years, and I've been on a countdown to this night from the moment I fled Colorado for Oregon.

Thankfully, things went my way, and the bastard is now rotting behind bars. He took a few gangsters down with him, so I don't think there is anyone left on the outside to do his bidding for him anymore. For the first time in years, I am safe and free to see Vander.

"It's okay, chica," June says, propping me up. "You can do this. You've been waiting so long to make things right." She turns to me with tears in her eyes. "Tonight is the night you reclaim your life. It's time."

I pull her into a hug. "Thank you for doing this with me." She holds me tight, rubbing her hand up and down my back to soothe the tremors wracking my body. I ease back, taking my friend's hands in mine. "I don't just mean offering me support tonight. I mean everything you have done. You are a true friend. Carly too."

I took June into my confidence before I left Colorado Springs because I was worried about her working in the same building as that snake. She quit on the spot, and four months after I moved to Portland with Ridge and Stella, newlyweds June and Carly took the plunge and joined us.

"I love you, Ken." She squeezes my hands. "But no more deflecting. It's time to get your man."

I'm sure the pretty young woman at the door can tell I'm terrified because I can't stop shaking and my palms are sweaty as I take the booklet from her. That's the only way I can explain the strange look she's giving me. "Today's showing is an exclusive first look at Vander Henley's new Rebirth collection," she explains, as June and I trade a knowing look. "Beginning next week, the gallery will exhibit a curated selection of artwork from new and upcoming talent." Her gaze rakes up and down my body, and I'm starting to feel uncomfortable.

It can't be what I'm wearing because I went all out to look my absolute best. Stella did my makeup, and I had my hair blow-dried and styled into soft waves at the salon on my way home from work. I'm wearing my soft, gray three-quarter-length wool coat over a blush-pink dress with tiny crisscrossing spaghetti straps, a fitted bodice, and a skater-style skirt. It hangs just below my knees. Silver and black stilettos and a black-pink-and-gray-striped purse complete the outfit. I know I look good, so her haughty expression must be for some other reason.

Perhaps I don't look wealthy enough to afford one of Vander's paintings, which is probably true at the minute. Our bakery business is thriving, and we make a comfortable living, but it doesn't extend to buying expensive artwork to hang on the walls of my new five-bedroom home. I used up most all of my savings to move us to Southwest Hills, and the rest will be needed to pay for Ridge's college education now that my ex-husband is broke and not in a position to cover it. I could sue, because it was a condition of our divorce, but I won't bother. As long as I can afford to send our youngest to college, it doesn't really matter who pays. I put Curtis Hawthorne behind me a long time ago, and I want him to remain permanently in the past.

June urges me to remove my coat, and I'm in a bit of a daze as I take it off. The woman gasps, her gaze locked on to my wrist. She says something to me, but I've already tuned her out. My skin is tingling, and my heart is going haywire inside my chest. My fingers twitch, and my limbs burn, urging me to move.

June thrusts our coats at the woman before grabbing my elbow and pulling me into the room. My bestie leads me over to a waiter walking around the room carrying a tray with flutes of champagne. She snatches two, handing one to me. "Do you see him yet?" she whispers in my ear while my gaze darts around the space.

"No, but I feel him." Most other people would probably have me institutionalized for the weird shit that regularly pops out of my mouth, but June knows everything. She knows all the dreams and visions I've had these past few years, and I tell her everything my psychic relays. Leaving Dee behind was hard because I'd grown attached to her, but she recommended a colleague in Portland, and I've been attending an annual reading with Tessa since we moved here.

The room is large; much larger than it looks from the outside, and it's divided into sections, separated by handcrafted partition walls with laser-cut panels depicting the same butterfly design on Vander's logo—the one that matches the ink on my wrist. The place is packed, and I'm torn between scanning the crowd looking for Vander and staring at his paintings. I take a healthy sip of the amber-colored liquid, needing it for courage, as I stare at the picture of an Ouroboros. My heart is pounding so loudly I'm sure everyone must hear it. "He is so talented."

"He is." June gulps back her champagne as we wander around the room inspecting his artwork. My heart is a swollen mess as I realize what I'm looking at. "This whole exhibit is a shrine to you," June whispers, looping her arm in mine.

"He was seeing them too," I say, stopping in front of a picture of the Taj Mahal. The couple looking into the reflecting pools, fed from the Yamuna River, in front of the building, look nothing like us, but they are us. I've seen this vision in my dreams too. "Water is one of the most traditional emblems of rebirth," I murmur as we continue walking around.

"It's all very clever. No one would guess it's so intimate. This is like a giant love letter to you." She squeezes my arm. "You were worrying for nothing. He's just been biding his time too."

"I hope you're right, but unless he's been dreaming about Iris, he's in for one hell of a shock, and that could change his feelings for me forever."

"Nonsense." She yanks me around the corner, and I notice a few people staring at me. "You two are written in the stars. It's the last hurdle to overcome, but it will be the easiest one. When you explain, he will understand you had no choice and you did the best you could."

Slowing my pace, I stop and watch the small crowd gathered at the end of the room, surrounding the tall, impressive broad-shouldered man standing in front of the largest canvas in the exhibition. I raise a trembling hand to my mouth as my entire being strains toward Vander. Even without his imposing

Always Meant to Be

presence, I would still know it's him because the pull between us is too strong to ignore. Knowing we have spent more years apart than together, it urges me forward, and I'm putting one foot in front of the other and walking toward him before I have consciously chosen to move. June keeps pace beside me as I head in his direction. Vander's shoulders tighten and his back stiffens, and I know he feels me approaching.

Nerves fire at me from all angles as I inch closer to my destiny. But at the same time, a serene sort of peace washes over me, and my anxiety fades into the background. The people surrounding Vander step aside as I approach, peering inquisitively at me. My heart is careening around my chest cavity, and blood is pumping ferociously through my veins when I stop beside Vander. Heat rolls off him in waves as we stand, side by side, staring at the magnificence of the Temple of Hephaestus. It's an almost perfect replica of the most prominent vision I see in my dreams.

In the picture, Vander is chasing me in the garden surrounding the temple. My long, wavy hair is streaming behind me as I laugh, my face radiant with happiness, while the hot sun bathes us in glorious rays of bright light. All around me, Vander has painted hundreds of blue morpho butterflies. It's the most intricate painting on display and the most colorful one too. It's also the only one where he has depicted our images as we are now.

I clear my throat and attempt to ignore the fluttering in my belly. "The temple dedicated to Hephaestus, the ancient god of fire, and to Athena, goddess of pottery and crafts." I recite from memory because I have learned everything about ancient Athens in the time since the visions first started coming to me. "It stands on top of the Agoraios Kolonos hill on the northwest side of the ancient Agora of Athens." I lean into his side, feeling a cavalcade of shivers skittering over my skin. "I do believe you missed a shrub right beside that column, painter boy." My voice trembles a little as I point at the painting, but I don't touch it. "I like the imaginative use of a butterfly clip in my hair though I don't believe I actually wore one in reality," I add in a lower tone, conscious we have some nosy bystanders.

A strangled sound escapes Vander's mouth as he slowly turns around, lowering his head and staring at me. Our gazes connect for the first time in eight years, and emotion seeps into the air. Tears glisten in my eyes as I drink him in.

He is even more gorgeous, if that's possible. Vander was an adult the last time I saw him, but he was still clinging to the vestiges of youth. Now, he is all man, and his commanding presence has magnified a hundred-fold. He's wearing sharp black dress pants and a brilliant-white clean-pressed shirt, rolled up to the elbows, demonstrating the strong arms that always made me feel safe and his exquisite ink. The top button of his shirt is undone, highlighting the new ink on his chest and around his neck. He has definitely had more work done, but my Google snooping over the years already confirmed that.

His emerald-green gaze dances over my skin as he checks me out too. His hair is shorter than he used to wear it, though still long on the top, with an artful skin fade on both sides. The eyebrow ring is still intact, but the nose ring has been replaced with a black diamond stud. His strong jawline and high cheekbones are the same, but the scruff on his face is heavier than he wore it back in high school. My eyes fixate on his mouth, and prickles of desire ghost over my skin as my body hums in a way it hasn't for a long time.

Murmurs and hushed conversation filter around us, but I tune them out, keeping my gaze secured to Vander's. "Kendall," he whispers, reaching out for my hand. "You haven't changed at all. You're still every bit as beautiful as the last time I saw you."

Our fingers thread together, and I swear I feel the fissures in my heart knit together. His touch sends warmth shooting up my arms and all over my body. "I have missed you so much, Vander." Tears spill out of my eyes and trek down my cheeks. "It has been far too long."

Without hesitation, he reels me into his arms, placing his hands on my lower back while hugging me close. His lips move in my hair, and my heart is so full it feels like it might burst right out of my chest. "I have missed you too. Every day, I've been on a countdown until we were reunited."

I'm not sure what I was expecting, but it wasn't this. I didn't dare to dream this much. He has spent years thinking I betrayed him, and though I hoped he remembered all the promises we made to one another and hadn't forgotten the powerful connection we shared, I'd been afraid to hope too much. Even with Tessa's predictions and assurances. So much is resting on this. I'm not out of the woods yet, but as I look up at his smiling face and the love pouring from his eyes like liquid sunshine, I allow myself to let go of my fear and permit myself to fully hope.

To believe and trust in destiny.

To accept that this is our time.

Chapter Fifty

Kendall

"I can't believe you're sitting across from me, and I'm finally looking at your beautiful face again. It feels like we've been apart forever, yet it also seems like barely any time has passed," Vander says after the waiter has taken our order and left. We are tucked into a corner table of one of Portland's most expensive restaurants, and it's very romantic. This place is renowned for its succulent food, delicious cocktails, and anonymity, and this is my first time here.

"I know what you mean. It seems that way to me too." I agree as he slides his hand across the table and links our fingers. Warmth seeps into my skin from his touch, and a bone-deep contentment settles over me. This is everything I've been craving for years. Vander hasn't missed an opportunity to touch me from the instant we reconnected at the gallery, and I get an inordinate thrill at how natural it feels to be together again. I thought it would be awkward, considering how we parted, but it's been the complete opposite, and I find myself regularly pinching myself. "I still can't believe you ditched your own exhibition."

He shrugs, flashing me a boyish grin that takes me back in time. "What good is being my own boss if I can't do what I want?" He tilts his head and smiles. "You're more important." He squeezes my hand. "I've been waiting a long time to see you again."

"You knew I was coming," I surmise, raising my wineglass to my lips. *How else did he know to make this reservation in advance?*

He nods. "West came to see me. He wanted to ensure I didn't do anything to upset you."

An automatic smile graces my lips hearing about my son's thoughtful gesture. "He's been very protective of me lately. It took him time to get over our betrayal. He didn't speak to me that entire first year, and it took another couple more to get us back on track. He stopped speaking to Curtis completely after what he did." Pain tightens my chest as I think back to those difficult first few years after I left Colorado. "His only contact was with Stella and Ridge."

"That must've hurt you deeply."

"It did, but that was the risk I took when I agreed to sneak around with you behind his back."

"Neither of us could've predicted how it would turn out or that there were other forces working behind the scenes to destroy us."

His words hint at things we haven't discussed yet. I know we need to talk about the heavy stuff, but I want to enjoy being here with him before it all implodes. "I hope you get the chance to patch things up with West. He could use a good friend."

"I was sorry to hear about the accident and how it derailed his plans." Vander leans across the table. "I want to reconnect with him, but I don't know if it'll ever be the same."

A veil of sadness shrouds me, and I hate it might be true. I have regrets in life, and one of them is ruining the friendship between my son and his best friend. "You won't know unless you try. Things have been hard for him. He moved here after the wreck. He was so broken, physically and mentally. Seeing his dreams die overnight sucked the joy from his life. Hazel ditched him when he was at his lowest point, and I'll never forgive her for that." I gulp back a mouthful of my wine, and it feels bitter sliding down my throat. "At least it opened the door for us to fully reunite, and we gradually repaired our relationship that year."

"I read an article about him six months ago, and it sounds like he's made a good career for himself as a sports agent," Vander says, unlinking our fingers when the waiter arrives with our appetizers. He sets plates down in front of us and leaves.

"He has, and he likes it, but I know he still struggles to accept the path his life has taken." I cut a piece of scallop. "I'm very proud of him though. He fought hard to recover after the accident and to rebuild his life." I pop the scallop in my mouth, blushing when I realize Vander is not eating and just staring at me.

"I'm still partial to that color on your cheeks," he says, maintaining eye contact as he picks up his knife and fork. "I can't stop looking at you. This feels surreal."

"I know," I say when I have finished chewing. "You look amazing, Vander, and I'm proud of you too. Look at everything you have achieved."

We chat while we eat, keeping it casual. He tells me about college, his digital art, and his ambitious plans to expand his galleries so he can offer more aspiring and new artists a platform. I explain how June and I set up our JuKe Bakery business, expanding to five stores in Oregon, and now that Carly has come on board to help us set up a franchise business, we plan to open bakeries all over the US.

"I'm not surprised you ended up doing something like that.

You were always far too good in the kitchen to waste those talents and smart too. I read about your success over the years, and it made me proud."

"You were keeping tabs on me?"

He nods, reaching over the table to take my hand again. "I wanted to ensure you were doing okay."

Tears prick my eyes. All these years, I worried he'd forgotten me. Terrified he couldn't get over my supposed betrayal, I feared he might hate me. I had no idea he was checking up on me like I was checking up on him. "I did the same," I softly admit. "I'm so sorry about your mom. I wanted to go to the funeral. I wanted to be there for you so badly."

"But you couldn't. Because of my dad."

My brows climb to my hairline. "You know?"

Lifting my hand, he raises it to his lips, brushing his mouth against my skin, sending fiery tremors skating across my knuckles and up my arm. His touch still does enchanting things to me. "I don't know the details. I'm hoping you'll finally tell me." He sets our conjoined hands back down on the table. "I was so angry at first, and I couldn't understand it. I knew the kind of person you were, and I struggled to accept you'd been playing me all along. I couldn't believe everything we'd shared, the connection we both believed in, was a lie. I spent the time before Yale in Canada with Mom. It gave me the headspace I needed, and I realized it couldn't be true." He squeezes my hand, and his chest inflates as his face floods with emotion. "I woke one morning, and I just knew he'd blackmailed you in some way. That it wasn't the way it looked." His face floods with sincerity. "I'm sorry, Kendall. I'm sorry for believing the lie so easily. For not trusting in you. For not going with my gut when it was whispering it wasn't true and that Dad was somehow involved. I let my hurt overrule common sense. If I had reacted differently, everything could have been different."

"It's not your fault. It's not mine either. If it makes you feel better, I wouldn't have let you come after me. I wasn't going to let you throw your dream away. I didn't want that for you."

"I was supposed to protect you. It was never meant to be the other way around."

"We have both done things to protect the other, and that's the way it should be." I don't want him feeling guilty for anything that happened.

"After I had my 'come to Jesus' moment, I phoned Jimmy. I had no one else to talk to who knew us. I told him I was going to book a flight to Oregon and go see you. I intended to demand the truth."

"He talked you out of doing it." It's what I asked him to do, and I know Jimmy is a man of his word.

"He did."

"How is Jimmy? I have missed him."

"He's getting old. Boner finally convinced him to retire and sell him the boxing club."

"Viola told me."

"I can't believe they got married, but Jimmy says they're very happy."

"They are. I hated missing their wedding, but I couldn't risk attending." It was clear Greg had eyes and ears on us over the years, and I didn't know what he might do if I stepped foot in Colorado Springs. I came clean to Viola before I left town, so she understands why I haven't returned and why I had to bail on her wedding.

"You have sacrificed so much for me, Kendall. I won't ever forget it." Vander's piercing green eyes lock on mine, and I can barely breathe. The intensity of the way he's looking at me knocks all the air from my lungs, and I'm back in the past, reliving every intimate moment we've ever shared. His lips kick up, and the biggest smile crests over his mouth as he points between us. "This is ultimately what kept me going. I knew we had the kind of love that would never die. I chose to trust in it and what we'd learned together about our past and what we suspected and hoped for our future."

I sniffle and swipe at the tears pooling in my eyes. "That is the only way I survived our separation, Vander. Knowing we were always meant to be, but I honestly didn't know if you'd given up on that. On us. I wouldn't have blamed you if you did."

"Never, Kendall." He stretches across the table and sweeps his lips against mine. "I would never give up on you or on us." He settles back in his seat. "Tell me what really happened. I want to know."

So, I do.

Chapter Fifty-One

Kendall

The waiter brings our main courses to the table while I am filling Vander in on everything that went down back then.

"Jesus, Kendall." He sets his silverware down and takes my hand again. Pain is etched upon his face. "I can't believe you went through all of that alone. I'm so upset he did that to you, and I'm ashamed of how I reacted. I should've known. I should have trusted you more."

"Don't do that. You have apologized, and I don't want you to blame yourself. You were eighteen, and while you were always more mature than your peers, our relationship was your first, and it was intense. I mostly forgot that because being with you was so natural, but it was a lot to take in. You were on the cusp of fulfilling your dreams. You were trying to protect your mom and me, and that man had put you through hell your entire life. You thought I'd cheated on you with him. You can't help how you felt or how you reacted. It killed me letting you believe that, but I knew if I told you the truth you'd either kill him or agree to whatever demands he made to protect me from prosecution."

"I would have," he says, pushing his dinner aside the same time I do.

"I didn't want you to throw everything away. I didn't want you to lose the future you had worked so hard for."

"A future I had thanks to you." His eyes shine with love, and my heart melts. "You sacrificed your happiness so I could pursue my dream. I know you secured me the financial aid. I can never repay you for all the ways you have supported me and supported my dreams. Though I look forward to trying."

There is no hesitation in his tone or his expression, and I want that for us so badly. I just hope he feels the same when he knows everything. "That's what you do for the person you love more than life itself. I loved you enough to walk away, but it wasn't easy, Vander. It destroyed me. None of it has been easy."

"I know, baby." He rubs his thumb over the back of my hand, and it's wonderfully soothing. "Jimmy eventually told me about that night. It was my junior year, just after I found out you'd spoken to Yale on my behalf. I called him up. Told him I was going to get you back. None of his usual reasoning placated me. I was determined to speak to you and clear the air, once and for all, until he told me what you said, and the gravity of the situation hit home. I knew then, conclusively, that my father was behind it. I confronted him, but he denied it. Continued to spout the lie. The only way I walked out of there without throttling him with my bare hands was the knowledge you had sacrificed our happiness and walked away from our love because you felt you'd had no choice."

"He never let me forget the deal. Every year, he sent me an image from his evidence file. It reminded me he could still get me sent down, and it drove the knife into my heart harder. He always chose a picture or a video that was one of our most precious moments. Every year, it threatened to destroy the progress I'd made, but anger and retribution are powerful motivators too, and it only made me more determined to see him brought to his knees."

"He threatened me as well," Vander says, topping off our wineglasses and emptying the bottle. The waiter approaches, and he orders another one. "I decided I'd had enough the year after I graduated. I couldn't go on any longer without you. I got on a flight to Oregon, and when I stepped outside the terminal building, I was ambushed by armed men and taken away in a van with a black bag over my head."

Shock shuttles through me, and I stare at him with my mouth hanging open. "He could have killed you!"

"Nah." He continues rubbing circles on the back of my hand as he stops to take a mouthful of his drink. "I was pretty famous for my digital art by then. I'd opened one gallery and was in the process of opening a second. He couldn't have taken me out without an investigation. If anything had happened to me, he'd be the first person they looked at. I knew he wouldn't kill me. Beat me to a bloody pulp and threaten your life if I went near you? Yeah. But he wouldn't murder me."

"He threatened you to stay away from me?"

"He said he'd kill you and your family, and he scared me enough that I never attempted to visit you again. He was playing us both off against the other. I didn't know what he was holding over you, and he never alluded to it. He made it seem like this was about me not getting what I wanted from life. His form of a twisted life lesson. He really is a sick son of a bitch."

"I have never hated anyone as much as I hate your father."

"I know the feeling though Curtis is a close second." He smirks. "I see karma kicked him in the ass."

"It did. He only defrauded his employer because Ingrid placed such demands on him. Then she divorced his ass the second he was arrested. When he got out of jail, she was already remarried, and she'd offloaded their son to Curtis's parents. He's forty-four and living back home again because he's broke, and no one will hire him. He lost everything including his other three kids."

"West, Stella, and Ridge don't speak to him?"

I shake my head and curl my fingers around his, needing to feel closer. "He basically cut them out of his life after we moved. I arranged a few visits for Ridge, and Curtis always canceled at the last minute. I blame Ingrid, but he never stood up to her. He never fought for them. West hated him for the cheating, and after he told him about my relationship with you, he broke away from him for good. Curtis said that to hurt West. Sure, he did it to hurt me too, but ultimately it hurt our children. One part of me feels sorry for my kids because it has messed with their heads. West and Ridge in particular. But another part of me is relieved he is out of their lives so he can't hurt them again."

"I'm glad my father is finally out of our lives so he can't interfere anymore." Lowering his voice, he casts a quick glance around. "After the time I tried to visit you, when he left me bloodied and bruised, I almost hired a hitman to kill him."

"Why didn't you? And by the way, I'm not shocked because I've had similar thoughts."

"I didn't go ahead with it because then I'd be no better than him. I didn't want my soul carrying a black mark, and I was wary of his criminal contacts. I also didn't want to risk getting caught and spending my life in jail. My goal was to find a way back to you, not to end up behind bars. I knew the only way to beat him was to find evidence of his crimes and get him put away for it. I was working that angle when I heard rumblings of a case being built against him." He takes my other hand in his

Always Meant to Be

and peers deep into my eyes. "You were behind that, weren't you?"

I nod. "I came to that conclusion far earlier than you. I had been working that angle from the time I left Colorado. When I first moved here, I worked with my friend Lynette at her law firm. She helped me set things up so I was pulling the strings anonymously in the background. A girl named Tania, who I used to work with at Bentley Law, held the mantle, but I did all the legwork behind the scenes. We identified more women he had harassed and assaulted in other law firms your father worked at over the years and gradually started building a case, but it was slow, painstaking work. A lot of them wouldn't talk to us; some of them couldn't because they had signed NDAs."

I pause to take a sip of water before continuing. "We had enough evidence to go after him, but then we couldn't get anyone to take on the case. Everyone we approached declined. Gregory's reputation preceded him, and most firms were too afraid to go up against him because his criminal ties were pretty widely known. That's the point where I got very depressed," I admit. "It had been six years, and I was missing you so badly. It all seemed like such an uphill battle. I began to wonder if I could ever defeat him. If I would ever get to see you again." Tears prick my eyes. "I almost gave up, and then a miracle happened."

A ginormous smile lights up his face, and I realize now it wasn't luck or coincidence. "It was you!" I clutch his hands for dear life. "You found Jenna Layton."

He bobs his head. "When I discovered there was a group working diligently and privately to take my father down, I hired a PI to find Jenna. I knew about her. She was the reason we had to move to Colorado. Greg was obsessed with her to the point he murdered her fiancé when she wouldn't agree to dump him and start an affair with him instead. Then he raped her and left her half dead. She went to the police, and he was questioned, but they couldn't prove anything because his mob friends had helped him commit the crime and dispose of the body. No one believed Jenna, or if they did, they refused to help. She disappeared overseas, assumed a new identity, and tried to move on with her life. Until I found her and begged her to help."

"Jenna was the turning point we needed," I confirm. "She had a personal story, but she also had evidence of his mob connections. We were able to link him to several murders and other perversions of justice. Things did a complete one-eighty after we joined forces. Then law firms couldn't wait to take our case. They were practically beating our door down. Everyone wanted to go after him and one of the biggest criminal organizations in the US. Everything fell into place after that."

"I'm glad he's locked up with no chance of parole. I'm only sorry it took this long."

"Don't be sad." I run my fingers back and forth across his hand. "Things happen for a reason, and maybe this needed to happen for you to achieve your dreams."

"Do you truly believe that?"

"I do. We knew we'd face roadblocks like we have in every lifetime. I put my trust in destiny. I might have lost faith a few times, but ultimately I believe we are here now because this is the way it had to be." I bite down on my lip while trying to pluck up the courage to direct this conversation where it needs to go. "I've been dreaming of you. Reliving the memories of our past in my dreams, and that gave me the strength to go on when things seemed impossible."

"Me too."

"I recognized all of your paintings, Vander. I was seeing those visions too."

"I had planned to visit you tomorrow. I was going to give you a private showing. I wanted you to see how inexplicably woven you are in my life and how you have always been with me, even when we were separated."

"Still such a poet." I reach out and touch his hair because I have been dying to all night. "And your talent is awe-inspiring, Vander. You are truly gifted." His smile matches the dreamy quality in his eyes as I skim my fingers through his hair. "I have the picture you painted of me framed and hanging in the closet at my new house." Although I'm incredibly proud of that drawing, I won't put it on full display because children should never see their mother like that. It was also one of the most intimate, erotic moments of my life, and I don't wish to share that with anyone but Vander. "And the painting you left for me at Jimmy's, the one with the lines and the hidden faces, occupies a proud space in my living room. Whenever Ridge brings dates home, he likes to brag we have a Vander Henley original on our walls."

Vander chuckles. "How is Ridge? I'm guessing he's about eighteen now?"

"He is almost eighteen and in his senior year of high school."

"And what about Stella? How's she doing?"

"Stella is a nurse, and she's been in a relationship with Amanda for the past two years."

"Okay, wow, didn't see that coming."

I shrug. "She came out as pansexual her freshman year of college. She's dated men and women over the years, but Amanda seems to be the one. They have a great relationship, and I've never seen Stella so happy. Amanda is cool. You'd like her. She's a tattooist by day, and she sings vocals for a rock band at night."

"What about Stella's daughter?" he asks, and my heart almost stops in my chest.

I was hoping we could go back to his place and talk about

this in private, but I'm not going to lie to him. I swore to myself I will never lie to Vander again. Swallowing my nerves, I lift my chin and stare him straight in the eyes. "Stella doesn't have a daughter, Vander."

His brow puckers. "But I've seen a couple of pictures of them online?"

I'm going to kill Stella. This is the very reason I put a social media ban on sharing pics of Iris.

"They look so alike. She has Stella's long dark hair and big blue eyes."

I wet my dry lips as blood rushes to my head. I don't want to have this conversation here. "Can we go somewhere more private to talk about this?"

Vander stares at me, his eyes penetrating mine in that piercing way of his, and I know he's searching for the truth. His chest heaves as he retracts his hands. He grabs his wineglass and knocks half of it back in one go, and I notice how badly his hand is shaking. When he sets it back down, he levels me with a serious look. "We're talking about this now, Kendall." His Adam's apple jumps in his throat. "Who is the little girl? If she's not Stella's daughter, whose daughter is she?"

I can tell he already knows. He has worked it out, but he needs me to confirm it. "Iris isn't Stella's daughter, Vander. She's yours. Yours and mine."

Chapter Fifty-Two

Vander

"She's mine?" I croak as all manner of thoughts and emotions ping-pong through my head.

Kendall nods with silent tears streaming down her face. "I discovered I was pregnant a few weeks after I moved to Portland. My first instinct was to tell you, but how could I?"

"This changed everything, Kendall."

"I know," she whispers.

"Do you?" I hate seeing her cry, but damn it, she should have told me. I should've been the first person she told. I know there were risks. I know my father didn't make idle threats. But we could have figured something out together. It's all such a mess. Propping my elbows on the table, I bury my head in my hands. I don't want to get mad at her, but fucking hell!

She was pregnant with my baby.

My baby that's now a little girl.

A little girl I know nothing about because she kept that knowledge from me.

My eyes sting as I lift my head and stare at her. "How could you keep this from me? It's been eight years!"

She slides her hand across the table, reaching for me, but I shake my head, and she withdraws it. "I was afraid, Vander. Afraid he'd hurt you, me, or Iris."

It's such a pretty name. What a pity I had nothing to do with naming her. "We could've worked something out," I say, snapping my gaze to the waiter and motioning him for the check. I'm about to lose it, and I won't do that in public or in front of Kendall. I know she wouldn't have kept my child from me if she'd felt there was any other way, but that doesn't make any of this right! I need time to wrap my head around this bomb she's dropped, and I don't want to lash out at Kendall and say something I'll regret until I've had time to process it. "I've lost eight years with my daughter."

I feel an instant protective urge and an insatiable need to meet her, but I need to get my shit together before I consider that.

Wow.

I'm a dad.

My mind is well and truly blown.

"Seven," Kendall softly says, yanking me out of my inner monologue. "Iris won't be eight until December. Her birthday is two weeks before Christmas."

"Something I should already know," I say through gritted teeth, handing my platinum card to the waiter without even looking at the check.

"You think I don't know that?" Pain is etched on every gorgeous curve of her face. "You think it hasn't killed me keeping her from you and you from her? That I haven't cried myself to sleep at night as each year rolled around because you were missing out on so many special moments?" She thumps her chest. "It's devastated me, Vander."

"As much as this is devastating me." I add a tip and punch in my code on the card reader, keeping my lips closed until the transaction is done and the waiter has stepped away from the table. "I need to be alone." I stand and grab my jacket off the back of my chair. "I don't want to say something that will hurt you, Kendall, because I know deep down you did what you felt was right, but I'm struggling to accept that. All I can focus on is how much I have missed. I didn't get to watch Iris grow in your stomach. I wasn't there to hold your hand when you delivered her into the world. And I haven't been around to help raise her." I choke on a sob as I pull back her chair and help her to stand. I brush the dampness from her cheeks. "That hurts so much."

"I'm sorry, Vander," she says in a defeated tone as I escort her from the restaurant.

"I know." I open the door and let her step outside first.

She turns around, facing me with tension bracketing her face. "I know you're shocked and upset, but we need to talk about this properly." She rummages in her purse, removing a business card and handing it to me. "Call me when you're ready to hear what I have to say."

Nodding, I hail a taxi and hold her hand as the car pulls up to the curb. "This wasn't how I saw tonight ending," I say, pulling her in for a brief hug.

She smells so good.

Feels so good in my arms too.

And she's pretty as a picture in her gorgeous pink dress with her hair styled in soft waves the way I have always loved it.

She hasn't aged a day. She still looks young and beautiful, and when I first saw her tonight, I couldn't wait to kiss her and hold her and tell her how much I still love her. I planned to get down on my knees and plead for forgiveness for failing her when she needed me the most. I imagined the night ending with us firmly reunited and rolling around my bed. Now everything is shot to shit, and I can't unscramble the mess in my head.

"I'd like to say me either, but I knew something you didn't."

She pins me with the saddest eyes, and I can't let her leave like this. "This doesn't change my feelings for you, but it's a lot to process, Kendall. This feels like the ultimate betrayal."

She cups my face as the taxi idles by the curb. "I understand, but you need to give me a chance to explain."

"Just give me some time." I put her in the back seat before handing a fifty to the driver and asking him to take her home.

Kendall rolls down the window and peeks out at me. "Don't take too long, Vander." Snatching my hand, she places a photo on my palm. "I have an excited little girl at home who's been waiting a long time to meet her daddy."

I park my car a few blocks from Kendall's flagship bakery the next afternoon, making the rest of the journey on foot. My head is still cluttered, and I've thought of nothing but my daughter and the circumstances of Kendall's pregnancy since she dropped the bomb last night.

I stared at the picture of Iris for hours when I was lying in bed, unable to sleep. She's beautiful, just like her mom. She has my dark hair and Kendall's blue eyes. Wearing a big smile, she looks like a happy little girl, and the fact she's well cared for comforts me. I know the kind of mom Kendall is, and I know she'll have gone overboard to compensate for my loss in our daughter's life.

Pain slices across my chest like it does every time I think of all I have missed. But it's like Jimmy said on the phone earlier. I

Always Meant to Be

can't change the past, but I can shape the present and influence the future. Instead of looking at all I have lost, I need to focus on what I stand to gain. Berating Kendall for making the decisions she has made won't give me back lost time with her or my daughter. She tried to protect me, and I've no doubt she did her best to protect our daughter. Dad's threats were not flippant. He must have known about Iris. That he went to such lengths to keep Kendall and me away from one another proves he was determined to deny me the family I have always wanted with the only woman I love. His need for power and control would never have ended if Kendall hadn't worked tirelessly to put him behind bars.

Continuing to hold on to my anger and my frustration won't achieve anything. All it does is give that psycho more power over our future, and I refuse to do that. I could spend weeks going over everything in my head, trying to make peace with it, or I could choose to forgive Kendall and to move forward with our lives.

I don't want to lose another second with my daughter. I want to get to know her and for her to have her father in her life.

I was so tempted to call West, get Kendall's address, and show up at her house because I'm dying to meet Iris. But I don't know what Kendall has told her about me, so I can't just show up on her doorstep and demand to see my daughter. We need to discuss it and work out a plan, but I'm not holding back. I want to be in her life.

In both their lives.

I moved to Portland with the intention of making Kendall my wife, and that hasn't changed. Yes, we have a lot of baggage to work through, but she is the other half of my heart and soul, and we belong together.

Iris is the icing on the cake, and instead of agonizing over lost time, I'm going to make it up to her. I'm going to ensure the rest of her life is so full of my love she doesn't remember the years she spent without me.

I've been so lost in thought I haven't even noticed the walk until I'm standing outside of JuKe Bakery, and the moment of truth has arrived. Drawing a brave breath, I push through the doors and approach the counter. The two women working there stop talking, their eyes widening as I step up to them. "I'm looking for Kendall. Is she here?"

They both nod, staring at me like I'm an apparition. My lips tip up in amusement. "Could you get her for me?"

They nod again, and the older woman nudges the younger one. "Go on. Go get Kendall." She races off while the other woman openly gawks at my ink and my piercings. "Can I get you anything while you wait?" she offers after a few beats of awkward silence.

"It's okay," Kendall says, appearing in the doorway behind her. "I've got this." She walks toward me and lifts a side panel of the counter to let me through to the back. "Hi." Her soft smile conveys relief tinged with hope. "I wasn't expecting to see you so soon, but I'm glad you're here."

"Me too." Being in her presence soothes something inside me, and I know I've made the right decision in choosing to let the past stay in the past and to focus on the future.

Chapter Fifty-Three

Vander

Kendall fixes us some coffee, and I follow her up a narrow set of stairs into a long hallway. "This is our main office space. Those are June's and Carly's offices," she says, pointing at two doors as we pass. "But neither of them is here today. Carly set up a meeting out of state with our first potential franchisee, and June went with her." She's babbling a little, and I know that's nerves.

I slide my hand into hers as we walk toward the door at the very end of the hallway. "Don't be nervous, sweetheart. I'm here because I want to sort everything out."

She squeezes my hand before letting it go to open her office door. I step inside the large, warm open-plan space, and she closes the door behind us. "Let's sit over here."

Kendall escorts me to a seated area in the corner rather than leading me to her desk or the round meeting table in the middle of the room. My eyes flit to the small desk and chair tucked against the wall.

"Iris comes here after school some days, and she does her

homework while I finish up," she explains, noticing where my eyes have wandered.

I walk up to the wall over the desk, scanning the myriad of family photos covering the space. "She's beautiful," I say, running my fingers over a gorgeous photo of Kendall with Stella and Iris. "And she looks happy."

"She is. On both counts." Kendall beams, and I slip my hand into hers again as we stand silently, side by side, while I examine every photo. "She loves drawing," Kendall supplies, pointing to the side wall where a ton of colorful pictures adorn every inch of space. "I have kept every single drawing from the time she was little. I have them at home for you. I have documented every milestone, and I have boxes upon boxes of photos. I printed them all out because I didn't want to risk losing a single photo or miss capturing a single moment."

My heart is full to bursting point as I listen to Kendall speak while I'm inspecting my daughter's artwork and drinking my coffee. It pleases me to no end that she shares my passion and my gift. "She's talented," I choke out, my voice swamped with thick emotion.

"She's an all-rounder," Kendall explains, taking a sip from her coffee. "She loves baking too, and she's an avid reader. She loves the movies and outdoors, and West and Ridge have taught her to play football. There's a big park near our new house, and we go biking and walking and hiking."

Pulling myself away from the wall, I keep a hold of her hand as we move toward the small leather couch and sit down. We are silent for a few seconds as we drink our coffee, lost in thought. "I never wanted to do this without you, Vander. You have to believe me." Tears well in her eyes as she stares at me while setting her paper cup down on the coffee table.

I drain my drink and toss the empty cup in the trashcan.

Always Meant to Be

Gripping her hand tighter, I say, "I know, Kendall. I understand, and I forgive you though there really isn't anything to forgive." I drive these words home because I know she'll carry this guilt around with her otherwise, and that is the last thing I want.

She blinks at me in shock. "You do?"

I tuck a piece of her hair behind her ear. "I don't want to play the blame game. I want to know what happened, and I want to know everything about her, but I don't want to dwell on the past because that'll only prolong our agony and delay the inevitable." I palm her cheek, and she leans into my touch. "The fact is, there were mistakes and wrongs on both sides. I didn't protect you from my father like I promised. You shouldered the entire burden, and I'm not going to be the asshole who criticizes you for that. I know you would've told me if it hadn't been dangerous to do so."

"I tried to tell you," she says, hiding nothing as she peers deep into my eyes. "I was six months pregnant and I couldn't bear it any longer. I wanted you by my side. I felt so lonely going through the pregnancy alone. Yes, I had Stella and June and Carly, but it wasn't the same as having you." She presses her palm to mine over her cheek. "I booked a flight to Connecticut. I was going to tell you. I figured we could try to work something out, and at least if Greg made a false report to the police and I was arrested, you'd be there to take care of our baby. I felt guilty knowing you'd most likely have to walk away from your dream, but I knew you'd want to know. I knew you'd rather take that chance than not know."

"What happened?" I ask because I know my father did something to stop her.

She drops her hand into her lap, and I let mine fall to my side. "I was packing my weekend bag the following morning when I received a text. It was from an unknown number, but I knew it was Greg." She worries her lower lip between her teeth and her brows scrunch up. "It was a picture of a pregnant woman lying on the ground in a pool of blood with a bullet hole in her skull." Her lower lip wobbles, and I pull her into my arms, unable to quell the urge to comfort her. "I was terrified, Vander. I threw up repeatedly, and I couldn't stop shaking and crying."

I smooth my hand up and down her back, loving the feel of her against my chest but hating the pain emanating from her every pore. Even now, after all this time, with the threat passed, I feel her distress. "I couldn't get on the plane, Vander. I couldn't take that risk." She pins troubled eyes on me. "I wanted to tell you but not at the expense of my life and our unborn child's life. I knew Greg was psychotic enough to go through with it. The fact he even sent me that picture confirmed he didn't care about his grandchild. Nothing mattered more to him than hurting you. I will never understand why he was hell-bent on hurting you or how someone can be so evil."

"No sane person can understand the mind of a psychopath. There's no way of comprehending how people can do such evil things. I lived with him a long time, and I spent most of my college years in therapy trying to figure out why he hated me so much, but we'll never have the answers because we're not evil. We're not devoid of empathy or normal human emotions. We'll never be able to relate to a monster like him."

"The only good he ever did was bring you into the world." She slides her hands up my chest and circles them around my neck. Her spicy, floral scent lingers in the air, and I tighten my arms around her and squeeze my eyes shut.

This, us, is all that matters.

Always Meant to Be

My father tried to deny me a life with Kendall and my daughter, but he hasn't succeeded.

"West tried too," she adds, brushing her lips against my cheek. "It was three years ago. He flew to New York for the opening of your gallery there. A lot like your experience, he was ambushed, kidnapped, and beaten within a block of your studio." She eases back so she's looking into my eyes. "I'd hoped he might have forgotten about me, but he hadn't. I felt so guilty for agreeing to let West try."

"I'm sorry, Kendall."

"It's not your fault. You don't ever apologize for what that man did to us."

I tip her head back. "That's not what I'm apologizing for. I'm apologizing for last night. For doubting your actions. All you've ever done is protect those you love." I hold her face in my hands. "You couldn't have done anything else. You tried, and I can't fault you for prioritizing your safety and Iris's." I press my lips to her brow. "I love you," I say against her soft skin. "I never stopped."

She eases back, tilting her chin up, fixing me with glassy eyes. "I love you too, Vander. I never stopped either. I've been waiting for you. I've been counting down the days until we could be together again. Even during my darkest days, I still believed in us."

My eyes lower to her lush mouth, and I can't wait a second longer to taste her. I kiss one corner of her mouth, silently fist pumping the air when she visibly shivers. My heart beats steadily against my rib cage as I kiss the other corner of her mouth. She whimpers, melting against me as I glide my lips against hers, just as the door to the office bursts open.

"Mommy! I got student of the week!" a girl with a cute little voice says.

A messy ball of emotion lodges in my throat as I drag my

lips and my arms away from Kendall and look over at my daughter.

Stella stands behind Iris with her mouth hanging open and her eyes out on stalks.

Iris stares at me, and I'm rooted to the spot as I look at my daughter for the first time. My heart is pounding furiously, and the vein in my neck is throbbing like crazy. Iris is even prettier in the flesh, and she exudes goodness and light and everything right in the world. Her blue eyes get bigger as she stares at me, neither of us breaking eye contact. Kendall hasn't budged beside me, waiting to see how Iris reacts before she makes a move, I expect.

"Daddy?" Iris says as a huge smile breaks out on her face. "You came home!" I barely have time to register my shock at her words before she runs at me and throws her slim arms around my neck.

My arms encircle her automatically, and I hug her close, inhaling the scent of strawberries and peaches from her hair, basking in the warmth of her little body clinging to mine. My eyes meet Kendall's over our daughter's head, and I'm not surprised to see she's crying. Very gently, I lift Iris onto my lap so I can slide one arm around her mother. Stella discreetly exits the room, closing the door. "Does it hurt?" Iris says, tugging not too gently on my eyebrow ring.

"Sweetheart, be careful," Kendall says. "It will only hurt if you pull on it."

"Oops." She giggles, and it's the best fucking sound in the world. Her small hands land on my cheeks, and she smiles. "Hi."

I can barely make my vocal cords work. My daughter is putting me to shame. "Hi, Iris." I press a kiss to her hair, and when she rests her head on my chest, I have an uncharacteristic urge to burst into tears like a teenage girl. Kendall is barely holding it together either.

"Daddy," Iris says, and I'm practically a puddle of goo on the floor at this stage.

"Yes, princess." I dust more kisses into her hair as Kendall leans her head on my shoulder, and I tighten my arm around her.

"I have an art studio in my new house, just like the one Mom says you used to have." She lifts her head, staring at me with so much trust and confidence in her eyes I am completely blown away. "Can we paint together when we go home?"

Kendall opens her mouth to say something, but I get there first. "Absolutely. As long as it's okay with Mommy."

She jumps around on my lap, turning to face her mom. "Can we, Mom? Pretty please." Her eyes dance with excitement as she claps her tiny hands together and pins pleading eyes on her mother.

"Sure."

"Yay!" Iris flings her arms around Kendall. "You're the best mommy in the whole wide world." Turning to me, she throws her arms around my neck and plants a wet kiss on my cheek. "And you're the best daddy ever. Now you're here does that mean you won't be traveling for work ever again?"

I don't know what Kendall has told her, but the fact my daughter knows things about me warms my heart. I should not have doubted Kendall would tell her who I am.

"Sweetheart." Kendall interjects before I can speak this time. "Let's not bombard Daddy with questions until after you've done your homework. Daddy and I are going for a walk, and Stella will help you."

She frowns. "My daddy's coming with us though, right, Mom?"

"Right," I say because this isn't in any way negotiable. Wild horses couldn't drag me away.

Kendall pins me with warning eyes, but I stare back at her, letting her see everything I'm feeling. Iris babbles away to me as she takes books out of her book bag while Kendall calls Stella. I can't stop staring at my bright, beautiful, confident, little girl, marveling at this perfect little creation crafted from unflinching love that has survived successive lifetimes. If there is anything I have done right in this world, it's contribute to her existence.

Ten minutes in her company and I already know she is the best thing to ever happen to me besides her mother.

"Hey, Van." Stella slinks into the room, immediately enveloping me in a hug. "It's so good to see you. We all missed you."

"His name is Vander Henley," Iris corrects, looking up from her seat at her sister.

"I know his name, silly," Stella says, tweaking her nose. "You know your daddy was West's best friend and my friend too when we lived in Colorado."

"Well, he's *my* daddy." Iris puffs out her chest, and I crouch in front of her, unable to resist hugging her again. She can be territorial all she likes, for as long as she likes, and I will never tire of it. My heart is so swollen behind my chest it feels like it might burst.

"And you're my princess." I dot kisses all over her cheeks, and she giggles. The sound is infectious, and I make a silent promise to make her giggle as often as I can.

"I love you, Daddy," she says with a big smile on her face, like it's the most natural thing in the world to say to a man who is a virtual stranger. Kids are so adaptable, and I love that she's so confident and loving and trusting. Every kid should grow up in an environment where they feel safe and comfortable expressing their feelings. Kendall has done an amazing job with her, and whatever guilt she is carrying needs to be eradicated.

"I love you too, Iris." My voice is thick with emotion. "I promise I'm going to see you all the time from now on." I sweep my fingers down her cheek.

"Silly Daddy." She tweaks my nose. "I already see you every night in my dreams."

Chapter Fifty-Four

Kendall

"You've got to give me some answers," Vander says as we walk one of the paths at Holladay Park, hand in hand. "How does she know who I am, and what did she mean about dreams?"

"I was faced with some impossible decisions," I begin explaining. "I had to make choices no parent should have to make." I scoot a little closer to him. April in Portland is still quite cold, and I'm grateful for the warmth of his hand in mine and the heat emanating from his body. "When I knew I couldn't tell you, I decided Iris was going to know who you were." I lean into his side because I crave being near him.

I was desolate last night, crying into my pillow, afraid I had ruined everything with the choices I'd been forced into making. I have always known Vander would do right by Iris. Given the childhood he had, I know he would never neglect his flesh and blood. My tears were selfish tears, and I was sobbing for a love I thought I might have lost forever.

Vander turning up today has reinforced my belief in destiny and the strength of the love between us. I wasn't lying when I said I have never stopped loving him. No one else has ever compared to Vander, and I know they never will.

"I'm listening," he says, pressing a feather-soft kiss on the tip of my nose. "Go on."

I don't blame him for being hungry for every detail. Seeing them together was probably the most emotional moment of my life, next to birthing my babies. "I chose to tell her about you, but I couldn't tell her the truth about why you weren't living with us and why she'd never met you in the flesh. I don't like lying to her, but there was no other option."

"I understand, Kendall, and you don't have to apologize. We're past that."

Vander yanks me out of the way as a man on a bicycle speeds toward us. I use the opportunity to slide my arm around his back, and he does the same. I like being all pressed up against him as we talk about our daughter. I have waited so long to tell him how amazing she is. "She's an incredible little girl, Vander. She brings such joy to my life, and besides our bond, Iris is the one who has helped me the most." My other kids and my friends have too, but every time I look at her, I see her father, and it helped to remind me of why I needed to keep fighting the good fight. That, and Iris's effortless positivity and constant joyfulness has pulled me through some of my darker days. Having children to care for stopped me from sinking into deep depression on many occasions when it felt like I couldn't keep going it alone.

I stop those thoughts before I put a dampener on what is a happy occasion. "Iris has a framed photo of you by her bed, and from the time she was little, I was pointing at it and telling her all about you. She knows you're a painter. She knows about your digital art and your galleries. I've read her articles and shown her pictures online. West and Stella have shared stories with her, and I've explained how we are in love but couldn't be together because you were busy studying and working to support us."

I glance up at him. "She readily accepted it, Vander. She has never questioned it or challenged it. She tells kids about you at school, and all her friends know the famous artist Vander Henley is her daddy. She tells me she misses you and she loves you all the time, but she never cries or whines or screams or tells me it's unfair. She has a picture of you with her at all times, and she wears the necklace you bought me for Christmas every day. She refuses to take it off even to shower."

"She's special," he says, immediately getting what I'm saying.

"Iris told me she saw you in her dreams for the first time when she was four. I'm not sure if she was seeing you longer than that, but it seemed perfectly normal to her that she was being visited by her daddy in her dreams. At first, I didn't even consider she was having visions or premonitions or whatever they are. I thought it's what she was conjuring up to cope without having you physically in her life, but she knows things, Vander. Things she shouldn't know. Like how the man who tattooed the butterfly on my wrist had gold teeth, and she says I was a scaredy-cat because I kept clinging to your arm. I almost fell off my chair the morning she told me that."

Shock is etched across his face as he pulls me over to a bench, yanking me down beside him. He bundles me in his arms, holding me close. "After that, I wondered if you were aware. If you were consciously visiting her in her sleep, but I know that's not the case now." He would've known she wasn't Stella's daughter.

"I'm astounded. If I was somehow doing it, it was completely subconscious because I haven't had dreams about her." Vander presses a lingering kiss to my brow. "Only dreams about you."

Gawd, he's as romantic as ever, and I never want to be without him again. I snuggle into his embrace and squeeze my eyes closed, committing the feel of being in his arms to my memory in case it all goes belly up and doesn't work out the way I want it to. "Baby." He brushes hair off my brow and tips my chin up. "I'm going nowhere." My eyes blink open, and I stare at him in amazement. "I can usually tell what you're thinking. You're clinging to me like a koala. Like you fear you'll never get to do it again, and I think we need to lay it all out in the open." He clasps my face in his palms. "I'd prefer to show you first."

Before I can do or say anything, his lips descend on mine, and he kisses me. The instant our mouths meet, an intrinsic change occurs deep within me, like a switch being flicked after years of being broken. My hands grab the back of his neck, and I hold on to him, angling my head and opening my lips to welcome his devilish tongue. He explores my mouth with a reverence that is both patient and urgent, casual and needy. My pulse throbs in my neck, and the parts of me that have lain dormant, waiting for my lover to return, restart with a ferocity that startles me.

Our kissing grows more frantic, hungrier, until we remember we're in a city park, and it's still bright enough to be seen. Slowly, we part as the realization dawns we can't do this here. Vander presses his brow to mine. "I love you, Kendall. I love you so damn much."

A sob builds at the base of my throat, but it's a happy one. "I love you too, Vander. You are my world. You and Iris and Ridge, Stella, and West." My kids have given me the greatest joy in my life, only rivaled by the time spent with this man holding me like I'm precious treasure.

Vander stares at me with so much love in his eyes it's impossible to deny. "I told you last night I came to Portland with a plan to permanently move here and make you my wife." My heart careens around my chest at his thrilling words. "Nothing has changed, Kendall. If anything, the timeline has just moved up. I already love Iris. It's impossible not to fall head over heels for that amazing little girl." He pecks my lips. "We made a gorgeous little human. A perfect combination of me and you, and I can't wait to get to know her completely. I don't want to waste another moment of our lives together. We have waited long enough. I want us to be a family, and I want it now."

He is saying all the right things, but I need to be sure he is fully committed. "I want that so badly, Vander, but you've just found out about Iris. Are you sure you don't need more time to think about it? Because it's okay if you do. This decision can't be rushed. It's not just us anymore. Every decision we make together from now on will impact our daughter. We can't rush into anything if you have even the slightest doubt about us. You will always be in her life, Vander. Now that she's safe from Gregory, I could never keep her from you. But we don't have to be a package deal."

"Silly Kendall." He tweaks my nose. "There is no you without her and no her without you." He slams his lips down on mine and kisses me passionately. "I'm all in, Kendall. I've been all in from the time I was fifteen. I don't need any more time. I know my mind. I know what I want, and it's you and my daughter."

Chapter Fifty-Five

Kendall

"I want you to read to me tonight," Iris says to Vander after she's dressed in her pajamas and ready for bed. She hasn't let her daddy out of her sight from the moment we returned from our walk. We drove to my house, and they painted while I made dinner. Then Vander helped me to bathe Iris while she chatted away about her siblings, her friends, her school, and her teacher. It's like she's on a mission to fill Vander in on every aspect of her life within the first twenty-four hours.

It's adorable, and my heart is full of love for my youngest daughter.

Stella arranged for Ridge to stay at her apartment to give us some privacy even though there was no need, but I appreciate their willingness to support me. Ridge and West both phoned me earlier to make sure I was okay and Vander was treating both of us right.

"Mommy." She tugs on my hand, peering up at me with her trusting face and jubilant eyes. "Can Daddy read me Iris Murdoch?"

I lean down and kiss her soft cheek. "Of course, honey. Go get it from my room."

Vander perches on the edge of her bed, stretching his legs out in front of him. "You named her after Iris Murdoch?" he surmises, taking my hand and pulling me down beside him.

"Yes." I run my fingers through the growth on his chin and cheeks, loving how velvety soft it feels against my skin.

"It's Mommy's favorite book," Iris says, skipping into the room with the dog-eared book in her hand. "You found it in a bookstore in Bridgeport the weekend you visited Yale," she adds, climbing up onto his lap like she does it all the time. Vander's arms instantly circle her small body, bundling her into the safety of his embrace. "Mom fell asleep listening to you read from it," she says matter-of-factly, as if she'd been there.

"I never told her that," I mouth at Vander as he raises a brow. Yikes. I wonder what else she's been seeing in her dreams. Whoever is feeding them to her, I hope they're keeping them G-rated.

"Night, Mommy." Iris flings herself at me, and I lift her up, hugging her tight.

"Night, my little angel."

Vander folds back the covers, and I set her down on her mattress. Iris moves to grab the photo of Vander beside her bed before collapsing in a fit of giggles. She buries her face in my neck. "I was going to kiss Daddy's picture good night, but I don't need to do that anymore. Now he's home I get to kiss him for real."

Vander's face softens as emotion swims in his eyes. "Come here, princess." He opens his arms, and our daughter crawls into his lap again. "Plant one on me." He points at his face.

Iris giggles into his neck this time. "Silly Daddy. I kiss you when I'm going to sleep *after* you read to me."

"I'm greedy." Vander nuzzles his nose in her neck, and she

shrieks. "I'm the kiss monster, and I'm going to claim all your kisses." He tickles her, and she writhes around, squealing and giggling, and I swear my heart is about to erupt from my chest. This is everything I have wanted for her her entire life. To see them bond instantly, to connect as if they have always been in each other's lives, is more than I dared to wish for.

"You're crazy, Daddy, but I love you."

"I love you too, princess. So, so much."

I leave the room watching Iris dot soft kisses all over her daddy's face, brimming with so much joy it feels like I could burst.

The kitchen is clean, and I'm sitting by the fire in the living room when Vander appears a half hour later. "She's conked out," he confirms as I pour a glass of red wine and hand it to him.

"You've exhausted her, and I let her stay up late as it was a special occasion."

"I'm already so in love with her." His face radiates happiness as he sits beside me, automatically snaking his arm around my shoulders and pulling me into his side. "It happened in the blink of an eye, just like with her mother."

I tilt my head back and ogle his mouth. Adoration glimmers in his eyes as he leans down and kisses me. It's soft and tender and imbued with potent emotion. "This is my every dream come to life," I admit.

Vander sets his wineglass down before plucking mine from my fingers and placing it on the coffee table with his. Then he lifts me onto his lap so I'm straddling him. "Mine too. I didn't dare to hope for a family, but now I have both my girls in my life I'm never letting you go." He plants tender kisses all over my face as I hug his shoulders and nestle my thighs against his growing erection. He lifts his face to mine, shielding nothing, conveying the strength of his feelings, and it's like basking in the glow of the most glorious rainbow. "We have lost so much time, and I don't want to waste another minute. We know what we want, and I say we go for it."

"So, it's not too soon to ask you to move in?"

He flashes me a blinding smile. "Definitely not. I'll arrange a moving truck tomorrow."

"I cannot wait to start living my life with you." I peck his lips, and my heart is overflowing. All of the suffering was worth it because it has led us to this moment.

"So, it's not too soon to ask you to marry me?" he says, extracting a small black box from his pocket.

I suck in a gasp when he pops the lid, revealing a gorgeous butterfly-shaped emerald and diamond ring, resting on a platinum band.

"Emerald is your birthstone, but it's also said to symbolize rebirth. I saw this in the window of a store the day I turned twenty-one, and I knew I had to buy it for you."

My heart jackhammers against my rib cage, and butterflies swoop into my belly. "It's stunning and absolutely perfect."

I watch him slide it on my ring finger with trembling hands as my heart jumps around in excitement. "I love you, Kendall." He holds my hand and brings it to his mouth. "I have loved you in every lifetime that has come before. I'll love you in this one and every lifetime that comes after." He kisses the ring on my finger before setting my hand on his chest, over the place where his heart beats. "I already consider you my wife. I always have, but I think we should make this official. I want to be your husband. I want to be Iris's dad, and I want to have the family I have always desired." He sweeps his lips against mine in a brief but tender kiss. "With you."

Always Meant to Be

Wrapping myself around him, I hold him close as I dust kisses all over his gorgeous face. "I want all of that with you too, and I can't wait to make it official. I want to be your wife, but I have always considered you mine, Vander. Our forced separation never altered how I feel about you."

He stands, cradling me against his body, and my legs wind around his toned waist as he carries me upstairs to the master bedroom.

Vander lays me down flat on the bed before returning to lock the door. He kicks off his shoes and lies next to me. Twisting on my side, I arch my neck, my lips seeking his, as my hands find purchase on his hips. We hold on to one another as we kiss, and it's a slow, deep, passionate reacquaintance. Our hips thrust together, and our hands explore as our kissing grows more heated, until we need more, because it's not enough. I need to feel him moving over me and in me, and I can't wait a minute longer.

Vander kisses every inch of my body as he slowly peels my clothes away. His eyes burn with emotion as he traces the outline of his name over my heart. I have my kids' names inked there too, keeping all my loved ones close. With great reverence, he sweeps his lips across the names, a knowing smile tipping up the corners of his mouth.

Our only communication is with our lips, our tongues, and our hands because words are redundant. We don't need to speak to convey how much we mean to one another.

I undress him until we're both naked, pressed skin to skin. Ink adorns most every part of Vander's upper body now, and our story is permanently etched into his flesh. My name is tattooed over his heart, just above the Ouroboros Boner inked all those years ago.

We share a secret smile as we appreciate how in sync we still are.

Even when we were apart, we still carried one another over and in our hearts.

Vander kisses my mouth before gliding down my body to reclaim what has always been his. I part my thighs and grip his dark hair as he feasts on my pussy, and it's like no time has passed. He remembers how to coax my desire to a peak in record time, and I bury my face in my pillow, muffling my cries of pleasure, as a powerful orgasm rips through my body.

Vander trails his lips up over my heated flesh before planting his mouth on mine again. I pull him down on top of me, needing to feel his skin flush against mine, and I can literally feel all the cracked, heartbroken pieces inside me knitting together until I feel complete.

He positions himself between my knees, tugging on his straining length as he asks a question with his eyes. I reply, asking one of my own, and then we're smiling again, our minds calm, our hearts healed, and our souls whole.

Maintaining eye contact, Vander slides carefully inside me, one delightful inch at a time. Emotion gathers in my eyes, clogs my throat, and soars in my chest as he fills me so fully I forget there was ever a time when we were separated. "I love you," he whispers, leaning down to kiss me as he holds his body still inside mine. "I love you for eternity."

"I will love you forever and ever until the very ends of time," I reply as he slowly starts to move, making love to me with an intensity and a depth that surpasses any intimacy we have shared before. As I peer into his gorgeous green eyes, holding his body against mine, while we arch and thrust in a perfect rhythm, I know no truer words have ever been spoken.

Epilogue

Vander

"Daddy, come on!" Iris says, charging along the cobblestone path ahead of Kendall and me. "You're both such slowpokes!"

Kendall giggles, snuggling into my side as I tighten my arm around her shoulders. "I think she gets her impatience from you."

"Not a chance." I playfully swat her ass as the warm Greek sun beats down on us. "I have the patience of a saint, or need I remind you how, in every lifetime, I have to wait years to be reunited with the other half of my heart and soul?"

"I never forget." She stretches up and pecks my lips. "I cherish every second with you, painter boy. The sacrifices we've made were worth it to get to this point. I'm living my best life with you," my wife says, beaming up at me, before she presses a kiss to my heart through my shirt.

It's been a little over three years since we got married, and I have never felt more content or more alive. My wife and my daughter have breathed life into all the frozen parts of me, and I can't remember the missing years because we fill every day with joy, making up for lost time. West and I have resumed our friendship, and I'm close with Ridge and Stella too. "You complete me, Kendall. In every lifetime, you are the very essence of my soul."

She sighs in contentment, and I am never happier than when I'm confronted with the evidence of our mutual elation. We slotted into a life together as easily as breathing. From the moment we reconnected, we haven't spent a single night apart. I know what it's like to be without this woman, and I never want to experience it again.

"I think we should buy a vacation home in Athens," she says as we quicken our pace to catch up with our excited daughter. Iris has shot up this past year, and she's the tallest in her class. She also looks much older than ten. Something teenage boys seem to have noticed, and I have spent half our vacation glaring at guys for even daring to glance at my beautiful princess. "I feel so at home here." Happiness fills Kendall's voice.

"I do too, and I agree. Let's book another week in the hotel and arrange to visit a few real estate agents." The beauty of being self-employed business owners is we can delegate work to others and take off whenever the mood suits us. We work hard, and taking regular vacation breaks is essential for our health and our sanity. We have spent every summer abroad, and we're enjoying exploring the world and visiting places we've seen in our dreams.

"It's a deal. You only get to celebrate your thirtieth birthday once."

I call out to Iris to wait as I squeeze Kendall's hip. "This has been the best birthday surprise ever."

"Come on, Mom," Iris drawls, rushing up to us, bouncing on her feet, physically unable to contain her excitement. "The entrance is right over there." She spins around, pointing at the small stone entry with open wrought-iron gates where a line of tourists is waiting to be admitted.

Out of all the places we have visited, Iris has loved Athens the most. It's fair to say it's true for all of us. I thought visiting Egypt would be the most pivotal moment, because of our Egyptian dream, but it doesn't hold a candle to how we both felt the second we stepped foot in magical Athens. Maybe it's the deeply spiritual vibe or the strong philosophical ties here, but the air feels different, and my skin tingles, like it's bursting with hidden knowledge that's dying to be set free.

The air is steeped with the history of the country, and no matter where we travel within the city, we are confronted with the evidence of the Athens of long ago. Excavations are still ongoing, and it's not unusual to stumble across an old bathing chamber or an ancient library or church, carefully preserved and protected, in between the vibrant stores, restaurants, and bars that make up modern-day Athens.

We have visited the infamous Parthenon—a historic elevated site overlooking the bustling city below—and the accompanying Acropolis Museum. We were completely enthralled wandering around the excavation of an ancient Athenian neighborhood, dating back to the fourth millennium BC. The exhibition is underneath the impressive museum building, and it's one of the most incredible things I've ever seen.

Today, we are visiting the Agora, which is essentially an old marketplace, and it was once the hub of the local community. The Temple of Hephaestus overlooks the Agora, and we're excited to see it in the flesh and hopeful it will conjure some past memory, in a way we were hoping the pyramids would. Now that we are together, Kendall and I don't dream of our past as much.

We spend an hour exploring the lower level of the Agora

before we begin our ascent to the temple. It's a stunning day. There isn't a cloud in the azure-blue sky, and buttery rays of sunshine illuminate Greece's most well-preserved temple, proudly holding fort, on a hill on top of the Agora. Kendall's excitement mounts as we walk up the stone steps, struggling to keep pace with our energetic daughter as Iris all but runs toward the ancient monument.

Kendall holds on to me when we reach the path at the top, and we walk hand in hand toward the cream-colored stone structure that is standing largely intact. The area around the temple is well maintained with manicured tall trees and shrubs and cut grass. Iris is shrieking, singing, jumping, and twirling as she makes her way toward the temple.

"My God, Vander." Kendall stops along the side of the temple, peering up at me with a wonderous expression. "Do you feel it?" She clasps both my hands in hers as a beatific smile breaks out on her face.

"I feel it." A surge of warmth and contentment sweeps through me, and tingles cascade over my skin.

"This was the place." Kendall looks all around as tears fill her eyes. "This was the start. This is where our souls first bonded on Earth." We move toward one another at the same time, our lips melting together in an electrifying kiss I feel in every part of my body. The outside environment fades into the background as a myriad of images flashes behind my eyes while I kiss my wife.

"Vander," Kendall whispers, happy tears rolling down her face. "Did you see?"

"Yes, *agapi mou*." I reel her into my arms, glancing ahead to where Iris is kneeling in the grass, looking up at the sky and singing. "Look at Iris." I turn my wife in my arms so she's facing our daughter. We watch as Iris holds up her hand and a beautiful butterfly floats down and lands on her palm.

"Look up," Kendall says, moving in my arms and tipping her head back. Light laughter filters from her lips as we watch a cluster of blue morpho butterflies descend upon us, out of nowhere. They keep coming, swarms of them, until we're surrounded in a colorful bubble that draws the attention of other people in the vicinity. "This is insane," Kendall whispers, smiling through her tears as she holds her palm out, letting butterflies cling to her hand and her arm.

"This is fate." I hold her tighter against me. "No matter where we end up or how many obstacles block our path, we will always be together because our destiny was sealed in this very spot, and there is nothing or no one that can ever keep us apart."

Want to read another emotional angsty romance? Check out **Say I'm the One**, the first book in my completed **All of Me Duet**. Free to read in Kindle Unlimited. Also available in paperback and audiobook format.

Subscribe to my newsletter to stay up to date with all my news. Type this link into your browser: http://eepurl.com/dl4l5v

I'm head over heels in love with my best friend. Although, I can't pinpoint exactly when Reeve Lancaster became my entire world.

Was it when we were little kids, practically brought up together, after Reeve's mom died during childbirth and his dad subsequently fell apart? Or when I doodled his name in my school journal at age ten? Maybe it was when we became boyfriend and girlfriend at fourteen or when we shed our virginity at sixteen, pledging our forever?

I was there as his star ascended—like I'd always known it would—and there wasn't a prouder person on the planet. As the only child of Hollywood's golden couple, I've lived my life in the spotlight enough to know it wasn't what I wanted for my future. But I sacrificed my own desires, because Reeve's happiness meant everything to me.

Until he crushed my heart into itty-bitty pieces, forcing me to fly halfway around the world just to escape the gut-wrenching pain.

The opportunity to study at Trinity College Dublin came at the perfect moment, and I jumped at the chance without hesitation. If I'd known fate was meddling in my life, perhaps I would have chosen differently, but my future was cemented the instant I laid eyes on *him*.

Dillon O'Donoghue was Reeve's polar opposite in every way, and perhaps, that's why I felt drawn to him. He was the dark to my light. The thorn in my side, irritating me with his cold disdain, wild recklessness, and a burning rage hidden deep inside him that spoke to a silent part within me. Yet Dillon showed me what it was like to truly live, opening my eyes to endless possibilities.

What happened next was inevitable, and I only have myself to blame. He warned me, and I knew my reprieve was temporary, because there is only so far I can run.

Especially when fate hasn't finished messing with me yet.

CLAIM YOUR FREE EBOOK – ONLY AVAILABLE TO NEWSLETTER SUBSCRIBERS!

The boy who broke my heart is now the man who wants to mend it.

Jared was my everything until an ocean separated us and he abandoned me when I needed him most.

He forgot the promises he made.

Forgot the love he swore was eternal.

It was over before it began.

Now, he's a hot commodity, universally adored, and I'm the woman no one wants.

Pining for a boy who no longer exists is pathetic. Years pass, men come and go, but I cannot move on.

Tell it To My Heart

I didn't believe my fractured heart and broken soul could endure any more pain. Until Jared rocks up to the art gallery where I work, with his fiancée in tow, and I'm drowning again.

Seeing him brings everything to the surface, so I flee. Placing distance between us again, I'm determined to put him behind me once and for all.

Then he reappears at my door, begging me for another chance.

I know I should turn him away.

Try telling that to my heart.

This angsty, new adult romance is a FREE full-length ebook, exclusively available to newsletter subscribers. Type this link into your browser to claim your free copy: https://dl.bookfunnel.com/521dpwbcnl

About the Author

Siobhan Davis is a *USA Today, Wall Street Journal,* and Amazon Top 5 bestselling romance author. **Siobhan** writes emotionally intense stories with swoon-worthy romance, complex characters, and tons of unexpected plot twists and turns that will have you flipping the pages beyond bedtime! She has sold over 2 million books, and her titles are translated into several languages.

Prior to becoming a full-time writer, Siobhan forged a successful corporate career in human resource management.

She lives in the Garden County of Ireland with her husband and two sons.

You can connect with Siobhan in the following ways:

Website: www.siobhandavis.com
Facebook: AuthorSiobhanDavis
Instagram: @siobhandavisauthor
Tiktok: @siobhandavisauthor
Email: siobhan@siobhandavis.com

Books by Siobhan Davis

KENNEDY BOYS SERIES

Upper Young Adult/New Adult Contemporary Romance

Finding Kyler

Losing Kyler

Keeping Kyler

The Irish Getaway

Loving Kalvin

Saving Brad

Seducing Kaden

Forgiving Keven

Summer in Nantucket

Releasing Keanu

Adoring Keaton

Reforming Kent

Moonlight in Massachusetts

STAND-ALONES

New Adult Contemporary Romance

Inseparable

Incognito

When Forever Changes
No Feelings Involved
Still Falling for You
Second Chances Box Set
Holding on to Forever
Always Meant to Be
Tell It to My Heart
The One I Want

Reverse Harem Romance

Surviving Amber Springs

Dark Mafia Romance

Vengeance of a Mafia Quee

RYDEVILLE ELITE SERIES

Dark High School Romance

Cruel Intentions
Twisted Betrayal
Sweet Retribution
Charlie
Jackson
Sawyer
The Hate I Feel^
Drew

MAZZONE MAFIA SERIES

Dark Mafia Romance

Condemned to Love

Forbidden to Love

Scared to Love

Mazzone Mafia: The Complete Series

THE ACCARDI TWINS

Dark Mafia Romance

CKONY #1 ^

CKONY #2 ^

THE SAINTHOOD (BOYS OF LOWELL HIGH)

Dark HS Reverse Harem Romance

Resurrection

Rebellion

Reign

Revere

The Sainthood: The Complete Series

DIRTY CRAZY BAD DUET

Dark College Reverse Harem Romance

Dirty Crazy Bad - A Prequel Short Story
Dirty Crazy Bad #1
Dirty Crazy Bad #2

ALL OF ME DUET

Angsty New Adult Romance

Say I'm The One
Let Me Love You
Hold Me Close
All of Me: The Complete Series

ALINTHIA SERIES

Upper YA/NA Paranormal Romance/Reverse Harem

The Lost Savior
The Secret Heir
The Warrior Princess
The Chosen One
*The Rightful Queen^*

SAVEN SERIES

Young Adult Science Fiction/Paranormal Romance

Saven Deception

Logan

Saven Disclosure

Saven Denial

Saven Defiance

Axton

Saven Deliverance

Saven: The Complete Series

^Release date to be confirmed

Made in the USA
Las Vegas, NV
29 October 2023